# MEDICAL

## Pulse-racing passion

**Healing The Baby Doc's Heart**
Fiona McArthur

**Resisting The Off-Limits Paediatrican**
Kate MacGuire

MILLS & BOON

HEALING THE BABY DOC'S HEART
© 2024 by Fiona McArthur
Philippine Copyright 2024
Australian Copyright 2024
New Zealand Copyright 2024

First Published 2024
First Australian Paperback Edition 2024
ISBN 978 1 038 90259 7

RESISTING THE OFF-LIMITS PAEDIATRICIAN
© 2024 by Kate MacGuire
Philippine Copyright 2024
Australian Copyright 2024
New Zealand Copyright 2024

First Published 2024
First Australian Paperback Edition 2024
ISBN 978 1 038 90259 7

MIX
Paper | Supporting
responsible forestry
FSC® C001695
www.fsc.org

Published by
Harlequin Mills & Boon
An imprint of Harlequin Enterprises (Australia) Pty Limited
(ABN 47 001 180 918), a subsidiary of HarperCollins
Publishers Australia Pty Limited
(ABN 36 009 913 517)
Level 19, 201 Elizabeth Street
SYDNEY NSW 2000 AUSTRALIA

Cover art used by arrangement with Harlequin Books S.A.. All rights reserved.

Printed and bound in Australia by McPherson's Printing Group

# Healing The Baby Doc's Heart
Fiona McArthur

# MILLS & BOON

**Fiona McArthur** is an Australian midwife who lives in the country and loves to dream. Writing medical romance gives Fiona the chance to write about all the wonderful aspects of romance, adventure, medicine and the midwifery she feels so passionate about. When she's not catching babies, Fiona and her husband, Ian, are off to meet new people, see new places and have wonderful adventures. Drop in and say hi at Fiona's website, fionamcarthurauthor.com.

Visit the Author Profile page
at millsandboon.com.au for more titles.

Dear Reader,

I loved the chance to spend a little more time with Malachi and Lisandra and the twins from the last book, *Father for the Midwife's Twins*, as in this story, they help their friends find love.

In some ways, this is an enemies-to-lovers story! Simon and Isabella do not get off on the right foot because they're both afraid to trust.

I loved Isabella. She's a wonderful character—strong, intelligent and caring despite some difficult relationships with men, including her workaholic father. But what she really needs, however, is a loving partner—though she doesn't know this yet.

It's no surprise that Simon finds her irresistible. Simon is such a heartthrob and impossible not to love! His path to love is not easy because since the death of his mother and his wife and child, he doesn't believe he has the power to protect the women around him. Instead, he finds his power and self-esteem from protecting his patients, which makes him incredibly committed to his job—a double-edged sword for Isabella!

I hope you love Simon and Isabella's story as much as I do. Wishing you a big happy smile at the end.

Love,

*Fi* xx

# DEDICATION

Dedicated to Jodie and her babies.

# PROLOGUE

*Vietnam, the first of May*

Isabella Hargraves pulled aside the curtains and looked down to the waking Hanoi street, seven floors below.

Warm air swirled around her fingers as she cracked open the window, yet the sky still radiated a pink glow from dawn. Her favourite time. Another hot day was coming.

An elderly vendor peddled below on a push-bike laden with multi-sized straw hats. These conical woven workers' hats could be seen in fields, sampans, on cyclists, and on the heads of tourists. On this pushbike, the towers of plaited straw rose behind the rider and out sideways, so he was encased in a cage of hats. He'd be on his way to sell them in the old quarter of the city.

One of Isabella's highlights for people-watching in Vietnam was noting the piles of drums, ladders, picture frames—in fact anything—on the back and front of push-bikes. Once she'd even seen a cow on a trailer pulled along by a motorcycle.

Nine million people and three million motorcycles. Such a crazy, wonderful place to live and work.

Of course, if you wanted to cross the road only a percentage of traffic would stop, and you needed to take your life in your hands. The trick, she'd found, was to walk slowly—no dashing—hand out, eyes open, and *voila*, the traffic avoided you. That was the local theory, anyway, and when she followed that it seemed to work.

From her window she could just see the pink sky lighting Hoen Kiem, the Lake of the Returned Sword, where an emperor had been said to use a magical sword to defeat the Ming Dynasty from China. The legends here fascinated her.

In this story, after victory, the Golden Turtle god had returned the sword to the bottom of the lake, and today the Turtle Tower stood on its own tiny island, on guard, as if to keep an eye out for the endangered turtles that were swimming in the lake.

Isabella pulled on her runners so she could circle the expanse of still water in the early morning before she went to the maternity wing of the Old City Hospital.

Circumnavigating the lake on the winding paths at daybreak had become Isabella's favourite start to the day. The streets were quiet, and the pleasure of watching groups of women on the grassed foreshore, line-dancing to boom boxes, bickering over which song to play and the exuberance once decided, seemed to bring some of their infectious joy her way.

She and her partner Conlon had another month of secondment here. She'd loved every second so far. Loved sharing it with Conlon. She'd even begun to hope she'd found a partner in life after she'd been alone for so long. Conlon had suggested she should become a full-time academic instead of fitting her research in blocks between her nursing work as an intensivist.

Her mood dipped. Yesterday's emergency in the neonatal intensive care unit—or NICU—had required all her skills to assist in saving the first-born son of a woman she'd befriended, and though she'd been present in the unit only for research, it had been her skills from the other part of her life that had helped to save the baby.

Isabella, an expert in the field, had been invited to participate in a study of neonatal outcomes for premature babies. Conlon, an ambitious lecturer at Sydney University, had been so eager to co-author the paper she was writing that he'd asked to join her. Their relationship had become more than collegial, and he now shared the flat she'd rented.

She was still getting used to the fact that Conlon had said he was there for her. It seemed hard to believe when she'd been let down so often by her father's work priorities while she was growing up. It had felt as if every single time she'd needed him that her father had been elsewhere, working.

Her phone rang and she glanced down to see the caller ID. Speak of the devil. Her brows furrowed. Dad? Six a.m. here... It would be nine in the morning in Australia.

Suddenly she felt as if she were a mother-less seven-year-old seeking an elusive hug, not a woman of twenty-seven.

She could count on the fingers of one hand how many times her father had rung her in the last year. Messages were usually sent via his very busy secretary at the Sydney Central Neurology Department.

A feeling of foreboding crept up her neck and circled her throat—because the last time he'd phoned had been to tell her about her brother-in-law's car accident, six months ago.

'Dad?'

'Isabella. I have bad news.'

No sugar coating. No, *How are you*? No, *I'm sorry to say this*. Not from Dad.

She felt her stomach roil with sick fear.

Was her widowed sister sick? Was it Nadia's pregnancy? The baby?

'It's your grandmother.'

Gran! The woman who had made up for the loss of her mother so long ago. The loss of her father, too, really. Because he'd morphed into a machine after Mum had died, and had only become more mechanical in his affections.

No. It couldn't be. Not Gran.

'An accident. Hit and run in Coolangatta. She's unconscious,' he went on. 'I don't believe she'll wake.'

Isabella closed her eyes as horror and the wash

of devastation began to saturate her insides along with cold fear.

'Isabella? Hello? Are you there?'

She jumped at the tone in her father's voice. 'Yes, sorry. I'm just trying to take it in. I'll come home, of course.'

'What?' she heard him snap. 'Why? There's nothing you can do.' His tone disbelieving. Sharp. Emphatic. 'No need. No. You must finish your work.' She heard the cold and clinical man for whom the god Work meant everything.

Her grandmother lay dying. Unconscious in hospital. Isabella wasn't leaving her alone.

'Of course there's something I can do. I can be with her. And with Nadia.'

Her father hmphed with exasperation. 'Your grandmother's not going to know you're with her.'

There it was. The impatience she'd grown up with. The inhuman being who was her father. He was probably already thinking about his next task.

'She's comatose. It's very sad. However, as I've said, it's unlikely she's going to regain consciousness.'

'I'm coming home.'

Or at least not home. Not to the cold, empty mausoleum her father lived in.

'I'll go to the Gold Coast. Be with Nadia. Stay at Gran's flat.'

*I will talk to my grandmother even if she's unconscious.*

It might help. Her grandmother might hear her at any point. Isabella would be there when she woke up.

*Oh, Gran.*

He huffed. 'You do what you need to do—though I can't imagine Conlon will be happy if you leave.'

She tilted her head at that. 'Conlon will come with me. Be with me. He'll support me.'

'Really? You both went there to do a job. Conlon knows your work is important and it's not finished. You should both stay.'

'We'll go back to Australia early. Come back to Vietnam later.'

*Of course he'll come with me...support me.*

God, she wanted him now, his arms around her, but he was already out jogging around the lake.

'I don't think you should. Nadia's there. She'll keep you up to date.'

She could almost imagine her father looking at his watch. Thinking he'd wasted enough time on this call.

'Thank you for ringing.'

*And not getting your secretary to do it.*

Isabella's fingers felt numb. Her lips clumsy as she said goodbye.

*Gran...*

A flash of sympathy for her father pierced her before he could hang up. 'Dad. Are you okay? Gran's your mother...'

'I'm sorry it's happened, of course.' He was silent for a moment. As if he was actually going to say he was upset. But no. 'There's nothing we can do. Your grandmother is eighty. She's had a good life.'

And then he was gone.

At first Isabella walked around the room in circles, picking things up and putting them down, trying to work out what to do. Trying to grasp the enormity of Gran lying in a hospital thousands of miles away. Alone. Possibly dying.

She thought about how much life, and love and laughter her grandmother had left inside her. Gran *had* to wake up. She couldn't bear the thought that her grandmother wouldn't be there. Wouldn't see Nadia's baby born.

The Sydney flights didn't leave until six p.m. from Hanoi to Singapore. And then a few hours later from Singapore to Sydney. They'd have to catch a domestic flight from Sydney to Brisbane and hire a car to drive to the Gold Coast. She'd arrange for her own car to be shipped up.

She thought of her sister. Alone in this. Poor Nadia… Six months pregnant and now she'd be losing two people she loved. Nadia needed her, too. No. Gran wouldn't die. She'd phone her as soon as she spoke to Conlon.

The door opened and Conlon breezed in from his run, bringing the heat from the pavements outside. His jet-black hair lay plastered to the sweat across his brows, which creased when he saw her face.

His long legs crossed the room to her quickly.

'What's wrong?'

She wasn't alone. Too many times in her childhood she and her sister had been alone...until Gran had stepped in. Thank goodness Conlon was here.

'My grandmother. She's in a coma. Hit and run in Coolangatta. We'll have to go back to Australia.' She reached forward and took his hand. 'We have to go home.'

He stared. 'I'm sorry... Run that by me again?'

How could he not have understood her?

She tamped down her impatience. 'My grandmother has been involved in an accident. I have to go home. I'll tell them we have to postpone our study. Put a hold on the paper.'

'Of course you have to go. But what do you mean, we have to postpone? We need to finish the project.'

He shook his head.

'I'm going home.'

'I know. I heard that. Your grandmother. You're fond of her.'

*Fond?* The word sat oddly.

'I'm terrified my grandmother is going to die,' she said slowly. Familiar dread was coiling inside her chest. 'I need you right now. You'll support me...?'

She hadn't meant to make it a question but it was too late now. She trailed off, looked at his face. Saw the truth. The distance that had grown between them in just minutes. That's all it took. Saw the selfishness she'd tried to ignore in all those little daily moments. Saw her father.

Conlon was looking past her, his gaze shifting away. He gave a more emphatic shake of his head this time.

'I'm not going to be any help. I'll stay and finish the project.'

This wasn't happening.

'They'll understand…we can come back. You don't need—'

He cut her off. 'No, it will only take a month for me to finish it. You go. Do what you have to do. Then come back if you can make it in time. If you can't, I'll tie it all up.' His chin went up. 'I'll still add your name on the paper.'

She shifted again at that. It had been her paper and she'd invited him to join her. He'd asked her to let him join. Now he was going to 'add her name' on it when she'd done eighty percent of the work?

She shook her head. Stung. Disgusted, actually. She narrowed her eyes as he avoided hers. But that was just work. Stuff to think on later. Later—when Gran was well. This was not important now.

Isabella shook her head. 'You're not listening to me. I want you to come and be with me. Support me. What if she dies?'

She knew she sounded forlorn and lost, and she hated it.

His face was screwed up, incredulous. 'You've flown alone more than I have. You'll be fine.' He waved a hand and glanced at his watch as it moved past his face. 'I'd better get moving.'

Isabella felt sick. And stupid. 'I don't want protection. I want support. There's a difference.'

'I would. If this was finished. But this work is too important, Isabella.'

She winced. Hurt. 'And I'm not?'

He'd already turned towards the bedroom. 'Don't be petty. Of course you're important. But I think you're not thinking right. Not thinking of our work. You're prioritising all wrong.'

Had he really just said that? Red-hot anger flooded through her. She could almost imagine her blood boiling like lava. Her father's favourite word all through her childhood. At school events and award nights. He was unable to come because he was 'prioritising'.

Conlon turned back briefly, oblivious to the fact that he wasn't in the right. 'Ridiculous for me to come with you. We're so close to finishing. This will be a breakthrough paper. Give us excellent credibility behind us.'

Through gritted teeth she whispered, 'My grandmother is dying.'

Oh, God. She saw it then. Why? Why was she attracted to these men who put work in front of everything? Like her father. She'd thought Conlon was safe. He was an academic, so at least he had no urgent calls taking him back to the hospital night after night. She'd thought—foolish her—that during every event or crisis, he would be there. For her. Would want to be.

If it hadn't been for Gran, she and Nadia wouldn't even have had a childhood. They would have spent their holidays locked in the house with part-time servants instead of going to visit Gran and flying up to her at the weekends when they were older.

And she'd thought she could make a life with Conlon. Thought they wanted the same things. Thought they'd be a caring family.

*Idiot.*

She'd have spent her life waiting for scraps of attention that didn't involve work. Just like in her childhood.

But she couldn't think about that now.

She said dully, 'You go and shower. When you come home I'll be gone.'

'Of course. That's fine. I'll give you a ring.'

Wow. So generous. Thoughtful.

Very quietly and clearly she said, 'No, don't bother.'

Conlon's dark brows drew together. He was irritated. His turn to be impatient. 'You're being foolish. We're good together. Our work is amazing.'

'*My* work is amazing.'

Because she was the one who found it easy. Made the connections and garnered the interviews that clarified the answers. She had a way with equations, and probabilities, always finding the right questions and writing everything down in the right words.

Conlon had let her down.

Hell, he couldn't even take the time to give her a hug of sympathy. What had she been thinking to attach herself to a man who was so like her father she'd have been starved for affection for the rest of her life?

Her heart wasn't broken—bruised, maybe— but her pride had taken a blow that had left her reeling.

She'd loved her time in Vietnam, had been honoured by the openness of the midwives and neonatal nurses she'd interviewed for her thesis. She'd ached over their stories, and enjoyed learning about a culture that was so different from her own. But she'd been here with Conlon and had thought something had been growing between them.

He'd been so enthusiastic about her scientific paper, and his handsome face had promised her a wonderful future at home and at work. She'd not seen what was now so obvious—that the man was selfish and egotistical.

Wow. Remembered his comment about the

paper. Seemed he thought it was generous that he'd let her share credit for her own thesis.

She'd almost loved him—or the man she'd thought he was—but now, as he turned to shower and change for the hospital, she felt as hollow and cast off as she'd felt as a child, when her father had immersed himself in his high-powered job.

She'd thought she'd got over that. Her gran would have scolded her for being dramatic. Would've said Conlon had done her a favour, exposing his shortfalls before she'd done something worse—like marrying him.

But after that Gran would have lovingly offered her a shoulder to cry on. Conlon hadn't.

It would take her twenty-four hours, but Isabella would be by her grandmother's bedside until she woke up. And Gran *would* wake up. She had to.

Alone, seven floors above the Hanoi street, Isabella said quietly, 'I'm coming, Gran...' To her sister whom she'd ring shortly, she promised silently, *Nadia, I've got your back*.

She'd find a job at the nearest hospital, visit Gran, be there for Nadia in the last months of her pregnancy. She'd get back to doing what she needed to do. Caring for those who loved and wanted her. Working with babies. She would leave behind Vietnam...this foray into academia... Conlon. Leave behind any silly little girl fantasies that men could be relied on.

She'd learnt that lesson. Oh, yes.

# CHAPTER ONE

*Three weeks later, Gold Coast, Australia*

NORMALLY DR SIMON PURDY, senior consultant paediatrician at Coolangatta Central, wouldn't notice a new nurse in the neonatal intensive care unit.

But today wasn't normal. Because seeing this new nurse hit him like a wrecking ball and he actually staggered. Mayhem exploded in Simon's chest and gut, and he could barely shift his gaze from the stranger across the room as he found his balance.

The unfamiliar sensations had begun when he'd seen her smile as she chatted with a newborn in an open cot—as if the baby could answer.

The tiny patient had done something that had made the nurse's mouth stretch softly until her whole face lit up with mischief.

She was so vibrant—good grief, she hummed with it. Visibly pulsing with life and vitality that made him see, and feel, the depth of his own emotional emptiness.

Now, suddenly and rudely awakened, he remembered he was alive. A man. A broken one. But still a man.

Then all he could think about was his inability to keep those he'd cared for safe. He didn't want to look at that frozen guilt that had been a part of his life for so long. His failure. His culpability that those he'd dared to love were dead.

Thankfully he'd made it to a dimmer corner of the clinical area before he'd been stricken by this strange paralysis and he'd had to force his hand up just to loosen his irritatingly constricting too-tight Tigger tie.

The new nurse, just for a moment, had looked like an angel. Blonde and gentle. Bathing him with healing light.

And then she'd turned side-on, and those curves had not made him think of his lost wife or celestial chastity. She was tall and strong. Like some goddess he had no right to covet. Someone else he would lose if he let himself care. Her thick plait of sun-and-sand-coloured hair swung and danced, with the end of the plait pointing to her backside like a neon arrow, as she floated across the polished floor checking the cots.

'Can I help you, Dr Purdy?'

Simon blinked. At least his eyelids worked again. He swivelled his head—though not his taut body—and looked at Carla, his good friend, and the neonatal nursery's unit manager. The woman who'd nagged him to get on with his life.

She'd spotted him and had her list of patients prepared for him, as usual, in order of urgency. But right now her head was tilted to the side and her eyes twinkled.

'Do you need help?'

He did. But nobody could help him. Where was his usual wall? His defences?

'No.'

The word came out unexpectedly. Just as the woman across the room was unexpected. He blinked again. 'Sorry, Carla. I'm off in another land. Thinking about a patient,' he lied.

Why did he lie? He never lied. Apparently he wasn't very good at it, either.

Carla snorted. 'That's Isabella Hargraves. Very experienced neonatal nurse. Her dad's Professor Piers Hargraves, the neurologist.'

'Head of Neurology at Sydney Central? Chair of Neurology Australia?'

Hopefully she was a socialite, then.

He was dreaming, A quiet, insidious voice inside his head whispered, *But maybe a one-night stand?*

'The same. Isabella's a midwife and neonatal nurse who loves babies. That's what she said when she interviewed. But she's also worked in retrieval, has five scientific papers to her name and has great experience across diverse units. She's moved from Sydney to here to be with her sick grandmother and pregnant sister.'

Simon shook himself.

*Loves babies? Good sister? Caring granddaughter?*

Despite her stunning looks she was a family

girl. Not for him, then. Danger with a capital D. Nothing to fancy there. He liked surfing alone, working hard and staying too busy with other people's babies to think about having any of his own.

That woman there could break hearts and he was not going there. Damn her. He'd already had more heartbreak than he could deal with. He turned his back on the unit. For some bizarre reason it made him angry with the newcomer.

'Let's see your list, Carla.'

Carla eyed him shrewdly. Handed over the patient list.

She murmured, 'I saw your friend Malachi Madden the other day. He even made a joke— a funny one. Seems having a family suits him.'

Simon raised his brows and side-eyed her without lifting his head.

'And your point?' he asked.

Carla pushed up one shoulder, her mouth kinking with amusement as she winked at him.

'Does there have to be a point, Simon? Could you perhaps think of something other than work? Just for a moment?'

# CHAPTER TWO

IT WASN'T UNUSUAL for Isabella Hargraves to feel a stranger's gaze, so she didn't take much notice of the tall man in the corner. Although she had to admit that he wasn't a bad piece of eye candy—despite the scowl.

She'd eased so joyfully back into working with babies in the NICU that it would take more than some random non-admirer to divert her from her tasks.

When the apnoea alarm sounded from Baby Jones she was at his open cot in an instant. Checking the time. Checking the monitor. Watching for breaths as the heartbeat slowed with a brief dip into bradycardia before righting itself as he eventually took a breath.

'Good boy,' she murmured.

She silenced the alarm, and by the time she lifted the chart to record the time and duration of the bradycardia, Carla and the tall man were next to her.

'Isabella.' Carla indicated the man beside her. 'This is Dr Simon Purdy.'

Ah, Dr Purdy... Isabella connected the name with the cot cards. She lifted her head and smiled. 'Nice to meet you, Dr Purdy.'

This man's name sat on the identification cards

of nearly every open-sided cot in the place. Obviously, here stood the favoured paediatrician. She'd heard the staff rave about his thoroughness, dedication and diagnostic abilities since she'd arrived here.

Up close? Oh, my... He was more than just eye candy. Broad-chested and broad-shouldered with tanned, handsome features and a crop of wayward golden hair. He was the full sweetshop. His eyes were the blue of the Coolangatta waves across the road from the hospital, but for some reason his gaze pierced her with surprising harshness. Her smile dimmed. Even his sinful mouth had been pulled into a taut line.

He nodded his blond head briefly—his face all carved cheek bones, patrician nose and strong chin—but his cool eyes swept away from her to the cot.

Obviously, he'd found her lacking in his previously extended perusal. 'Nurse Hargraves.' His voice was deep and dismissive.

Her brows furrowed. *Nurse?*

So, he was doing titles. Everyone else here was on a first-name basis. But he could call her what he wanted. She was actually a doctor of midwifery. She had a PhD. She gave a mental shrug. She could use professional focus against rudeness.

'Self-righting apnoea?' he questioned. Curt and clipped. Cool, even. Barely courteous.

'Yes. Self-stimulation. Sixteen seconds dura-

tion. Heart rate dipped to seventy beats per minute.' She handed him the chart.

Baby Jack Jones, his parents having only yesterday decided on his first name, was ten days old
and had arrived six weeks before his due date. He
lay pink and placid in the cot in front of them.

Jack's heart rate monitor read one hundred and
twenty beats per minute—directly at the lower
end of the perfectly normal range.

'When was his last feed?'

Although a full tummy often caused a baby's
heart rate to drop post-feeding, Dr Purdy's tone
seemed taciturn for a man so many had raved
about. Still, a chilly tone wasn't Isabella's problem, or even interesting.

She leaned forward and touched the chart,
pushing his long, elegant finger aside to lift the
top sheet. The feed chart lay underneath the observation chart. But he'd know that. So why ask
her the question?

'Thirty minutes ago,' she told him.

'No problems during the feed?'

'No.'

She glanced at Carla, surprised to find a glare
in her boss's eyes that was certainly directed at
Dr Purdy. Carla's brows were crinkled and her
eyes narrowed.

Was he acting out of character? And if so, why?

Did she care?

*Nope.*

Isabella smiled and moved away from the ward round that she would normally follow with attentiveness. Dr Purdy didn't like her for some reason, though how that could be when they hadn't met before, she didn't know. It was not something that happened often, she realised, giving herself another mental shrug.

She glanced up at the big ward clock. Almost time for Baby Timms to be tube fed.

Cosette Timms was the smallest baby in the unit at the moment, weighing in at seven hundred and thirty grams. She'd been born premature at twenty-nine weeks, thanks to her mum's eclampsia, but had passed the fifteen-hundred-gram mark now.

Isabella would warm expressed breast milk from the fridge and prepare syringes to feed Cosette.

Carla had mentioned that Ellen Timms, Cosette's mum, phoned every morning and evening to check on her daughter.

Isabella had taken the phone call this morning. Mum wasn't coming in. She normally managed the three-hundred-kilometre round trip from the family farm twice a week—even with her other children and her husband's disability after a farm accident. But she couldn't make it today because of a home drama. There was plenty of frozen expressed milk, prepared by Ellen for just such an occasion.

Not at this feed but just before the next one, it would be Cosette's weigh time, and the baby would have to be stripped off and redressed for weighing. Being handled too often tired the premature infants—so it coincided with bath day. Isabella had plans to sending cute bath and weigh-in photos to Ellen from the ward's mobile phone.

Isabella pictured the mum's delight at receiving the pictures as she bustled around the milk room, preparing the feed. She checked the labelled container against the chart, hailed one of the other passing NICU nurses to confirm and countersign the chart, and withdrew the correct amount of milk into the syringe to heat up.

'Isabella?' Carla called out to her.

The nurse who'd co-signed the chart with Isabella reappeared and gestured to the apparatus in her hands.

'Carla said I should take over. She's got another job for you.'

'Oh…' Isabella put the syringes and the bottle of milk down and nodded. 'Okay. Thanks.'

She washed her hands, a small frown crinkling her brows until she let it go. Hopefully, she'd still get to bath Cosette later.

She crossed the room to where Carla stood with Dr Purdy and tilted her head. 'Do you need me, Carla?'

'Yes. I've been called to a managers' meeting and Dr Purdy wants to re-site Jack's IV cannula.

You know how unstable Jack can be, so I'd rather you assisted here for the moment.'

'Of course.' Isabella glanced around until she spotted the trolley they used for procedures and Jack's chart. And anything else she might need.

Dr Purdy glanced at his watch.

Isabella raised her brows at him before saying placidly, 'Give me a moment to set it up, Dr Purdy. Then I'll be with you.'

He seemed to drag his eyes away from his expensive diver's timepiece and nodded. Thankfully, he then turned to the last cot and picked up the chart.

Well, at least he wasn't going to stand there and watch her while she made everything ready. That was a good thing, but Isabella was way past worrying about nervousness with new doctors.

They came in such variety. She'd dated more than a few herself before she fell for Conlon, though most seemed to be obsessed with their own importance.

Probably Freud could have told her why she'd gone for those doctors. Daddy complex. It was a terrible thought.

But now? Hah! No more doctors or lecturers for her. She'd given up the idea of expecting anything from them except self-absorption and egotism.

She knew that was perhaps unfair. But she'd been to so many boring medical fundraising dinners with her father, and playing hostess at her father's house, she'd met many impatient doctors like Simon Purdy.

Most seemed to be in awe of their own intelligence, without observing that Isabella could have run rings around them. Though that didn't matter because she'd chosen midwifery and neonatal nursing.

She liked the hands-on patient care. She didn't want to sit all day in consulting rooms, only being allowed out for surgeries or emergencies—which mostly came during family time if her childhood had been anything to go by.

She wanted continuity of patient care. Being somewhere like here at the NICU, watching tiny newborns struggle, change and finally grow into good health. This was what she wanted to do.

That first rotation through a neonatal nursery had changed her life. She'd found her calling and taken herself to the top of her game as a neonatal intensivist. She'd been asked to join the neonatal emergency retrieval consultancy board, and through that had met neonatologists from all over the world. Which had led to her writing her thesis in Vietnam.

Conlon had jumped on board, seeing an opportunity to advance his own career by sharing the scientific paper she'd spent a year preparing.

She wasn't going there.

Deftly, she completed setting up for the procedure. She had at hand two different types of intravenous fluids, in case Dr Purdy wanted to change the intravenous concentrations. She washed her hands again.

Dr Purdy wasn't obviously looking at her, but she still felt his scrutiny despite that. It was as if he couldn't grasp something he should be able to see.

Well, she had things to do.

'When you're ready, Dr Purdy...'

# CHAPTER THREE

SIMON WATCHED NURSE HARGRAVES out of the corner of his eye, refusing to think of her as Isabella. Although, grudgingly, he had to admit it was a beautiful name.

He couldn't help his strange fascination, or being impressed by her. She moved gracefully, efficiently and without hesitation as she gathered supplies and opened them onto the sterile field. Her obvious experience seemed to be at odds with her apparent youth.

Maybe she wasn't as young as she looked—but she was younger than him. And she was full of life and energy. Unlike him. She made him feel old.

As he glanced at her long, graceful neck, his breath caught again, until he had to force his eyes back to the chart that he hadn't even read once.

He wasn't that old. Just sleepwalking through life…until now.

What was it about her?

Dispassionately, you might say her eyes were too big—yet they shone like pools of jungle-green and gold, like a lioness guarding her small cub. Her nose was too straight. No, not straight… refined. It suited her face perfectly. Darn it, he wasn't going to say her mouth was too big…because seriously that mouth was to die for.

*Was he sixteen years old?*

'When you're ready, Dr Purdy...'

He'd sworn he would never be ready again. He wasn't ready now. He wasn't.

His mouth felt dry—parched, like the sand across the road at the beach. And he swallowed once before he answered, 'Thank you.'

Simon's critical gaze skimmed over the dressing trolley that looked to include anything he could possibly want. Forcibly, he cleared his mind of everything but the task at hand. He lifted Jack's tiny hand and studied the translucent skin and the tiny, thread-like veins beneath.

Simon noticed Nurse Hargraves had the tips of her fingers very gently resting on Jack's foot, as if reassuring him. He'd forgive her the disruption to his world for that.

'Thank you. Everything looks perfect.'

As they worked, she seemed to know what he'd ask for next. They didn't speak and, though they were both unhurried, the procedure was completed smoothly and successfully within minutes.

He frowned at the dexterous and innovative way she wrapped the insertion site.

'That's different. And better than the way I do it. Can you show me again? Please.' He handed her a small splint to mimic a baby's arm and opened another canula packet and held it up to her. 'On this?'

He poked at the facsimile.

'I like the way you've taped it down. Without any strain. And yet so secure. Teach me?'

Simon had forgotten for the moment that he was bizarrely attracted to her. His mind wanted to know how to perform this technique that looked far more comfortable for the infant.

'It's a trick I learned in Vietnam,' she replied.

He watched her fingers while she dipped and circled the cannula, then secured the tape to the imitation arm. Absently he asked, 'When were you in Vietnam?'

'Last month. Helping out in a neonatal unit in Hanoi on an exchange organised by the university in Sydney for a paper I was writing.'

Simon nodded as he began to wrap Jack, who'd fallen asleep. When the baby was secure, Simon tucked him gently back into his open cot, then ensured all the alarms for the monitors were switched back on.

'What's the paper on?' he asked.

'Outcomes in neonatal nurseries in Vietnam, and how to raise Vietnamese community awareness for screening and neonatal care for congenital abnormalities.'

She reeled it off as she worked, cleaning up as fast and efficiently as she'd prepared. She seemed to know where everything was in the unit already as she slipped things they hadn't used back into their correct place. She'd only been here a day. He knew that. He came here every day. Many times. He would have noticed her if she'd been here longer.

He liked her forethought in learning the layout of the unit—she'd ensured that she'd be ready for emergencies. Impressive.

Lots of things about her impressed him.

*Stop it.*

He murmured, 'I've never been to Hanoi. How was the unit? The staff?'

'The unit's not as high-tech as this one. But the staff are amazing. The aim of my study was to encourage more antenatal attendance with the advantage of picking up potential problems before they happen.'

'Sounds like an interesting study.'

'It was.'

Something in her voice said she wasn't happy with how it had ended.

Then another apnoea alarm began to chime, and she turned and calmly walked across the room to observe and record the event. The alarm stopped.

Simon glanced around the unit. He knew all their patients were stable for the moment. He also knew that he should get to his consulting room for the morning's appointments, but he felt strangely reluctant to leave. Which reminded him: he was supposed to be distancing himself from this woman. Their conversation had pushed her even further under his skin. He needed to stop that. Back away. Fast.

That might have been why was curt as he said, 'I'll be in my office if Carla needs me.'

She lifted her hand but didn't turn around. He guessed he was dismissed. But for some absurd reason he could still see her in his mind.

# CHAPTER FOUR

THE FOLLOWING MORNING the sun offered Isabella a pastel bouquet for breakfast—along with a text from Conlon, which she deleted unread.

On the horizon, the guava-pink sky hung with eggshell edges, and where the ocean fell off the edge of the world it turned strawberry around the glow in the east.

'Red sky in the morning,' Isabella murmured. 'Got the warning.'

*And it's nothing to do with my new job, the swanky and cranky Dr Simon Purdy, or anything else. Not today. No, siree.*

After Hanoi—and the disappointment caused by her ex—being back in Australia with Gran felt right. Her grandmother's condition had been labelled 'stable', but she was no closer to waking.

Isabella had found her sister Nadia to be well, and the promise of Isabella surfing just outside her door made this place feel like an adventure she wanted to live through every day of her life.

Except for Dr Simon Purdy.

Rainbow Bay, so aptly named, had settled into her mind as a sandy paradise. The ocean vista waved and frothed ahead of the break wall of rocks that lined the eastern edge of the beach and greeted each wave.

*This is the best place to be*, she mentally reassured herself.

No Sydney traffic snarling her up on the way to the beach. No disappointment waiting for her—like Conlon, who was still oblivious to his disloyalty. No daily hurt caused by her father's dismissal because he was far away in Sydney.

Gran's apartment, just a few steps to the beach and one floor from the top, gazed across the bay towards the tall skyscrapers of Surfers Paradise in the distance. The same skyscrapers that right now were blazing windows of blinding gold reflecting the sunrise from across the waves.

The drone of a plane rose above the din of the surf for a moment, until the plane disappeared behind the hill of apartments to her left to land at the hidden airport.

Why on earth hadn't she thought to come to the Gold Coast earlier, instead of working in Sydney? Why hadn't she stayed close to Gran—the most important woman in her life? Because now it might be too late.

She should have had more quality time with Gran. Especially now her widowed sister had bought a tiny courtyard apartment in her grandmother's small block facing the beach. The ground floor apartment seemed perfect for when the baby was born.

Isabella had moved into her grandmother's spare room in a bittersweet temporary arrangement while Gran lay unconscious two kilometres away, in the hospital's critical care unit. Isabella visited every day.

This morning, day two of her new job, she sat on Gran's balcony, watching the ocean and the world awaken. Drinking green tea with jasmine, she studied the water and tried not to think about the irritating Dr Purdy, who'd gone back behind his grim rock façade after the brief period of rapport they'd had while re-siting Jack's cannula.

She just wished she could remove his annoyingly handsome face from her mind, but he lurked and aggravated her like a jagged splinter in her finger. Maybe if she scraped him out and examined him under the light like a wood shaving the annoyance would go away.

*Nope. Not going there.*

As if to distract her, the currents and swells ebbed and flowed, whispering their secrets, and hidden rocks showed themselves briefly. Peace— at last—seemed to soak into her, like a rock pool into a sea sponge, until her disquiet eased.

As the light grew, she watched the first surfers run to the water. Watched a lithe and powerful man run out to the back of the swells, catch a monster of a wave and ride it like quicksilver skimming the crest.

*Nice.*

She watched the foamy lines of rips. Looked for the best places away from the rocks and the longest rides into the beach. She worked out where she wanted to take her first surf on Rainbow Bay, tomorrow. Then she rose to get dressed for work.

'So, Gran. Today was my second day at the hospital. I think I'll really enjoy working in the unit here.'

Her grandmother's chest rose and fell.

'Carla, the unit manager, is the best kind of boss. Calm and sensible, with one of those honest faces I really like. You know that she's really *seeing* you.'

Isabella glanced across the sheets to the wrinkled face so dear to her. Gran, who had always *seen* her and Nadia, giving boundless love without coddling them.

But Gran's eyes were shut now. The wrinkled lids hiding the faded green of her irises, probably like Isabella's would in fifty years. Gran's eyes were closed as they had been since the accident, when her head had suffered the blow that had silenced her. But Gran's chest rose and fell in those shallow breaths that Isabella tried to tell herself were good enough. At least she was breathing for herself and not through a machine.

'Anyway... The unit is state-of-the-art. There are babies in there I adore already. There's this little girl—Cosette. Her mum lives an hour and a half away. She runs a farm, but still comes to visit and drop off expressed breast milk three times a week. Her husband was disabled in a farm accident, and she has three other kids. I can't wait to meet her. She sounds like a champion.'

Isabella watched the red electronic trace of her grandmother's heartbeat on the monitor above the bed. Rarely, there was a variation that suggested she might wake. But there were no signs that Gran could even hear her.

Isabella's father—expert neurologist that he was—had reminded Isabella that the longer the oblivion continued the less chance there was that her grandmother would ever wake. So clinical, even when it was his own mother he was talking about. She'd wanted to hit him.

Even more so when he'd said, 'Or if she does wake, she will most likely be in a vegetative state.'

It had been three weeks and three days since the accident and her father had given what scarce hope he ever had, away.

Lately, even Nadia seemed to be accepting that Gran was gone. But Isabella couldn't.

It was Isabella who had begged her father to request that Gran stay here, in the high-dependency unit at the private hospital, which was not quite critical care but still well-watched, for another month before they transferred her to a long-term facility.

Isabella would come and talk to Gran for as long as it took. She knew that the last sense to go in an unconscious body was hearing. She came every day for at least half an hour, either before or after work, depending on the shift, and shared the events of her day.

'There's this paediatrician—Simon Purdy. I loathe him. Don't start me on him. If he wasn't such an excellent neonatologist...'

She frowned at herself.

She *thought* she loathed him.

'Actually, he's too good at intubation and cannulation with tiny babies for me to loathe him. He managed to intubate this twenty-nine-weeker today, in less time than I had to think about it. And he got the cannula in on the first attempt. Pretty incredible. But he's still a pain.'

There—that sounded right.

'But I'm not wasting any more of our time talking about him. I had my first surf this morning.'

Gran had taught her to surf.

'You would have loved this big wave I caught...'

On Thursday Gran's heart rate had risen by ten beats per minute. Isabella checked her observation charts. There was no sign of a temperature, and even her respirations had increased in depth.

Was she getting better? Closer to surfacing? Or was Isabella dreaming?

This was a good sign, wasn't it? Or was it an infection?

'How are you, Gran?' Isabella picked up the

limp, age-spotted hand and lifted it to her cheek. 'Are you okay?'

Gran's hand was cool and dry, so Isabella squeezed her fingers softly and lowered them to the bed as she sat.

'Well, this week flew by, with busy shifts at work. But these daily doses of Simon Purdy are getting harder to take. Remember I said that first day he'd started cold and then got almost civil after Jack's cannula re-siting? Well, since then he's barely said a word to me.'

Her grandmother breathed. In and out.

Isabella sat silently for a bit.

'It's weird… It's as if I can feel his eyes drilling into my back every time I turn around. Like he doesn't want me to catch him looking. But if I turn, he's spinning away. What's with that?'

She frowned at the monitor as she thought about it. And the heart rate rose for a few beats and then fell.

Isabella turned back to her grandmother and looked down at the small hand in hers. 'And of course he's as nice as pie to everyone else in the unit. So why am I getting the silent treatment? What did I do to him?'

She felt her own heart rate speed up as she thought of the unfairness of Simon Purdy's behaviour. Felt her eyes narrow. She'd like to kick him. Which was so unlike her she almost gasped.

Gran's chest rose and fell. The line on the mon-

itor didn't change again. But it was if a thought
had wriggled into her brain from the pillow beside
her. Almost as if her grandmother had answered.

Isabella said slowly, 'Me being there must be
doing something to him. But what?'

Of course she hadn't done anything. But the
thought sat there. Hanging. Germinating.

Isabella's brows drew together again. 'Seriously, Gran. The man doesn't seem to have a life
outside the unit. He's never impatient to leave or
to go home. He was there every morning before
I got in this week, and still there for the afternoon shift.'

She'd thought it often enough, and finally she
said out loud,

'He reminds me of Dad. Spending his life at
work. I pity his poor family.'

She sat back in the chair and thought about
that. She could actually imagine a quarter-sized
boy, the image of Simon, with the same ocean-
blue eyes and full mouth, blond hair and scuffed
knees. A little boy waiting for his father to come
home. It made her sad for that little boy...

She refocussed. Sad for an imaginary little boy?
What was wrong with her?

'Does he even have a wife?' she wondered
aloud.

She'd been there a week and she still didn't
know. Well, she'd know if she let people tell her.
But for some crazy reason she kept holding up her

hand when any colleague—and there were a couple who loved to gossip—started to wax lyrical about Simon and his life. She didn't want to know.

*Why was that?*

Friday dawned with another perfect daybreak in paradise, and Isabella needed the cool water in the bay to wake her after an unsettled night. Her feet slapped rhythmically on the cool sand as she ran towards the surf. Her board lay tucked securely under her arm and her anticipation rose, like the waves out there, as she carried it across the cool pre-dawn beach towards the water.

'Morning,' a chic, elderly woman called out as she passed, lifting her hand as her cavoodle chased seagulls at the edge of the water.

'Best time of the day!' Isabella called back.

The woman, Elsa Green, lived two floors down in the apartment building. She was a friend of her grandmother's.

Isabella's run to the surf slowed, as if a sea fog had rolled over her, as she remembered the cheeky, wise woman her grandmother had been for both her and her sister before that horrible day everything changed. She'd been such a loving set of soft arms when her father had been immersed in work. A rock in their childhood until she'd moved north to Rainbow Bay.

It was tragic. Unfair. But when were accidents ever fair?

She lifted her chin. Catherine Goodwin Hargraves would wake up.

Moving here had been one of Isabella's best ideas. And Nadia selling her ostentatious and heavily mortgaged house to buy the apartment under Gran's was a great move. Meanwhile Isabella could stay and mind Gran's apartment upstairs, so it would be perfect for when she came home.

And Gran *would* come home.

Isabella was already helping Nadia in the last months of pregnancy. Which only bolstered her need to be close to her sister and Gran. Rainbow Bay worked perfectly. Isabella could surf and Nadia could photograph endlessly. And soon there would be a baby—Nadia's baby. And Isabella wouldn't be in her sister's pocket because they had the separate apartments. She might even buy her own apartment in the block if one came on the market.

She just wished Gran was there with them...

The first wave slapped her knee as she jogged deeper into the breaking wash. The water soaked her thighs and waist and she sucked in a breath at the delicious coolness.

Her gaze scanned the distance and she let thoughts of the past and the present fade. She observed about two dozen riders out there with the waves, but she was concentrating on the swells. Rollers that were big enough to give a nice run in towards the beach but with no need to concentrate excessively on avoiding others with her unsettled mind.

It was Simon Purdy who had caused all this twitching and turning through the night. It didn't matter which shift she worked, he turned up at least three times and never seemed to be in hurry to leave.

He took up so much space—and not all of it physical. Though his shoulders and big bronzed arms could block the light, his hands were always gentle and capable.

She could almost see the way his mind zeroed in on their small charges, making him aware of the status of every baby in the unit. She could see it because she did the same.

An ill baby could keep him there for hours. And now, for some illogical reason, he'd apparently decided he needed Isabella as his private assistant for the trickier procedures. Even when she would have preferred not to be called upon because she was doing something she particularly enjoyed.

Especially as he still didn't talk to her.

If he hadn't been so good at what he did she'd have lost patience with him long ago, but she wanted those babies to be well as much as he did.

It was the fact that he talked to everybody else except her that made her seethe. He treated all others with friendliness and respect, while she got the serious looks, the furrowed brows, the unsmiling mouth and gestures rather than words. Hand signals. Head-nods. It wasn't fair. And, if she was honest, it was more than a little annoying.

Yet at other times she caught his glance on her and felt his attention on her back. It was as if he didn't trust her. Which was ridiculous when he'd said himself she was easily the most experienced neonatal nurse in the unit alongside Carla. What was there not to trust?

A wave slapped her in the face—she hadn't seen it coming. And there he was again, intruding on her special time. *Grr...*

Isabella put her head down and paddled, her hands digging into the water, shooting past other surfers as she arrowed through swells and crests and pushed for the back of the sets. She was using up the energy that seemed to be zinging around her body like some electrical conduit of annoyance.

She looked up. There was just the ocean in front of her, all the way to New Zealand, and she finally stopped. As she sat back on her board, legs dangling in the clear blue water, she twisted to face the beach a couple of hundred metres away, then looked back to the far horizon.

She was alone, except for the guy to her left with his back to her, who seemed to be checking out the route to New Zealand as well.

But there wasn't time to think of him. The largest swell she'd seen this morning was rolling towards her and she lifted her feet and pressed her belly and breasts into the board and began to paddle, timing the connection.

Out of the corner of her eye she saw the other surfer shift to do the same. Plenty of room between them. This wave was a monster—one of those walls of water that people didn't notice but came every couple of sets and washed fishermen off rocks. The type of wave that gave surfers the best rush. A wave that reminded her that the sea was royalty and she just its subject.

The power and height of the wave surged swiftly and smoothly and she did the same, springing to her feet and tucking her board on the shelf of water like the bow of a boat. Wind dragged at her hair. Her eyes watched the water shoot below her and around her.

Blue everywhere—above her and beneath her. The sky, the wind... The world was condensed into this ride along the shoulder of a magnificent wall of myriad coloured water.

Her feet danced as she adjusted angle and weight, almost flying as she shot faster and closer to the beach, until the water monster collapsed under her and she slid out at the back and surfaced in a wash of foam and clinging magic.

Isabella lifted her chin, tilted her face to the sky and whooped.

She turned to see if the man at the back of the waves had made it, to share the moment, but he was already paddling away. He must have made it, because he was close, but she had been in a world of her own.

# CHAPTER FIVE

SIMON HAD NOTICED the glorious woman before she'd entered the water. Hell, every man out at the back of the waves had noticed her in those bikini bottoms under a short-sleeved surf shirt. Her board sat under her arm as if it was a flimsy paddle-pop stick, rather than a finned, fibreglass weight. Her long, luscious legs bronzed by the sun, glided smoothly as she ate up the distance between the sand and the launch point.

She hadn't been looking his way—her eyes had been fixed on the sets of waves, the wash, the horizon—but he'd been drawn, then, to her face.

His stomach had twisted as if a shark had come up from beneath him and chewed on his intestines.

*Not happening. Couldn't be.*

His breath had hitched as his chest went tight. It was *her.*

He'd almost fallen off his board—not something he would have lived down with his peers—but he'd stopped himself wobbling in time to absorb the shock. Might as well have been slapped in the nose by a neighbour's board. But his eyes had stayed glued to her.

Isabella Hargraves had run into the waves and launched herself on top of the board and then begun to paddle towards him, squashing her beautiful breasts. Which had meant the taut globes of her tanned buttocks had been there for all to see as her strong, feminine arms arrowed through the swells towards the quieter water.

The force of the biggest wave in the world couldn't have stopped him watching.

*Me and all the rest of the guys out there*, he'd thought sourly, as he'd glanced around.

Yep. She was poetry in motion. And the last thing he needed to see. Or feel.

But, dammit! This was *his* beach—*his* sanctuary—and now she was here to destroy the peace he'd fought for all week.

Another ghastly thought intruded.

*Was he going to bump into her every morning when the surf was up as well as at work?*

This was wrong. Already she was taking up too much headspace just by him seeing her in the NICU. He didn't need her glorious backside and her long, lean legs to kick him when he was down.

Since that first day he hadn't been able to ignore her, no matter how hard he'd tried. And he had tried. He'd managed to shore up his defences by barely speaking to her, so that he didn't get any closer, but he couldn't keep his eyes and his thoughts away.

Thankfully, his ridiculous fascination had kept his mouth shut. But, bizarrely, his brain kept going back to that brief rapport they'd had that first day, and how she'd felt like the easiest person in the world to talk to. How much more he'd wanted to know about her... How he'd wanted to lose himself in her fiercely intelligent eyes and revel in the elusive dream he'd vowed would never be his again.

That was when he'd really panicked.

Carla was on his case for giving Isabella the cold shoulder and apparently singling out a staff member she really, really wanted to keep, so he'd agreed yesterday afternoon that he'd try harder to be civil to Nurse Hargraves.

But his whole psyche had screamed *danger* right along with *hot, hot, hot* when he looked at Isabella.

Simon would not let anyone close again. His own mother had died giving birth to him. And he would not put himself out there to risk the grief, the loss and the monumental guilt he still carried from three years ago when he'd lost his wife.

Louise had been his first love, the first woman he'd allowed to get close to him. He'd sworn to protect her and keep her safe.

Probably another guilt trip left over since his seventh birthday, when his father told him that *he'd* been the reason his mother had died. A fact that his older, medically trained self knew was spurious, but it was still so hard to convince the seven-year-old kid inside him.

Then Louise and their son had died. When he

had been absent—working. And despite his best friend—his wife's doctor—telling him that nothing would have changed the outcome, Louise's death had damaged him. Adding to the loathing his father had heaped on him in the dark times of his childhood.

In short, he was not going down the route of attraction, falling in love, planning a life together and then losing the one he'd pinned his future on ever again. *Ever.*

Never.

No matter how glorious Isabella Hargraves was. No matter how much poetry in motion he saw in her.

He just wasn't sure how he was going to stop himself.

# CHAPTER SIX

WHEN ISABELLA WALKED into the unit later that morning, the ferocious glower she received from Simon Purdy could have shrivelled her on the spot.

She froze. Stared. Glared back at him.

The calmness and tranquillity from her amazing surf this morning seemed to trickle away like seawater down her back, leaving her cold and chilled. And then red-hot with fury. She was *so* over this.

Isabella marched across the unit. Stopped in front of him and asked very quietly, so nobody else could hear, and very clearly, so he would understand, 'What is your problem?'

'You,' he replied.

His blue eyes were stone-hard and his mouth was a thin line.

She narrowed her eyes at him. It was a measure of the build-up of tension over the last week that she allowed her hands to come up to her hips.

'What have I done?' she shot back. 'Or did you just get out on the wrong side of the bed? *Again.*'

Before he could answer, Carla glided up and stepped between them. 'What's going on?' she asked them both, but she was looking at Simon.

Isabella said quietly, and with impeccable calm,

'I don't care if Dr Purdy is the best paediatrician this side of the equator. I expect to be treated with the respect I deserve and the politeness he so easily gives to everyone else in the unit.'

Carla nodded. 'Fair call, Isabella. Simon...?'

Isabella's and Simon's eyes were still locked— neither had looked at the unit manager. Isabella held his gaze—his hard and blue, hers determined not to give in—until he flinched.

She heard his breath heave out and for some strange, stupid reason she actually felt sorry for him.

*What the...?*

'You're right,' Simon said.

He lifted his chin. Straightened his shoulders. Stared at the wall past her head.

'I apologise, Isabella. Something happened this morning that I shouldn't have brought to work.'

His gaze drifted briefly to Isabella's face. She saw the briefest flicker of searing pain there until he looked away to Carla.

'I'll do better.'

Then he walked out of the unit, leaving Isabella staring after him, still not understanding why she wasn't angry any more and confused as to why on earth she was wishing she hadn't said anything.

Carla must have read her expression. Or else she was prescient.

'It needed saying. And he wasn't listening to

me,' Carla said as she patted Isabella's arm. 'He knows he wasn't being fair.'

'Hi, Gran. How are you today?'

As Isabella leaned over and kissed her grandmother's soft cheek she inhaled the faint, sweet rose scent. Gran still smelled the same as she had for as long as Isabella could remember and the fragrance always made her feel hope that her grandmother would wake up.

That was why Isabella replenished Gran's favourite soap when it shrank, and why the nurses promised to continue to use it during her care.

Isabella sat down. 'Work was fine…'

Gran's chest rose and fell.

'Although this morning, when he came in, Simon Purdy was in a foul mood.' Isabella scoffed. 'He actually glared at me as if I'd done something wrong. So I confronted him. That's not like me, I know, but I was so over the dirty looks. He did apologise. But he looked strange…'

She shook her head.

'I still have no idea what his beef is, and if he wasn't one of the best neonatologists I've ever seen I'd have made a formal complaint. Still, maybe he'll be better now.'

She listened to herself. Gran did not need to hear this.

She blew out a breath. 'Luckily, I had such a great surf before work. So it was like water off a seagull's back. You would have loved this huge wave I caught. It was so good...'

It had been an amazing start to the day.

And then that man... Her mind drifted back to Simon Purdy. It was disconcerting. She'd never had someone take an instant dislike to her before. And then there'd been that look of agony she'd seen.

Gran didn't need to know about that, either. But she felt agitated at the thought of him, and grimaced.

Isabella leaned forward and opened the drawer beside the bed. Her fingers found the tube of rose-scented hand lotion and she reached to pick up her grandmother's hand. She squeezed the tube and gently swirled the lotion onto the papery skin of Gran's hands.

Isabella did this often—sat and gently massaged the long, thin fingers of Gran's hands with the lotion while she talked. As always, a sense of peace settled over her.

'Anyway... Nadia's been getting headaches. I don't think it's pregnancy-related, but her next antenatal appointment isn't until next Wednesday. Hopefully she's going as an outpatient today to get checked, as I suggested, but you know what she's like. Stubborn.'

As Gran breathed in and out her heart rate did that little rise and fall thing again, but Isabella was used to it now.

'You always said we were both stubborn, but I think Nadia's more obstinate than me. I'll find out whether she went when I get home.'

*Home.* To Gran's apartment without Gran. It was getting harder and harder to imagine her grandmother ever being there when she came home from work. She hated that and hoped she wasn't losing faith like everyone else.

No. She wouldn't. She'd use some of her own stubbornness to stay positive.

'Your flat's looking fine. I haven't killed all your plants.'

*Yet*, she thought ruefully. Most were drooping, and she didn't know if she was giving them too much water or not enough.

*Or maybe they needed more sunlight?*

'I mentioned my concerns to Mrs Green…'

Isabella thought about that, and a smile tugged at her mouth.

'So cool that her name is Green and she's good with plants.'

She waited for her grandmother to smile, but of course she didn't.

She shook her head at herself.

'Mrs Green said she'd use her spare key and come up and water the plants on the veranda every other day, when she knows I'm out. She always asks about you. I keep telling her you'll be home soon.'

Gran continued to breathe. In and out.

The monitor continued to trace her heart rate.

By the time Isabella parked her car under the apartments it was nearing four-thirty. Instead of pressing for the lift she climbed the stairs, turned left, and knocked on her sister's door.

When there was no answer, she knocked again. And again. Until she heard Nadia's voice inside. Faintly.

'I'm coming… All right… Give me a minute.'

A cold flicker of worry ignited in Isabella's chest at the dull timbre of Nadia's voice. But at least the shuffling noises were coming closer, and finally the door opened.

Her sister leaned against the door frame like a droopy sunflower, with her yellow hair falling over her face and her long neck bent as if she could barely hold the weight of her head up. Let alone the big belly out front.

'Isabella. It's you.'

*Who else would it be?*

Isabella pushed the door open and gently turned her sister, nudging her back into the lounge room and into a chair. 'You look terrible.'

'Gee. Thanks, Sis.' Nadia's voice trailed away listlessly.

'Did you go and get checked out today at the hospital?'

'Didn't have the energy.'

'How's your headache?'

'There all the time. All over my head. It's weird...' Nadia lifted a tired hand to rub her scalp.

Isabella peered down and examined her sister's ankles. No, they didn't look swollen. But oedema could happen quickly.

'Are you going to the toilet as much as you normally do?'

Nadia sighed. 'Probably not. But then I'm not drinking or eating either, so there's nothing to pass. I'm a bit sick in my stomach.' She rubbed her abdomen under her breast. 'Probably picked up a bug from somewhere.'

All nebulous symptoms, but worrying. 'I want to take you in and get you checked out in Maternity.'

Nadia shook her head—gingerly. 'Not now. I've just taken two headache tablets. I'm going to go and lie down.' She closed her eyes, as if the light was too bright. 'I was lying down when you knocked.'

'I don't like the look of you... Really. Something's not right.'

Her sister made an effort to sit straighter in the chair. Forced her eyes wider. 'You're a worry-wart. How about I have my sleep, then you come and see me in a couple of hours? Use your key so I don't have to get up. If I'm still no good, I'll go then.'

'I'd be happier if you went now...'

Nadia waved her away. 'But it's not about *you* being happy, is it?'

Time for the big guns.

Isabella's instincts were screaming.

'No. It's about keeping your baby safe,' Isabella said quietly. Her voice was firm and she watched her words finally sink in.

Understanding flooded Nadia's face. And then her green eyes widened in fear. 'Yes. It's about the baby. I'll go now.'

Half an hour after they arrived at the hospital Nadia began to see flashes of light in front of her eyes, and then she started to seize uncontrollably.

Suddenly the clinic was full of people and Isabella retreated to the back of the room. She gave thanks for the hospital policy of one support person being allowed to stay at all times where possible.

Then a tall, dark-haired doctor suddenly strode in and organised everyone in seconds, giving quiet orders that were instantly obeyed.

Isabella's terror receded as Nadia's hypertensive crisis was brought swiftly under control and a care plan commenced.

The new doctor turned to her and introduced himself. 'I'm Malachi Madden, the consultant obstetrician on call today. You're Nadia's sister? And a midwife?'

'Yes.'

'Excellent. So, Nadia has eclampsia—you'll know what I'm talking about. We'll keep her in under one-on-one observation for the next twenty-four hours. If she settles on the medication, we'll see how long we can prolong the pregnancy. Thirty-two weeks is not a great stage for birth, but sometimes it's necessary. We'll start steroids now, to help mature the baby's lungs, with the probability of delivery in the next forty-eight hours.'

His manner was brisk and blunt—which she appreciated—and decisive.

He went on, 'With eclampsia, there's really not much benefit to prolonging the pregnancy, because the environment becomes dangerous for the mother and is no longer optimal for the foetus.'

'I understand. I work in neonatal intensive care.'

'Do you? That's handy.' He smiled at her and, unexpectedly, his smile was sweet and sincere. 'My wife and I have one-year-old twins, and I know babies do give you interesting moments. Your sister will be glad of your advice.'

# CHAPTER SEVEN

AT FIVE-THIRTY THE next morning Simon's phone buzzed. He rolled out of bed to sit up and answer the call.

Years ago, as an exhausted med student, he'd learned not to lie down and take phone calls. Though he knew at this time of day he wouldn't fall asleep, because the sun would be up soon and he'd be planning on hitting the beach.

In five out of the last six days he'd been called out before sunrise and had had to go to the hospital instead of enjoying an early-morning surf.

The only day he had made it, his longed-for peace had been slapped for six by a blonde bombshell in tiny bikini bottoms.

He glanced at the caller ID. His registrar. Not surprising. Henry was the most likely person to ring him at an ungodly hour, though he only phoned when he needed advice or help.

'Morning, Simon.' Henry's cheerful voice came down the line. 'Got a new prem. Thirty-two weeks. Female. Two thousand grams. Born an hour ago due to maternal eclampsia and requiring CPAP at the moment, plus a cannula that's proving tricky, but otherwise she's stable.'

'Nothing you can't handle. So what's the problem?' Simon didn't believe in babying his registrars. Because they were the next generation and one day, unimaginable as it was at this moment, he would retire.

'I've had two goes at inserting the line without success, and the baby's auntie said I had to get you.'

Simon's brow furrowed. 'Come again?'

He couldn't think of any of his friends due to have a baby soon. Though it sometimes happened with hospital staff. People recommended him for their grandchildren or asked him to be in charge of sick nieces and nephews. And he always agreed. There had to be some perks for these staff who cared so diligently for others. But those requests usually came when he was on duty. At handover or in normal working hours.

'She said I'm not allowed to try the cannula again.'

Simon mentally shrugged. He was awake anyway. 'Who's the auntie?'

His registrar lowered his voice. 'That new neo-natal intensivist... Isabella Hargraves. She said if the kid wasn't her niece she'd put the line in herself.'

Any lingering drowsiness in Simon's mind disappeared like mist in the sun and he remembered that first day, with Carla telling him Isabella had moved here to be with her grandmother and pregnant sister.

'Ahh. Her sister. I'm coming.'

* * *

The first person Simon saw when he entered the unit was Isabella, and his gaze stuck on her like a seagull spotting a lone potato chip. He forced himself to look away as he washed his hands at the sink. Her hair had been pulled back in a blonde ponytail, she wore no make-up, and yet she still looked as if she'd stepped out of a fashion magazine. It was the way she held herself as much as what she wore.

Hell, she looked like a model even when she was in scrubs.

His gaze shifted to the cot she stood beside, and he saw the small bare limbs under the heat lamp, and the monitors and paraphernalia of a prem baby in their care. He inclined his head towards Henry and the night shift nurse as he crossed the room to them.

'Thank you for coming,' Isabella said, her voice softly hesitant.

He wasn't surprised to see uncertainty in her eyes, as if she was not sure of her reception. Yesterday had been a day of fireworks, and they'd been careful to avoid each other since her accusations and his apology.

But it wasn't as if he would ever have declined the request. He realised he hadn't been particularly friendly, but...

'Of course I'd come.'

There was no missing her relief. Though it was

a surprise that she'd want him looking after her niece. And even more personally noteworthy that he found he didn't want anyone else doing it, either.

'Thank you for trusting me.'

He turned to Henry.

'Run me through the history.'

Henry did, and when he was finished Simon nodded. Then another thought intruded.

He looked at Isabella. 'Where's your sister? Is she okay?'

The beautiful woman in front of him sagged a little, and he wanted to put out a hand in sympathy. Badly. But his sense of self-preservation wouldn't let him.

'Nadia's still in Recovery. She had a caesarean section after escalating eclampsia. But she should improve soon, with the end of the pregnancy.'

He could see the concern in the creases of her brow. It must be a big worry for her to carry, and he wanted to ease that burden. He felt the urge to reassure her. Comfort her. Dammit, he wanted to help her in any way he could.

'I'm sorry to hear she's unwell. Who's her obstetrician?'

'Malachi Madden.'

She searched his face for reassurance, and he felt the consolation of being able to give it freely. Relief expanded inside him. His long-time friend was the best.

'Ahh. Great. Excellent choice. He's sharp. He'll look after her.'

'And you'll look after Kate?' she asked.

He could see she'd recovered her usual calm façade, as if he had already helped with his endorsement of Malachi.

'I will,' he told her. 'Absolutely.'

Simon was soon feeling along the edges of the tiny baby's body, skimming the abdomen and watching the equal rising of both lungs.

'Her mum had called her Kate? Great name.'

'Named after my grandmother—Catherine.'

He looked up and saw her gaze had clouded again.

'Gran's not well either.'

He nodded. Said sincerely, 'I'm sorry to hear that.'

Then he shifted his gaze down again. 'Let's have a listen to this little lady.' He raised a brow at Henry. 'You go. I'll stay.'

'Thanks, boss. Been a long night.'

The young man lifted one finger to his forehead in a salute to Simon and tipped an imaginary hat to Isabella. He was grinning as he strode away.

Simon positioned the buds of his stethoscope in his ears and examined his new patient.

He said quietly to the night shift nurse waiting, 'Do we know how the placenta looked? Was it failing? Were all vessels present?'

'The theatre notes haven't arrived, yet.' The nurse was young, nervous, and kept darting glances between Simon and Isabella. 'I'll let you know when they come through.'

'Maybe give them a ring now?' Simon suggested mildly, but the nurse got the message and took off.

He looked at 'Auntie Isabella'. The thought made him want to smile, but there was nothing funny about what she was going through.

'Is there any history of pre-eclampsia with your sister?' he asked.

'No.'

She shook her head and her ponytail flopped over her shoulder. He could see more clearly that she looked tired and a little strung out. Not surprising. And no thanks to him.

In a flash of insight, he regretted the barriers he'd been putting up since he first saw her. She was new to town. She needed kindness, not his prickly defences, and she had a lot going on in her life. He hadn't realised how much. He'd been an arrogant idiot, only thinking about himself and his own insecurities. His own demons. Which wasn't like him.

So why was that? Why act so much out of character? And why had he targeted someone he knew didn't deserve it?

He was afraid he knew why. Fear. Of himself.

For himself. And, riding on the back of that, fear for her if she relied on him.

He had a sudden urge to reach out and touch her shoulder...apologise. Hell, he wanted to pull her into his arms and give her a hug. Of course he couldn't do anything so stupid. But he could breathe in the scent of her. Could watch the expressions cross her face as she looked at Kate.

Thankfully, her eyes were fixed on her niece, not on him.

'When I got home yesterday afternoon Nadia was complaining of a headache,' she explained. 'She looked so unwell I dragged her into Maternity. She started seizures half an hour after we arrived.'

Close call. And scary. She had to be imagining other scenarios.

'Lucky you did what you did.' His voice was soft. He understood the fear of others. He'd been there in the worst way. 'That's nasty. Dangerous for both Mum and baby.'

She started, as if surprised. For a horrid moment he thought she was going to cry. And then she lifted her chin.

'Yes.'

He dragged his eyes from her face, glanced towards the desk, but the young nurse was still on the phone.

'She's in the best place now. Let's have a look at this cannula...'

'Want me to help?'

Isabella had already begun to douse her hands with the cleanser clipped to the sides of all the cots.

Of course he wanted her help. She was the best to work with. But it wasn't fair when it was her own niece.

'You're okay with that?' he asked.

'As long as you don't mind that I called you in.'

He did smile at that. 'No. Never. Though Henry probably would've got the cannula in on the third go.'

'I wasn't willing to risk his next attempt.' She narrowed her eyes. 'Send him to me next week and I'll adjust his technique.'

'I'll do that.'

Simon laughed. Something he hadn't done for a while, except maybe with his friend Malachi and his wife, Lisandra. Henry did tend to rush when he was nervous. Isabella might have made him nervous. Hell, she made *him* nervous—but for a different reason.

That thought sobered him.

'If Kate was my niece, I probably wouldn't have let him try again, either.'

'Yes… Thank you for coming.'

'You're welcome. She looks good, Isabella.'

Suddenly it was easy to talk to her. Like back in the beginning, before he'd put up his great wall. It was something he'd been avoiding thinking about like the plague, because that one time he'd listened, he'd been drawn to her so strongly. He'd backed away in an absolute wild panic, and hadn't wanted to repeat the experience. It hurt too much to care for people and then lose them. So, he'd vowed to keep that wall way up during work—to make it unlikely he'd do anything stupid.

Anyway, she was experienced enough to know what he wanted during procedures without him having to use words. All it took was a lift of his brow and she knew what he wanted. Which made it easier. And harder.

Aside from that, the more he discreetly watched and listened to her, the more he suspected she might be one of the smartest people he'd met.

But now she was a concerned relative. And he talked to her because it was part of his job. She needed to hear what was going on. He passionately believed in not holding back information from those who had the right to be told.

'She's got a heart murmur. Did you hear that?' he asked her.

Isabella had a stethoscope around her neck, and he assumed she'd have listened to her niece's chest.

'I did. Sounds like a PDA. Hopefully, because she's prem, her patent ductus will close as she grows.'

'My thought too.'

Ha! He known she'd pick that up.

'And we both know that children born after twenty-eight weeks of pregnancy, and with a weight like this little lady, have a big chance of having no long-term problems.'

'We know eight out of ten do,' Isabella corrected him.

He smiled to himself, and didn't look at her as he studied the lack of creases on Baby Kate's feet and the cartilage growth of her ears.

'But she's a good weight for thirty-two weeks, so the pre-eclampsia hasn't been a long-term issue she'll have to recover from.'

Her shoulders rose and fell in a sigh. 'When it's your own sister's baby, she looks more tiny and delicate than everyone else's baby. I'm used to seeing babies without toenails and hair, and she has both, but she's so fragile. What do you think of her breathing?'

'I think she's doing well for the day she's had.'

'I know. Don't tell me.' She waved her hand at him, apparently aware he'd been about to say something reassuring. 'Albert Einstein was born two months premature and look at what he achieved.'

She smiled, and he couldn't help smiling back. He'd bet she'd heard that so many times. They'd dined on that story in med school, and he suspected midwives did too.

'Exactly. We'll get her started on some broad-spectrum antibiotics. Do you know if Nadia's going to breastfeed?'

He saw Isabella was looking better for their conversation. More herself. Not so shattered.

'She intends to.'

'Great. She'll have you to help her.'

# CHAPTER EIGHT

SIMON PURDY WAS being nice to her, and now she felt like crying. Felt like burying her nose in his big, beautiful chest and sobbing. Of course it was just emotional overload from the last twelve hours. Her sister and niece could have died—highly unlikely in the modern day—but the risk had been there.

And then Isabella had demanded they get Simon. She didn't know how it had happened, and she wasn't normally a pushy person, but she'd stood there watching his registrar's second attempt at placing the cannula and known he wouldn't get it.

She needed Simon on board for her niece. She didn't care if she was being demanding. Didn't care if Simon hated her guts. He was the best. This was all about Nadia's baby and Nadia couldn't be there. Isabella was. And she would be Kate's champion until her mother recovered.

And so here they were. Back to working on a baby together—although she was pretending it wasn't her flesh and blood lying there.

Her hands moved confidently, with muscle memory, as she assembled fresh equipment and Simon prepared Kate's tiny arm for another attempt at the cannula insertion.

He'd come when she'd asked, she thought. So fast. He must live as close as she did. And Henry, the registrar, hadn't been offended, which was a good thing for future professional relationships. Although, even if he had been miffed she would still have demanded Simon.

All these thoughts played in her mind as she watched his long, slender, yet strong hands. Piano player's hands...calm, capable, hands, she thought, her eyes glued to them as they very gently tilted Kate's skin this way and that to catch the light and expose the minuscule thread of veins below the skin.

'One there,' he said, and she peered with him. She inhaled his man scent and felt her pulse jump and her heated skin react to his nearness.

She ignored the sensations. She didn't want to think about them. She returned her mind to Kate, and allowed the relief of seeing Simon's skills to flow over her.

The vein was faint, but clear to see. Henry hadn't seen that one. The tension in her shoulders and neck released. The responsibility had shifted to the man beside her.

Simon Purdy had this all under control. She could relax.

He was here and—surprise, surprise—finally treating her the same way he treated the other staff.

She thought about that. No. Actually, he was treating her as if she was the relative of one of his patients. With reassurance and an unspoken promise to do his best. And yet there was professional appreciation for her as well. She'd seen a glimmer of it before, when they were working together, but it was a little hard to feel appreciated if the person you worked with didn't speak to you.

If her niece wasn't so fragile she'd be thinking all her Christmases had come at once. But for the moment she just wanted to see this cannula in and working.

Within seconds the procedure had been completed successfully and their eyes briefly met in relief. Held for a couple of seconds longer than necessary.

She taped the tiny tube down while Simon held it still. Then they both stood back as the machine began to count the slow drops of fluid running into Kate's arm.

All tension her released and relief washed over her. 'Thank you.'

He smiled at her. His teeth white, his mouth curved and that beautiful, strangely sexy nose of his pointed her way.

'You're very welcome. As always, you're a great right hand.'

'As always, huh?' She tilted her head at him and

raised her brows. Her voice just a little mocking. 'Can't say I've felt that appreciation much over the last week.'

*Good grief. Not now.* She closed her lips.

Not when he was doing her and Kate a favour.

But he had the grace to look away. 'Some personal stuff,' he murmured. 'Not your fault. But, yes, you copped some of the fall-out. I apologise again for that. My behaviour hasn't been fair.'

That made her blink. She had not expected a confession and another comprehensive expression of regret.

Off balance, she said quietly, 'Why were you so foul yesterday when I came in?'

Lord, it was as if her filters had been lost sometime in the long night.

It was her turn to look away. 'Sorry. Ignore that. It's been an emotional twelve hours.'

His whole body went rigid. His mouth pursed. And then he sighed. Shook his head and turned his gaze to her. He studied her face and then shook his head again. His expression was resigned... even slightly amused.

'Would you like to go for breakfast after this? I know a place that opens early. I can explain.'

And that was another thing she had not expected him to say.

She glanced at the clock. Twenty minutes until

the day staff began to arrive. She was on the afternoon shift today, and she had to sleep. But…

'I guess I need to eat. I've drunk lots of coffee. But no food since lunch yesterday.'

'We'll wait to hand over to Carla…get the morning staff here first, if that's okay with you?'

'Of course. Actually, I'd prefer that.'

'Thought you might.'

He smiled, and she felt that ridiculous urge to cry again.

She didn't think he would notice, but he said softly, so nobody else could hear, 'You'd be eligible for compassionate leave, you know. Next of kin. You should take a day or two, get some sleep, come and go to see Kate and your sister without having to concentrate on your patients.'

That did sound like heaven, and she was so tempted—but she was new here, and couldn't let Carla down. The unit had already been busy before Kate, and a new premmie would stretch their limits.

'I think they'll need more staff…not less.'

'I thought you might say that too.' His blue eyes were too kind. 'We'll see.'

He walked away a few steps, picked up a chair and placed it gently beside Kate's cot. 'Sit here, watch your niece and enjoy her. She's stable, if early in her adventures. I'll do a quick round to check everyone else while we wait.'

So she sat. In the chair he brought for her. And the overwhelming facts finally sank in. She was an auntie. Nadia was safe. And Simon had come to care for Kate.

They'd walked to breakfast. They went to the coffee shop that sat perched above Rainbow Bay, with its high stools and tall benches under red umbrellas, all facing the waves. Jars of pretty purple-blue knives and forks sat in the middle of the tables. Very beachy...

Simon had said he lived too close to the hospital to drive—it was only a block—so he didn't take his car to work. She said she didn't either.

Isabella hadn't realised there was a place so near to where she lived that was open this early. She studied the menu briefly—*yum*—and put it back down. Her stomach rumbled.

The waitress, a young woman with a dozen piercings and her hair shaved so close to her head she was almost bald, grinned at Simon. 'Yo, Doc. The usual?' She patted her pocket and pulled out a pen and notebook.

'Yes. Thanks, Lulu.'

He turned to face her. That lovely, debonair nose of his—which for some reason she liked too much—was suddenly too close to hers and his face, too handsome, was filling her vision.

'You ready to order?'

*Order. Right. Stop looking at the pretty man.*

'Smashed avocado and eggs, thanks. Plus, your rainbow juice. No coffee. I need to sleep soon.'

'On the way,' Lulu said, and winked at Simon. He was obviously a regular patron.

'I think the waitress likes you.'

'Lulu's the proprietor. I looked after her twins when they were born. Twin-to-twin transfusion, and the smallest one struggled a bit at first. They're both at preschool now and doing well.'

'No wonder you're a favourite. A story around every corner. Or around every cafe.' She waved her arm towards the other stools. 'Great to know this is here, though. Thanks.'

He lounged in his chair, relaxed, soaking in the sun and the admiration of passers-by like a darned rock star. Not looking as if he'd been dragged from his bed by her. Drat the man. No doubt she looked as if she'd been raking her hair and sleeping in her clothes for the whole night.

'Despite how I look now, I do like to get up early,' she said.

'Me too,' he said, with an odd tone in his voice. 'I've been surfing here for the last three years. It's where I find my peace.'

There was a definite note of pique there. Plus, a strange twist to his beautiful mouth. And why she was noticing all these masculine attributes she did not know.

That was the last thing she needed to do. She needed to eat and go to bed. And put the intriguing Simon Purdy, currently being so pleasant to her, out of her mind. Another workaholic she was drawn to. What was wrong with her?

Then his actual words sank in.

She turned to face him. 'You surf?'

'Mm-hmm,' he said, very dryly.

She crinkled her brows at him. Now that she thought about it, he did have more of a laid-back, world-class surfer look than a rock star gleam, with his blond hair slightly ruffled and his skin tanned bronze. The way his azure-blue eyes crinkled at the corners could be from watching hundreds of promising ocean swells roll his way.

And suddenly she knew.

'You were out at the back of the swells when I was there yesterday.' She should have recognised those shoulders. That hair. 'And later that was you paddling away after that amazing wave.'

'It was.'

She frowned. 'I've been surfing every morning this week. I haven't seen you...'

Then she remembered that first surfer she'd watched, and suspected that had been him as well. How could she have missed him? She couldn't believe she hadn't recognised him yesterday. She guessed on a surfboard was not a place she'd expected to see him. But surely, she hadn't missed him day after day, every morning?

'I've had a run of early call-outs that have impacted on my surf time this week.' He breathed in slowly and let it out. 'Since my wife died, and since I moved to the beach…' He lifted his shoulders, and then his chin. 'The waves and work. That's where I find my peace.'

'You lost your wife?'

Heck. That explained a lot. He was broken. He had a right to be moody.

'I'm sorry for your loss.'

'Three years ago. Louise and our baby both died. Amniotic fluid embolism.'

Disasterous. That happened when amniotic fluid crossed the placenta into the mother's bloodstream. How awful for all of them.

He was looking at her as if he didn't believe her. 'You didn't know? Hospital staff usually make sure everyone knows everything.'

She shook her head. 'I make an effort not to engage. I come from a high-profile family and I dislike gossip.'

'Yes. Carla told me about your father on your first day.' His mouth quirked. 'Apparently, I do listen to gossip. She could see you had made an impact on me.'

She had made an impact on him? When? How?

But he didn't add to the statement. Maybe she had heard him wrong.

Something else bothered her. 'You said you'd tell me what happened yesterday. Why did I get the super-snarly Dr Purdy?'

He rubbed his chin with his knuckles, and looked relieved when their drinks arrived.

Lulu stood for a minute, examining Simon's face. 'Haven't seen you for a while...'

'We've been busy in the NICU. This is Isabella. She's one of those hotshot neonatal nurses—like the ones who came in the helicopter to scoop up Lily when she was transferred.'

Lulu looked impressed and Isabella felt the heat in her cheeks. He'd known that about her, too?

'Cool.' Lulu grinned, and the tiny diamond in her tooth glinted. 'You people are amazing. I hope we see you again another day.'

Isabella smiled back, even if it was a tired smile. She could feel herself wilting.

'You will. I live around here. Or my grandmother did...' *Not did.* 'Does. She *does.* She's in hospital at the moment.'

Why had she started this? She was too tired to be sensible.

'Anyway, thanks...'

Lulu nodded and went off to answer the bell at the kitchen window. It looked as if their food was ready.

Lulu arrived back with their plates just as Simon asked, 'What's wrong with your grandmother?'

His concern warmed Isabella more than it should have, but still she felt the tug of old grief and shock. 'She was knocked over by a hit-and-run driver a month ago. She's still unconscious.'

Simon closed his eyes briefly and muttered, 'I've been stupid...' He shook his head. 'Mrs Hargraves...' He turned his shoulders and pointed to where her grandmother's apartment block was just visible through the trees. 'You're living in her flat?'

'Yes. And my sister bought one in the same block.'

He said something she couldn't quite hear, but it sounded possibly like *Fate is conspiring*.

'Sorry?'

'Nothing.' He lifted his hands and said to the sky, 'Should I just bow to the inevitable? That I'm going to see you everywhere I go?'

Isabella stifled a yawn. 'You're being annoying.'

He tilted his head as if he changed his mind about what he was going to say and gestured for her to eat. 'I'm guessing you've been up for twenty-four hours. You need a sleep.'

He still hadn't told her what his problem had been yesterday, but at that point she just didn't care. She'd got to the stage when she was almost too tired to eat, but she'd better—she'd need some energy to get home.

# CHAPTER NINE

Simon finished his breakfast and sipped his coffee while his companion finished hers. Really, there was nothing he could do except make sure Isabella made it to her apartment.

He might as well tell her he lived upstairs, even if she was too tired to comprehend, because it would be stupid to put her into the lift and not get in after her.

Lulu brought the bill and he paid it. Isabella didn't notice as she stared unfocussed into the distance.

Yep, she'd crashed.

'Come on, sleepyhead, I'll walk you home. Can't have you falling asleep in a bus shelter.'

'I will not fall asleep in a bus shelter,' she said with just a little fuzzy haughtiness that he found surprisingly cute. She gathered her bag and slung it over her shoulder. Then she turned back and said, 'Thanks, Lulu. That was wonderful.'

He thought it sweet that she'd appreciated the service. They walked side by side along the path towards the square apartment building that soon loomed over them.

He couldn't believe he hadn't run into her in the lift. But then, he had been keeping odd hours lately. Pretty funny that he'd spent most days with her at work, though, and yet they hadn't realised they shared an address.

As they reached the ground floor entrance she fumbled in her bag and he touched her shoulder. 'I've got it.' He pulled out his keys from his pocket, opened the door, and gestured for her to go in front of him.

She frowned. 'Why have you got a key to this building?'

'Not that sleepy, then?' he said, amused by her suspicion.

She tilted her head back, stared at him with narrowed eyes. He noticed her gaze had lost its dozy inattention.

'I live on the eighth floor,' he said succinctly.

Her eyes widened. 'You're kidding me?'

'I was surprised, too, when I worked it out at the café.'

'So you know my grandmother?'

Her eyes were an incredible shade of green with gold flecks. The world shifted as he stared. His gaze drifted to her mouth, where the words had come from. So soft. Tempting. He could just kiss… And then he woke up. Hot. Bothered. Mentally smacking himself.

She said, 'Hello…?'

Simon stepped back to make more space between them.

*Oh, whoa, lost it there for a second.*

What the heck had happened?

He'd known this was a bad idea.

He reorganised his thoughts and played back the conversation. 'Yes. Mrs Hargraves? I've met her many times in the lift. She's a lovely lady. I was very sorry to hear about her accident.' He pressed the lift call button and stood back with her to wait.

'She's still unconscious,' Isabella said, in a normal voice.

Maybe she hadn't noticed he'd almost kissed her, he thought. Hoped.

*He had almost...what?*

'I see her every day, depending on my shift. I'm still praying...' Her voice trailed off.

This was not about him. This was about her world and he had no idea about it.

'You've had a tough month,' he said.

'You have no idea,' she said, as if she'd read his thoughts.

There was just a touch of bitterness that seemed very unlike her, and he wondered what else could have gone wrong for her.

He knew about ghastly times. Things had gone horribly wrong for him.

'Where there's life there's hope,' he said. A trite saying that tasted bitter in his mouth.

During his ghastly time he hadn't even had that—hope. His wife and child had both been gone within minutes. When he wasn't there. No hope. But he was finding a little more distance from the shock as the years passed. And even more since he'd met Isabella.

*What?*

He took another step back as the lift doors opened. He was suddenly very conscious of how small the lift was, and how close they'd be. Maybe he should dash back to the hospital to check on Kate?

'Get in. I won't bite,' she said, and the super-confident woman he'd first met was back in place.

He felt his cheeks warm. He hadn't blushed since high school. But he stepped in and the doors closed.

She pushed buttons seven and eight. 'You never told me what happened yesterday.' Her eyes widened. 'And I didn't pay for breakfast.'

'I settled the bill. You were half asleep. You can pay next time.'

*Next time? Was there going to be a next time?* Heaven help him.

The lift stopped and he put his hand across the doors to prevent them closing prematurely on her.

'Phone me directly if you're ever worried about Kate. I'll come as soon as I can.' He opened his wallet and gave her his business card, so she'd have his cell phone number.

Suddenly her eyes glittered with tears, and he saw her throat shift as she swallowed. She nodded. 'Thank you.' Her voice cracked. 'I appreciate that.'

'Sleep well.' He pulled his arm back and the lift doors closed as she walked away.

# CHAPTER TEN

'NADIA'S HAD HER BABY, Gran. A little girl.'

Gran's serene expression didn't change.

'She's called her Kate after you. Catherine and Kate. I think it's a gorgeous pairing.'

Isabella had slept for four hours. She'd spoken to her father again, as she had before she'd gone to sleep, and deleted another text from Conlon. Then on the way back to NICU she dropped in to the high dependency ward looking after her grandmother.

'You're a great-grandmother.'

Gran breathed in and out. Her eyes were still shut. Hopefully one day soon they'd open.

'I'm going to see her again now. She weighs two kilograms—that's four pounds four ounces in your terms—and she's gorgeous. Big eyes like Nadia.'

No twitch from Gran and Isabella sighed.

'Still, she's so tiny and fragile-looking. But Simon Purdy—that doctor in the unit I was telling you about—is going to look after her, so I'm happy about that. Turns out he lives one floor up from you.'

The penthouse, she guessed. Funny to think of Simon in a penthouse...

She thought about what she'd said about Simon before to her grandmother.

'And even though I was cross with him yesterday...' Had she been? Yes, actually. She'd been cross that he'd been so cold towards her when she didn't deserve it. She'd still not found out what had upset him. He'd said he'd tell her at breakfast. He hadn't!

'Anyway, he is an excellent paediatrician, and my niece—your great-granddaughter,' she added, trying to break through her grandmother's silence, 'has to have the best. Simon said he would be there whenever Kate needed him.'

She sat back and thought about the relief that gave her. And the fact that Nadia had been pronounced as 'improving' as well. Soon she'd be well enough to visit her baby. It must be so hard for her sister to be stuck in intensive care as a new mum.

'When I phoned just now they said I can see Nadia even though she's still in Intensive Care. I'll have to hurry, because I start work in an hour and a half. I'll drop into the neonatal unit first, and check that Kate's fine, and take a few more photos for Nadia on my phone before I visit her.'

She stood. Looked down at the now familiarly sleeping face.

'It's time you woke up, Gran. We need you to meet your namesake.' She leaned down and kissed the soft wrinkled cheek. 'Love you.'

* * *

When Isabella reached the NICU, she saw Simon, tall and far too eye-catching, beside Carla at Kate's cot. He looked up as she washed her hands at the sink and smiled.

Carla turned Isabella's way as well, as she crossed the room, drying her fingers on a paper towel. 'Congratulations, Auntie,' she said. 'She's beautiful.'

Isabella looked down at the baby with her naso-gastric tube and IV line, and the electronic pulse oximeter sensor strapped to her foot. 'Thank you. She is, isn't she? Has she been a good girl?'

She addressed the last question to Simon, who nodded.

'She's behaving like a typical thirty-two-weeker, so she'll have her moments of unusual in-terest. But she's stable. Have you seen your sister?'

'I phoned the ward when I woke up. They say she's stable and improving. I thought I'd take a few more photos before I went up. I'm allowed to see her in Intensive Care.'

'She's awake,' Simon said. 'I went up after I'd checked on Kate. I explained Kate's condition and said that we were happy with her.'

Of course he would have done that. Bless him. Not something she would have thought about Simon Purdy a few days ago.

Isabella pressed her lips together to hold back the rush of words. Seemed she was still emotional.

That had been very kind, and she wasn't used to it from him.

'Thank you. She must have been so relieved.'

'She was.' He smiled, and she could see he understood she was still feeling fragile from the fright.

Carla spoke up. 'It's not sensible for you to work this afternoon. You should take the day off today—and tomorrow as well. Family and carer's leave. Though you won't get paid. If you agree, I've found someone to replace you, so no guilt trip needed.'

'Thank you. That would be...' she waved her hand vaguely '...great.' She flicked a glance at Simon and then away—had he asked Carla? 'I'll catch up on sleep.'

'Of course a substitute won't really replace you,' Simon said, and she realised, with a little spurt of shocked amusement, that he was teasing her. Now, that was a first. She furrowed her brows as he grinned and turned back to the cot.

She looked at her boss. 'Thanks, Carla. I was planning on coming in this afternoon, but it's probably safer this way, as I'm still fuzzy from lack of sleep.'

'I do prefer my staff awake,' Carla said mildly. 'No need to rush away after you visit your sister. Take all the time you need and we'll see you as a visiting auntie for the next couple of days.' She tilted her head at Simon. 'As long as Dr Purdy can do without you?

'He managed perfectly well before I came. I'm not worried,' Isabella said dryly. Though it was interesting that Simon had been the first one to suggest she have time off. For someone who had barely spoken to her, he'd made a reversal of interaction with her, even with teasing thrown in. It was all too much to take on board, but right now she didn't want to think about it, because she desperately wanted to see her sister.

Isabella snapped several photos of Kate on her phone—one accidentally, with Simon looking gorgeous in the background. She should delete that, but didn't.

She said her goodbyes, but once she was outside the unit she realised she wasn't sure which way to turn or which floor to get off the lift.

Simon appeared beside her. 'Do you know where you're going?'

'I just realised I don't. I can ask at the reception desk.'

'Follow me. If you don't mind moving fast, I'll show you.' They set off at a rapid pace until they got to the lift. Stepped in. 'I'm going to Theatre to check on a newborn. I'll drop you off on the way.'

'So many words... Who is this chatty person I've met this morning? He's quite a nice fellow.'

'Ha! Nice? I heard he's moody,' Simon said.

Isabella glanced up at him from under her eyebrows. 'Really? Imagine that... I wouldn't have believed it.'

'Cheeky!' Then his voice became more serious. 'What about your parents? Do they know?'

'I rang my father this morning, and then again when I woke up. After I'd spoken to the ICU staff this afternoon. He's flying up tomorrow. Of course he's too busy to come today.'

She heard the underlying bitterness and frowned at herself. It had been unrealistic to expect him to drop everything. She should be used to that now.

'I guess he has to rearrange his schedule,' Simon said, but Isabella could hear the surprise in his voice.

Suddenly she was defensive. 'You should talk. Being married to your job.'

'Not always. I had a life. When I had a wife.'

Suddenly Isabella felt sick. She'd known about that. His loss. His wife. What had she said?

'Heck, Simon, I'm sorry. That was unforgivable of me. But unintended, I promise.'

The doors opened and they stepped out of the lift.

'Don't worry about it. Intensive Care's just there on your left. Say hello to your sister for me.'

He strode on, leaving her feeling like a callous cow.

*Damn!*

She stared at his rigid back as he disappeared

fast. Then looked back at the closed doors of the intensive care unit. Later she'd find him and apologise.

Again.

# CHAPTER ELEVEN

SIMON WINCED AS he sped away from the truth and the pain that slithered around his body like a snake in a box.

Isabella's words had stung. Because it was true. He *had* put his work before his family when Louise was alive. Hell, he'd missed most of the pregnancy, rushing to and from work. She'd never complained. She'd been a saint. And if he'd paid a bit more attention—if he'd been there more—then maybe his wife wouldn't have died alone.

Malachi had told him time and again that nothing could have saved Louise. That it had been quick. An anaphylaxis from a bolus of amniotic fluid, later found in her bloodstream at autopsy, and the allergic response causing rapid cardiac arrest.

But she'd died alone.

And the baby?

Malachi hadn't been so sure, though his friend had said that the chance of survival would have been slim even if someone had been there.

But Simon knew. If he'd been there, his son would have had greater than a fifty-fifty chance. Simon knew that.

If he'd been there, instead of at work, his son might be alive now. They just might have been able to save him from the wreckage of his mother's body before his life was lost.

He knew Isabella hadn't meant to hurt him. But he didn't need anyone else to say it because he reminded himself every morning and every night, getting in and out of bed. The words of his father from long ago—'*It's your fault your mother died giving birth to you.*' And it was his fault for not being there for his wife and child.

Malachi had said he should let it go. And over the last day or so he'd actually thought he was. But it had all crashed back with Isabella's words. Of course he was married his job, and to saving others. He had to make up for the past.

Simon quickened his pace. That was his life. Best thing, really. He needed to work.

Simon left the operating theatre fifteen minutes later. The baby girl he'd gone to see would be transferred to the ward with her mother and he'd check on them both later. After a forceps delivery, the baby had been slow to turn pink after respiration started. But he was confident she had it all worked out now.

He guessed he could go and see Nadia, and ask if she had any questions about Kate, but in his head he knew if she had questions she'd only have to ask her sister.

Still. It couldn't hurt. Any new mother would love to hear about her baby from the baby's doctor. He couldn't avoid Nadia just to avoid seeing Isabella.

Simon felt like slapping his own forehead. He was having so many internal conversations he was twisting himself up in knots.

It all boiled down to the fact that he was being drawn like a lemming to the edge of a cliff—the cliff being Isabella Hargraves—and to the stark reality that he had nothing to offer a woman like her except a sliver of time that would never be enough. And would leave her at risk should she need him.

But Isabella Hargraves had crashed into his world. She would be there in his face at work, in the freaking surf, and even in the lift to his own apartment. The mischievous angels in heaven must be laughing their heads off.

Not his fault. It was fate. He'd tried to stay away.

He pushed open the swing doors to Intensive Care and spoke to one of the nurses there. She told him that Nadia was improving and would probably go to the ward tomorrow morning. He encouraged her to find Nadia a room close to the NICU, and when she agreed to try, he took himself to the sink to wash his hands.

Funny how he couldn't help turning his head towards the room where he knew Nadia had been put… As he'd expected, he noted two blonde heads together.

Isabella was still there. Of course she was. He'd only been gone twenty minutes.

'Here's Simon, now,' he heard her say.

Just hearing that woman speak his name made him stupidly warm.

'Spare me...' he muttered to himself. This was getting out of control. He needed to stop.

He crossed the room and kept his eyes on Isabella's sister. 'How are you feeling, Nadia? Pain under control?'

'I'm getting better all the time.'

Nadia's voice had similarities to Isabella's—he heard them—but her confidence didn't come across as much as Isabella's did.

Could be the fact that Nadia was a patient in a hospital after a traumatic illness and birth.

Or the fact that her husband had died.

He'd discovered she was a widow, and he knew all about that knocking the stuffing out of you. But he suspected it was something else. Perhaps the reason her elder sister was so protective. Had something else happened to Nadia?

He frowned at himself. What was he doing? He should back away from these women and not get more embroiled than he already was.

He didn't want to think about loss. Guilt. Or regret.

'I just dropped in to see if you had any questions. Though I expect your sister can probably answer most of them anyway.'

'None for the moment,' Nadia said, smiling wanly. 'And you're right—Izzy knew the answers to all the ones I had. I loved the photos.'

*Izzy?* What a travesty to shorten a beautiful name to that. Perhaps Bella? Meaning beautiful. But not Izzy. Sacrilege...

'I sent the pics to her phone,' Isabella said, and he could see in her eyes the anxiety she tried to hide as she watched her sister's tired face. 'As long as you leave it on aeroplane mode, you can look at them as much as you need—until we can get you to her.'

Isabella stood up.

'And on that note...' She kissed her sister's cheek, said softly, 'You need a snooze. I'll be back this afternoon.'

'Say hi to Gran for me,' Nadia whispered, and Isabella nodded.

Mrs Hargraves. Yes. Isabella went every day to see her unconscious grandmother. Somewhere in his chest he felt a twist of empathy that made him want to reach out to her and say he thought she was amazing. She was doing it tough but still thinking of others.

Unlike him. He suspected his attempts at selfish self-preservation hadn't helped her at all this last week. It was hard to remember that she'd only begun in the unit such a short time ago. It felt as if he'd been watching her for way longer.

Simon saw a man in the dark suit striding

swiftly towards them and his mouth quirked up. One of the ICU nurses followed the newcomer, trying to catch him up with a chart.

'Malachi.' Simon held out his hand and his friend shook it warmly.

'Simon. Come to see my patient, have you?' Malachi leaned past Simon and smiled at Nadia in the bed. 'I won't stay long and interrupt your visitors,' he told her.

# CHAPTER TWELVE

MALACHI MADDEN, THE man Isabella had seen when Nadia had first been admitted, was clearly Simon's friend. He looked nice, if in a hurry, and she recognised the consultant's fierce intelligence and wanted all those brains directed at her sister.

'Nice to meet you, again.' she murmured. 'Thank you for looking after my sister so well. Please don't rush—I'm just leaving.'

Before she could move past him, Simon said to Malachi, 'Isabella is one of the NICU nurses in our unit here. And a midwife.'

'Yes, I know. Nice to meet you again, Isabella.' He glanced at Simon and raised his brows, with a twinkle in his intelligent eyes. 'I've heard the team are pretty good down there.' She watched their rapport. It was easy and were obviously used to teasing each other.

Isabella glanced at Simon. 'Yes. We're very fortunate.'

Simon said, 'Do you remember Mrs Hargraves? That friend of your grandmother's who lives in the flat below me?'

Malachi frowned, and then nodded. 'She was injured in that nasty hit-and-run accident a month or so ago. Millicent was very distressed to hear about it.'

'Nadia and Isabella are her granddaughters.'

Malachi's face softened, as did his voice. 'Oh…
How is she? I heard she's still unconscious?'

Isabella didn't know what to say. Why had
Simon shared this? She scrambled for a short response. 'Yes, she hasn't woken up yet. I see her
every day.'

'Of course.' Malachi nodded. His face was serious. 'I would visit if it were me, too. I must tell
my grandmother. You should come and meet my
wife, Lisandra,' he told her, with a searching look
towards his friend and then a smile. 'Simon, you
should come too. Isabella, maybe you can convince him to arrive for dinner instead of dessert.'

What? Dinner? With Simon? She felt as if she'd
just been steamrollered.

Malachi raised his eyebrows at his friend. 'If
you're done with Nadia, trot away with Isabella
so I can see my patient.'

Isabella closed her mouth on the open sag it
wanted to make. 'Goodbye, Dr Madden.'

He nodded vaguely, as if he'd already forgotten her, and walked instantly over to Nadia and
took her wrist.

She didn't realise Simon was behind her until
she went to open the swing doors out of the ICU
and he stretched out his arm ahead of her and
pushed the door until she was through.

'He's funny,' she said.

'Malachi is no-nonsense and a very good friend. We went through med school together.'

She still didn't understand Simon's blurting out of information. 'Why did you tell him about Gran?'

'No idea… I'm sorry if I shouldn't have. I think maybe because I think you'd like Lisandra, and I think you need a friend right now. She's also a midwife. You have that in common. They have twin boys who just turned one.'

'Good grief. How does she manage when he works all hours as an obstetrician?'

'Lisandra is one of the calmest women I know. As well as the best thing that's ever happened to Malachi—for which I am very grateful.'

She still didn't understand why he'd shared so much about her and Nadia with his friend. 'What made you think of my grandmother when you were talking to him?'

'I remember meeting Mrs Hargraves and Malachi's grandmother, Millicent, in the lift one day. Now, Millicent…she's a terrifying lady.'

Isabella couldn't imagine Simon being terrified by any woman. But she suspected he meant the comment fondly. His eyes twinkled.

Something made her ask, 'Do *you* have a terrifying grandmother?'

'I don't have any grandmother. Or a mother.'

There was darkness there in those words. Sorrow. Regret. Something she wanted to find out more about.

'In fact,' Simon went on, 'Malachi's the closest thing I have to a relative and he's not even blood-related.'

Oh... More sadness. Simon had baggage she hadn't even considered.

'I'm sorry to hear that. My family might not win any happy-all-together awards, but at least I have them.'

'Yes—and they have you.' He cast a sideways glance at her as they walked to the lift. 'I'm beginning to see that you're the person who worries about everyone else.'

How the heck had he deduced that? It wasn't true. Was it? He barely knew her. And apart from Nadia, he didn't know her family at all.

The lift arrived and deposited them on the ground floor. 'Are you coming to check on Kate before you go home?' he asked.

And suddenly she was awkward again. 'I'd like to. Is that okay? Even though I'm not working?'

He waved her in. 'Of course. You're officially a relative. Next of kin to his mother. You can visit any time.'

It still didn't feel right to go outside of regular visiting times. 'But there are specific visiting hours for non-staff members. I don't want to be a nuisance.'

He wrinkled his brow at her, as if he couldn't

believe what she was saying. 'I don't think there's any risk of you abusing your position.'

And he held the door open for her so she had no choice. Not that she wanted one.

Shoulder to shoulder, they washed their hands at the sink until Simon, who'd finished first, tore off some paper towel and then went off to see Carla.

Isabella crossed the busy unit, past open cots and rolling cots, and past the staff working on the tiny inhabitants of both, to check on Kate.

Her niece lay on her belly, leads sneaking from under her chest at each side. Her left foot now sported the pulse oximeter probe that had previously been attached to the right foot. She was sleeping and serene. Warm under her heater. Her breathing steady and sure.

Isabella's quick survey of the monitors suggested her vital signs were stable. She picked up the chart, not sure whether she was allowed to, but not letting that stop her.

She confirmed everything looked normal for the moment, though she suspected a tinge of yellowing jaundice in Kate's skin. She expected there'd be a need for phototherapy soon, to assist her body to rid itself of the extra bilirubin. And the use of purple lights to help disperse the toxic by-products.

Once born into the outside air, babies normally discarded unneeded extra oxygen-carrying blood cells. But, as Kate was a prem, her liver would struggle to break down the products left behind. Hence the build up of jaundice.

Simon didn't need her mentioning it—he'd already be on top of it all—and it was truly strange how relaxed she was feeling about Kate's progress. There were still so many obstacles that could catch her tiny niece out as she grew, like infections and breathing difficulties, or a need for nasogastric feeds of expressed breast milk—something she and Nadia had discussed and would address again this afternoon.

It was almost a shock, how calm she felt now that Simon was in charge of Kate's care. How reassured. Though his very competent registrar would have been just as good. She needed to remember that.

It just went to show that sometimes too much knowledge could be a problem.

Maybe she should go home before she said something else out of line. Again.

She would drop in to Gran as well—tell her about Malachi Madden's grandmother. Maybe that would be something that might stimulate her.

Then she'd have a sleep herself, she supposed, and she'd better polish Gran's flat and clean the bathroom in case her father decided to stay there. But knowing him, he'd book a suite at the nearest hotel, so he could be on his own. That was more his style. But maybe she'd have a chance to be his host and they could really talk.

Who knew when he would come? He hadn't known himself when she'd last spoken to him. But she couldn't help being glad that he would. For Nadia. For Gran. And for her. Because if it wasn't for Simon she would be feeling very alone amongst all these medical dramas.

Simon…the kind-eyed Simon…who was suddenly her friend.

Simon returned with Carla and Isabella felt awkward again. In the way. Superfluous. Without a real job. A third wheel because she wasn't working this afternoon.

'I'm going now,' she told them.

Simon frowned, as if he'd read her thoughts, and she saw him close his mouth as if he was about to say something.

Carla lifted her head from a chart. 'I'm sure we'll see you later.'

Isabella nodded. She glanced once more at her niece and then left, feeling suddenly rootless.

# CHAPTER THIRTEEN

SIMON'S GAZE FOLLOWED Isabella as she opened the door and left. There was something about the droop in her shoulders that hinted she felt a little lost.

Funny how much that thought troubled him.

Which was a very good reason for him to turn around and concentrate on the baby in front of him.

'Do I sense a change with you and Isabella?' Carla's voice was quietly discreet, and didn't carry, yet he wished she hadn't voiced the question at all. It meant that others could see that things were noteworthy between them.

'No. Not really.' He lowered his brows at her, but she knew him too well to be bothered. 'Why would you ask that?'

'Uh…because everybody can feel the friction between you two and it would be good if you could clear the air.'

He huffed. 'I have. We had breakfast together this morning and I apologised for my moodiness with her.'

'Simon, I'm impressed.' But her eyes twinkled and he suspected she was more amused than impressed. 'That was brave.'

He pulled a face. 'That's the end of this topic.

Back to work,' he mock-growled, and Carla dipped her head to hide her smile.

Simon pointed to the prem in front of them. 'I think Kate's becoming jaundiced. I'll order a serum bilirubin. Has she started on EBM yet?'

'Yes. Mum's started expressing and the ICU sent down the first colostrum. You happy for us to start that?'

'Absolutely. ASAP. The usual regime.'

Carla made a note. 'Yes, we'll gradually increase the expressed milk and decrease the IV if she tolerates it.'

'Has she passed meconium?'

'Yes. And voided twice. Clever baby.'

All looking good for the moment, then. The extra relief he felt was interesting.

'Excellent. All systems working. Let me know if there's problems. Tell the night staff to ring through straight to me for Kate.' He avoided meeting Carla's raised brows. 'Anyone else you're worried about?' he asked.

'Nope. All up to date. We'll let you know if we need you.'

'Fine. I'll head to my rooms, then. I've got appointments all afternoon, so I'll be there if you need me.'


By four-thirty Simon was with his last patient.

Young Reece had unstable diabetes. He was

thrilled with his new insulin pump, which meant he could play with the other kids more than he'd ever been able to before.

Simon had known Reece for the last three years, and always enjoyed talking to the boy and his mother.

By five p.m. he was waving them farewell at the door, and he was just about to head for the children's ward when his phone rang.

'Dr Purdy.' Malachi was in good spirits, it seemed.

'Dr Madden. You sound chipper.'

'My wife requests the pleasure of your company tomorrow night for dinner.'

'Does she? Are you home from work already, Malachi? Things have certainly changed.'

Malachi had been worse than Simon for staying at work all hours.

'You should try it,' his friend said. 'The twins are waving at you. They want to see their uncle Simon.'

Simon shook his head. But he couldn't stop the big smile on his face. 'Who are you? What happened to the workaholic?'

But Simon knew what had happened. Lisandra had changed his friend's life, and his priorities, for the better. And even though the twins weren't Malachi's, he adored his new family and revelled in being a father.

Malachi said, 'I've seen the light. So, how

about you shift your last appointment and get your rounds done early tomorrow?'

Simon considered that. 'My secretary hasn't left, yet. I'll see what I can do.'

'Lisandra said to bring Isabella.'

Good grief. Malachi—or Lisandra, more likely—was matchmaking, and the idea scared the daylights out of him.

'I'm not sure about Isabella's shifts.' Except he knew she was off. He'd seen the staff rota.

'How about you give me her number and Lisandra can ring her? Midwives stick together, you know.'

Malachi wasn't fazed or worried about Simon's feelings. It wasn't in his make-up—and hadn't Simon accepted that years ago?

Served him right. He'd been the one to tell Isabella she would like Malachi's wife. But now it was happening, old doubts and insecurities slithered in. Was this really a good idea? The one situation he'd thought he wouldn't bump into Isabella was socially, with Malachi. Now Malachi was changing that.

Without permission, the words slipped out. 'Seems there won't be anywhere I can go and not meet this woman.'

'Explain?'

Simon sighed. Bowing to the inevitable. 'She lives in her grandmother's flat—which, as you know, is one floor below mine. We work together in the NICU. And guess what she does in her off time.'

Malachi laughed. 'Don't tell me...she's a surfer.'

'Yep.'

Malachi laughed again. 'I can't wait to tell Lisandra.'

Simon couldn't help smiling. Not so long ago even one Malachi laugh would have been a reason for celebration.

'Tell me what...?' Simon heard Lisandra ask in the background.

'Simon's being stalked by a midwife.'

Simon grimaced as Lisandra laughed. 'I am not. She didn't even know any of those things.'

Malachi chuckled. 'Who knew Simon's relationships could be so much fun? Six p.m. You'll be kicked out at eight. You know we like to go to bed early.'

The phone went dead.

Simon stared at the receiver in his hand and gritted his teeth. Served him right for dumping all that information about Isabella on his friend. Malachi wasn't stupid—too freakin' smart. But usually not so intuitive.

Of course introducing and giving the back story on a woman was out of character for Simon.

Too late. Lisandra had the run of it now.

He shrugged and went to make peace with his

secretary about changing his appointment times tomorrow, then took himself off to the children's ward.

After work that night, Simon took his car from the garage underneath the building and did something he hadn't done for a long time. He went to the cemetery where they'd buried Louise and Lucas, his son who had never breathed.

It was sunset. And between the trees lay shadows. Although above the canopy the sky was alight with an orange glow that made the headstones sparkle as the last rays sank into the sandstone blocks.

He walked to the row he needed, and six graves along, until he came to Louise and Lucas's. There. A cold stone where once a sweet woman and the promise of a young life had been.

Just twenty-eight, and so gentle in spirit had been his kind and loving wife. He'd thought that there would never be another woman for him. That what they'd had was too special. Too perfect.

But mostly it had involved too much guilt.

Because the ending had been anything but perfect.

She'd been so happy in her pregnancy. And he couldn't remember how many times since her death he'd railed at himself for not spending more time at home with her.

Three years. A long time to mourn. Or not long enough?

His friends had been pushing him to look for happiness again, but he'd felt so guilty. So disloyal. So uninterested.

Until now. When suddenly he was swamped by the feelings that were growing for Isabella Hargraves. What if he let them flower? What was his plan? To fall in love again? Have a baby again? Already his head was shaking at the thought. What if he lost another wife? What if Isabella died in childbirth?

No. He couldn't. He wasn't ready.

# CHAPTER FOURTEEN

Isabella's phone buzzed with a text at six o'clock that evening.

Hello, Isabella. My name is Lisandra Madden. Is this a good time to call you?

Isabella read it again. Then she remembered Malachi Madden inviting her and Simon for dinner.

Good grief. They didn't let any grass grow underfoot.

She texted back.

Now is fine.

The phone rang within ten seconds.

'Thanks for the quick response,' came a lilting woman's voice. 'It's Lisandra here. I've got twin boys and they're asleep at the moment. I try to do everything in the quiet times.'

*I bet you do.*

Isabella could imagine. And she smiled at the thought.

'Malachi tells me you're a midwife and new to the area. He also says you work with Simon Purdy. Well, those boys are great friends, and it's always a struggle to get Simon to come out. We're having a dinner party tomorrow night. Malachi's grand-mother will be there, and we'd like to invite you both as well—if you're up to it.'

Before Isabella could answer Lisandra said quickly, 'It won't be a late night. We call them "six to eight" parties.'

Isabella laughed—how funny—and replied, 'I'd probably run on the same hours if I had twins.'

She could absolutely fit that in.

'My father is flying up tomorrow, to see my sis-ter, but he won't be here till late. I've been invited to his hotel at nine, and I was wondering what I'd do until then.'

'Good grief, we'll all be snoring by that time,' Lisandra murmured with disbelief.

Isabella laughed again. She liked this woman already. 'Then thank you. What can I bring to-morrow?'

'If you can bring Simon on time, I'd be very grateful. The man doesn't seem to know the meaning of punctuality. Everything else is cov-ered. I'll text you the address, in case Simon gets called away. You can park underneath the apart-ments in the visitors' parking and then take the lift straight up—I'll send you the codes.'

'You've thought of everything.'

'Good. I'm looking forward to meeting you. I haven't had a good chat with a midwife for ages.'

'I'm more of a neonatal nurse, right now. But I look forward to meeting you too.'

'Great. Bye.'

'Bye.'

*Good grief,* Isabella thought as the call ended. A whirlwind had just blown past, and she'd been caught up in it. She wondered what Simon thought about going with her to dinner. Her mouth twitched.

Someone knocked on her door.

Was she about to find out?

There weren't many in the block who knew her well enough to knock on her door.

Isabella peered through the peephole and saw Simon on the other side, staring off to the left.

Yep. She was about to find out Simon's response to the dinner invitation.

While she watched, he lifted his hand to the back of his neck and rubbed. *Tired or uncomfortable?* she wondered, and opened the door.

'Hello.' She opened her mouth to say more, when a horrible thought crashed into her. 'Nadia...? Kate...?'

'Both fine,' Simon said quickly. 'If they weren't I would have phoned immediately.'

She blew her breath out. 'Of course. Sorry— mild panic attack came up out of nowhere.'

'I get it. But I'm here about Malachi and Lisandra...' He put his hand over his face as if he was embarrassed. 'Have you had the call yet?'

She opened the door wider and swept out her arm to indicate that he could come in. 'Yes, I've just finished. Lisandra's a force to be reckoned with.'

'Lisandra's a delight, but when she's determined on something, it's hard to get away.'

She chewed her lip to stop the smile. 'My task is to get you there on time,' she said.

'Well, I'm to take you and a bottle of wine.' He met her gaze fully, concern in his. 'So, you're okay with this?'

'Sure. Sounds like fun.' She smiled reassuringly at him. He looked as if he needed it. 'My father is arriving tomorrow night, and I'm to meet him at nine at his hotel. Saves me sitting here, watching the clock.'

She saw his gaze slide over the room. And the hallway beyond. 'He's not going to stay here with you? It's three bedrooms, isn't it?'

She sighed. 'Yes. And I've just cleaned in case he comes.' She shrugged. 'But no. He'll feel much more comfortable arriving late at a hotel.' She could see that he thought she might be hurt by her father's choice. 'It's fine with me. I told you we don't do *happy-all-together*.'

He nodded and she went on.

'I'm a little bit nervous about meeting Malachi's terrifying grandmother now you've told me about her.'

Simon laughed. 'Oh, she'll love you. You won't have any problems.'

And what did she do now? With Simon in her flat? Looking scrumptious. With the scent of freshly showered man, damp hair and that subtle woodsy cologne she was coming to recognise.

'Would you like a drink? Tea? Coffee?'

'Tea would be great. Black. No sugar, thanks.'

Same as her. And why would that make her want to happy dance? Weird...

She flicked the kettle on. 'Got it.' She started rifling through the cupboards. 'I think I've got some biscuits here.'

'No, it's fine. My housekeeper leaves me dinner in the fridge to heat up.'

That made her pause, her hand on the cupboard door. 'You have a housekeeper?'

'I spend a fair bit of time at work.'

He looked just a little embarrassed, and that made her smile. As if he was a bad person for not wanting to keep house.

'I'd rather surf waves than clean.'

She nodded. She thought of her afternoon of rubber gloves and bathrooms and grimaced. 'Me too. Speaking of surfing... Have you had a chance to get back out there since yesterday morning?'

'Was that only yesterday morning?' His hand pinched the bridge of his nose. 'It feels like a year ago.'

She narrowed her eyes at him. 'I've been thinking about that.' She poured boiling water into a cup. 'And I have a theory.'

'Oh, yeah?' He took the cup from her, removed the teabag and put it in the bin.

She liked the fact that he was making himself at home here, opening cupboards until he found the garbage.

'Yes, I think the reason you were bad-tempered with me at work is because I was surfing in your spot.'

'I don't own the surf.'

But it sounded as if he wished he did.

Then he smiled. Held out his hands in a *What can I do?* gesture. 'I told myself you were an incredibly intelligent woman and I'd have to stay at the top of my game.'

'True.' She nodded slowly. 'You do. Is the rest true, you were bad tempered because I was surfing in your spot?'

'I confess.'

'The ocean is big enough for both of us,' she mused.

He was watching her. 'It should be.' There was a small, ironic smile on his mouth. 'But if I want to try not to expose myself to the fact that I find my new colleague compellingly and breath-stealingly attractive, it's very difficult when she pops up not only at work, but also in the one place I go to escape work.'

She opened her mouth, but he held up his hand.

'Oh, it gets worse. She even lives in the same block as I do.'

She opened her mouth again.

He said, 'And one more thing. Let's add to that. My friends have now included her in their circle. So, I'm going to be exposed to Isabella Hargraves in every part of my day.'

'Poor you,' she said.

'Or poor you? I'm not cross any more, because I've given up fighting the inevitable.

That made her blink. 'What's the inevitable?.'

Did she sound petulant?

'Being drawn to you. Attracted. You know you're delightful.'

He must have seen her brows draw up into her hairline. Because he went on.

'And, yes, I would like to be your friend. Please.' The humour left his face. 'I need to say that because of the past I'm in no hurry to be more than that. And I think it's only fair that I tell you I live for my work.'

Wow. That was pretty brave. And a downer. Because she was attracted right back, and he was married to his work. Still, she appreciated his honesty—even if she was a little bit disappointed.

But she had the feeling this was a big admission for Simon. So she held out her hand. 'To friendship.'

# CHAPTER FIFTEEN

SIMON TOOK ISABELLA'S slender hand in his and solemnly held it. Her fingers felt warm, silky, and
suddenly fragile in his. He didn't want to let go.
But he had to. Now. He'd ease his fingers away as
soon as they weren't Velcroed onto hers.

'Are you surfing tomorrow?' he asked.

She pulled her hand away, picked up her mug
and sat at the small table.

'Yes, because I don't have to go to work. Thanks
to Dr Simon Purdy, who has told my supervisor
that I require two days FACS leave.'

He laughed. 'I did do that.'

'Well, I appreciate it. Thank you. I would have
pushed myself to turn up, but it wouldn't have
been a sensible thing to do with no sleep.'

'They're moving Nadia down to a room near
the NICU tomorrow. Did you know that?'

Her face lit up and he saw again her love for
her sister.

'No. That's good. She's still improving, then?'

'Blood pressure is settling well.'

'And my niece?'

'I'd say she'll be under phototherapy by tonight.'

'I thought that.' She nodded and he could see
she'd expected it.

'You didn't say anything.'

Her mouth kinked up and drew his gaze.

*That mouth.*

'I have great faith in you. But I would have said something tomorrow,' she told him.

He laughed and thought, *Oh, yeah, I'll have to watch myself, or I could fall hard for this woman.*

He was not going to do that—for her sake, not his.

At five forty-five the next evening, after he'd ensured Isabella's sister and niece were both stable and improving, and he'd dressed appropriately enough to satisfy Malachi's grandmother, Simon pressed the bell on Isabella's door.

The NICU had been busy today, with the new admission of twins at thirty-four weeks. But he'd put Henry in charge and suggested, for once, that he only be called for his own patients instead of the usual—being called by anyone who needed him for a paediatric consult.

The door opened and Isabella stood there, stealing his breath, then his words. And he hoped not his heart, as his chest felt clamped in a vice that made cardiac output difficult.

'You look beautiful...' The words escaped in an awed murmur.

And, my glory, she did. The flowing silk trousers and jacket floated over a cream blouse in soft shades of lilac that brought out the green of her eyes while they hugged and skimmed the length of her body. The feather-light material shifted alluringly as she moved.

Her gaze skimmed his outfit and then finished at his face. 'Looking good yourself, Dr Purdy. I like the Tigger tie. And you're right on time.'

She pulled the door shut behind her. He stifled disappointment. So, he wasn't going in?

'Malachi's boys like this tie,' he said, struggling for normal conversation. A 'date' with Isabella was having way more impact than he'd been prepared for.

They'd finally agreed the previous evening to go in her car, against Simon's preference. She'd argued that she was driving on to the hotel afterwards to see her father. She would drop him home on her way.

Now, as he waited beside the driver's door for her to unlock the car, she slanted a sideways look at him. 'Are you planning on driving my car?'

The lock clicked and he reached down. 'No, I'm opening your door for you.'

She lifted her head and laughed up at him. The sound was sexy as hell, and sent blood pounding all over his body in ways he'd forgotten existed.

'Well, thank you, kind sir.' She pulled her beautiful mouth into order, as if holding back more mirth. 'Do I have to come round to your side and open *your* door?'

'It would have been easier if we'd taken my car,' he said.

'But not more sensible.'

'And if I get called out?'

She shrugged, with a *not my problem* attitude he also found sexy.

He sighed. 'It's close... I can always get a taxi.'

She settled into her seat. 'Or I can drive you. Let's go.'

He closed her door, his mouth twitching, because he was so unused to this kind of rapport where she could fire back. Shaking his head at his own smitten-ness, he walked around the car. It was cleaned and polished enough to show she cared about it.

'Nice car,' he said as he climbed in.

'This is Rosa.' Isabella patted the leather dashboard. 'She's my friend. Buckle up.'

Once Simon had himself settled, trying not to deep-breathe the now familiar scent of her delicate perfume, Isabella pulled smoothly out of the garage and into the busy street.

It was still light outside, and there were families wandering across the road to the beach and people dog-walking after work. Her driving style was smooth and confident, like everything about her, and he could feel himself relax. Maybe he could cope with her driving. Louise had been a timid nightmare...

She glanced at him. 'So how did Malachi and Lisandra meet? Was she working as a midwife?'

Simon laughed. He couldn't help it. It was funny. Though he was sure it hadn't been at the time.

Isabella turned her beautiful face his way briefly and arched her brows. 'Was it that good a meet-cute?'

*Meet-cute?* He'd seen that movie. Ha!

'They met in a stuck elevator at the hospital. Lisandra's waters had broken and Malachi almost delivered the twins in there.'

Thankfully they'd pulled up at a red light. Because he could see his driver was having trouble concentrating.

Something lodged in his chest as she stared at him. She looked so cute, blinking incredulous green eyes at him. Then she turned back to the road. He could see the smile on her face, and he just had to lean forward to see her full expression, not just in profile.

He felt as if he could actually see her imagining the scenario. 'Crazy, huh?'

She inhaled with amusement. 'That's different…'

'There's a long story there that's not mine to tell, but they're the happiest couple I know. Lisandra changed Malachi's life for the better, and for that I'll always be grateful to her.'

'Well, I'm sure he's changed hers too. He seems very nice.'

'He is.'

They drove through busy Coolangatta, along the beachfront and around the headland to Kira Beach. The waves rolled in as the road curved around the bay.

He pointed. 'The underground car park is up ahead. Just past the lights. Yep, turn left here.'

They pulled under a tall white building with beautiful gardens full of red hibiscus in flower.

He watched her press the code numbers into the keypad and the boom gate lifted smoothly, so they could drive past and park beside the elevators in the visitors' parking.

'If I ever come back here to visit Lisandra, I'll know how to find the place.'

He hoped she would. 'It's easier for her to have visitors here, with the boys, than it is for them to go out.'

They went to the lifts, and he pressed in the code, and then she was next to him again in another closed space. Alone. Just the two of them. Close.

*There would be time for a kiss*, his crazy inner demon told him, as he stared straight ahead at the doors.

Diversion needed. His mouth dried and he had to moisten it before he could speak.

'You'll enjoy the view from Malachi's apartment.'

When the lift doors opened, they were in an entry foyer with only one closed front door. Thankfully, as he stepped out, Simon could breathe again. He took a couple of extra, subtle inhalations before he knocked.

# CHAPTER SIXTEEN

A BLONDE WOMAN in her late twenties opened the door, leaned forward and kissed Simon's cheek. This had to be Lisandra, Isabella thought. She had a fine bone structure, a pink bow of a mouth and big, deep turquoise eyes.

'Simon. Welcome.' She smiled at Isabella, her face warm and happy. 'And you must be Isabella.' The woman kissed her cheek too. 'That's for getting him here on time.' She laughed at Simon and ushered them in, saying, 'It's so lovely to meet you. I'm Lisandra. Come in... Come in... Malachi is just bathing the boys.'

And after that whirlwind introduction, reminiscent of the phone call she'd shared with Malachi's wife, Isabella just knew she could become firm friends with this woman.

Their hosts' apartment seemed to stretch for ever—probably because the sea air flowed seamlessly through open sliding doors to a wide terrace instead of a narrow balcony. She guessed there was a big drop to the ground below, but in front of them the horizon stretched over the waves.

White marble tiles ran from the floor to the terrace rail, past white furniture with blue accents, a wall-length television screen and a small curved bar with stools.

'Come through and meet Malachi's grand-mother, Millicent. She's out on the terrace.'

A tall woman, possibly in her early eighties, stepped away from the rail and turned their way. Not quite as tall as Malachi, she was wearing peach silk trousers and a paler peach sleeveless tunic, almost white. The silk draped softly over her reed-thin body. Her make-up glowed with per-fection, and her short, curly, snow-white hair was artfully tousled. Her smile shone warm and genu-ine as she came towards them.

'Simon,' she said, and her voice was huskier than Isabella had expected. 'A pleasure as always to see you.'

She kissed his cheeks in the French style, but her eyes were on Isabella.

'My dear, you have a look of your grand-mother—those fine eyes and cheekbones. I'm Millicent Charles. A friend of Catherine's.'

It felt so long since she'd heard someone actu-ally refer to her grandmother by her first name and a lump formed in her throat. She swallowed and smiled. 'It's lovely to meet you, Mrs Charles.'

'Likewise. And, please, call me Millicent. I've been so distressed since Catherine's accident. Any sign of improvement? I've asked your father, but he had nothing to offer.'

Isabella tried not to wince. *Yes, that sounded like dear old Dad*, Isabella thought grimly.

'She's breathing for herself. The hospital is

maintaining intravenous nutrition. And...' she spread her hands '...we're just waiting.'

'Malachi says you visit often?'

Had they been talking about her? No, probably just about Gran. And it was good to talk about her grandmother with someone who knew her.

'I visit every day. Sometimes I think she can hear me. Hopefully I'm not driving her mad with my chatter.'

Kind, yet faded eyes shared sympathy and understanding. 'I'm very sure she loves your visits.'

'Well, I told her yesterday that I would be meeting you tonight. Now I can tell her tomorrow that I did.'

'Excellent. Would you mind if I visited her as well? I didn't get the impression from your father that it would be possible.'

'He's arriving tonight. I'll make sure he knows that your visits certainly are permitted. The staff have been wonderful at welcoming me. She has an IV, and monitors, of course, but nothing that jumps out at you too much. I think it's a lovely idea.'

Malachi appeared out of a side hallway, carrying two blonde-headed toddlers in zip-up sleep suits, one in each arm. One of the boys leaned towards Simon as they drew close, and Simon scooped him out of his father's hold and perched him against his chest.

Malachi leaned across and shook Simon's hand. He smiled at Isabella. 'Welcome to our home.'

Lisandra lifted the other little boy from his father and perched him on her hip. 'Isabella, these are our boys, Bastian and Bennett. Bennett is the one who grabbed his uncle Simon.'

The little boy had caught Simon's tie and was tugging it.

'That's his favourite tie. Simon bought him a stuffed Tigger and Bastian a stuffed Winnie-the-Pooh bear, which they sleep with.'

And there was Simon—gorgeous Dr Simon Purdy—so at ease and delighted with the little boy in his arms. Of course, he was a paediatrician, so he was good with kids. But, dammit, she could see him being a fabulous dad with a pack of his own.

Except he'd said he would never marry again or be a dad. That was sad. For him. Not for her. That tragic fact had nothing to do with her. But her heart still hurt.

Millicent had taken herself to one of the large white sofas, and Lisandra carried Bastian across to her and settled him in her lap. His grandmother tucked her chin down to talk to the boy, and for a minute Isabella thought she was going to cry.

That was what she wanted Gran to do. She wanted Gran to be there for Nadia's baby, like she'd been there for Isabella and Nadia. Like Malachi's grandmother.

Why couldn't her grandmother be here, too? She'd already lost her mother. She wasn't ready to lose Gran.

Isabella felt a sympathetic touch on her shoulder. A touch that filled her with comfort and strength. Then Simon lifted his hand and let it fall. He had followed her gaze. As if he knew what she was thinking. She shoved the emotion away. He couldn't have. But she glanced at him with gratitude because that touch had helped.

'Come through to the kitchen, Isabella.' Lisandra intruded on her thoughts as well, and she was glad to step away from the sadness. Maybe not so glad to step away from Simon's side...

'I'd love to. What can I do to help?'

And that was how the evening went. Every time she felt even a tiny bit sad, or a little out of place amongst these people who knew each other so very well, Lisandra was there to bring her into the conversation or ask her a question. Or Simon would catch her eye and smile. Touch her briefly. Make sure she didn't feel as if he didn't understand.

When the meal was over, Isabella helped Lisandra stack the dishwasher while Malachi and Simon took the boys to their bedroom to read them a story.

'There's no excuse for you not to visit me,' said Lisandra. 'You know where I live and now you know all the codes.'

'And I have your phone number,' Isabella agreed, with a grin.

'While the boys are little, I'm not thinking about going back to work.' She dropped the volume of her voice so she wouldn't be overheard. 'Malachi would be happy if I never went back to work, but I loved being a midwife.'

'It is special,' Isabella agreed.

Lisandra shrugged. 'No rush. I'll get there. Malachi says you work in the neonatal nursery?'

'Yes, with Simon. He's very good. The unit's excellent.'

Lisandra's bright eyes closed briefly. 'It is. And I know. We had a scare with Bastian and Simon was there for us.'

'I'm sorry to hear that.'

Lisandra glanced towards the bedrooms. 'We try not to think about it.'

'Then don't.' Isabella changed the subject. 'Simon's looking after my sister's prem baby.'

'That's right. You're an auntie. First time?'

'Yes. And a first grandchild for my dad.'

She hadn't really thought about that, and wondered if there was any chance Kate could change him into a more human, human being.

'You said your father's arriving tonight?'

'Nine o'clock,' Isabella confirmed.

'I won't even be awake to think of you.' Lisandra mimed sleep.

'Yes, but you're a lot busier than I am.'

Lisandra shrugged. 'I'm not working… Malachi tells me you surf?'

'Yes, I've just found out Simon does too.'

There was a definite sparkle in Lisandra's eyes. 'I know… Are you good at it?'

Isabella knew she was good. But she didn't boast. 'Good enough to enjoy it.'

'Will you teach me?'

Ah… Hence the questions? 'Of course. I'd love to. My grandmother taught me.'

Lisandra looked ridiculously happy. 'That's a date, then.'

Malachi and Simon returned to sit with Millicent in the lounge room, and the women joined them there. Lisandra touched her husband's arm, her fingers resting lightly on his shirtsleeve, and they shared a smile. The look of connection in their faces made Isabella look away. She wanted that too. Connection. Silent communication.

Her thoughts stilled. Narrowed. Wasn't that what Simon had been giving her all night?

Dimly she heard Lisandra say, 'Are the boys asleep?'

'Out for the count.' There was a satisfied smile in Malachi's voice.

'Then I'm going to show Isabella the angels through the doorway.'

Lisandra took her arm, and they turned left up the corridor to where a door stood ajar at the end.

Soft light spilled into the hallway. It had an odd bluish tinge.

Isabella leaned her head around the doorway and could see a blue nightlight shaped like a fishbowl, with tiny imitation fish swimming in a blue ball. The light allowed her to see two blond heads on the pillows in twin beds. One tiny boy was tucked under his cover with his Tigger, and the other had already thrown his quilt off, one arm flung out, holding his Winnie the Pooh.

Isabella stepped back. Mouthed, *They are gorgeous.*

Lisandra smiled and drew her back down the corridor. She sighed theatrically. 'Even more so when they're asleep.'

It wasn't much later when Simon stood up. 'Gone eight o'clock. Looks like it's time for us to be kicked out.'

Malachi glanced at his watch. 'Oh, you sneaked in an extra five minutes there. Luckily someone was watching.'

Simon laughed. 'Did you bring your car, Millicent, or would you like a lift?'

Isabella lifted her head to smile.

Simon put his fingers over his face and dragged them down comically. 'I mean would you like a lift in Isabella's car, because she won the discussion on who was driving tonight.'

Millicent smiled approvingly at Isabella. 'I have

my own vehicle, thank you.' She nodded. 'Always good to keep them guessing who's boss.'

'It's a democracy,' Simon said dryly, and shook Malachi's hand.

Millicent laughed.

'Dinner was wonderful, as always.'

Simon kissed Lisandra's cheek and stood waiting patiently for Isabella to say her goodbyes.

*It had been perfect*, Isabella thought. Not a boring dinner party at all like her father's events.

Everything had been a pleasure, and she thought Lisandra might be one of the luckiest people she knew.

'Thank you so much for a wonderful evening.'

'First of many, hopefully,' Malachi said briskly.

Lisandra hugged her. 'Ring me when you're ready for a surf on a weekend. Malachi and Simon can mind the boys.'

Suddenly she and Simon were standing close together again, in the lift going down to the car park. She felt as if she'd glimpsed a family the like of which she wanted so badly her heart and arms ached with emptiness. But it did feel like that warmth would never be hers.

'Did you enjoy that?' Simon asked, and Isabella turned her eyes to him.

She couldn't articulate how much. Instead, she nodded and asked, 'Did you?'

His tie looked crumpled, where Bennett had mashed it with his pudgy fingers and Simon had tried to straighten it. It needed an iron. She leaned across and tugged it, to pull the creases out, and then stepped back. That had brought her very close to him. She probably shouldn't have done it.

He was looking at her quizzically, and she hurried into speech. 'It was a wonderful night. I love your friends—and Millicent is wonderful.'

*Two 'wonderfuls'? Brain, brain...where is my brain?*

She concentrated on the evening, because that was safer than dwelling on the fact that the lift was slow, and that they were alone in the small space. And that she'd just touched him without invitation.

His shoulders loomed next to her but it wasn't just his big body taking up space—it was his personality. The one she'd seen tonight. The friend. The uncle. The charming escort. The man who cared if she felt sad. She almost couldn't believe that side of him.

Thankfully the lift had arrived at the underground car park, so she stepped out, unlocked her car, slid past Simon's door-opening arm, and sat behind the wheel as her mind mulled over the conundrum of her thoughts.

Earlier, she hadn't noticed being overwhelmed by Simon in the car because she'd been driving. But watching Simon tonight, listening to his jokes with Malachi, seeing his kindnesses and the way he'd handled the little boys, as if they were the most delightful thing he'd seen all day, it was hard not to be awed by him. Not to want to hug him. To feel his arms around her, too.

This was the Simon Purdy she'd hoped would be inside him. Tonight she'd seen the real man. Why on earth was this glorious nurturer standing behind his decision not to embrace life and a family? Yes, he'd lost his wife, but... There had to be another reason she didn't know.

But, again, like his tie, Simon's life wasn't hers to straighten.

*None of your business, Isabella.*

If she started on trying to convince him she might cry.

Instead, she talked about her family. 'It was good to talk about Gran. Even for a little bit.'

He nodded thoughtfully as he slid into his seat belt and snapped it shut. 'Must have been.'

He tapped his watch. A high-pitched electronic voice said, 'It's eight-fifteen!'

She pushed back in the seat and turned her head briefly. 'What was *that*?'

He laughed. 'Mickey Mouse. The boys love it when I change my watch to Mickey.'

'You have a Mickey Mouse watch?'

'I'm a paediatrician. Of course I do.' He grinned at her amused face. 'I meant to change it back to silent when they went to sleep.'

'You're full of surprises.'

'You have no idea...' He waggled his brows.

'It's still early. Would you like a drink at the hotel bar until you see your father? I can just get an Uber home at nine.'

She'd like that. She wasn't sure how sensible it was, because the way she felt towards Simon Purdy right now she needed to take two steps back before she did more than straighten his tie.

She started the car and drove out of the car park towards the airport.

'Company at the hotel sounds good. If you don't mind? I'd love that. Saves me sitting by myself, watching the clock. You could even come with me to see my father, if you don't want to wait for an Uber. I'll only be there half an hour. If that. I'm sure he'll be interested to hear straight from a paediatrician about his new granddaughter. But he'll be keen to get back to work on his computer.'

'Easily done,' he said, and turned his head briefly to study her face. She felt his gaze on her. 'Barring Henry calling me,' he added.

Oh, heck. She'd forgotten about Henry. About Simon's world. Being on call. She'd lived with being on call with her father. Even been on call herself when she'd worked for retrievals. She remembered how much that impacted on life—more than expected.

That was why she'd gone for an academic, like Conlon. No on call. No emergencies. No need to be constantly aware and ready to go at a moment's notice. Being there when families needed you.

Right… And how had *that* worked out for her?

Not so good. She'd deleted another text from Conlon today without reading it.

'Dad's at the airport hotel. We can park underneath. Apparently, there's a bar on the top floor with excellent views, open till eleven tonight.'

'Perfect. We'll wing it when your father arrives.'

'Was that a pun?'

'I'm a funny guy.' He smiled at her. 'You just haven't met him yet.'

And that was how she found herself on the top floor of a beach-themed hotel, looking over the lights of the Gold Coast with Simon Purdy. On the horizon, the lights of ships glowed as they chugged up and down the coast. Behind them the planes were coming in to land.

Simon put two steaming chai teas down and slung his big frame into the high stool.

'You're buying for me again. Thank you.'

'You're welcome. You've had a big week with your sister. So Kate's the first baby in the family?'

She took a sip of the tea. Hot and soothing. 'My niece? Yes. I've only the one sister. Our mother died when we were young.'

'Like Malachi and me. Both our mothers died early too, and if it wasn't for Millicent, Malachi would have had no warmth in his life at all. That's why Lisandra is such a joy.'

'Makes sense.' Isabella huffed a sad laugh. 'Sounds like my world. My father was too busy for either of us after my mother was gone. If it wasn't for my grandmother...' Her words trailed off as she thought of Gran then and Gran now.

'That must make it doubly hard for you to see her so ill.'

Simon's words were quiet, not over-sentimental. It was as if he knew not to be too sympathetic or she might cry.

The thought eased the tightness in her throat caused by his words.

Isabella lifted her chin and looked at him. 'We went to boarding school, but Gran was the one who took us on holidays. Made sure we knew about cuddles and hugs. She's the person I love most in the world.'

'I bet she has some stories about you.'

Isabella surprised herself when she laughed. He had such a way of lifting her up. 'She does. But what about you? You lost your mother? What was your childhood like?'

His face closed. 'No memories of my mother. She died when I was born. I don't think my father ever forgave me for that.'

# CHAPTER SEVENTEEN

SIMON COULD NOT believe he'd just told her his deepest secret. Malachi was the only other person who knew. And probably Lisandra now, because Malachi would keep nothing from his wife.

Hopefully, Isabella would let it go.

'I'm sorry, Simon. Did you have any mother figure who gave you hugs? At least I had Gran.'

He sighed. Nope. She wasn't going to let it go.

'There were housekeepers. My grandmother died not long before my mother.'

'Well, you wouldn't know it from the way you interacted with Malachi's family. You look very balanced.'

'Do I?' He smiled at her. 'Diplomatic... Especially after the way I treated you last week.'

'We'll come to that—but not here. Ah...here comes my father. And soon I'll introduce you to my grandmother.'

'It is unlikely your grandmother will wake, Isabella.'

Simon heard the voice behind his right shoulder. He stood, sliding to the left and moving closer, instinctively, to Isabella, as if to offer her protection from the coldness in the man's words.

Isabella stood up as well. 'Good evening, Dad.' She inclined her head.

There wasn't even a hug between them. It had to be the coldest father-daughter reunion he'd ever seen, and Isabella wasn't a cold woman. He'd known that from the first moment he'd seen her. In fact...

No, he didn't want to go there.

Maybe her dad had realised his lack of warmth would reflect badly, because the man stepped forward and touched Isabella's shoulder. 'I'm aware how fond you are of your grandmother, but you need to be realistic. I spoke to the staff yesterday and there's no change. That's not good.'

Isabella ignored his comment and turned to Simon. 'Dad, I'd like to introduce you to Dr Simon Purdy, a consultant paediatrician where I work. Simon, this is my father, Professor Piers Hargrave, Director of Neurology at Sydney Central.'

Simon put out his hand to the older man and Piers shook it briefly, but Simon was marvelling at the strength and composure in the woman beside him. He could only imagine the distress her father's comments would have caused her. Good grief! Had he heard the man actually say he knew Isabella was *fond* of her grandmother, when anyone could see she adored the woman?

'Are you the consultant for my granddaughter?'

It looked as if Piers Hargraves had finished on the topic of his mother. Maybe that was for the best.

And Simon could do composed, too. 'Yes. Kate

is as stable as any thirty-two-week prem can be. At the moment, we see no reason to expect more complications as she grows. But of course everything is fluid.'

'More complications?'

The question was fired at him.

'She's undergoing phototherapy at the moment. But has successfully commenced EBM through her NG tube. We're pleased that she doesn't require supplemental oxygen or respiratory support now.'

Piers nodded at Simon and then looked at Isabella. 'How's Nadia?'

Nice that he'd asked, thought Simon—but maybe he was doing the man a disservice.

Isabella remained steady. 'We expect her to be discharged from Intensive Care tomorrow morning and transferred to a room near the NICU. Her blood pressure is coming down. It was a rapid onset of eclampsia, as I said on the phone. Dr Madden is the consultant looking after her. He seems happy with her progress. You should call him tomorrow.'

'Excellent. Thank you for the update.' He glanced at his watch. 'I expect to be here until the flight out tomorrow afternoon. I'll see Nadia and...' he hesitated over his granddaughter's name '... Kate.' He looked at Isabella. 'Is that her full name?'

'Yes. Though it is a derivative of Catherine.'

He frowned. 'Right... I imagine I'll see you tomorrow, Isabella?' He inclined his head at Simon. 'Dr Purdy.'

Then he was gone.

Isabella watched him go and then Simon heard her say softly, 'And that stellar conversationalist was my father. All warm and fuzzy, as usual.'

Simon studied the expressionless face beside him and his mouth quirked. 'As you say, I need to meet your grandmother. Because you are nothing like *him*.'

Isabella turned her face to his, and despite the tinge of sadness in her eyes he saw her lips twitch.

'Apparently, I have his brains. But I refused to go into medicine when he wanted me to. Things got even cooler then.'

She looked a little lost, and he didn't want her father to do that to her. 'Nursing's gain and medicine's loss. Now, would you like another drink? Maybe a stiff one? Or would you like to go home?'

She laughed. Which surprised him and possibly her, too.

'Thank you, Simon. For being here.' She raised her brows at him. 'Actually, I'd like to go home and have a stiff drink.'

That was dangerous, but wild horses couldn't drag him away from such an idea.

'Let's do that.'

Isabella drove. He'd opened her door for her,

then strode round to the other side to climb in. Neither had said anything but they'd both smiled.

He watched her handle the car beautifully, slipping through the traffic and down into the parking garage as if the car was on rails. When she'd pulled up they sat there for a few seconds, letting the engine tick as it cooled down.

'Your place or mine?' he said as he looked across at her from the passenger seat. She looked small and tired. And a little bit wounded. Which was a contrast to the confident woman he'd seen in the rooftop bar, talking to her father.

He felt the privilege of her allowing him to see her distress. He didn't want to take advantage. But he also wanted to be there for her. So the dilemma... Too much or too little being there for her? That was why he'd passed the decision to Isabella.

She said quietly, 'I'd like you to come up. To Gran's apartment. With me.'

Simon nodded. 'Stay there,' he said, and slipped out of the car and went around to her side and opened the door.

'You don't have to open my door.'

'It gives me pleasure.'

And it did. He wanted to protect and nurture her, despite the complex, rippling ramifications of that. What he didn't know was what *she* wanted.

She shrugged and slid gracefully from the vehicle. 'Feel free.'

She smiled, and that smile shone a little more vibrantly than before.

Pleased, he walked with her across to the lifts and used his key to let them in. He stretched out his arm across the doors as she stepped through and then followed her.

He could see she wasn't thinking about the present moment, because she didn't even move to the buttons they needed to press.

He pushed seven. The doors closed.

'We've done a lot of lift travelling today, haven't we?'

*There's a conversation*, he thought. As a starter, it was pretty useless.

But she lifted her head. Glanced his way.

'We have.'

And there was something there, at the back of her voice, that he'd like to know more about. Follow up. Explore...

The lift stopped before either of them said anything else. Again, he put his arm in front of the doors as she walked past to her grandmother's door. Yep. Protective. He could feel his own need. It had started.

She used her key and didn't wait for him. Just left the door open behind her.

Simon followed and closed the door to temptation behind him with a click.

His heart went thump at that same moment.

# CHAPTER EIGHTEEN

ISABELLA PUT HER leather clutch down with tingling fingers. Her whole body was warm from standing next to Simon in the lift. She slipped out of the silk jacket she'd had tailored in Vietnam and took it through to the hanger in her wardrobe. The jacket and trousers had been one of those indulgences she'd promised herself.

Tonight, she'd dressed for dinner with friends, but the choice of outfit had been for her father more than Simon. Really it had. Of course, dear Dad hadn't noticed or commented on it. Though, she could tell Simon had admired it.

When she came back into the sitting room Simon still lounged against the door. Waiting for permission to enter further?

He said softly, 'You looked stunning tonight.'

It was as if he'd heard her thoughts. But he couldn't have.

'You still look stunning. That colour is amazing on you. I've never seen anything quite like it.'

The way he'd said *'never seen'* was almost as if he meant he'd never seen anything quite like *her*. And it was a very nice balm for her apparent insignificance to her father.

She rubbed her arms, because the warmth increased and suddenly her skin felt super-charged as he looked at her.

She could almost hear Gran scolding her for feeling slighted by her dad. *'Drama, drama, drama!'*

She tried to let it go. Gran had also said, *'Thank someone if they pay you a compliment.'*

'Thank you, Simon.'

She waved him to the little bar in the corner, where the sherry and the spirits lived.

Obediently, he shifted. As she watched his muscular body ease into motion, calm and unhurried, yet eating the distance from the door, that slow, primitive warmth settled low in her belly.

*Oh my. There goes a man who could help a person forget anything.*

She'd enjoyed the intimate side of her relationship with Conlon, but she'd never felt this heat Simon generated just by standing there in front of her. This awareness. This lust that was coiling deep inside. Yes, Simon had annoyed and frustrated her before yesterday, but she'd always been aware of her overwhelming physical attraction to him. After tonight at the Maddens' it was more than physical. It was a little too close to consuming.

As if he'd picked up on her thoughts, his voice sounded deeper than usual when he asked, 'What's your definition of a stiff drink?'

She felt the timbre of his quiet words slide into her bones. *Oh my.* She should *not* be going down this path.

'Gran has a lovely cognac...'

It was as if they were both playing a part in a play. Pretending to be normal.

Then she thought of her father's comment.

'I'll replace it when she comes home.'

She heard the harshness in her tone when she said that. But, damn it, her father was wrong.

'As I said before,' Simon murmured as he poured, 'I can't wait to meet Catherine.'

Isabella crossed the room. Simon still had his back to her as he poured the drinks, and she gave in to the urge to slip her arms around his waist and rest her cheek against his broad back, looking for the comfort she knew she'd find there.

He was warm—hot, really—and muscularly hard. He smelled like cinnamon and the wind out on the ocean.

She closed her eyes and breathed him in. Letting go of the tension that had risen higher every day and coiled deep inside her, with Gran not waking, her sister's crisis, Kate's frailty, and tonight waiting for her father.

'Thank you, Simon. Thank you for being with me tonight. Thank you for being there during that incredibly painful five minutes my father could spare me. Thank you for understanding that I need to hope Gran will be back here.'

He put the crystal glasses down on the silver tray with a gentle *ting* that seemed to shimmer in the air like the sound of Tibetan bowls.

Very, very slowly, he unfastened her hands from around his waist, slid them to hold in his, and turned to look down on her so that the front of her body lay against his chest. He studied her face and then leaned down and kissed her lips gently, until he pulled back to stare at the spot he'd just saluted.

His gaze darkened to midnight-blue as it met her eyes. Her heart tripped. She could still feel the imprint of his mouth, hot against hers, and taste the chai on his breath.

In that deep gravelly voice that sent tingles through her, he said, 'You, dear Isabella, are very welcome.'

She loved the way he said her name. And he didn't step back. Didn't let her go. Didn't push on.

All it would take was one lift of her chin up to his mouth and she could forget. Escape from so much. Lose herself in Simon Purdy until tomorrow. She searched his eyes, but he wasn't giving her any pressure. This was her decision.

And what of tomorrow? What then? What of now? What about her needs? The comfort she needed right at this moment? Had needed since she'd landed in Australia?

Simon was offering that. *Simon.* He'd already

said it wasn't a relationship thing. But he would be gentle and kind and most likely a wonderful lover.

And tonight she'd feel warm and cared-for.

She searched his face. What if Simon needed it too? How long since he'd felt cared-for? She suspected it had been far too long.

With that thought she lifted her mouth to his.

Thankfully, he didn't need to be told twice.

Simon's strong hand lifted to her neck and he tilted her head back to expose her throat. His fingers slid down her cheek, down her throat, past the side of her breast and down to the small of her back in a hot trail, coming to rest just above the crease of her buttocks.

He pulled her in against him. Gently, but firmly. He was interested, too. Very interested.

'You taste like chai and sunshine,' he murmured into her hair.

'You taste like chai and the waves out on the beach.'

'Just one night…' he murmured against her mouth as he tilted his face down at her. 'I need you to know it's just one night.'

She stared into the depths of his eyes. Saw the fear in his. The need for mutual comfort.

'One night, or one night at a time,' she breathed. 'Either is fine.'

The hand that rested in the small of her back slid down until he caught her under the swell of her hips and swept her up against his chest.

'Lucky it's Saturday tomorrow and I'm not on duty till the afternoon,' he said. 'Because I'm planning on a late night.'

# CHAPTER NINETEEN

DECIDING TO SPEND the night with Simon was like surfing the first wave she'd ever ridden.

A leap of faith that she wouldn't fall flat on her face and get hurt.

And, like that first exhilarating wave, carnal pleasure with Simon had been everything she'd hoped for and more as she'd lifted her face to the sky and flew.

It had turned out to be a mutual delight and an unexpected healing. But both of them knew it wasn't happily-ever-after.

Now it was morning. The pillow was cold beside her. Like the space under her ribs as she realised he wasn't there and she didn't know why. He'd said one night but she'd not even had that. Just hours. And then he'd left.

In the early hours she'd dropped into a boneless sleep in his arms. It must have been some time after that when he'd slipped away. Had he left to avoid talking when they woke? Had she not been good enough? Or had he been called out?

This was why she didn't have one-night stands.

How had this seemed like a good idea last night?

For pity's sake. She had to work this afternoon and face the man.

What she needed was the fresh start of the ocean, but she wasn't sure she wanted to meet Simon face to face in the waves either.

His pique at her invading his surf-space suddenly became more understandable.

But maybe that was the best place to meet him. Floating on a board. A distance apart. With the excuse of looking forward as well as behind them to see a promising wave.

So that was what she did.

The sand flew cold and grainy from her bare feet as she ran towards the breakers. The seagulls were squawking, as if they knew there was juicy gossip to be had, and she squinted up at them balefully.

'Go eat a chip.'

She'd been avoiding it, but now, as she drew closer, Isabella narrowed her gaze to the waves. The space where Simon had been last time and she hadn't recognised his face.

Well, that wasn't going to happen now. She'd identify him, all right.

She'd traced the lines of his cheekbones. And his mouth. *Oh my*.... That mouth could do wonderful things. She'd gripped the hard muscles of his body and...

Nope. No forgetting Simon Purdy—today or probably ever.

Her cheeks warmed even with the cool breeze

on them, but her lips curved as the water sloshed up her ankles and knees and she jogged into the waves. Leaning down, she pushed the surfboard in front of her and launched herself along it, to push the water past with her hands.

Her breath caught as she saw a lone figure ahead. She wondered what time he'd come out. Because he was just sitting there. Like a lone pirate surveying the world. Now he was surveying her.

She paddled towards him, but not too close, always leaving a distance between their boards.

'Good morning, Dr Purdy,' she called as she sat up on her fibreglass island.

'Good morning, Isabella. A beautiful morning.'

But there was more in his voice than a remark on the weather, and his blue, blue eyes were looking at her as if she was the best thing he'd seen since he got here.

Her cheeks heated again, and she glanced away from him to the horizon, and the movement of water towards them.

She gestured with her arm. 'Nice swells coming in. Had some good rides?'

She did not just say that. *Shoot*. Her face scorched this time, and she spluttered and shut her mouth.

Simon was too much of a gentleman to laugh, but his eyes danced.

She turned her back on him, paddled quickly,

and caught a wave, even though it wasn't as perfect as she would have normally chosen. Right now she needed space.

Surprisingly, considering the mediocrity of the ride, Simon followed her. When she slipped off the back of the wave he paddled strongly towards her, white teeth gleaming, all rippling muscles, brown skin and big arms bringing him closer.

When he'd closed the distance he paddled up beside her and murmured, 'We said it wasn't going to be awkward.'

'It's not,' she lied.

He raised his brows at her. 'Do you regret spending the night with me?'

She looked up then, and forced herself to hold his gaze. 'Do you with me?'

He laughed. 'No, gorgeous. How could I? You were amazing.'

Oh. That was all right, then.

A weight fell off her shoulders.

'Then, no. You were pretty wonderful, too.'

And suddenly the awkwardness between them slipped into the water beneath them and she smiled.

His teeth gleamed again. 'Although perhaps what we shared last night could be a little more distracting than either of us expected.'

'Sorry.'

*My word, it was certainly distracting.*

'I'm not much of an expert at morning-afters.'
She put her head down, suddenly shy.

She heard his voice, but she still wasn't looking at him as they paddled side by side, up and
over another wave.

'Surprisingly, neither am I. Henry rang me not
long after you went to sleep. I left to speak to him.'

Isabella sucked in a breath.

He held up his hand. 'Not about Kate. Your
niece is fine.'

And that allayed two concerns in one. He hadn't
left because of any awkwardness or because he
was uncaring. He'd left for work. And he'd reassured her about Kate before she could jump to
wrong conclusions.

'Thank you, Simon. You're a thoughtful man.'
She lifted her head and risked looking into his
face. 'Race you to the back?'


When they'd surfed the early morning away, they
stopped at Lulu's café for breakfast.

As Simon was off duty, and Isabella was not
working until the afternoon, they had time—unless their phones rang.

Lulu swept up, pencil behind her ear and notepad in her hand, her usual exuberant self. 'Good
morning, you two. How's the surf?'

'Nice swells, thanks, Lulu.'

Simon leaned back in his chair and Isabella
tried not to stare at his strong throat and chest

above the open neck of his shirt. It was as if everything about him had taken on colour and tactile recognition and scent and memory, but he was still talking to Lulu.

'How're the twins?'

'Full of mischief. The usual for you, Simon? And what about you, Isabella? Smashed avocado and eggs on rye? Orange juice and coffee?

Isabella smiled up at the woman. She'd remembered her name and her previous order. 'Great memory, Lulu. All of the above, but a skinny cap, please.'

'Done.' Lulu swung away with her notebook.

'Why does she carry a notebook if she remembers everything?'

'For the chef. I've seen Lulu take an order from ten people at a table and bring out the correct food to everybody without writing a thing down. That's her superpower.'

'I think her personality is her superpower. She's amazing.'

Simon was looking at her with a smile on his face.

'What?' she asked.

'Some people might judge her for the piercings and the tattoos.'

'She's vibrant and happy and amazing. All the while loving twin babies. No judgement.' Isabella shrugged. 'So, what was the problem in the unit last night?'

She could do this. Talk to Simon normally after a night of incredible, bone-melting... She didn't like to call it sex. It had been more than that. How about mutual appreciation? Tenderness? Gentleness? A little bit of wildness. And lots of healing. She felt as if every knot in her body had been undone.

'Earth to Isabella?' Simon was watching her face and his blue eyes had darkened to ocean-depth-blue. 'You might want to stop looking at me like that...'

Her face flushed. Her neck heated. She closed and opened her eyes. 'Oh, dear.' She raised her gaze to his face. 'This is your fault.'

He laughed. 'I am not taking all the blame. No way. And last night at work it was the new twins.'

Lulu brought their coffee and juice and put their cups down. She didn't say anything, but she waved her hand at her own face as if fanning it. The smile in her eyes said, *It's smokin' hot over here!*

Once Lulu was gone, Isabella said quietly, 'So where do we go from here, Simon?'

'I'll go back home. I imagine you'll visit your grandmother, get ready for work, and visit your sister before you start. And I'll run into you this afternoon in the unit. At least we have two days before Carla is back with her eagle eyes, ready to tease us. Everything will be fine by then.'

She wondered if he really would *imagine*, daydream, or think about her while she was doing all that.

'You have experience in all this,' she accused.

He'd just laid out a very sensible plan, but it was sweet that he'd paid enough attention to know what her movements would be.

# CHAPTER TWENTY

SIMON WASN'T EXPERIENCED. Not with what had happened last night. He'd played around a bit before he'd met Louise, but since her death he'd been in cold storage. Now Isabella Hargraves had swooped in, and lust had taken him by dangerous and heated surprise.

Last night, while incredible, had been so momentous he knew without a doubt it had been a mistake. No way could he do that again and walk away.

Not with how amazing it had been and how hazardous it was to his resolution to stay single and safe from the type of pain he couldn't even contemplate going through again.

Isabella would want it all. She deserved it all. He just couldn't give it to her. He couldn't keep her safe.

He would remain focused on his career. He would not go down the route of falling in love.

Isabella Hargraves had all the makings of an addiction. And he knew where that led.

A place he wasn't going. Hadn't he told himself that before? Didn't matter. It had never been as important to remember as it was this morning.

They would finish breakfast and go their separate ways. And when they met in the unit he would be pleasantly friendly, because she deserved that. But he would pretend nothing had happened.

Eventually, she'd get it. He hoped.

Except he was kidding himself.

Simon grimaced into his coffee and pushed that thought away along with the cup.

The food arrived and they both tucked in.

It seemed neither of them had eaten for a week, because there was no word said as they shovelled the nourishment down. He hadn't been this hungry for years. Three years, in fact.

They sat back at the same time and looked at each other, and then looked down at their empty plates. And he couldn't help it. He laughed when she did.

'Apparently surfing works up an appetite,' he said.

She pushed her gorgeous lips together, as if holding words back, and he just knew what she was going to say.

Surfing wasn't the only thing that had given them an appetite.

He needed to run away. Tried to say, *I have to go*.

The one time he wanted his phone to ring and it wouldn't do it!

His phone rang.

*Thank you, heaven.*

His pulse rate settled.

*There we go.*

He stood up.

She said thoughtfully, studying his face, 'I'll pay for this. You go.'

And, contrarily, just for a moment he didn't want to leave.

# CHAPTER TWENTY-ONE

THAT. THERE. THE TWITCH. The flicker she'd seen in his eyes. He'd wanted to get away, to get to work. That was her father all over again. She felt the knowledge slide in, felt as if she'd been stabbed with one of the happy, beachy purple knives off the table, straight in her heart.

Simon wanted to leave her behind and get on with more exciting business-like work.

It stung. She'd told herself that she was fine for a one-night stand. And on one hand it had been a good decision to sleep with Simon—apart from all the benefits of the best sex she'd ever had—because now she knew, without investing in any more wishy-washy thoughts of the future. Even after what they'd shared, Simon wanted work more than he wanted her!

Message received.

Isabella watched as Simon ate up the distance to the apartments in big strides, even more quickly than if he'd run. And, yes, it all underlined the fact he wanted to get away.

'He's a nice guy,' Lulu said at her shoulder.

'Wonderful.' Isabella sighed and finished her coffee. 'But married to his work. I had a childhood like that. Not doing that for the rest of my life.'

She wasn't sure why she'd told Lulu that, except

Isabella needed to hear it out loud. Her statement solidified in her mind as she reached for her purse.

'And it's grateful I am that he is,' Lulu murmured, and there was emotion and a hint of Irish brogue under that sentence.

She got that. Oh, yes, Dr Simon Purdy was great at his job. And right now she was glad of that too. She had a niece who needed him.

'Hello, Gran. It's Isabella. I've brought you flowers. Deep purple with a subtle perfume.'

She subconsciously waited for a greeting that never came. Shook her head at herself.

'Violets. Your favourite. That's right...'

She tucked the small vase next to her grandmother on the side table and tweaked one of the blooms more upright.

'They say gently stimulating the five senses might help you to wake up.'

*Please, Gran*, she thought as emotion clogged.

She swallowed the lump in her throat.

'It's four weeks now, so that's enough of this sleeping for you.'

She pulled open the bedside drawer and took out the hand cream. She sat down and picked up her grandmother's thin, wrinkled hand in hers.

'Anyway, back to the five senses. I'm trying to stimulate your hearing, not drive you mad with my babble. And later your friend Millicent is coming to chat as well. Would you like that?'

That made her think about Simon.

She glanced across at her grandmother's face and for a moment she'd thought her eyes were open. They weren't. Her heart thumped faster and then settled down.

*Wishful thinking.*

Her brain wasn't working properly with images of Simon intruding with every second thought. She'd have to do something about that.

'The flowers are to stimulate your sense of smell…'

She began to smooth the cream into her grandmother's soft hands.

'And I'll spend a little time rubbing your fingers to stimulate your sense of touch.'

With a hint of asperity that wasn't solely directed at her grandmother, thanks to her father and Simon, she said, 'It's a beautiful day outside and you need to wake up.'

There was so much she wanted to tell her grandmother. Wanted to pour out into her ears.

But she was not going to talk about Simon. All she said was, 'The nurse said Dad has been in to see you. Did you recognise his voice?'

When Isabella walked into the neonatal intensive care unit the first person she saw, for a change, was her father. Tall and strangely gaunt-looking, and almost seeming old. She hadn't noticed that last night.

The second person was Simon, too darned handsome and full of stamina, standing beside him, talking beside Kate's cot.

Two tall men. One dark-haired, one light-haired. Both standing there with that consultant doctor attitude. An *I've studied a long time to be able to help this sick patient* look on their faces. Both married to their work. Both saving the world.

Blow the both of them.

She was early, so she had time to have a quick word before she officially started.

She put her bag away in the small staff room and crossed the room towards them.

They stopped talking as she approached. 'Hello, Dad. Simon...' She addressed her father. 'You went to see Gran? What did you think?'

She suspected he wouldn't even have said anything if she hadn't asked.

Her father's cool gaze held a hint of concern, which wasn't like him, and she focussed her attention on him while her stomach dived.

'There's a possibility she's not as deeply unconscious as she has been earlier, but I hesitate to give you false hope. Extensive brain damage is likely.'

And there it was. Did the man not have any heart?

Simon's gaze raked her face and she felt his sympathy. She didn't need it. She was becoming even more disenchanted with her father.

She narrowed her eyes at him. 'Thanks. Don't hold back. I need all the hope I can get.'

She turned to Simon before she said something she'd regret. Her voice softened and she searched his face. 'How's Kate?'

That was the question for now.

She plastered on a cool, calm expression for all to see. She looked down at her sleeping niece and asked, 'All going well?'

Simon spoke quietly. 'Kate's temperature control is erratic. We've had a couple of bradycardias and two occasions of apnoea. We've stopped the feeds for the time being.'

Stopped the feeds? Her stomach plummeted.

'Infection?' That was the most common cause of problems with premature babies. 'Her breathing?' She was certainly breathing a little faster. 'Not NEC…?'

Her brain rifled through the options. Infection they could treat with antibiotics. Kate had already been started on some. Could be anything. Worst-case scenario it could be the beginning of a Necrotising Enterocolitis, but it was very early.

She studied Kate's belly. Was the tiny tummy a little more bloated? It was the third day. That was a horrifying concept.

Simon studied her face as if he could see the thoughts chasing through her mind. 'There is some decrease in bowel sounds,' he said.

She nodded. Ignored her father. Fished her

stethoscope from her pocket, where she kept it to keep it warm, and wiped the membrane and casing—the listening end—with an alcohol swab from her other pocket. When she was done with meticulously cleaning it, she looked for somewhere to put the discarded swab and debris.

Simon held out his hand. Their eyes met and she saw the understanding in his. She settled the wrappings carefully in his palm, as if doing so equalled crossing her fingers behind her back and therefore she could keep Kate safe.

'Thank you,' she murmured, before leaning down to very gently put the stethoscope on Kate's belly to listen. She was hoping Kate's belly would gurgle. Or hiss. All she got was a tiny trickle. The rest was…silence.

She took the stethoscope away. Fear clutched her throat but she pushed it down.

'Do you think her abdomen is swollen?' At Simon's nod she asked quietly, 'How's the gastric aspirate trending? Has it increased?'

'Five mils removed last time.'

'X-ray?'

His intent gaze never left her face. 'There is a small collection of gases.'

'Treatment?'

'Change antibiotics. Nil by mouth for three days and fingers crossed.'

Okay. Standard protocol.

'When did you first notice it?'

'On my round an hour ago.'

He'd called over a radiologist for the X-ray.

No doubt he would have ordered blood tests as well.

Pre-empting her question, Simon added, 'Blood results aren't back yet. Not even the preliminary ones.'

Simon was worried—which meant she was worried.

She glanced towards the nurses' station and the staff who had gathered there. 'I'll take the handover report and come back.'

She didn't say it, but she wanted him still to be there. She glanced at her father, but uncharacteristically he didn't say anything. She nodded and left.

# CHAPTER TWENTY-TWO

PIERS HARGRAVES SAID, 'My daughter was always very quick on the uptake.'

Simon heard the pride in his voice. And he guessed that he, himself, was a little impressed that he hadn't been wrong about Isabella's ability to take in the situation instantly.

'She could have been a doctor, you know. She chose midwifery.'

Simon heard the curl of disgust in her father's voice. He was liking this guy less and less.

He lifted his chin and met the man's eyes. 'I have no doubt she's an amazing midwife. She's certainly brilliant as a neonatal intensivist. We're very lucky to have her.'

'Yes, you are. Hopefully she won't stay. I'm keen for her to move back to Sydney.'

Simon hoped Isabella's father didn't mean after Piers's mother had passed away. That was just too cold.

Either way, he couldn't see Isabella leaving. Not with Nadia here. And Kate. Even though Kate's situation was worrisome, Simon was quietly confident the baby would rise to the challenge. He thought this would only be a small setback, because they'd hit the problem quickly.

No doubt Isabella would think that too.

But he wasn't saying that out loud. He wasn't going to guarantee anything or make promises he couldn't keep.

And that went for other things as well. No promises anywhere about anything.

But was that just like Isabella's father?

Simon changed the subject. 'How's Nadia?' He hadn't seen Kate's mother today though he planned to go there now. Now that he'd seen Isabella.

'The oedema is receding. And her blood pressure is stable. It appears there is no sequalae. She's said she'll try to walk to the NICU late this afternoon.'

'Of course. I imagine she's been waiting for Isabella's shift. I'll ask them to bring her in a wheelchair.'

Piers dropped his voice. 'What is your intention with my daughter?'

Simon almost said *Nadia?* just to annoy him. But he didn't. And as for Isabella... He wished he knew.

'We have a mutual respect,' he said gravely. And left it at that.

Anything else was not her father's business—especially after the cold way he'd treated his daughter in the bar at that airport hotel.

Simon didn't want to think about why he was feeling so protective.

He saw the good doctor glance across at the

nurses circumnavigating the unit, stopping at each cot to discuss progress and treatment. He glanced at his watch.

Surely Piers wouldn't…?

'Let's go over and you can say goodbye. That'll be better than just slipping away. She's finding it tough,' Simon said, pre-empting Isabella's father's obvious intention of getting Simon to pass on a farewell message. Words that might sting Isabella with dismissal.

No. Simon wasn't going to let him do it.

He turned and crossed the room, and guided Piers to where the nurses were gathered to discuss their next patient.

'Sorry for the interruption, ladies,' Simon said. 'Isabella?' She looked at him. 'Could I borrow you for a moment, please?'

Seeing as he tended to do that all the time, nobody was surprised.

She detached herself and came to where he'd moved, back to Piers's side.

Her father's lips were pressed together. 'Goodbye, Isabella. You're doing a good thing, being here for Nadia. For everyone. Thank you.'

Simon saw her surprise and the quickly veiled pleasure at her father's words and breathed out a little deeper in relief, fiercely glad he'd leant on the other man to make a formal goodbye.

'Thank you,' she said quietly, and leaned forward to kiss his cheek. 'Safe flight.'

Her father nodded and strode away.

Simon saw the questioning look in her eyes. 'Yes. I'll still be here when you finish.'

It was her turn to nod, but he saw that same satisfaction flare briefly, and his own pleasure at her response sat warm in his chest.

'Thank you.'

She turned and walked back to the group and he went to the desk to call Pathology, to see if any results had come through for Kate.

# CHAPTER TWENTY-THREE

IN THE END, just before tea, Simon went to the post-natal ward and brought Nadia back in a wheelchair himself, to sit beside Kate.

Isábella didn't know what he'd said to her, but Nadia looked calm and composed, and she understood that her baby had issues that needed dealing with.

For Isabella, her concern was shelved as she watched her sister reach out and touch her daughter's hand for the first time. A baby too sick to travel up to visit and a mother to unstable to be transported down from the intensive care. But Nadia was in the new room on the same floor now. Everything would be easier. That small, tentative mother's touch brought tears to Isabella's eyes.

Hospital policy made it against the rules for its staff to care for their own relatives, so Isabella wasn't looking after Kate. But while she was not responsible for her care or observations, she could—and did—keep an eye on her from her side of the unit.

Thankfully, it seemed a quieter afternoon in the unit. Nice, Isabella thought, because it meant she could slip over and talk to her sister when she had questions. Also, it would be her break time soon, and she would spend it with Nadia.

Simon had disappeared to the emergency department, to treat a three-year-old girl with epilepsy, but had promised to come back.

Her sensible brain would have preferred he went home and got some sleep, just in case he was needed for her niece...

'Has Dad gone?' asked Nadia, glancing at her watch.

*Nadia. Think about Nadia. Be present.*

'Yes, he left not long after I started shift. I guess that means he didn't drop in to see you on his way out?'

Nadia shook her head and Isabella could see the quickly veiled hurt.

*Darn him,* Isabella seethed. What would it have cost him? Three minutes? Nadia was five doors away from the NICU.

'He said he was going to see Gran today, but he didn't come back to tell me what he thought about her prognosis.'

Isabel wanted to grind her teeth. The man had real issues with being a parent, and for the first time she wondered how many times her grandmother had actually forced him to do things that they'd thought he'd instigated himself.

'Did he tell *you* how Gran was?' Nadia asked.

Isabella said gently, 'He said he thought she wasn't as deeply unconscious as before, but he's not optimistic.'

She didn't say that she'd thought their grandmother's eyes had opened. Or that their father thought brain damage would be a problem.

'Imagine that…' Nadia drawled grimly. 'Dad not being optimistic…' She glanced up at Isabella, said softly, 'I'm sorry I didn't go more often to see her before Kate was born. It just upset me too much.'

Isabella leant down and hugged her. 'It's okay. I understand. Being pregnant mucks with your emotions.'

Right then Kate's cardiac monitor alarm went off, and Isabella watched the screen as her niece's heart rate slowly dropped. She glanced across to the nurse looking after her, who nodded and slipped across to watch as well.

Isabella said softly in Nadia's ear, 'We don't want to stimulate her—we want her to stimulate herself. But we will if her lack of breath and falling heart rate goes on for longer than thirty seconds.'

Nadia paled, and Isabella squeezed her sister's shoulder.

After seventeen seconds Kate breathed in, and her cardiac output increased as her heart rate went back up.

'Good girl,' Isabella said, and the nurse next to them smiled.

'She didn't need stimulation,' the nurse explained to Nadia. 'She's managing.'

'Yes, thanks… I see,' said Nadia, but her eyes

tracked back to Isabella, who nodded encouragingly.

'Jesse has this. She'll watch her,' Isabella said, and then continued, 'I'd better get back to my own babies. See you soon. Let me know when you want to go back to bed.'

Nadia nodded unhappily. 'I'll stay another ten minutes, but I'm getting sore...'

Isabella frowned. 'If you're in pain, only stay a few minutes more, while I phone an orderly to take you back to your ward. I'll come and see you in your room when I go on my next break.'

Forty minutes later, after all her babies were fed and their observations were up to date, Isabella went along to Nadia's room with the packed dinner she'd brought from home.

Nadia was just finishing off her own tray of food.

Nadia's first words—'Kate's good?'—made Isabella smile.

'Kate's good.'

'Great. And now, because I'm dying to know...' Her sister sat back expectantly. 'How was your date at Dr Madden's house with the hunky Dr Purdy?

Isabella smiled. Her sister had been very patient. 'Hunky Dr Purdy, eh?'

She was thankful this conversation hadn't come up on the unit, with everyone within earshot.

'Not my type.' Nadia tilted her head. 'But definitely hunky.'

She looked crestfallen for a second, and Isabella guessed Nadia had just remembered her late husband. The man had been not a happy partner in life for Nadia. A gambler and unfaithful. It would take time, and someone very special, for Nadia to trust a man again. Her sister did not need to go there yet, and Isabella could sacrifice a little privacy to cheer her up.

'It was fun,' she said, pretending she hadn't seen Nadia's punctured mood. 'And Lisandra Madden is a lovely woman I hope I see more of.'

'That's nice...' Nadia surreptitiously wiped her eyes.

'Yes. And I even met Dr Madden's grandmother. Millicent. She's a friend of Gran's.'

Nadia opened her eyes wide. 'Is she?' She smiled and shook her head. 'It's like a small town here.'

Isabella laughed. 'Probably because we're all connected through the hospital. Anyway, it was a lovely dinner, great conversation, and Lisandra's twins are gorgeous.'

'I'm jealous.' Nadia sounded wistful. 'You're making new friends and I haven't made any.'

Isabella opened the tucker box on her lap. 'It will happen.' She popped a cherry tomato into her mouth.

'But what about Simon?' Her sister shifted on

her pillows as if trying to get comfortable. 'Did he kiss you goodnight?'

Isabella's mind flew back to that long look in the lounge room of Gran's apartment, and the way, after that, Simon had carried her to bed. She slowed her chewing to give herself time to answer.

My word, he'd kissed her.

Her stomach curled, kicked and rolled.

She looked down at her food box.

He'd kissed her so many times. In so many places. She didn't think she'd ever forget that night. Or his mouth...

Instead of answering the question, and fighting down the heat that wanted to flood her cheeks, she offered, 'Simon and I called into the airport hotel after we left. He even came with me when I spoke to Dad. He met us in the bar.'

Nadia opened her eyes wide. 'Did he?' Thankfully she was diverted. 'That's above and beyond for Simon.' Then she frowned. 'How did Dad take that?'

'Didn't blink an eye.' Isabella grimaced. 'But then it didn't take very long. I was out of there in five minutes.'

Nadia shook her head. 'What do you think is wrong with our father? Do you think we'll be like that when we're old?'

Isabella couldn't help but laugh. 'He's not old. But no, I'm not turning into an antisocial pessimist. I refuse. And neither will you. I'm starting to think Gran is the only reason we're both turned out so well.'

That brought the mood down again. They were both thinking about Gran, lying there unconscious, her eyes closed. Not what she'd intended. But at least it diverted Nadia from asking about Simon kissing her goodnight again.

'Do you think she'll wake up?' asked Nadia.

'Yes. I do. When she's ready.'

Strangely, her dwindling hope had taken off again.

Isabella took a bite of her sandwich, because she needed to eat before she went back to work and she only had fifteen minutes left.

'Did you see Dr Madden today? Sorry I haven't asked before.'

Nadia nodded. 'Yes, just before lunch. He says I'm making good progress, but they need to keep checking my blood pressure.'

'I think you're in the golden light of Simon and Malachi now.'

And because that wasn't a bad place to be from Nadia's point of view, she smiled. Nadia and Kate needed the care.

'Also, it's great that we live close for later, as Kate grows up.'

Nadia sighed, long and loud, and then held her aching stomach. 'How long do you think Kate will be in hospital?'

That was the question most asked by parents in

the NICU, Isabella thought, and her sister was no different. 'I always tell people that however early the baby is in weeks is the general length of time they're going to stay in hospital.

'It could be eight weeks?' Nadia sounded forlorn.

'Could be… But probably closer to five. There'll be ups and downs, like today, so it's hard to tell.'

She pointed her finger at Nadia. 'But her mother and her auntie will be here for as long as it takes, and the time will pass. She just needs to be well and grow up. It will happen.'

# CHAPTER TWENTY-FOUR

SIMON DROPPED BACK into the NICU after the emergency department's call, hoping to catch Isabella before he went home. He'd planned to give her the pathology results personally, but she wasn't there.

He knew where she'd be.

On her break with her sister. Caring.

He should go home. The result would be in Kate's records soon, and the staff would let Isabella know when she came back. That would be in less than half an hour. He didn't need to go looking for her all over the hospital.

Except his feet carried him out of the NICU and along the corridor to the postnatal area and Nadia's room. He could hear Isabella's voice as he approached.

'It will happen.'

*What will happen?*

He couldn't help thinking of last night, and paused at the door to gather himself as memories tried to break through the wall he'd erected. Yes, it had happened. He squeezed his eyes shut, trying to hold back the images.

*My word, it had.*

He knocked. Two blonde heads turned his way, and two pairs of green eyes: one pair sleepy and owl-like because of the drugs, and the other alert, cool, and too beautiful for their own good. How did he find one of these sisters totally pole-axing and the other merely pleasant? Nadia was a beautiful woman, too, but Isabella stole his breath.

'Pathology back?' Isabella said softly as her brows rose in question.

He hadn't really noticed people's brows before, but hers were arched, darker than her hair. They drew the eye to the angles of her face. Perfect.

What was he doing? Spending seconds he didn't need to thinking thoughts he shouldn't be thinking. He should be walking in the opposite direction. Jogging? Sprinting?

The thought soured in his mind, and he pushed it away.

'Pathology? Yes. Not looking too bad. If Kate has an inflamed bowel, it's only just started, and hopefully the antibiotics will stop any spread of infection. We'll keep her nil by mouth and wait. She'll get IV nutrition.'

'Thanks, Simon.' Isabella smiled at her sister. 'That's good news, Nadia.'

Nadia breathed out a sigh. 'Wonderful. So, when will her tummy work again? Should I carry on expressing breast milk?'

He watched Isabella tweak the covers straight on her sister's bed, making sure she was snuggled in.

'You keep expressing every few hours, like you have been. We'll store the milk. There won't be much at first, but it will meet Kate's needs when she's ready. We'll sort that.' Isabella glanced at her watch. 'Thanks for the update, Simon. You going home now?'

He felt dismissed. Maybe she did have a bit of the old man in her. The thought made his mouth twitch. Isabella was nothing like her cold father.

'Yes.' He had a sudden uneasy thought. 'Did you bring your car? How do you normally get home at night after a late shift?'

He walked the block and a half home at night. The fresh air after the air-conditioned hospital felt good. But he didn't like the idea of Isabella out at eleven p.m., when her shift ended, which coincidentally was not long after the pubs shut with all the drunks and revellers emptied onto the streets.

It was dark on the road towards their apartments, even with the streetlights.

'I walk fast,' she said. 'Like you do. And I carry an alarm.'

He opened his mouth and closed it again. Fair enough. Except he wasn't happy. His neck crawled with how unhappy he was.

'She has a black belt in karate,' Nadia said with a wicked, sisterly grin. 'Which she doesn't tell anybody about.'

That made him blink. Why was he surprised? Why did that make her even hotter?

'I should ask you to walk *me* home, then,' Simon quipped, but his brain spun with relief...

and maybe some graphic imaginings of Isabella
flying through the air or kicking out at an assail-
ant.

His body stirred. *Hot, or what?*

Nope. Not going there.

It wasn't strange that his mind was on alert—
he had feelings for Isabella...complicated feelings. But she was a friend. They'd agreed on that.

Friend with benefits? his libido whispered.

No. No more benefits.

But maybe he'd watch for her out of his balcony
tonight and just make sure she was safe.

'I'll leave you, then,' he said, wishing his phone
would ring. Why was he still here?

'I'll come with you.' Isabella leaned down to
kiss her sister. 'You need sleep, missy. I'm not far
away if you need me.'

Ah, Isabella would want to talk to him about the
results. That was why he hadn't left. He'd known
she'd want that.

It was as if another Simon lived inside him—
one tuned to Isabella and Isabella's needs.

He waved, and Isabella said, 'See you tomorrow, Nadia.'

He walked to the door and Isabella followed
until they were out in the corridor and halfway
back to the NICU. Then she stopped.

'Thanks for being here today, Simon.'

He saw her concern, her worry, and his heart
ached a little at the load she carried. But he needed

his walls to stay up. Especially when she looked at him like that.

In response, he made light of his part. 'Easy done. I don't have a life.'

That was true. But the statement fell flat. She didn't smile.

'Why is that? Why don't you have a life? You deserve one.'

Her voice was more intense than he'd expected.

His brows furrowed. 'I told you why. I've had my time.'

*Because I'm scared that if I allow myself to care and something happens again...*

He wasn't going to say that. So he batted the question back to her. 'Why don't *you* have a life, apart from worrying about your family? Where's your home life?'

He hadn't wondered about that before, and suddenly the answer was very, very interesting.

She looked away. Which wasn't like her.

'I tried that in Vietnam. His name was Conlon. He let me down, too.'

He saw the subtle shake of her head, as if she was calling herself a fool for believing in fairy tales. She deserved the fairy tale. He just couldn't give it to her either.

The man must have been a fool. He wanted to say so, because standing there with Isabella he felt as if they were in a bubble, insulated from the world.

Except they weren't alone in the bubble.

An orderly pushed an empty stretcher around the corner and they had to separate to let him through. It broke the spell.

'I'm sorry. It's none of my business. I'd better go.'

Before he said something else stupid.

He turned and left, but he could feel her gaze on him as he walked away.

At ten past eleven that evening Simon stood on his balcony and watched the road between the hospital and the apartments.

He'd never really thought about the fact that he could see his place of work from where he lived, but for the purpose of watching for Isabella it was perfect.

There she was. Right on time. Walking under the first streetlight with a brisk pace and a cross-body bag tucked in front of her. There was something in the droop of her shoulders that said she was unhappy.

He scanned the streets, but there was no one around. Still, he didn't like it. He wanted to slip down in the lift and stand outside, open the door for her.

Crazy on top of crazy. He needed sleep.

He stayed watching.

He'd phoned half an hour ago to check on Isabella's niece, and she'd been stable, so nothing new to worry either of them there. They should both sleep.

But why was she unhappy? Was it him? Had he done this to her?

She must have felt his attention on her, because she glanced up at his balcony and shaded her eyes from the streetlight. He reached his hand back into the apartment and flicked the light on and off.

She offered a tiny wave and he smiled. Felt his whole face crinkle with satisfaction from one miniscule hand lift. *Idiot.*

He texted her. Fingers moving before he could stop them. He hadn't even realised that he had his phone in his hand.

Do you want to come up?

And that was why he was standing there. God, he was such a fool. He hadn't realised that was what he was going to do.

She texted back.

Two minutes.

His libido whispered that he could be fast, if that was what she wanted. Against the door, maybe?

He closed his eyes.

No. No. No. He wasn't going to do this. They weren't going to do this.

He was just there to hear about her night. Be an ear and listen to her, because she didn't have anyone else. Let her unwind so she could sleep without her brain reeling in the night with suppressed conversations she couldn't have on her own.

Like he did. Nearly every night.

He went back inside to the kitchen to put on the kettle. Absently checked there was ice in the freezer in case she wanted something stronger. Put out two mugs. Threw in two sleepy-time teabags.

Because then he wouldn't have to spend time in the kitchen, when really he wanted to look at her, talk to her, not have his back to her making tea.

She knocked at the door before he had time to put everything back and tell himself to stop being stupid, so instead he crossed the room in long strides.

He took a breath to fill his lungs and opened the door, so he could search the features he was coming to know so well.

He'd missed her face.

He frowned when he saw the worry in her eyes. The concern in the pull of her mouth. The weariness. He wanted to hug her.

'Come in,' he said.

She eased past him, bringing the smell of the hospital and handwash in with her.

He shut the door and followed. 'How was your night? I thought you might like a quick debrief before you went to bed.'

Her chin lifted and he saw the glitter of tears. 'Nadia had another seizure. Malachi's with her and she's back in Intensive Care.'

This time he didn't hesitate before he stepped up and pulled her to his chest, wrapping his arms around her. The hug was long and firm. She shuddered with distress under his hands.

'I'm so sorry, Isabella. No wonder you look stressed. I'm glad you came up.'

He tucked his chin on top of her head and breathed in the scent of her hair. Herbs. Flowers. And Isabella.

'What time did it happen?'

'Nine p.m. Malachi came down to see me afterwards. Very kind of him. He said she's stable now, but will have to stay in the ICU for another forty-eight hours at least.'

She lifted the back of her hand to wipe a tear off her cheek.

'I rang Dad. But he was in a late meeting, so I left a message.'

Of course he was. Useless man. Or useless to Isabella, anyway.

She pulled away and he let his arms fall so she could step back.

'Sorry.' She turned her face away. 'You don't need all this drama.'

'Hey...' He lifted a finger and turned her chin back. 'You're the lone lighthouse here, for all these people. It's tough being you. You just keep on being an incredible rock for everyone and I'll help hold up the foundations when you need it.'

She sniffed and lifted her chin, but her mouth trembled. 'I don't feel very rock-like at the moment.'

'How about you roll your rock my way?' He patted his chest. 'Let me be a refuge you can come to when you need it.' He stepped closer and pulled her in again. 'Another hug won't hurt.'

She let him, but she mumbled against his chest, her words vibrating between them.

'You couldn't wait to get away this morning,' she said.

And, yes, he had wanted to get away. He'd actually bolted. And he was ashamed of that. Yet, strangely, he didn't want to escape at this moment.

'But not now,' he said by way of apology.

Because she needed him now. And he couldn't dispute the fact that he needed to be there for her.

'Doesn't mean we're not friends. Just means I'm trying not to promise something I don't think I can give.' He dropped a kiss on her hair. 'But this is now. I can give this. The other is for the future. Would you like a sleepy time tea? Or something stronger?'

She stepped back again. When she looked up at him her mouth had firmed and her eyes were clearer. 'I'll take the tea.'

He nodded and pulled her over to the long sofa

with all the cushions, and made sure she was comfortable before he turned for the kitchen.

He was back less than a minute later, with the tea poured, and a small empty bowl for the tea bag when she was happy with the strength of her beverage.

'Do you need something to eat?'

'I couldn't eat,' she said. 'I've been feeling sick since nine.'

'Understandable. But you know what? Sometimes food helps. How about I make you some cheese on toast cut into soldiers?'

She leaned her head leaned back at that, and stared up at him quizzically.

He shrugged, his face a little warm. 'Malachi made it for me after my wife died and I was doing zombie impersonations. I find it really helps when things get bad.'

She shook her head, as if she couldn't imagine what he described, but then a small smile bloomed on her beautiful mouth. 'Truly, that sounds wonderful. I'd love to try Malachi's soldiers.'

They sat together for the next half an hour, munching on crunchy toast and melted cheese, and drinking sleepy time tea as the clock ticked towards midnight. He'd dimmed the lights, so they could see out through the door towards the twinkling lights of Surfers Paradise across the wide bay.

Outside, the sound of the waves on the beach

made a rhythmic hum as the traffic died away. His arm lay across her shoulders, pulling her into him, and her skin was like silk against his, warm and wonderful. Gradually Isabella relaxed beside him. His own stomach unwound as the tightness in her neck loosened and her head sank back into his arm. Good.

'I checked on Kate at half past ten and everything was fine with her,' Simon murmured quietly, not wanting to upset the mood but giving her the option to talk if she wanted to.

She shifted her head to look at him. She was so close. Kissably close.

'This is nice. I feel better,' she said, off-topic. Then, 'Yes, she looks good. I think you've nailed the danger after that first sign of inflammation. Nipped it in the bud.'

He stared back at her. Her eyes had deepened to emerald in the low light. 'I hope so. When are you on shift again?'

'An evening shift tomorrow.'

He fought with his body to lift his arm from her shoulders, because it really didn't want him to move. 'I, on the other hand, am on duty at eight. And you, missy...' he smiled as he remembered her addressing her sister like that '...need to go to bed.'

*And not with me, despite how lovely that would be.*

But he didn't say that out loud.

'You need sleep.'

'So do you,' she said. She turned her face and kissed his cheek. 'Thanks for the listening ear. I needed it.'

When she stood, she looked better somehow. Stronger. As if she'd regrouped. And he hoped that he had been a small part of that, even if he couldn't be anything else.

# CHAPTER TWENTY-FIVE

ISABELLA'S HEARING SEEMED bizarrely attuned to hear when Simon shut the door after her. But when she got to the lift there had been no sound, and she turned back. He was still waiting.

She furrowed her brows at him. He smiled and waited until she'd slipped inside the elevator and the doors began to close before closing his own door.

That had been lovely interlude after a mad day. Simon had cosseted her. Not something she'd experienced often—someone looking after her.

Gran was bracing. Fun as she was, she expected the girls to look after themselves.

Simon making her cheese on toast soldiers, instead of Isabella doing the nurturing, sat oddly, but was warmly comforting—as it had been intended to be. There was no doubt she felt more serene than she had when she'd walked through Simon's door forty-five minutes ago.

But yes, she was tired. Needed to sleep. And not in Simon's bed. There was no future there. She wasn't going down that rabbit hole before trying to sleep. It would be too easy to get used to it.

The next morning Isabella launched her surfboard into the ocean and let the clarity of the waves wash away the fog, drama and fear of yesterday.

By the time she left the water she felt awake and alive. Ready for the day. Simon wasn't there, though. She'd spent a lot of the time looking. She tried not to worry about Kate just because he was missing. He had promised to call and her waterproof watch said she hadn't missed any attempts of communication.

She jogged back to her apartment with her surfboard under her arm, feeling her body lift and respond as if eager for more of a workout.

Nadia had told Simon about her karate. She hadn't thought about joining a martial arts class up here but that would be a great idea to give her another outlet. A place to stretch her muscles, keep fit and expend extra energy. Distract her from thinking about Simon.

Yup. She'd look into classes after Nadia was home and safe.

She'd phoned the ICU this morning. Her sister was stable and there'd been no more seizures. Kate was unchanging, according to the night shift in the NICU, though Simon's absence from the beach made that less reassuring.

She'd see Gran soon. Something about today felt positive, instead of a day spiralling down into worse and worse, and Gran was a good place to start.

'Good morning, Gran.'

Isabel placed another bowl of tiny heart-shaped

purple flowers on Gran's bedside table. This time they came with succulent leaves as well.

'Mrs Green has more violets for you.'

She glanced down at the familiar face and froze.

Her grandmother's eyes were open. Isabella shut her own eyes and held them shut for the count of three. She slowly opened them, terrified of what she'd see.

Gran's eyes were still open. They weren't vague and staring. They were lucid. And warm.

Isabella's mouth opened in wonder as two single tears slid from the corner of her grandmother's eyes.

Isabella watched, barely daring to breathe, as Gran moistened her lips and whispered hoarsely, 'Bella…'

And then she closed her eyes and drifted off. But this time there was a smile on her face.

'Gran?' Isabella called, her voice frantic. Her gaze flew to the heart rate monitor above her head and she saw the rise in the heart rate begin to settle down again from the faster rhythm to the usual seventy. She hadn't noticed it when she'd arrived.

Gran had woken up.

Spoken and been lucid.

She'd recognised Isabella.

Isabella sank into the nearest chair. She put a hand to her mouth and silent tears ran down her face.

When she lifted her head there was a nurse there. Ella—the one she saw most mornings.

'What's wrong? I saw the monitor change,'

Isabella turned damp eyes to the young woman she'd spoken to nearly every day for the last month. 'Ella... Her eyes were open. And she said my name. Then she went back to sleep.'

Isabella heard herself say the words, but even she couldn't quite believe it.

Ella nodded with delight. 'They all said I was mad when I said she was less deeply unconscious than before.' Ella reached down and quickly hugged Isabella and then stood back. 'I'm so pleased for you all, Isabella. I'll phone the doctor.'

The room quickly filled with people and Isabella found herself tucked into the corner of the room, her heart still pounding.

She needed to tell Nadia.

And her father.

But, strangely, the person she really wanted to tell was Simon.

Ella said, 'They're going to take your grandmother down to have another CAT scan. Probably other tests as well.'

Isabella understood. Ella meant she'd soon be sitting in an empty room. 'I'll leave and come back on my way to work.'

Ella nodded. 'I'll phone you if anything changes.'

'Thank you.'

Her voice cracked. Time away was probably a good idea.

She walked away, her head full of improbabilities and hope and dread all mixed up so that she could barely think. When she reached her car, she sat in it, but didn't turn on the engine. Couldn't bear to drive away.

She looked down at her phone and her fingers flew as she texted before she thought too much about it.

Gran opened her eyes, Simon. And said my name.

She sent it just like that, and a text flew back within a minute.

Where are you?

She texted back.

Sitting in my car outside the hospital. I can't seem to drive away.

His reply.

I'll be there in ten minutes.

He was there in eight. He must have run to the apartments to retrieve his vehicle. He parked three car spaces down and was out of his car and at her door faster than she would have thought possible.

He opened her door and she climbed out and into his strong, warm arms. They wrapped around her. Wrapped her with kindness, understanding, and the big-heartedness she desperately needed right at that minute.

'But what if that was her last lucid moment before she passes away?' She whispered her worst fear into his chest.

He rubbed her back. Up and down, up and down, soothing her like a child with a skinned knee.

'What if it's the beginning of her waking up properly?' he said quietly into her hair. 'I think we should go for that one. Don't you?'

The sob in Isabella's throat turned into a strangled hiccup of a laugh.

'I like your optimism,' she said. 'I desperately *need* your optimism.'

His big warm hand, still rubbing up and down her back, patted her. 'Maybe she regained consciousness because she knew you'd be here, waiting for her.'

Isabella sobbed until his shirt was wet. Big, ugly, heart-wrenching sobs of relief that she hadn't allowed herself before.

As she quieted, he pushed a big, folded square

of soft white material into her hand and she glanced at it. Her shaky laugh was a good exchange for the tears. 'I didn't think people carried handkerchiefs anymore.'

'I'm in a job where I sometimes need more than a tissue. Fragile paper just doesn't cut the mustard when your baby is sick.'

She sniffed, opened out the handkerchief, wiped her saturated eyes and cheeks, and blew her nose soundly.

He laughed. 'You can keep that.'

She offered him a wobbly grin. 'I'll wash it and give it back to you.'

He stepped away. The warmth of his hand falling away from her left a gap in her world and she missed it.

'Feel better?' he asked.

She sniffed again, but she felt as if she'd dropped a neck yoke and two full buckets off her shoulders.

'I do.'

Then she saw the way his damp shirt clung to the muscular ridges of his chest and abdomen, and suddenly she wanted nothing more than to trace the lines and hollows of his torso. She pulled her hand back as soon as it began to reach out.

'Um…you're wet. Sorry.'

'I didn't have time for a swim this morning. Must be my quota of salt water.' He was smiling, but there was heat there, too.

'Cute,' she said.

She eased away. Further. Until her back was against the closed door of the car. It felt warm from the sun, but not as warm as her belly. 'You got here quickly.'

'My friend needed me,' he said.

*Friend.* Cold water. That put out some of the flames.

'But I have to go back now. Are you going to be okay?' he asked.

She was used to standing on her own. But she appreciated the thought.

'Yes,' she said. 'I'll be fine. I'll go home now. I'll visit Gran again this afternoon, before I come to work.' Then another thought intruded. 'How's Kate? I was worried when you didn't come surfing.'

'The new twins are playing up. Respiratory issues. But I've pulled them into line,' he said with an easy smile.

Yet still his eyes remained serious and concerned.

About her?

'That's good. And I'm good. Now.' She met his gaze. 'Thank you, Simon. For coming when I needed you.'

His mouth opened and closed again. As if he'd thought better of what he'd been going to say. Instead, his lips formed different words. 'Have you called your father?'

No, she hadn't. She'd called *him*.

'Not yet.'

He smiled, and she suspected he liked it that she had called him first.

'I have to go. I'll see you later.' He turned towards his car, then spun back. 'Text me if you need to talk.'

# CHAPTER TWENTY-SIX

SIMON LEFT ISABELLA at the hospital and his mind spun with what seemed suspiciously like delight.

She'd contacted him before her father.

To share her news and her fears. Because she'd trusted that he'd understand and be there for her.

She couldn't have known that he'd come, and he wondered what had been going on inside her head that had made her think texting him would help.

He lifted his chin as he drove back to the hospital. He had helped. Judging by her face. But when he'd first arrived—heavens, she'd looked like a fragile crystal vase about to smash into a million pieces.

He guessed she had finally broken against his chest, judging by the dampness of his skin. But the idea of Isabella—beautiful and tough and, yes, astoundingly fragile—needing him made him glad she'd called him.

In fact, the idea of Isabella seeking comfort anywhere else made his eyes narrow.

Simon wondered just how deeply he was falling for Isabella Hargraves...and if there was any hope at all that he could extricate himself before it was too late.

\* \* \*

Simon should be in his office with his afternoon appointments, but his two-thirty had called to cancel. And instead of catching up on paperwork—which he always needed to do—he was striding through the hospital to the NICU, to be there for when Isabel started work.

He watched her push through the door, totally put-together, showing no hint of the life-altering change that had occurred for her that day. Maybe there was an extra spring in her step. Certainly there was a smile in her eyes when she saw him.

He smiled back. Must be good news with her grandmother—but he'd have to wait. She'd only just made it in time, because the shift handover was about to begin.

While he waited, he finished typing up the changes he'd made to one of the twins' treatment and checked through the notes for the rest of the tiny patients in the unit.

Fifteen minutes later the nurses had finished their walk around the patients and Isabella arrived at his side.

He was still typing on the rolling computer in front of the cot. 'Are you looking after these boys today?' he asked her.

She nodded. 'Yes.'

'Good,' he said.

They talked about the twins. Their treatment. The results of the latest blood tests. They compared thoughts on an X-ray and Simon realised he didn't even have this kind of in-depth conversation with Henry, and he was supposed to be his registrar, able to keep up.

Isabella mentioned something that might lead to a breakthrough.

He looked at her sideways. 'Good insight. I hadn't thought of that. Thank you.'

She lifted a hand, brushing it away. 'I love X-rays—they can show so much. So, you're welcome.'

He nodded, and knew he would think more on that later, but for the moment they had more important things to talk about. 'How's your grandmother?'

As he asked the question he studied her face and saw that her eyes were sparkling.

'She woke up again. She's incredibly weak, of course. But her doctor seems to think that because she recognised me and spoke again, making sense, she should just get better every day.'

'That's wonderful.' It was. Mind-blowing, really. 'Have you told Nadia?'

'Yes. I dropped into Intensive Care just before I came here. Malachi has her on some pretty strong drugs, so she's vague. But she's as thrilled as I am.'

'And your father?'

'My father told me not to expect too much.'

Simon was relieved to see she didn't look too disappointed. 'Of course he did...' Simon muttered. And then pressed his lips together. *Oops*. 'Sorry, that was judgmental.'

Isabella laughed. 'But true.'

He touched her shoulder. 'I'm very happy for you all.' *Especially you.* But he didn't say that out loud. He looked up as the phone rang and Carla called his name. 'I have to go. But I'll see you before I go home.'

He watched her beautiful mouth curve and her eyes lighten. Yes. She was glad that he'd said that. Which was good. Wasn't it...?

But Simon didn't make it back to the NICU before he went home because he spent the evening in the ICU with a young boy who'd came into Emergency with a severe asthma attack. It was touch-and-go as to whether they could save him. Simon couldn't leave the child until he was stable.

He had managed to lift his hand in a wave to Isabella when she'd entered the ICU to see Nadia. Isabella had waved back.

He finished in the ICU at ten-thirty that night, tired, rumpled, with his shirt slightly bloodstained from a tricky cannula.

On seeing the time, his first thought was Isabella, but it was too early to walk her home, and a bad time to talk to her as she prepared to end her shift and hand over. Instead, he decided to go to his own flat and shower. With luck he could walk and meet her on her way home.

Which was how he managed to find her under that first streetlight just outside the hospital, in his fresh attire and with damp skin. He'd had to rush.

Isabella met his eyes as she walked up to him. 'Fancy meeting you here.' She looked him up and down, taking in his different clothes and wet hair. 'I'm guessing you had a busy night?'

Before he could speak a huge yawn overtook him and his hand lifted to hide his cracking jaw. 'I did. But the good guys won, so that's what's important.'

She bumped his shoulder with hers. 'You're the good guy.'

*Nice.* He smiled at her. 'Thank you. But this good guy is exhausted.' He side-eyed her and thought, *I'm exhausted, but loving the view.* 'And starving. I didn't get dinner. Fancy sharing a late-night snack?'

'I'd like that—but how about you come to Gran's apartment? I've got some homemade pumpkin soup, half a cooked chicken and some sourdough I'm happy to share.'

'Sounds even better. What shift are you on to-morrow?' It wouldn't be fair to keep her up if she started at seven a.m.

'A two-thirty start.'

'Excellent.' And he realised as he walked along the dark street with Isabella by his side that he was very, very content.

When Simon stepped inside Catherine Hargraves' apartment his eyes skittered to the bedroom he could see through the open guest room door. The bed was made. It hadn't been before. The last time he'd seen that room Isabella had been well loved and asleep amidst tumbled sheets.

His body stirred at the memories of that night, and when he looked away he saw she'd caught the direction of his interest.

Her voice conversational, she asked, 'You regretting that?'

'Lots of emotions,' he said soberly. 'But none are regret.'

'Good.' Her gaze left his and she walked into the kitchen, as if he'd given her the right answer. 'Do you want your sourdough toasted or soft?'

# CHAPTER TWENTY-SEVEN

'Soft, please.'

Isabella turned away to hide her blushes, because she had lots of emotions about that night, too. None of them regret. And none of them soft. Mainly she felt caution, the possibility of peril, and the absolute fear of never finding another man she cared about as much as Simon.

Maybe he would change his mind.

But she was trying to keep a lid on fantasising until she heard or felt something positive back from Simon.

She understood he was wounded. Battered by the loss of his wife. And probably scared of losing another someone he might possibly build a life with. She could see why. But there had to be more.

She had her own fears. She thought about Conlon. How he'd let her down when she'd needed him most. Thought about her father and how he'd let her down so many times when she'd been desperate for a shoulder to cry on. And she thought about Simon itching to get away at breakfast the other day.

But also she remembered today. When he'd come and held her while she'd been at her most vulnerable.

Had Simon changed his mind? Let himself become more accessible to her? It did look as if he wanted her to call on him if she needed support.

Or was she dreaming the fact they were getting closer because that was what she wanted? That he might reconsider them being more than friends?

Or maybe the guy just wanted more sex since he'd broken his drought.

But she didn't think Simon was shallow, and she suspected he knew she was protecting herself from expecting more than he offered.

Which left her vulnerable again.

Maybe inviting him here tonight hadn't been her most sensible idea.

Through all these thoughts and tortured paths of indecision her hands were busy heating soup, buttering sourdough and pulling the chicken from the fridge to cut up onto a larger plate. She threw on a couple of cherry tomatoes and a handful of spinach leaves, along with a baby cucumber and sweet yellow capsicum, sliced quickly. Then she gathered a knife and fork and a bottle of mayo and put the plate down in front of him at the table.

'You start on this while the soup heats and I'll butter more toast.'

He glanced up at her. His eyes twinkled and her belly kicked.

'So...you're one of those women who can make something out of nothing in less than two minutes?'

*Stick to this conversation.*

'I've had years of grabbing quick snacks. And I don't like commercial fast food, so I always have the makings.'

Simon opened his eyes wide. 'You don't like fast food? Wash your mouth out.' He reached for the plate and the cutlery.

He laughed and ate, and by the time she brought out the toast and soup he was scraping the plate.

'Hungry, much?'

'I have been wasting away,' he acknowledged, as she put a blue mug filled with steaming soup beside him, along with a plate holding two big slices of sourdough and real butter.

She considered his wide shoulders, gloriously broad chest—and those arms! *Oh, my.* This man was *not* wasting away.

Luckily, Simon missed her long, hungry examination as he looked at the soup with eager anticipation. 'Now I might live.'

Smiling, damping down the fire that had burst into flame in her belly, she went back into the kitchen and returned with her own soup and bread. She sat down opposite him. 'So? What happened in ICU?'

He was the one who was strung up this time. She, for a change, was feeling calm—or as calm as she could be with Simon across the table from her late at night, looking scrumptious. It was a nice change from her meltdown against that particular awesome chest earlier today.

But she had a feeling he'd had some trauma that still bothered him. Horrors lingering after the close call she'd heard about tonight, when one of the ICU nurses had spoken to her during her break with Nadia.

'Was it the young boy? Arlo? Asthma?'

Simon shook his head. 'Horrid disease. I hate it. Sometimes they get so shut down you just can't break through to their lungs.' He blew out a big sigh. 'We were lucky. We managed in the end.'

'Good job.'

He shook his head. 'I still can't believe the kid didn't even have an asthma plan for his mum to work through if he started to get sick. I'll have to contact his GP. Have a word with the practice about patient safety with asthmatics.'

She listened as he ranted a little. And then talked about the scariest bits. The fact that the boy's eyes had watched him, terrified, as he'd struggled for breath, and how Simon had thought he'd been going to lose him. And that wasn't even mentioning the distraught parents.

'But we won,' he finished, as if it had been a huge battle.

She could see that it had been. 'They were lucky to have you,' she said.

'It took a team,' he said. And looked away.

He seemed uncomfortable with the praise, and she wondered about his childhood. About his in-ability to take a compliment graciously. Not losing a patient seemed vitally, intrinsically imperative to him. It was the end goal for all health professionals, but to Simon it seemed more. As if his own life and death was in the balance.

'I'm lucky to have you to listen to me. And feed me. That was delicious.'

They'd both finished, and the empty plates had been pushed to the middle of the table.

Suddenly it felt as if the air had been sucked from the room. Which was crazy, because she had the door to the balcony open and the curtains were floating in a soft sea breeze.

She licked her suddenly dry lips. 'You should go to bed, Simon.' She stood up. 'You need to sleep.'

He rose, and Isabella walked towards the door. He followed her closely—which was good, wasn't it? But so was the fact that before she could undo the lock he had rested his hand on her shoulder and turned her to face him.

Yes. She wanted this.

Stepping close, he put both hands above her head against the door. Caging her loosely. But not holding her.

As he gazed down into her face she knew she should slip under his arm and away, but there was a lot of heat coming from his body that was now so close to hers. And she liked that heat. All she had to do was say the word, though, and she knew he would let her go.

But that was hard to do when she didn't want to. 'Is this a friends-with-benefits moment?'

He winced. He lowered his face, resting his forehead against hers. 'I don't know what this is.' Then he straightened, kissed her very gently on the lips before he pulled back. 'But right now I think I want to find out.'

His lips had been warm…seeking and offering. But his words stopped her.

They made Isabella lift her chin higher and move her head towards the door a little, increasing the gap between them.

She caught and held his gaze, her eyes narrowing. 'Are you sure about that Simon?'

There was challenge in her words…regret in her stomach. Because she knew how this would end. 'Because "I think I want to find out" isn't good enough.'

She scooted under his arm and put some distance between them before she did something that she, and apparently he, would regret.

'Nowhere near good enough. You should get some sleep. Goodnight.'

# CHAPTER TWENTY-EIGHT

SIMON FELT THE absence of Isabella as she moved out of his reach like a gap in the universe. How had it come to this so quickly? So quickly that his head spun?

While his sense of loss urged him to answer her question the way she wanted, he knew that wouldn't be fair. Because it was true. He was still thinking about this. And he was a fool for pushing it.

'Thank you for being the sensible one,' he said.

He moved his hands from the door where she'd been. Returned them to his sides.

'Good call, Isabella. I need to sleep.'

He reached forward, opened the door, and let himself out before he could promise something he still wasn't convinced was true.

All the way back to his apartment he remembered her face, and the narrowing of her beautiful eyes as she demanded an honest answer.

She was amazing. Incredible. A way more put-together person than he was. Hell, he probably didn't deserve her anyway.

His father had said he wouldn't amount to much. And that parting sneer had driven Simon out of the only home he'd known to push himself at his studies until he could prove the man wrong.

The old martinet had died before Simon had been admitted to med school, which had left Simon a little skewed about his self-worth. But he'd hung out with the other misfit in college—Malachi Madden—and together they'd been a force to be reckoned with. The bond that had grown between them had turned out to be rock-solid, and Malachi—the brother he'd never had—always had his back.

Was his lack of self-worth stopping him? Was that why he was holding back from Isabella? He didn't know. Maybe he'd ask his pseudo-brother tomorrow. Because Malachi had been worse at relationships than he was—until Lisandra had taken control.

Simon woke at dawn. For once, his phone hadn't gone off overnight. He jerked on his board shorts and grabbed his board. If he hadn't had two metres of fibreglass under his arm he would have jogged down the fire escape, to get a bit more exercise. But surfboards and narrow stairwells didn't go well together.

As he stepped out into the dim, cool morning, he breathed in the fresh salt air and decided to stop beating himself up about his vacillations over Isabella.

It would take as long as it took for him to get over his bereavement...be normal again.

In fact, he had come a long way towards 'normal' since Isabella Hargraves had first smashed through his barriers nearly five weeks ago.

Had it even been five weeks?

She'd been like a steamroller through the barriers that he'd thought impervious. She'd pushed through his defences as if they were putty.

And that had been just her looks.

Her brilliant brain blew him away, too.

He thought about the way they were so synchronised in their thought processes when discussing sick babies and possible prognoses. That was hot too.

Then he'd seen the big family-centred heart of her and he'd been a goner.

A goner? *Was* he a goner?

He thought about the way she caught his eye every time she moved. He thought about the softness of her skin against his. Glorious. And she knew karate. His mouth kinked up. He wanted to explore that!

But questions and commitments and answers were all in play, and he couldn't go through another heartbreak. His father was right. He couldn't even keep the people he cared about safe. And Isabella didn't deserve the kind of person he was.

Simon walked into Malachi's office at eight-thirty, with his hair still wet from his post-surf shower.

There'd used to be days when Malachi was there at seven a.m., but family life had trained him out of that. Now the man even left before five in the evening some nights. Simon wasn't quite sure how Lisandra had achieved that, but there was no doubt that Dr Madden had more balance in his life now than Simon had.

Malachi looked up to see him at the door and raised his brows. 'What are you doing here?'

'Lovely greeting for your best friend.'

'*Only* friend apart from my darling wife.'

That was probably true. 'I've come for advice.'

The twinkle that materialised more and more often in his friend's eyes made Simon feel as if his ears were burning.

'You've fallen for Isabella!' Malachi appeared disgustingly delighted.

It wasn't a question. He hadn't even had to explain. Which was a relief of sorts.

'Not like you to be so observant, Malachi.

He shrugged. 'Lisandra told me.' It was a statement of fact.

Simon sighed. Of course she had.

'Thing is, I don't know if I want to do that whole *I would lose my world if anything happened to her* scenario.'

'You're scared.'

Malachi was known for his straight shooting. And for his ability to miss the concept of tactful advice. That was why he'd come here, wasn't it? Maybe...

Malachi sat down at his desk and leaned back in his chair. 'How long have you known her?'

'Less than five weeks.'

'Plenty,' said his now superior friend. 'Even I, stunted relationship guru that I was, only took a week to realise that Lisandra was the one I didn't want to get away.'

'You're saying take the risk? Put myself out on a limb?'

Malachi arched a brow. 'You won't be out on the limb by yourself. Isabella will be there. But you're the only one who knows whether you're ready, Simon. Lisandra says you've taken too long as it is.'

His friend tilted his head at him and shooed him out of his office.

'Get a move on.'

# CHAPTER TWENTY-NINE

AFTER ANOTHER BUSY SHIFT, with two new prem babies admitted to the NICU and Kate improving, Isabella finished work and stepped out into the night with a smile. She wasn't surprised to see Simon under the streetlight outside.

'We really have to stop meeting like this,' she quipped.

It was funny, considering they'd spent about four hours together on and off throughout her shift.

'Was there something you couldn't tell me in the middle of the NICU?'

He didn't answer her facetious question. Instead, he said, 'I've started to really like this time of night.'

'Really? Angling for another invite? Well, I'm on the morning shift tomorrow. No midnight snacks for you.'

He smiled easily. Which meant he hadn't been expecting that scenario but had decided to come and meet her anyway. Curiouser and curiouser...

He glanced up at the moon overhead. 'That's okay. I just thought I'd walk you home.'

'Thank you. I may be your *friend*...' she emphasised the word '...but I don't need protecting. You know that, right?'

He looked struck for a moment, and she wasn't sure why. But then he went off on another tangent. 'I see Malachi is transferring Nadia back to the ward again tomorrow.'

She thought about her sister's excellent progress and it sat well. Such relief.

'Yes. He's pretty sure she'll be fine this time. She's still on heavy-duty antihypertensives, but at least the blood pressure is staying down now.'

'And I assume you'll be happy that Kate's back on oral feeds tomorrow?'

'I am.'

She wasn't making it easy for him, which wasn't like her, but Isabella was still a wee bit irritated about last night. Her mind had circled around Simon's intentions. What were they if he didn't feel that there was a relationship in the future for them? Just sex?

Today, when they worked together, they'd both remained very professional. Even Carla hadn't made any cheeky comments. So why was he here? Apart from his notion that near-midnight rambling was a pleasant idea.

'I didn't get a chance to ask—how's Catherine? Has there been more progress??'

Her crossness evaporated. She loved the way he called her grandmother by her name. Highlighting that he saw her as a person, not just as a patient recovering from a head injury or, as in her father's case, a hopeless invalid. She appreciated that sub-text of support more than he probably knew.

Relief and pleasure rolled over her as she thought about Gran. 'She was sitting up today. In the chair. Not for long, but they've stopped the parenteral nutrition and she's drinking and eat-ing soft foods.'

'That's amazing.' His delight seemed genuine, and she hugged that to herself.

'That's what the doctors are saying. They can't believe how fast she's recovering. Even Dad's gob-smacked. He's flying up at the weekend to see her.'

'I really am thrilled.'

And his smile, which was pleased for her as well as Gran, warmed her more.

'Nadia might even be discharged by then,' he added.

'I know. My world is changing. Things are fi-nally going right.'

She should not have said that.

They were almost at the apartments, and up ahead she could see a man sitting on the low wall at the front of the block. She was glad that Simon was beside her.

Simon saw the figure as well, and stiffened. He stepped closer, until his shoulder touched hers.

As they neared, the man stood up. She recog-nised him. Though he seemed smaller. Slighter. Compared to Simon. Her light-heartedness disappeared. So much for everything going right for a change.

'Conlon. Hello. What are you doing here?'

She felt Simon's stillness. Did he remember her mentioning him?

Her ex glanced at Simon, and then back at her. His brow furrowed. 'I flew into Brisbane. You didn't answer my texts.' It sounded like a complaint not a statement.

She felt Simon relax slightly beside her.

Conlon was whining on. 'Your father said you were finishing at eleven and gave me your address.'

Still whining. Had he always whined?

Isabella closed her eyes for a moment. *Thanks, Dad.* She could feel Simon looming beside her, radiating distrust and other emotions. She wondered what he saw when he looked at Conlon. Judging by the expression on his face, not something he liked.

'Simon, this is Dr Conlon Brazier. We were working on a scientific paper together in Hanoi. Conlon, this is Dr Simon Purdy. Simon is walking me home in the dark.'

Conlon put his hand out. 'Great idea. Thanks for that.'

Simon jammed his hands in his pockets. The action quite forcible, as if had he not performed it, he might do something he regretted. 'Didn't do it for you, mate.'

Isabella suppressed a smile. 'No, you did it for me.' She looked up at him and smiled. 'Thank you, Simon. But I'll be fine now.'

She thought for a moment that Simon wasn't going to leave, but he nodded, stalked into the porch to unlock the door, and disappeared. The door didn't click shut behind him, staying open a crack. She suspected Simon was making sure Conlon wasn't going to annoy her.

She hid her smile. Her over-protective friend. That said more about Simon than he probably realised.

Had Simon been jealous? She'd think about that later.

First, she had to shake off her ex. Permanently.

'I'm on a morning shift tomorrow, Conlon. There's no need for us to talk. Anything between us is well and truly over.'

Conlon came closer. Into her space. *Idiot.*

'We had something, Isabella. We were good together in Vietnam.'

She stared into his arrogant, handsome face with a coolness she wouldn't have believed possible a month ago.

'Maybe. Briefly. But…' She shook her head as if msystified. 'It's gone now.'

She shrugged and saw him flinch. She wanted no misunderstandings. No comebacks. She doubted it had ever been more than superficial, now that she knew what real, world-shaking attraction, lust and magnetic draw was. Like she had for Simon.

She resisted a glance towards the door he'd disappeared through.

Conlon eased closer. 'I should have been more supportive. I'll try to do better. I flew all this way to see you.'

*Yep. Whining.*

'Conlon. Not happening. You let me down when I needed you. There's no going back.'

Isabella stepped past him—though really she wanted to push him onto his backside. Instead, she huffed out a small puff of amusement. He'd just think she accidentally shoved him. The guy was oblivious.

She said, with finality, 'It's been a big week for me, and I desperately need sleep. You can go now.'

His horrified eyes widened. 'You're just going to leave me out in the cold?'

She almost laughed. Except none of this was funny. 'It's the Gold Coast, Conlon. Twenty degrees Celsius.'

He huffed in disgust. 'I hoped you'd at least put me up.'

She teetered for a moment. Maybe she should take him in? They had been more than friends. But then common sense flooded back, and a wave of tiredness over the top of the shock of seeing him. Unannounced. Unwanted. Unsupportive Conlon.

*No.*

'You're a big boy. The airport hotel has twenty-four-hour check-in. That's where Dad stays when he's up here. I'm surprised he didn't tell you that.'

Conlon had the grace to look slightly embarrassed. 'He did.'

'I *would* drive you, but I'm done. Call a taxi—they respond fast here. Do you want me to wait here with you?'

'Not if you're too tired to talk to me.'

Sarcastic and definitely with the assumption that she would stay, and he'd keep trying, Isabella decided.

He'd be fine. 'Excellent. Goodnight.'

How had she ever thought she had a future with this petulant man?

She turned and left him, relief expanding inside her as she walked away. Simon wasn't behind the door inside, but the lift was still going up. He had just been there. She smiled.

Riding up in the elevator herself, Isabella felt briefly tempted to keep going all the way to the top and tell Simon that she and Conlon had no future. Ever. But Simon... Well, Simon was still *thinking* he wanted to find out what could grow between them.

Let him think about Conlon. She really was tired.

At last Isabella allowed herself to acknowledge the strain of the last weeks.

Tonight, seeing Conlon, she'd remembered the first moment her father had called her in Hanoi to tell her of Gran's accident.

She hadn't had any support as she'd rushed to Gran's side. And she'd had to be the strong one and drag Nadia to the emergency department when she'd suspected pre-eclampsia.

It was her belligerence that had requested Simon's consultancy when Kate was born.

She'd even refused to believe her father's dire prognosis, and stayed with the faith Gran would wake.

Now that Gran was improving, Isabella wanted to stand down. Stop being the rock, always on her own against the odds.

But maybe she wasn't truly on her own anymore.

Simon had stepped up.

He'd taken over with Kate, ensuring her excellent care.

He'd been her sounding board when her father had let her down, as usual.

He'd been there when Nadia had been readmitted to the ICU and Isabella had been so scared.

Most of all she remembered him driving fast to the hospital, when Gran had opened her eyes and Isabella had melted down against his shirt.

The elevator doors opened.

There, beside her front door, stood Simon.

Despite the fact that she'd just decided he could stew in his own juices, it was good to see him. Wonderful.

She couldn't help the crooked smile she gave him. 'Fancy meeting you here,' she said, echoing the earlier greeting. She crossed the hallway to him.

'I'm sorry,' he said. 'I was a jealous idiot downstairs and I behaved badly. And I eavesdropped.'

She looked at him. Blond. Strong and beautiful. Hopefully hers.

She touched his cheek. 'Don't bother worrying. He won't be coming back.'

'Why is that?' Simon asked, but she saw that he knew.

'You were listening?'

'In case you needed me.'

'I didn't.'

'I heard that.'

The relief in his eyes shone plainly. Along with a furnace of heat.

'Because he let me down.' This was important. It had to be said. 'That's the one thing I won't have from the man in my life. Never again.'

Simon stepped closer. 'And if I promise not to let you down?'

'There's no "if", Simon. *Do* you promise that?'

His chin went high. He lifted his hand to his heart to rest on his chest. 'Yes.'

His voice was firm. His eyes held hers. There was no doubting the sincerity. The inherent promise.

'If you'll let me into your life?'

'I know—I don't *think*,' she said, using words ironically, because he'd used them last night, 'that you're already in my life, Simon. You're the one who needs to remember that I'm in yours.'

She passed him and put her key in the lock and slipped away.

The door closed behind her.

# CHAPTER THIRTY

SIMON STOOD OUTSIDE Isabella's door and thought about knocking. Asking her what she meant.

He imagined kissing her.

Then he thought about the tiredness in her eyes and in the droop of her shoulders.

Shook his head. No. Not tonight.

He played back what she'd said about Conlon—that he would never come back after today. He'd heard that dismissal. *Ouch.* Okay, then. He acknowledged the fact that she was willing to trust that he would never let her down if she let him in. That she'd said he was a part of her life.

She'd also said he needed to realise she was a part of his.

Suddenly it wasn't hard to be certain that he wanted Isabella Hargraves in his life—for now and for always.

The other thing he'd come to realise—painful, but true, and just a bit enlightening—was that Isabella didn't need his protection. She would protect herself. In fact, he thought with a smile, she could probably protect *him*.

She didn't want protection. She wanted a partnership. With him. She wanted support as an individual. But with him.

His darling Louise had always been soft. Gentle. In need of protection. Thus, when she'd died, his soul had whispered that he was the one at fault for not protecting her.

That whisper had coiled around him, merged with the guilt his father had left him with, and stolen his smile. His faith in himself. He'd built up his walls so that he could never fail to protect anyone ever again. Those conjoined whispers had kept him from trusting his heart to find someone he wouldn't let down.

Isabella had restored his faith. Isabella didn't want protection. She wanted a man at her back as well as by her side. Through thick and thin. She wanted him, and he had no idea how he could have been so lucky.

He could do what she needed. Because it was what he needed too. He wanted to be there always for the woman he loved.

He loved her. She'd been a wrecking ball he hadn't expected—stealing his breath and his heart.

He'd been finding his self-esteem in protecting his patients. Being there for them twenty-four-seven at work had given his life meaning. What Isabella offered was so much more than that…so much more sustainable.

Maybe now he could understand his friend's soul-deep happiness. And his advice to get a move on.

It was time to start wooing his love. Building

trust. To ensure that his Isabella knew he would always be there for her. Proud to be by her side.

The next afternoon, late in the day, as he walked back into the unit, Simon acknowledged that it had been a good day. He and Isabella had a professional working relationship that ran smoothly, and he was planning to court her with his charms when work was behind them. He even had a plan.

Nadia had moved back to the ward and was looking well. Simon felt pleased for her, and Kate, but also for Isabella, who had been so worried about her sister.

Malachi had assured him that Nadia would continue to improve now, as all her blood results had settled down—Simon had checked with him so he could reassure Isabella if she needed more.

Kate was back on tube feeds, and had had her first skin-to-skin kangaroo care with her mother, tucked under her mum's shirt against her bare skin.

He'd gone down to the unit for the event, and had smiled with everyone else when Kate was settled, with her head poking out of her mother's shirt. He'd been watching Isabella the most, and the joy he'd seen on her face had warmed his heart and filled him somewhere he hadn't realised he'd been empty.

There'd been three babies discharged from the unit as well, going home happy and healthy.

With those babies gone suddenly there was time to breathe—until the next rush of patients arrived. These moments gave the dedicated staff time to be satisfied with the job they were doing, caring for their tiny charges.

He'd timed his return to the unit now for just before Isabella walked out through the door. He caught her as she was saying goodbye to her niece and she didn't see him coming.

He touched her shoulder. 'I know you don't have to see Big Boy Conlon when you finish here...'

She flashed a grin at him, remembering that she'd told Conlon he was a big boy and could find himself somewhere else to sleep. 'Funny man...'

He smiled. 'Well, I used to be a funny man. And I'm finding humour again. Because there's this woman I fancy so much that I'm willing to change. And Carla tells me the sadness I've been wallowing in has grown really old.'

She smiled at that too. Watching his face with that careful attention she gave to anyone she spoke to.

'But that's not why I'm here,' he said.

'Goodness,' she said—a little facetiously, he thought. 'Why *are* you here?'

'Anyway,' he continued quietly, 'when you leave here, are you going to visit Catherine?'

'Yes.' Those lovely brows arched. 'Why?'

'Would you mind if I came? You could text me and I could meet you there.'

He wasn't sure what he would do if she said no.

She tilted her head at him. 'Sure. I can leave at five.'

'Great. I'll be on time.'

She looked startled and pleased. Good. He'd ticked one box on his mental list.

'And afterwards...' He tried a winning smile and her lips twitched. 'I'd like to take you on a dinner date.'

'A date?' she said. 'Haven't we moved past that?'

'Not officially.'

She cocked her head. 'We've had breakfast together... I've met your friends...we've had dinner...' She waggled her brows. 'And more!'

'Yes, but this is me asking you to dress up and come out to a flash meal with me for the purpose of getting to know each other better. With nobody else present.'

'Simon Purdy—' she started, but Carla had crossed the room to them with a small piece of paper for Simon and she stopped.

'Yes, I know,' he said. 'We'll talk about it tonight.'

He saluted her and turned to Carla.

And that was how he ended up at the hospital just after five.

Now that he really observed Catherine Hargraves, he decided she looked like he imagined Isabella would look in fifty years. Snow-white hair had been brushed back off her face in soft waves. She had a long neck, like her granddaughter, and the same angled cheekbones and the same large green eyes, though faded.

But mostly it was the bright mind lurking at the back of those eyes that made him think of Isabella.

He picked up the wrinkled hand, stroked his thumb over the soft skin and bowed over it.

'Mrs Hargraves… You're obviously made of stern stuff,' he said. 'It's wonderful to see you looking so alert.'

'As opposed to comatose?' she said, a quirk of amusement tilting her mouth.

'Isabella never gave up on you,' he said.

'No. She didn't.'

He watched Catherine Hargraves glance at her granddaughter.

'She's a strong woman. She's had to be.'

There it was. That mutual appreciation between Isabella and her grandmother. A precious thing that he envied.

'I know,' he said softly.

He squeezed her hand gently, rested it back on the covers and stepped back.

Isabella had been talking to the doctor at the door, discussing discharge dates and reminding the doctor that she lived with her grandmother and would be able to help with the heavier tasks that might be difficult for her at the moment.

When she returned to the bedside her smile was reflected in her eyes. 'Possibly Monday. How do you feel about that, Gran?'

'Sounds fine.'

'Great! I'm off Tuesday and Wednesday. I could pick you up after work Monday afternoon. Then we'd have two full days together.'

Her grandmother pretended to slump in exhaustion against the pillows. Or most of it was pretend. 'Not full days, child. Your energy would drive me batty.'

'I'll take her off your hands when she's too much, Catherine. Just let me know.'

Simon watched Isabella's face as he said it, and saw how she tucked in her chin and looked at him from under her brows.

'Will you, now?' she asked.

'Surf, sand and avocado on rye as necessary,' he agreed. 'But now I think I've stayed long enough. I'll wait for you at your car. No hurry.'

He watched Isabella shoot a quick glance at her grandmother. 'No. I'll come too. We've both stayed long enough.'

Which was what he'd hoped she'd say. Because he knew that even in Isabella's excitement she would not have missed the droop of exhaustion in the older woman's shoulders. But he didn't think she'd mind him creating the opportunity to leave.

As they walked out onto the street, he said, 'So...? Dinner? Do you like Greek?'

'I love Greek food.'

'Is seven p.m. enough time for you?'

He couldn't wait.

'Sure.'

'I'll pick you up at six forty-five. We'll take my car.'

She laughed, and her face filled his vision. She leaned in and kissed him. She tasted of sunshine and mint. 'You haven't got over that yet. Have you?'

Her mouth against his made him melt. But this wasn't the place. Or the time.

Instead he said, 'Smart Alec.' She filled him with joy.

'I'm willing to be persuaded to take your vehicle occasionally, but you'll need a good argument,' she told him.

He wondered if even Hanoi traffic had fazed Isabella.

She patted his arm. 'You can be the driver tonight.'

# CHAPTER THIRTY-ONE

SIMON BROUGHT FLOWERS. Wildflowers. Her favourite kind. A huge bunch of beautiful proteas, flannel flowers, waratahs and everlasting daisies.

The armful lay against his white shirt like a frame for his smile until he handed it over. The bouquet almost sang with exuberance—glorious and perfectly set off by native leaves and grasses.

'So beautiful... And they will still look gorgeous when Gran comes home.'

'I thought about that,' he said, smiling around his pleasure at her obvious approval.

'That's thoughtful.' He *was* thoughtful.

'Thank you.'

He had no idea how much she appreciated his kindness.

'I love them.'

And she knew, now that she'd allowed her dreams to surface, how much she loved *him*.

His expression—the tilt of his stubborn chin and the beautiful smile on his face—said how pleased he felt as he watched her reaction.

He slid a small blue paper packet out of his pocket. 'I also brought chocolates.'

This was a real date, then. The whole hog.

She widened her eyes at him. 'Thank you. I

love chocolates. As long as you help me eat them later.'

His eyes said he could do more than that.

*Oh, my.*

His lips formed the words. 'I can do that.'

She nodded for him to put them on the table while she took the flowers into the kitchen and hugged them to herself. She breathed them in to steady the excitement that had ramped up since he arrived. Her date really was pulling out all the stops. She wondered if she should thank Conlon for Simon's over-eagerness to pursue her and suppressed a grin.

She pulled the largest vase from under the sink and filled it with water. 'I'll pop the whole lot in here until later, and sort them out when we come home.'

She heard the echo of those words…*when we come home.* Presumptuous—maybe ambitious— but her belly kicked in anticipation.

Simon must have caught on to the concept, too, because his eyes darkened. 'We should go now…'

His voice had dropped to that deeper, hungry, gravelly tone she was coming to recognise.

'Or we'll be late.'

She glanced up at him. Saw the craving, heard the unspoken *really late*, and smiled as she grabbed her small clutch with her keys inside.

She said a little breathlessly, 'Coming.'

They didn't speak on the way to the restaurant, but the car simmered like a pot on the stove with the unspoken heat between them. His shoulder and hers were close, and buzzing even without touching.

The restaurant had dressed itself in blue and white, which was funny because Simon was wearing a white shirt and she was wearing an Aegean-blue trouser suit in silk.

'You look beautiful,' he murmured. 'Did you get that in Vietnam?'

'Thank you. And, yes, I did. My friend is a tailor there, and she kept pushing them on me after I nursed her son. We're very colour co-ordinated in here.'

He lifted his glass to her.

They'd ordered two flutes of sparkling Greek rosé and they clinked crystal in a toast.

'To the future,' he said.

'The future…' she murmured.

That was…unexpected. And bold. She met his eyes and sipped. She tasted the explosion of fruit in the underlying rose petals and set the glass down.

'Lovely wine.'

'Malachi tells me it's Lisandra's favourite. I thought you might like it.'

'I do.'

So he'd discussed this dinner with his friend. Interesting... Very interesting.

'What else did you discuss with Malachi Madden?'

'Apparently, Lisandra told him I was taking too long to make a move on you.'

Isabella spluttered, glad her wine was on the table. 'Did she, now? I'll tease her about that when I see her next.'

His hand reached across the table and captured her fingers in his. 'I was a fool the other night. I don't want to be a fool again. I'm moving now. Forward, I hope. Not letting go.'

The dinner passed in a blur of heated glances, brushing fingers and hot knees touching beneath the table.

Isabella didn't remember much about the food. She remembered the wine, because the cool touch of the glass against her lips put out some of the heat from Simon's gaze. His hot, hungry gaze that rested so often on her mouth...

When she opened the door to her grandmother's apartment, he backed her into the room and pulled the door handle from her fingers gently. He didn't turn on the light, letting the glow from the moon be the only illumination in the room.

She'd left the curtains open and moonglow spilled across his face. It turned him into a silver god, and her into a woman so very willing to surrender.

His hand captured the back of her neck, warm and possessive. The other cupped her cheek as he leaned her against the wall.

'Do you have any idea how much I want you?'

His words caressed her skin, murmured against her throat, heating her nerves from throat to toes. His dark, dark eyes drilled into hers with such awe and possessive need. She hadn't dreamt that so much wanton, fiery desire would ever be directed at her.

She waved her hand in front of her face. 'There's a lot of heat coming from you,' she whispered. 'Perhaps we'll both burst into flames.'

The idea had merit.

Simon growled, 'I'd like to find out. You know I'll want you for ever? You up for that?'

'I was hoping...'

And that was the last almost full sentence she managed to utter for a very long time.

# CHAPTER THIRTY-TWO

*Three months later*

ON THE MORNING of Simon and Isabella's wedding, Isabella watched the last of the wedding preparations from her bedroom in Gran's apartment. The temporary lights set up on the beach allowed the wedding planners to scoot around and set up before sunrise.

The path to the beach held an avenue of tall white wedding flags with silver hearts dangling from their ends. Isabella would walk through them and the newlyweds would return that way.

The sand hadn't found its sunlit gold yet, and the still, indigo ocean lay flat, a lazy mini swell all that hinted at the possibilities Lady Ocean could offer. Later she would glitter and spin with the sunlight under the gentle breeze.

Down at the water's edge and to one side, a huge white circular umbrella gently flapped, tipped with the same silver hearts dangling from each flag. The umbrella was planted above a white table covered in the same material, flanked by potted palm trees. Two pristine deck-chairs waited for after the ceremony, when Simon and Isabella would sit and sign the marriage certificate.

Five rows of white chairs, four each side of the aisle, waited for the guests. More palm trees in pots graced each row on the outside edge.

The whole thing was like a tiny chapel at the edge of the sea.

Isabella blinked back unexpected prickles in her eyes. *Stop it. No time to redo mascara.* But the setting below had sprung up even more beautifully than she'd imagined, and would look wonderful when the sun rose.

'Isabella? Darling, nearly time to go.'

Her grandmother stood at the door in a pale turquoise sheath. Her eyes were clear and bright. She had recovered most of her vigour and all of her sharp wit.

'You look beautiful, Gran,' Isabella said as her grandmother came into the room.

Gran's make-up lay perfectly, and her white hair, professionally styled, was soft about her face.

Isabella knew that Lisandra had been the instigator of quite an organisational campaign in the early hours, from five a.m., when a team of stylists and make-up artists had arrived to prepare the wedding party.

Catherine murmured, 'You look beautiful in white, darling. You should wear it more often.'

Isabella glanced down at the floor-length sheath, studded at neck and hemline with the luminous pearls that her seamstress friend from Hanoi had wanted to sew on as a gift.

'Thank you.'

The long slit that ran to Isabella's tanned thigh would make her walk up the sandy aisle easy. Her feet were encased in tiny silver slip-ons which she would leave at the edge of the sand and go bare-foot—she and Simon wanted to be the only ones who would go unshod.

'I never imagined myself in a white wedding dress, Gran…'

'And why not? Today is the start of your beau-tiful life with Simon. Mutual love such as yours should be celebrated with distinction.'

Distinction? Yes. Her gorgeous, generous Simon deserved distinction. Their joy in each other had grown and spread like foam on the ocean, diffusing through their world and reach-ing out to bubble into everything. And everyone. Even her father looked happier sometimes.

She loved Simon so much…admired him, de-lighted in his brilliant brain, and in his quirky sense of humour that still caught her at unex-pected intervals and seemed to grow each day. She loved him so much she couldn't imagine not having him by her side. At her back. In her bed. For ever.

Two more figures crowded at the door. Nadia in cornflower-blue and Lisandra in lapis lazuli.

Her three matrons of honour matched the shifting blues of the ocean. Each carried a small spray of multi-shaded blue flowers, with baby's breath backed by blue-green gum leaves, and wore silver slip-on sandals like Isabella's.

She'd wanted to be there before dawn, when the beach colours were the most ethereal, but they'd compromised for the non-morning people and had gone for sunrise instead.

It had taken three months for Catherine Hargraves to re-establish her strength well enough to be able to enjoy a wedding as a principal player, and Isabella and Simon had waited patiently for her grandmother to be one of the bridal party.

Now it was time.

Professor Piers Hargraves appeared at the door, with a serious face that said he couldn't see any good coming out of this match. The women in the room glanced at each other and pressed their painted lips together.

'For goodness' sake, Piers! It's a wedding, not a funeral. Smile!' his mother ordered.

Isabella had to stifle a laugh. The more time she spent with Simon, the less her father's dourness affected her. Simon had helped her realise that her dad's emotional distance was his default. And not her fault. It didn't matter. She still loved him, despite all his doom and gloom. But that didn't stop her winking at her grandmother.

* * *

Simon stood barefoot at the edge of the water, watching the path through the flags for the woman he loved.

'She'd better hurry or we're here early for nothing and we'll miss the sunrise,' Malachi murmured sagely. He had shoes on.

Simon shook his head. 'She won't be late.'

Just then the music began—gentle flutes playing the 'Bridal March' in the morning air, the notes soaring and sweeping like the gulls above.

The first of the bride's attendants swayed into view and he heard Malachi suck in a breath. When he glanced at his best man, he saw Malachi's attention was focussed fully on his wife. Lisandra swayed onwards, in a dress coloured with the shifting, vibrant blue of a lapis stone.

'So beautiful…' his friend sighed.

There was an amused huff from Simon. 'You're supposed to be supporting me.'

Malachi flicked him a glance, and then his gaze ricocheted unerringly back to his wife. 'Don't need to. I'm surplus. You've got this.'

Nadia sashayed into view. Isabella's sister looked so good in a dress the paler blue of a cloudless afternoon sky.

Then came Catherine, slow and gracious, in her dress which was the turquoise of ocean shallows in the sunshine.

Isabella had told him she'd chosen the colours because those were what she saw when they were out on their boards. So fitting. So beautiful. So deep and thoughtful, his Isabella...

Catherine looked well, and the rosy bloom of her now healthy skin colour made him think briefly of the unexpected delight of his being treated by her like a favourite grandchild.

But the sky was getting lighter.

Sunrise was approaching.

And finally he saw a figure in white. His Isabella. His future. The woman who held his heart in her sure hands and promised him a partnership he'd never even dreamed was possible.

His chest tightened as his vibrant, joyful bride—so vital, like the first day he saw her, his Isabella—came closer. She slipped off her sandals and stepped on to the sand.

She'd said having bare feet together meant the beginning of a promise...casting off the world to come together bare of protection, open to the sand below their feet. Connected to each other and only each other, with their bare feet joined in the golden grains that had been there for millennia.

He loved her so much.

Emotion swelled. His eyes prickled and he blinked away the sting of tears at the memory of her serious, heartfelt explanation.

Their gazes met and she smiled just for him,

her face lighting with love and excitement and the *joie de vivre* that was so much a part of the woman he'd fallen in love with that first day.

He reached out his hand and finally her precious fingers slid into his palm as they entwined their fingers and their lives for ever.

\* \* \* \* \*

# Resisting the Off-Limits
# Paediatrician
## Kate MacGuire

# MILLS & BOON

**Kate MacGuire** has loved writing since forever, which led to a career in journalism and public relations. Her short fiction won the Swarthout Award and placed third in the 2020 Women's National Book Association writing contest. Medical romance has always been her guilty pleasure, so she is thrilled to publish her first novel with Harlequin's Medical Romance line. When she's not pounding away on the keyboard, Kate coruns Camp Runamuk with her husband, keeping its two unruly campers in line in the beautiful woodlands of North Carolina. Visit katemacguire.com for updates and stories.

*Resisting the Off-Limits Pediatrician*

is Kate MacGuire's debut title for Harlequin.

Visit the Author Profile page
at millsandboon.com.au.

Dear Reader,

Greetings! I'm thrilled to share my debut novel for the Harlequin Medical Romance line!

John and Charlotte's story was inspired by the real-life doctors and nurses who care for homeless teens. Whether they work in a strip mall clinic, mobile medical unit, or by strapping on a backpack and working on foot, I knew these doctors deserved their own love story!

Welcome to the Sunshine Clinic, where John heals the homeless teens of Seattle. Gaining guardianship of his spirited niece has forced John to hire Charlotte, a beautiful locum tenens pediatrician, until his life settles down.

Charlotte is equally resentful at being stuck in Seattle to settle her absentee father's estate. Life has taught her to trust adventure over love, so she's fighting her attraction to the brooding, sexy doc with everything she's got.

They're both deeply committed to living life on their terms. If it weren't for an accident that forces Charlotte to share her home with John and his niece, maybe they would have escaped love's healing touch.

Then again, when two people are meant to be together, love always finds a way.

I hope you enjoy John and Charlotte's journey to happily-ever-after!

Love,

*Kate*

# DEDICATION

This book (and my heart) is dedicated to Patrick.
Thank you for believing in me. Love you…Always.

# CHAPTER ONE

SANDY WHITE BEACHES as far as the eye could see... Early-morning sea-kayaking adventures... An elegant evening at the world-class opera house.

Charlotte thumbed through the images on her social media feed. She knew her friends meant well, but every photo of their amazing vacation in Sydney, Australia, was like an icepick to her heart.

Thunder cracked overhead as she waited in line for her rental car. No sandy white beaches here, thank you very much. Instead, she was stuck in her former hometown of Seattle, Washington, right in the middle of one of its legendary rainstorms. She took one last longing glance at her missed vacation before closing her social media feed. That was enough torture for one day.

Every few years she and her friends—all traveling doctors like her—planned an amazing trip to take a break from their locum tenens medical assignments. For their first trip they'd gone to Bora Bora. Then came Madrid, Rome, and

Singapore. These trips, along with her doctor assignments, were captured in her travel blog, *GypsyMD*. She had a small but loyal group of followers who loved her work-hard-play-hard lifestyle as a locum tenens physician.

But the Sydney trip had been the hardest to plan. More of her friends were finding partners, getting married, and settling down with full-time permanent jobs. None of which interested Charlotte, but it sure did make it harder to get enough people interested to justify the expense of the Sydney trip.

Just when she'd solved that problem, her life had taken an unwelcome detour. From out of the blue, a man claiming to be her father's estate attorney had called her.

*"It's important that you come to Seattle,"* he'd said. *"There are some matters related to your father's estate that must be settled."*

*Your father.*

Two words that sounded so foreign to a girl who'd grown up without one. Once upon a time, when she was much younger, she had daydreamed about her missing father. Was he a rock star who spent every night in a different city? Or maybe a navy captain, steadfastly determined to protect her country's borders? Or a reclusive mountaineer who climbed the world's most treacherous peaks and slept in a yurt?

But in her favorite little-girl dream he was a powerful but despondent king, who used every resource at his disposal to find her. No one would rest, he'd bellow, until his precious, long-lost daughter was returned to her family, safe and sound.

Eventually she'd outgrown those silly day-dreams and accepted her fate. Her father had no idea she existed. So when her mother was killed in a terrible car accident, Charlotte had found herself orphaned at thirteen, with no one to claim her and nowhere to go.

"Ma'am?"

A voice behind her shook Charlotte from her reverie. She mumbled an apology and moved forward with the line. Another crack of thunder overhead released a torrent of rain that fell in sheets against the windows of the airport rental car office. This unexpected trip home was getting better by the minute.

An hour later, Charlotte had finished an over-sized coffee and made her way to the address the estate attorney had texted her. The rain had let up a bit, and she paused to gather her thoughts before meeting him. Her view of the house was partially obscured by the steep sloped front yard and its landscaped features of rocks and vegetation, all there to protect against the soil erosion and landslides that came with living in one of

Seattle's hilly neighborhoods. The house appeared to be a two-story split-level, with a large fir tree dominating the front yard.

Someone rapped hard on the passenger window, startling her. A small man with a hooked nose and small, beady eyes peered through the window. "Charlotte? Dr. Charlotte Owens?"

She nodded.

"I'm Jeffrey Bain, your father's attorney."

She nodded, still taking in the home and its upscale neighborhood. She remembered this neighborhood from her childhood. Located northwest of downtown Seattle, the Queen Anne neighborhood was built on a hill with amazing views of the Puget Sound, an inlet of the Pacific Ocean. It was an enclave for Seattle residents who were far more affluent than she and her single mother had been. Once, on a dare, she and a few other teens in her foster care group home had tried trick-or-treating here, to see if they really gave out full-sized chocolate bars, as was rumored. Only one house had.

"Shall we?"

The attorney indicated the house with a short wave of his hand. He seemed to be in just as much of a hurry to get these estate matters settled as she was.

She followed the attorney, navigating the stone steps that climbed the hilly front yard. "You have

a beautiful home," she said, noting the professionally designed garden beds and hand-painted ceramic pots along the walkway, though many of
the flowers and plants seemed to be languishing.

The attorney gave her a strange glance over
his shoulder. "No, ma'am," he said. "*You* have a
beautiful home."

Charlotte stopped in her tracks as her brain
scrambled to make sense of his words. She had
assumed this was the attorney's home, because
it didn't make any sense that her father would
live here.

*"He was just a silly summer fling,"* her mother
had said, when she could be enticed to say anything at all about Charlotte's father. *"He was
never going to amount to much."*

All the questions she'd had as a child about her
father were swirling in her mind like nosy summer gnats. The attorney unlocked the door and
beckoned her inside where the possibility of explanation waited.

She followed him for a breakneck tour of the
five-bedroom home. Architecturally speaking,
the house was perfect in form and function, design and style. But the wood floors were dull and
the windows were dirty. Dust lined the window-
sills and spider webs wafted in the corners when
she and the attorney passed. Despite touring both
floors, she found nothing that explained what her

father had become after his summer fling with her mother. There was no evidence of a family. No tick marks on the wall marking a child's growth, no holes in the wall where a teen would have hung posters. Instead, the air was stagnant and sour. Like no one had ever lived here other than ghosts and dust motes.

The tour ended in the kitchen, where the attorney hoisted his oversize briefcase onto the perfect marble countertop, displacing a small cloud of dust. He combed rifled through the files in his briefcase until he found a gray and white folder marked with the emblem of his law firm.

"This is your father's last will and testament, along with his living trust and other important legal documents for your records. Now, as you may be aware, your father lost a great deal of his wealth due to a series of business failures over the last decade of his life. I'm afraid this home is his only real asset, and he has specifically left it to you."

No, she was not aware of any of this. And how could he leave his home to her when he didn't know she existed?

She was about to ask that very question as she thumbed through the legal documents— there were so many! But one caught her attention: *Form JU 04.0100 Petition for Termination of Parent-Child Relationship.*

Charlotte's breath went shallow as she withdrew the document and read it slowly. She was a pediatrician, not a lawyer, but if she understood this right her father had signed an agreement with the state of Washington to forfeit his parental rights. Time slowed as she searched the document for his signature.

It was dated six months after her mother had died.

She continued staring at the document, but the words were blurred, and a horrible rushing sound filled her ears as if a massive runaway train was bearing down on her. Had he known about her all along? Or not until Child Welfare Services had contacted him, informing him that he had a daughter? Either way, he'd known she was orphaned when he'd signed his rights away.

She set the pages down and stepped away from the counter, her chest so tight it burned.

So, her daydreams hadn't been so far-fetched after all. She *was* the long-lost princess daughter of a quasi-king. But knights had never been dispatched to search for her because the King had never yearned for her return.

*Inconvenient. Unwanted. Go away.*

Anguish uncoiled from deep in her core, its tendrils finding every painful memory of her foster care years that she wanted to forget. How she'd grown up always feeling like an outsider, unwanted and unwelcome. The social workers who'd shown up without warning, giving her a donated suitcase and ten minutes to pack for her next placement. Knowing she would never, ever, find a home of her own. Because everyone knew that families wanted babies, not teenagers.

She squeezed her eyes shut and wished it was ten minutes ago, when she'd thought her painful past was a casualty of fate.

But the petition said otherwise. It said that her father had signed away his rights knowing full well that she would slip into foster care. Shock and hurt quickly gave way to anger. A deep, red-hot rage that demanded to know one thing.

*Who does this to a child?*

Especially when he'd clearly had the means to care for her.

As if on cue, Charlotte heard the hiss of air brakes. Through the large picture window in the living room that looked out to the street and the Puget Sound beyond, she could see a bright yellow school bus stop in front of the house. Its doors whooshed open and a half dozen kids spilled out, wearing raincoats and rubber boots, whooping with joy as their backpacks bounced with every step that took them back to waiting parents and warm, dry homes.

That could have been her.

*That could have been her!*

"Why?" she choked out, not trusting her voice to form full sentences.

Why would her father not claim her?

Was there something wrong with her?

She didn't realize she'd spoken the words out loud until the attorney gently slid the folder from her grasp and thumbed through the documents.

"Here," he said, pressing something into her hands.

An envelope, its ivory paper thick and expensive. *Dr. Charlotte Owens* printed on the front.

"Maybe this will explain things," he said, his tone gentle and sympathetic for the first time since they'd met.

Charlotte stared blankly at the letter, as if she had forgotten what envelopes were for. She felt utterly uncertain about what to do next. She considered the contents of the envelope. Good grief, was this her father's attempt to explain himself? To make things right? How dare he? He'd had years to write, call or find her. To do something. To do *anything*! And now he was going to put this on her? Just leave her a letter so he got to have his say while she had none?

The very thought repulsed her so much, it felt like she was holding a snake. She pushed the letter aside so vehemently it would have slid off the counter had Jeffery not caught it first.

"Sell it." Her voice was flat, but steely, her hands curled into fists.

Jeffrey looked at the letter. "Sorry?"

"The house," she clarified. "Just sell it and donate the money to charity."

She wanted nothing to do with anything her father had touched. Why had he even bothered to leave her this house? Was it some kind of torture to make sure she understood all that she had been denied?

She checked her watch and gathered her things. This trip had been a waste of her time. But it wasn't too late to salvage her vacation. If she was lucky, she might catch a late flight to San Francisco, so she could start the long trip to Sydney the next day. With any luck she'd be able to join her friends by the weekend. She could really use some time on a beach chair with a fruity drink before she started her next assignment as ship physician aboard *The Eden*, a massive cruise ship that traveled the Caribbean.

"Wait," Jeffrey said, combing through his briefcase. He fanned a stack of documents before her. Home inspection reports, market analyses, and other incomprehensible paperwork that seemed irrelevant to Charlotte. Until he explained that, despite its desirable zip code and near-perfect facade, the home had been neglected for quite some time. It needed a new roof, there was pervasive mold in the basement, and some structures on the property, like the greenhouse and the pool house, had fallen into such disrepair it was considered hazardous for anyone to enter.

"I'm sorry, but I don't see what this has to do with me." Charlotte shook out her coat, preparing to leave.

The lawyer tidied the pages into a neat stack before clipping them together. "To be blunt, you can't sell the home. I mean, you can try, but no insurance company will cover a house with these problems. And without homeowner's insurance no bank will issue a loan. So, unless you have a cash buyer, this house can't be sold."

Charlotte frowned, her mind racing. "So, are you saying I'm stuck with his house?"

The attorney flicked some invisible lint from his jacket. "Not necessarily. You could sell the property 'as is' to a real estate investment firm. You'll only get a fraction of the home's market value, but you'd be free and clear in a few weeks. In fact..." he rummaged through his seemingly bottomless briefcase "...our firm has an investment division that would be happy to take this property off your hands."

He pushed yet another document her way.

Charlotte's heart leapt at the chance to escape. Just one signature and she could join her friends in Sydney, where the steady tempo of the surf would chase her stress away. Warm sun, cold rum, and friendly locals would help her forget everything that had happened here.

But when she saw the offer amount her pen froze mid-air. She knew a steal when she saw one. Even in its current condition, this house was easily worth three or four times what the firm was offering.

*So what? You're going to donate the money to charity. Why do you care?*

Maybe that was why she balked. Because this money could do some real good. Charlotte didn't know much about her father, but if he could live in a house like this and not claim his daughter she doubted he had supported many charities. Selling his home and donating the money might be the first good he'd ever done in his life.

It would be wrong to let this attorney lowball her out of the home's true worth. Jeffrey's financial gain wouldn't benefit anyone other than opportunistic investors.

But giving up her travel plans to oversee the renovations felt like a handful of salt in a wound that had never healed. When she'd turned eighteen and aged out of foster care she had vowed that *never* again would others decide her fate. No more social workers and no more donated suitcases. Now she went where she wanted, for as long as she wanted, and stayed only as long as it felt right. That was the beauty of being a traveling doctor. No long-term commitments and she was in total control of her fate.

But what if she had a reason to stay in Seattle beyond renovating her father's home? A purpose that would allow her to leave Seattle with some sense of closure for the harm her father had done? What if she spent *his* money and *her* time helping kids who were in the same situation she'd once been in—alone, vulnerable, scared. Then maybe she would feel justice had been done.

Surely her recruiting agency could help her find a short-term assignment here in Seattle. There had to be a public health clinic or community hospital that could use an extra pediatrician for a few months. If not, she would just volunteer.

Either way, she'd be able to board *The Eden* with a sense of pride. She didn't need her father's wealth, but she could make damn sure that his money would benefit teens who needed it.

She pushed the contract back to the attorney. "Thank you for the offer, Jeffrey. But I have other plans."

The Sunshine Clinic for Kids was a humble brick building that claimed the corner of Fifth and Monroe. Charlotte's heels clicked against the aging sidewalk where stubborn weeds managed to grow in the cracks formed by years of Seattle's rain and low-grade earthquakes. This part of the city was old and industrial, with little concern for aesthetics.

But Charlotte wasn't focused on the factories or the weeds. She was more interested in the clinic itself. The stout little building didn't have the same left behind feel of its neighborhood. Its glass door was polished and flanked by two blue ceramic pots that were spilling over with lush verbena flowers. Lace curtains softened the windows, and in a burst of creativity someone had drawn a bright yellow sun above the clinic's name. There was a relentlessly optimistic feel about the place that appealed to Charlotte. As if the clinic refused to be dragged down by its shabby surroundings.

"Good for you," Charlotte said out loud.

She didn't normally talk to inanimate buildings, but the past few days of being stuck in her father's house was making her a little crazy. Every minute there was a reminder of her father's utter disregard for her well-being when she was still a child.

But finally, she could put all that behind her. The recruiting agency had been thrilled to place her with The Sunshine Clinic, a satellite clinic of Seattle's main hospital, dedicated to providing care for the city's at-risk and homeless teens. She didn't know why her recruiter had been having a hard time finding an interim pediatrician for the clinic, but she was more than ready to lose herself in the demands of a busy day seeing patients. Work and travel had always been her escape from stress and painful emotions. That was how she had sailed through high school with top grades and landed full scholarships to college.

Today was special, so she had chosen her favorite dress. It was light blue, fell just below her knees, and had been handmade by an artist in Sedona, Arizona, where Charlotte had worked at a pediatrics clinic for one summer. When she hadn't been treating the tourists' kids for sunburn and dehydration, she'd used her free time to hike and explore the legendary red rocks of a mountain town reputed to be home to four powerful energy vortexes. Wearing this dress felt like a promise that as soon as the house was ready to sell she'd be back to living life on her terms again.

She struggled to open the clinic door, one arm balancing a box of office supplies and framed diplomas.

"Hello!" she called, but the security system chirped at the same time, obscuring her greeting.

A man was hunched over the reception counter, his back to her, with a phone pressed to his ear, oblivious to her presence. She took in his dark jeans and motorcycle boots, along with a leather jacket that strained to contain his broad, muscular shoulders. Was he a patient or an employee of the clinic? She couldn't tell. But the open ladder near the counter made her think he might be something to do with maintenance.

Whoever he was, he was not having a good day.

"But Mrs. Winthrop, at least she used her words, right?" The man forced a chuckle. "No, I agree. It's inappropriate for an eleven-year-old to use *those* words." After a few *mm-hmms* and *yes, I sees*, he suddenly straightened. "Oh, no, that won't be necessary." There was a silence as he pressed the phone harder to his ear. "Well... yes, but you see..." His shoulders slumped in defeat. "Mrs. Winthrop, please. I'm begging you. This is Piper's third school this year..." There was a long pause before he suddenly brightened. "Oh, thank you! I appreciate that." He ran his thumb along the edge of the counter, smoothing an imperfection that was invisible to Charlotte. "I promise that we *will* be working on this at home."

His leather jacket shifted when he hung up the phone, revealing the V-shape of his back and waist. Charlotte bit her lip as she watched him pinch the bridge of his nose. It was obvious she had overheard a private phone call. She hated to intrude on his apparent distress, but today was her first day and she didn't want to be late. She needed to report to Dr. John Bennett, the clinic's director, as soon as possible.

She cleared her throat. "Hello?"

The man spun to face her. For several long seconds Charlotte felt a kind of shock to her system that momentarily stole her words and purpose. The strength she had seen his leather jacket struggling to contain was also found in the thick muscles of his chest and neck. He had a handsome, honest face and wore his chestnut-brown hair long to his collar, the waves still shower-damp. He was rugged and masculine, and maybe a bit intimidating with that intense scowl.

Or maybe it was his eyes that pinned her in place. Greenish gold, like the eyes of coyotes and cougars, his gaze was so intense she felt like a rabbit that had wandered too far into apex predator territory.

She swallowed hard as she noticed the stethoscope around his neck. Though he bore little resemblance to the bland headshot posted on the hospital's website, this was Dr. John Bennett, her new colleague.

*For heaven's sake, Charlotte. Stop staring and say something!*

But he saved her the trouble. He folded his arms across his impressive chest and assessed her with a measured stare. "Dr. Owens, right? The locum doctor?"

Charlotte wiggled the lapel of her lab coat where her name was embroidered in black thread. "Guilty as charged!" she said, hating her too-cheerful tone.

The first day of a new job was the worst. She loved the freedom that came with being a traveling doctor, but being "the new doc" took its toll.

"Paperwork, please," he said, finally shifting his focus from her to rummage through his tool-box. "So we can get you on your way." He found whatever he was looking for and started to climb the ladder.

"Paperwork?"

"You know… Whatever the courts gave you to track your community service so you can get your medical license reinstated. I'll sign off to say that you're making a good faith effort to find a service site and you can be on your way."

Charlotte had felt off-kilter ever since she'd walked through the door. This conversation was not helping. "I'm sorry, I don't know what you're talking about."

He paused, a screwdriver gripped between his teeth. He removed it to ask, "Then why are you here?"

Charlotte was starting to wonder if Gina, her recruiter, had made a mistake with this assignment. Only that would explain this surreal conversation.

"Because you need a locum pediatrician. At least that's what I was told."

Her new colleague chuckled and shook his head. "Depends on who you ask, I suppose."

As if that should satisfy her curiosity, he tucked the screwdriver in his back pocket and climbed back up the ladder.

What did that mean? And what was she supposed to do next? The box she was holding was growing heavier by the minute. She'd like to set it down on the counter, but the strange man was occupying that space, so she chose one of the orange vinyl chairs near the picture window instead. Then she found her phone and contemplated calling Gina, to make sure she was in the right place. But she'd worked with Gina for years, long enough to know that Gina double-checked every detail before sending one of her doctors to a new assignment. There was no way she was in the wrong place or had the wrong information.

Whatever was wrong here, her new colleague seemed to be at the heart of it.

John Bennett started whistling a tune—something familiar, but she couldn't quite place the melody. And she didn't care because she was getting annoyed. For Pete's sake, she was standing right here. Why was he refusing to talk to her or deal with her?

Before she knew exactly what she was going

to do, she strode over and gave the ladder a tiny shake. "Hey!"

"Hey!" he yelled back. "Do you mind?"

"Actually, I do. Do I have a job here or not?"

She braced herself for a fight, but from this angle, looking up at him, she could see a slight crook in his nose, hinting that he was no stranger to fights much worse than what she was bringing.

He leaned one arm on the ladder and studied her like she was a specimen under a microscope. "Well, that depends. Because so far everyone interested in the job has been a pretty desperate character. Either they need community service hours to get their medical license reinstated or they are serving probation for some kind of legal trouble." He tucked the light fixture back in the ceiling and started tightening screws. "We don't need any of that nonsense around here."

"I'm not a desperate character!" Unless you counted her desperation to get away from her father's house and all of its painful memories.

John paused his tinkering long enough to indicate her entire person with a wave of his screwdriver. "I don't know about desperate, lady. But that dress definitely makes you a character."

A flare of heat bloomed in her cheeks as she realized this John didn't want her in his clinic. Just like her father hadn't wanted her in his life. Which was fine by her. She was sick of being pushed around by the inexplicable whims of men who wielded their power with a reckless disregard for how they hurt others.

She stalked back to the window and grabbed her box of personal belongings. A familiar bravado infused her core. Gina could find her another noble cause to keep her busy while she was stuck in Seattle. Or maybe she should abandon this plan to do some good while she was here. It wasn't too late to follow her first impulse and sell her father's house "as is" and get her derriere over to Sydney.

She was halfway to the door when she spied that shaky yellow sun hovering above the clinic's name. Who had drawn that? Had it been one of the teens who'd passed through here, desperate for something pretty and warm to brighten the world? Or an employee—perhaps the same employee who had planted flowers at the front door and hung lacy curtains in the windows?

Someone was working awfully hard to make this clinic a refuge for the teens who found their way here. It wasn't Dr. Sunshine-on-a-Ladder over there, that was for sure. But someone here had known darkness and loss. And also that the tiniest gesture of hope could pull you through the darkest nights.

Her shoulders slumped as the fight left her. What kind of doctor would she be if she turned her back on vulnerable teens after a little friction with a grumpy doctor? She huffed an exasperated sigh as she set her box back down on the orange vinyl chair.

John was off the ladder now, rummaging through his tools. If he'd noticed her near-exit, he was keeping a pretty good poker face about it.

"So." She crossed her arms. "Where's my office?"

He glanced up, a tiny glimmer of surprise in his eyes before he recovered his stoic expression. Had she had surprised him? If so, good. John looked like he needed someone to rattle his cage once in a while.

He closed his toolbox and latched it shut before turning back to Charlotte, arms folded across his chest. "If you're going to stick around, we have to fix this first." He indicated her entire person with a chin-thrust.

"Pardon me?"

His gaze moved like an elevator from her head to her shoes before he shook his head. "Didn't the agency tell you how to dress?"

Her urge to snipe back was strong, but if they were going to get anything done they needed to have an actual conversation.

"Here, give me that." He proffered his hand, clearly wanting something from her, and she detected a hint of his cologne. Clean, with musky male undernotes and hints of spice and surprise.

"Give you what?"

"Your lab coat." He beckoned with a quick wave of his fingers.

The man made less sense by the minute. Why on earth did he want her lab coat? Still, he was at least speaking to her now, and that seemed like progress.

She shrugged off her coat and handed it over.

"Do you have anything else you could wear? Something less…bohemian?"

That familiar quick flash of anger flared again. "This isn't bohemian. It's practically a work of art. It was hand-stitched in Sedona by a textile artist whose work is in high demand."

But that wasn't why she'd bought it. She just loved the whimsy of a blue dress printed with sycamore trees, pink owls tucked in their branches.

"Is that so? Well, you don't see many hand-stitched works of art around here, which means you're going to stick out. Not the effect we're going for, Dr. Owens, so please, follow me."

Curiosity compelled her to follow him down a narrow hallway to a storage closet where he dragged out several boxes labeled *Donations*. Then he dug through the clothing, checking tags and tossing items aside, until he held up a pair of faded green cargo pants. "These might work," he said.

Charlotte hooked a finger through the belt loop. "For what?"

He didn't respond. He was too busy digging through the box until he found a salmon-hued graphic tee shirt. After years of washing, its letters were faded and peeling, but she could still make out *Fort Lauderdale, Florida. Est 1911.*

He pointed to a door behind her. "You can change in there. But I can't help you with the shoes."

Charlotte looked down at her simple flats.

"From now on you need to wear closed-toe athletic shoes."

Her head was spinning. What was happening here?

He grabbed a box of baby wipes from the shelf. "The lipstick—it's got to go. And the earrings. And the bangles." He paused and assessed her with a critical eye. "And your hair." He indicated her long, dark hair, which she wore in loose waves past her shoulders. "Just try to draw less attention to yourself. Be like a lamppost— there, but not really seen. Okay?"

"You want me to look like a lamppost?"

He shook his head, exasperated. "No, I don't want you to look like a lamppost. Just be less... striking, okay?" He groaned as if he hadn't meant to say that, running a rough hand through his hair.

Charlotte caught a glimpse of herself in the hallway mirror, crumpled clothes and baby wipes in her hand. "Dr. Bennett, this seems very unprofessional."

His green eyes softened for the first time since they'd met. "Good. Then maybe the kids will talk to you. Tell you where it hurts."

He headed back to the waiting room, leaving Charlotte alone. She went into the small bathroom and tried to recover her equilibrium. It wasn't like she'd expected a parade just for showing up. But she sure hadn't expected to be butting heads with her new colleague on day one.

She puffed an errant strand of hair away from her eyes. "So much for saving the world," she said to her reflection.

Was this why Gina had had such trouble filling this position? Who knew how many well-meaning doctors had been here before her, wanting to help, only to get run off by a good-looking but grumpy doctor?

She slipped off her dress, trading it for the tee shirt and cargo pants. John had guessed her size just right. She liked the shirt, soft and cozy after years of washing, but it was hard to shake off the unwanted flashback to her younger self, when she'd had to take whatever hand-me-downs were given to her.

"So go," she whispered to her image. "You don't have to stay…"

*Easy-breezy* was her life's motto. *Travel light and keep things casual and fun.*

That was how she'd stayed one step ahead of the heartbreak and loss that had stained her teen years. But Dr. Bennett looked like he was anything but easy-breezy.

Conflicting thoughts swirled in her head. This assignment was going to be tough, for sure. But life was full of tough challenges. That was what it took to reveal true character. And if she missed this opportunity to make a difference in the lives of teens who needed her, then she'd be a lot more like her father than she wanted to admit.

She took a deep breath to steady herself, then started arranging her hair into a French braid.

She wasn't going anywhere—whether John liked it or not.

# CHAPTER TWO

JOHN CLIMBED BACK up the ladder to finish his repairs. He didn't have time for these extra tasks, but filing a work order with the hospital's maintenance department meant waiting weeks for someone to show. Out here, deep in Seattle's industrial district, his little satellite clinic wasn't a big priority for the administrative types.

Which was fine by him. If being the king of his clinic meant doing the maintenance, so be it. It kept the top brass from breathing down his neck and let him do things his way. The same way he'd been doing things since his father had walked out on his family, leaving John charged with keeping his little brother Michael out of trouble while their mom worked two or three jobs to keep their heads above water. Not an easy task for John—especially with Michael's iron will and mad Houdini-esque escape artist skills.

But Michael wouldn't be escaping anytime soon. He'd been sentenced to five years in prison on drug charges, making John the legal guardian of Piper, his eleven-year-old niece. But, despite his best efforts, Piper was not settling into her new life with her bachelor uncle on his live-aboard sailboat very well. She was frequently in trouble at school, which meant now the hospital was breathing down John's neck plenty, on account of his many missed shifts so he could meet with Piper's principal or fill in when an exasperated sitter quit on the spot.

Those missed shifts had eventually caught the attention of the chief of pediatrics, who'd decreed that adding a locum doctor to the clinic would be better than relying on on-call doctors to fill in. John had done his best to assure the pediatric team that he had everything under control. The last thing he needed was another doctor in his space, messing up the systems that he and Sarah, his receptionist and medical assistant, had spent years perfecting.

And most of the locums who had applied so far had had their own agenda—like documenting community service hours to get a medical license reinstated. He had worked too hard to earn the trust of Seattle's vulnerable teens to let anyone like that through the front door. And the good doctors just didn't stick around. The long hours and limited resources made it too tempting to accept positions with the main hospital or pediatric private practices.

So he probably didn't need to worry about the tall brunette who was now carefully folding her dress. Two weeks—four, tops—and she'd be one more doctor who'd ghosted him for a better opportunity, leaving him alone to take care of everything.

At least she looked better now that she had changed. Not that she'd looked terrible before. She was actually quite stunning, with that Grecian profile and soft blue eyes. But the rumpled tee shirt and casual braid made her more approachable, which the teens needed. Many had trust issues with adults, so he had learned to ditch anything that made him look like an authority figure.

She hoisted the box and turned to face him. "Where's my office?"

So she was sticking around despite his unsolicited wardrobe consultation. *Interesting*.

"You don't have an office. Sorry." He'd had to sacrifice his own to create a second exam room for the steady parade of locum doctors who had come and gone before her. He folded the ladder and leaned it against the wall. "But I can add some shelving to your exam room if you want."

"Where am I supposed to do my charting? Or phone in scripts and consults?"

He pointed behind the reception desk, where he had set an old door across two sawhorses.

Two computers and a single phone marked the office space.

She narrowed her eyes and he braced himself for another clash. He liked how her blue eyes darkened when she was irritated. A man could learn to read a woman like that, he thought, the same way a sailor could read the skies for signs of trouble.

But Sarah saved him from the impending squall by breezing into the clinic. She hustled behind the front desk, organizing her coat and purse before she noticed Charlotte.

"Oh, honey!" she exclaimed. "You must be the new doctor!" She set Charlotte's box on the counter so she could pull her into one of the famous Mother Bear hugs the teens loved. Then she stepped back, her hands cupping Charlotte's shoulders. "Ready for some coffee and a tour?"

Now, why hadn't he thought of that? Coffee and a tour would have been a far more civilized way to start the day.

John half listened as Sarah led Charlotte on a tour of the real-estate-office-turned-medical-clinic. They had maximized their small space by using office partitions and creative design to create two exam rooms, an onsite pharmacy and lab, and a food pantry where kids could grab snacks and drinks to go. It was half as much as John had wanted when he'd started the clinic five years ago but, as Sarah often reminded him, Rome wasn't built in a day.

"And here we are, back where we started," Sarah said, her hands set low on her hips.

Charlotte rounded the corner and he caught her eyes for a moment. Everything about her—from her resume, which read like a travel brochure, to her sun-kissed smooth skin—hinted at freedom, wanderlust, adventure. She was like a telegraph from his Before Times, when he had been free to spend his time as he liked. Mostly that had translated to long hours at the clinic, then spending his free time rehabbing *The House Call*, the sailboat he called home, to prepare for his next trip into the open waters beyond the Puget Sound. It was a little too easy to imagine Charlotte's long, lithe body at the helm of *The House Call*, the wind whipping her dark hair and her eyes wild with delight.

But there would be no voyages now—nor wild-eyed women on his boat or in his bed. Not with Piper as his charge. The mistakes he had made with his brother had robbed Michael of his freedom and his future. Mistakes he would not repeat—which was why it didn't matter that Charlotte smelled like jasmine and rain. He'd be sticking to his side of the clinic until the trade winds that had blown her into Seattle blew her somewhere else.

By noon, the clinic was in chaos. The waiting room was standing room only, with teens laughing and buzzing like a swarm of cicadas. A tower of mail and magazines threatened to spill off the reception counter. Sarah was running triage, somehow taking calls and screening walk-ins without losing her mind.

John walked his last patient to Sarah for checkout just as Charlotte left her office. She had Matthew with her, a quiet boy John knew from his previous visits. Something about Matthew's uneasy expression and the stack of prescription slips in his hand tripped John's radar.

"For starters," Charlotte said, "you'll need to avoid triggers like smoke, pollen, and cold weather."

John willed himself to stay on his side of the clinic, as he had vowed. He didn't need to get in the middle of every single thing that happened.

Matthew squinted at one of the slips. "What's a nebulizer?"

Okay, maybe he did. Cripes, she'd prescribed a *nebulizer*? Didn't she know some of these kids didn't have…?

No, of course she didn't. This wasn't her world—it was his. And whether he wanted a partner or not, he had one now. It was up to him to make sure she understood what she had signed up for.

He joined them at the reception counter. "May I see those?" he asked, indicating the prescriptions. He thumbed through them one by one. "Advair disks...excellent choice." He crumpled the slip and stuck it in his pocket. "If state insurance covered them."

Charlotte's brow furrowed.

He looked at the next slip. "Steroids—good. Let's add an antihistamine and a generic bronchodilator. Sarah can find those in our pharmacy." Which wasn't a pharmacy at all, but a storage closet stocked with the medications they prescribed most often. "Now, let's talk about your digs."

Sarah swiveled in her chair, a phone receiver pressed to her ear. "I've got the House of Hope on the line. He's got a bed."

"And a caseworker?"

"Working on it!" She patted the chair next to her, indicating Matthew should sit with her while she worked.

Suddenly Charlotte's hand was on John's arm, squeezing hard. "How am I supposed to help these kids if I can't give them what they need? You know as well as I do that Matthew needs more than steroids and allergy meds!"

The intensity of her expression matched the pressure of her grip. Was she a Type A person, then, intent on excelling at whatever she tried?

Or did she actually care if Matthew got the help he needed?

John sighed and slid his pen behind his ear. "You prescribed a nebulizer, right? Which requires electricity?"

"Of course."

"So, does Matthew have consistent access to electricity?"

She frowned. "I don't know."

"And the Advair disks? Insurance doesn't cover the branded version, so he'll need the generic—which we don't stock. So where is the closest pharmacy? What bus routes does Matthew need to get there?"

Her grip on his arm loosened. "I don't know that either."

He reached behind the counter, then slid a bus route planner in front of her. "Well, study up, Doc. Because this is part of your job too."

She looked up at him, her hand still draped on his arm, her eyes shiny—with anger or distress? He couldn't tell. "Why is he even on the street? Why not in a shelter or a foster home—someplace safe?"

Because life was inherently unfair. End of story. There was no point dwelling on *who* or *why* or *should* and *could*. All that mattered was being there for the teens who needed them and doing what they could for as long as they could.

"Kids like Matthew have it tough. There are only a few shelters in Seattle that are certified to accept unaccompanied minors, and they have long waiting lists. That's why they need meds they can stuff in their pockets or shoes. It's not ideal—I know that. But if we can help, they'll start to trust us. That's when we can make a difference."

Charlotte stepped away, her gaze avoiding his as her fingers fidgeted with a loose thread on the hem of her shirt. Her forehead puckered, as if she was working something out. He'd seen that look before, in the doctors who had come before her. He braced himself for The Talk, full of reassurances that *It's not you, it's not the kids...it's me.*

But she surprised him.

"You know what we should do? We should set up an area where kids could come by for breathing treatments when we're open." She was stalking the clinic now, looking through doorways and assessing every room.

John felt like a puppy as he trailed her. "I'm sorry...what? We don't have the budget or the space for..."

"And we should stock more brand-name drugs. Pharmaceutical companies donate drugs all the time. I'm sure there's a process—and lots of forms, of course. But we can figure it out!"

We? When had they become a "we"?

John cleared his throat. "I appreciate your enthusiasm, Dr. Owens. But we don't have the space to add a breathing treatment area. And Sarah doesn't have the time to set up and monitor a drug donation partnership."

"Just Charlotte is fine. It won't be difficult, I promise. If we move a partition here or there we can make the space. Then we could contact the university and become a practicum site for nursing students. They could oversee the breathing treatment area in exchange for getting firsthand experience in community medicine."

She was bold—he had to give her that. Bold and provocative and a little sexy, with those intense and determined blue eyes.

"These are very ambitious ideas, Dr. Owens, and I appreciate—"

"Charlotte," she corrected him again.

"Charlotte, I appreciate your enthusiasm—I do. But we have our hands full providing the services we already have."

Not that he didn't want to offer the teens more. When he'd started he'd been full of ambitious plans to grow the tiny storefront clinic into a full-service medical, dental, and behavioral health clinic, able to provide all the care Seattle's vulnerable teens deserved.

But there was only so much that he and Sarah could do on their own. And, while Sarah had been nagging him to start thinking about how he would replace her when she finally retired for good, he could not imagine entrusting the clinic and its teen patients to anyone other than himself and Sarah.

"I couldn't possibly ask Sarah to take on more—"

Charlotte flashed him an absolutely brilliant smile. "Sarah doesn't have to do a thing. You have me now! I'll start researching the medication program tonight."

Then she powered up her computer tablet and scanned the day's appointments as if she'd worked there all her life.

John stood for a moment, hands fisted at his sides, thoroughly annoyed at the flare of attraction that bloomed in his chest. Everything she'd suggested was exactly how he wanted to grow the clinic. Could it be different if he had a partner? Could someone like Charlotte figure out how to overcome obstacles that had stymied him?

For one long minute it was tempting to lean into the hope he felt stirring in his chest.

But no, he wouldn't do it. It was too risky. The teens and the hospital relied on him to keep the clinic running, day after day. The last thing he needed was to build something with Charlotte, only to have her take off when wanderlust struck, leaving him to pick up the pieces. It was better for him to stick to what he could manage on his own, year after year.

His musings were interrupted when the front door was flung open hard and fast, hitting the wall at the same time as the security alarm chirped twice.

"Hey, Doc!" a girl's frantic voice called. "This kid needs help!"

John knew who it was without looking. Angel was a frequent visitor to The Sunshine Clinic, often dragging along a kid who needed help while refusing any for herself.

Today was no different. She had one arm slung around the shoulders of a freckle-faced boy who wiped his nose on his sleeve, looking more confused than sick.

Sarah peered at the girl over her bifocals. "The door, Angel. We've discussed this, remember?"

"Right!" Angel dashed back and shut the door quietly, her long ponytail swinging wildly with every step. "Sorry."

Sarah oversaw the check-in process for the boy, Bruce, while John contemplated how to handle Charlotte's plans for the clinic. He didn't want to crush her enthusiasm for helping the teens, but he wasn't going to start anything with Charlotte that he couldn't finish.

"Angel, would you please take Bruce to Exam Room Two?" Sarah said.

John's head snapped up. That was Charlotte's exam room.

John willed himself to wait until Angel had led Bruce out of earshot. "Sarah, what are you doing? Angel's case is far too complicated for Charlotte's first day."

"Angel?" Charlotte asked, clearly confused. "I thought Bruce was the patient?"

Sarah explained Angel's habit of bringing other kids to the clinic. "But we're worried about Angel."

"Or whoever she is," John continued. "We don't know, because she won't tell us her real name. What we do know is that sometimes she presses her chest, as if it hurts. And she's admitted to having a few dizzy spells. She won't consent to an exam, but even if she did I can't treat her until she qualifies for state medical insurance."

Charlotte bit her bottom lip as she listened. "And you can't get her qualified for insurance without a real, legal name, right?"

"Right," Sarah confirmed. "That's why I think you should be the one to see her. You're brandnew here. Maybe there will be something about you that will get her to open up."

"But this is Charlotte's first day!" John protested. "She doesn't know anything about Angel's case. More importantly, Angel doesn't know her. There's no rapport there...no trust."

"I know she trusts you, John, but despite your best efforts you haven't been able to get Angel to consent to a physical exam. If we don't make progress soon, whatever's wrong with her could get a lot worse."

Every cell in John's body was on alert. It had taken him months to build a rapport with Angel, but despite his lectures and gentle cajoling Angel still would not agree to an exam or reveal her name.

Sarah was right. For Angel's sake, he had to give Charlotte a chance to get past Angel's defenses.

He gave a quick nod of agreement. "But be careful, Charlotte. No pushing her, okay? If she wants to talk—" *she wouldn't* "—great. But if not, just back off. Otherwise she'll run away and we may never see her again."

Charlotte nodded and headed down the hall. John followed close behind, feeling jittery with frustration. He knew Sarah was right to see if Charlotte could have a breakthrough with Angel, but it felt like just one more area of his life where he was losing control.

Not that his life before getting guardianship of Piper had been perfect. He'd worked long hours at the clinic and sailed alone on the sea. But it had been *his* life to live the way he saw fit, and he'd liked it just fine.

Now he felt his world churning beneath his feet, as if a fierce storm was headed his way.

Charlotte closed the door behind her and assessed her young patients. Bruce sat on the exam table, relaxed and curious. Angel stood in the corner of the room, her back up against the wall, arms crossed across her chest, her expression suspicious.

"Where's Dr. J?" she demanded.

"Busy with other patients," Charlotte answered truthfully, because the waiting room was about to burst at the seams. "I'm Dr. Charlotte Owens."

Then she cringed, because that sounded so formal. Was it better to introduce herself as Dr. C, borrowing the teen's shortened name for John? That didn't feel right. She realized she had no idea how to get things off to a good start with kids who didn't trust her as readily as the patients she usually treated.

It would be nice to ask John for some guidance, but apparently she didn't know how to get things off to a good start with him either. Was he this unfriendly to all the locums who'd come before her? Or was there something special about her that brought out his snarky side?

"So tell me, Bruce, what brings you in today?"

It wasn't Bruce who answered, though. Angel immediately responded, describing Bruce's sneezing, watery eyes, and occasional cough. She seemed very comfortable in the medical setting. *Interesting*, Charlotte thought. Angel had clearly been mothered by someone who'd taken her to the doctor. So where was that parent now?

"Well, let's take a look, shall we?"

Charlotte soon ruled out any serious infection or a virus. Bruce didn't have a fever and his lymph nodes were just slightly enlarged. Enough to indicate his immune system was on alert, but not fighting anything serious.

"Looks like seasonal allergies, Bruce," Charlotte said, making a note in his file.

"So he'll need antihistamines, then," Angel said, still serious and motherly. That was another surprise, because most teens didn't talk like that.

How old was she anyway? Charlotte did a quick visual.

Angel wore a lot of makeup, had big hoop earrings, and carried herself tall and strong. Late high school was Charlotte's best guess, maybe close to graduation. Charlotte remembered what it had been like to be on the cusp of graduation, on the verge of losing the fragile support she'd had through foster care. It hurt her heart to think that Angel was already fending for herself when she was still in high school.

"That's right, he will. Do you prefer chewable or can you swallow pills?" Charlotte asked Bruce.

"Pills."

She typed up the visit notes along with an order for a month's supply of allergy medication. "Bruce, take this to Sarah. She'll get your medication and get you checked out."

Angel stood to follow him and Charlotte held her breath, hoping for the best. "Hey, Angel, would you mind sticking around for a minute?"

Angel paused, her hand on the doorknob. She gave Charlotte a long, appraising look before she slowly walked back and stood in the corner, re-crossing her arms against her chest.

Charlotte slowly exhaled with relief. Finally, she had a chance to make a difference here—which was the whole reason she wanted to work at The Sunshine Clinic.

"What do you want?"

Charlotte took care to keep her distance, positioning herself away from the door so Angel knew she could leave whenever she wanted. But Charlotte hoped she wouldn't.

"I just wanted to talk a little, if that's okay."

"About what?"

"About you, I suppose."

Angel's eyes narrowed. Everything about her, from her tensed body to her focused gaze, spoke of distrust and fear.

"Dr. J told me that your chest hurts sometimes. And you also get dizzy?"

Angel shrugged. "It doesn't happen that often."

"That's good. But you're pretty young for chest pain. How old are you anyway?"

Angel gave her a knowing look and shook her head. "Nice try, Doc."

So Angel was withholding *all* personal information, not just her name. Did she not want to be found? Was it possible she had a head trauma or an illness that affected her memory so that she truly didn't know who she was? Or had she found one small way to seize control of something in a world that had spun hopelessly off its axis?

Charlotte continued. "Angel, there's a lot of reasons why you might have these symptoms, like dehydration, stress or fatigue. But there's also some pretty scary ones. I'd like to do an exam, if that's okay, or at least listen to your heart for a bit."

That only seemed to make Angel double down on her tough girl facade. She jutted her chin forward, more determined than ever. "I'm not scared."

But there was a flicker in her eyes that said otherwise, and she was starting to cast side glances at the door.

Charlotte's stomach fluttered with alarm. How

was she going to help this girl if the mere mention of a medical exam triggered her flight response?

*Stay calm and think. Find a way.*

Then Charlotte noticed Angel's necklace. She wore a pendant with four interlocked hearts. The first one was solid gold while the others were hollow. A hazy memory from Charlotte's foster home days slowly rose to the surface.

"That's a sister's necklace, right?"

Angel's hand reflexively flew to her neck. "I guess."

"And you're the oldest, right? That's why the first heart is solid?"

"Yeah."

Charlotte's mind sifted through the possibilities for connection. It was clear that Angel's need for control was too strong for her to accept help. Not for herself, anyway.

But maybe for her sisters, she would.

"I'm worried about them, Angel. Your sisters, that is."

Angel's brows furrowed. "Why? You don't even know them."

"True. But I know that many heart conditions are hereditary. So, if you're sick…"

"My sisters could have it too?" Angel's defiant expression melted into worry.

"It's possible. The only way to know for sure is to find out if your heart is healthy."

A great war of emotions played out across the canvas of Angel's face. Charlotte bit her lip, hoping against hope that her love for her sisters was enough to push her beyond her comfort zone.

"Okay, fine." She turned and jumped up on the exam table.

Charlotte quickly completed the exam, limiting herself to what was essential. Angel was thinner than Charlotte would like, and she would have loved to check her blood cell counts and nutritional status. But Charlotte limited herself to focusing on Angel's heart, warming the stethoscope drum before laying it against the girl's thin chest. She took her time, listening from all angles to make sure she was right.

"Thank you, Angel." Charlotte stood and draped her stethoscope around her neck, considering her approach.

"So?" Angel asked, adjusting her shirt. "Am I okay?"

Charlotte smiled. "Overall, you look really healthy, Angel. But your heart is beating faster than it should. We need to figure out why."

"Can't you just give me a pill or something?"

"That might be an option, once we know what's wrong. That's why I need to refer you to a cardiologist for an EKG." Charlotte silently chided herself for the doctor talk. "In other words, I'd like you to see a heart specialist. They'll want to do an

EKG, which is a painless test that gives us more information about how your heart is working."

Angel avoided Charlotte's gaze as she jumped off the table and headed for the door. For one moment, Charlotte feared Angel would just walk out the door and never return.

But Angel paused, her hair falling to block her face. "This would help my sisters?"

Charlotte's heart clutched with compassion. She wanted Angel to know it was important to help herself too. "It would be a good start. But it could lead to more testing to figure out what's really wrong."

For several long seconds, Charlotte stayed perfectly still, waiting to see what Angel would do.

*Come on, girl. Take a chance on me. I won't let you down.*

"Maybe," Angel whispered, before slipping out the door.

That was not the answer Charlotte wanted to hear. Tachycardia could be caused by a lot of things, some of them quite serious. If Angel had a congenital heart issue, her heart could be a ticking time bomb, just waiting for a day when she exercised too hard or was otherwise stressed to go into full cardiac arrest.

Where did Angel go? When would she come back?

Would she ever get another chance to help her?

Charlotte dropped her head to her hands, overwhelmed with the weight of this work. She'd come here determined to make a difference in the lives of teenagers who had no one looking out for them. But how could she help kids who didn't have a permanent address or phone number? Or a clean place to sleep or safe places to store their medicine?

And could she even help a girl so determined to live like a ghost?

Charlotte made her way back to her makeshift office. John was already there, recording his notes on the computer.

Charlotte dropped into the chair next to him.

"So, how did it go?" he asked.

Charlotte let her head drop back until it rested on the back of her chair. She didn't want to tell him he was right. But he was. "Exactly the way you said it would. Except..." She held up an index finger to mark her point. "I did get her to consent to a basic physical exam."

John's fingers hovered over the keyboard. "And?"

"You were right again. She has significant tachycardia that needs to be checked out by a cardiologist."

John spun in his chair to face her. "And she agreed?"

Damn it. Every cell in her body wanted to say

she had made the connection with Angel that John thought was impossible. For Angel's sake, of course. But also to prove that she belonged there, to John and maybe even to herself.

"No, she didn't," Charlotte conceded. "But she didn't say no either. In fact, I got a 'maybe' before she left the office. Kind of in a hurry."

"Was she freaked out?"

"Not freaked out. Just not happy."

John rubbed the back of his neck and looked off into the distance, as if he might be able to catch a glimpse of Angel before her tiny frame disappeared into the city.

"So what does that mean? Will she come back?"

Judging from his worried body language, John didn't know either. And that was when Charlotte realized she had signed up for something she didn't understand. How was she going to make this grand difference in the universe when she didn't even know who her patients were or when they would come back?

"All we can do is earn her trust over time…on her schedule," John said.

His sigh was heavy as he turned his bulky frame back to the tiny keyboard and resumed his hunt-and-peck technique. He was so earnest as he studied the screen, deliberately typing each word. It was tempting to tease him a little, but she wasn't sure if John was the teasing type. In fact, she knew very little about him.

If she was going to have any chance of making a difference at The Sunshine Clinic, she needed to understand the kids who came here. One person in this place clearly had that gift, and he was currently squinting at the screen with a pencil clasped between his teeth.

"So…" Charlotte said, fiddling with the pocket on her cargo pants. "If—I mean *when* Angel comes back, we should have some sort of plan for her EKG, right? Maybe we could work together on making that happen?"

John looked her way, a flicker of surprise in his eyes. He really was a handsome man when he wasn't scowling. Intelligent green eyes, smooth, olive-toned skin. And a sculpted jaw that would make Michelangelo weep.

Charlotte willed herself to look away, but her gaze lingered on his mouth a beat too long and her cheeks grew warm when he caught her staring.

Sarah paused in typing away on her keyboard and spun her chair to face them.

"Oh, John, you should take her to Guido's for lunch. It's been ages since you've had a real break from the clinic. And I think it would be lovely for you two to get to know each other."

Something in Sarah's tone sounded slightly

provocative, like she was suggesting a date rather than a working lunch between colleagues. Good grief, did John think that was what she was thinking? Because she wasn't! She just wanted to talk about Angel and how to get her to a specialist.

Did he feel put on the spot too?

If so, he didn't seem bothered. If anything, his moss-green eyes seemed a bit softer now as he studied her. Making her feel less like a specimen and more like a...a friend?

"Sure," John agreed affably. "I'd love to get to know my new colleague."

# CHAPTER THREE

IT WAS MORE than a week later before they could carve out some time for their lunch date. John kept a tight schedule, often skipping lunch so he could fit in one more appointment or spend extra time with a teen who had complex medical needs.

By the time they set out on the short, four-block walk to Guido's Mexican Cantina, Charlotte had been thinking about their lunch for days. John's plan to earn Angel's trust over time wasn't sitting right with her. Not with Angel's fast heartbeat and dizzy spells. They needed to be ready to help her as soon as she returned, whether she shared her real name with them or not.

Despite it being early, the cantina was crowded when they arrived. With its ombre orange walls and wrought-iron decor, the café felt like a Spanish Gothic man cave. On the back wall, near the kitchen, a stenciled jet-black bull posed, its nostrils flared, with one menacing hoof poised to stamp.

John found a wrought-iron table at the back of

the café. It was tiny and seemed more suited to a streetside coffee shop, but it was the only table available. Charlotte slid into one chair while John disappeared to place their order.

John glanced her way as he waited in line. He gave her a little nod. What that meant, she couldn't say, but it unleashed a flurry of goose-bumps down her back. She smiled in return, then dove for her water glass to relieve her parched throat. Why was she so nervous about this lunch? She'd completed dozens of assignments as a traveling doctor. Meeting new people, fitting in—it was all old news to her. So this edgy feeling she had around John made no sense.

It was also annoying, because she had some ideas for helping Angel get her testing done faster. She needed to stay focused if she was going to get past John's territorial tendencies, not stutter her way through her speech because of nerves.

Reflexively she groped through her handbag until her fingers found her lipstick and compact. She flipped it open to check her appearance and was just about to freshen her lipstick when she paused.

*What are you doing, Char?*

Her gaze shifted from the mirror to John, who had made it to the order counter and was oblivious to her gaze. He was a solidly built man, that was for sure, with a cool, streetwise vibe that the teens gravitated to. The woman taking his order was giving him lots of big smiles while twirling a strand of her hair. Even at this distance, it was obvious she was flirting.

Charlotte could see the appeal. John was a strong, attractive man, with a no-nonsense attitude that could make a girl feel a bit invincible by his side.

Her gaze shifted back to her mirror. Was that what she was doing too? Flirting a little with her attractive, vigilant colleague?

She paused to consider that scenario, then felt a rush of heat as she realized it was true. She snapped her compact shut. No need to give anyone the wrong idea—including herself. She had one simple rule when it came to romance on the road, designed to keep her career intact and her reputation stellar. *No. Dating. Coworkers.* As a traveling doctor, she needed excellent recommendations to secure her next assignment. She couldn't afford loose ends, bad breakups, or misunderstandings in her line of work.

So John could keep that stacked body of his on his side of the clinic—because romance was not in the cards.

Nor was it the point of this lunch!

She shook her head in frustration.

*Focus, Charlotte.*

She closed her eyes and mentally reviewed the lines she had practiced all week.

*John, I know I'm only here for a few months. So, I hope you won't think I'm speaking out of turn when I say that I don't think we can just wait for Angel to be ready to trust us before we refer her for testing. There must be some other way to get her EKG done...something we can work out with the hospital. I don't know exactly how yet, but I'm just not willing to take no for an answer...*

"Take no for an answer to what?"

John was back, holding two chilled fruit sodas in one hand and a basket of just-fried tortilla chips in the other. His bulky frame was less intimidating, now that it was paired with his relaxed, friendly smile.

Her flood of goosebumps returned, making her wonder if it really was nerves that made her body react this way.

Embarrassed, she grabbed a chip, eager for an excuse not to talk. "Mmm..." she said, waving her chip like an idiot. "Delicious!"

She moved over as far as she could to make room for him to settle into his chair, but his knee jammed hard against hers anyway. He muttered an apology as he moved left while she went right, both doing their best to navigate their postage stamp of a table. Despite their amateur gymnastics, she could still feel the heat of his leg next to hers, his jeans tickling her ankle. That set off another hot explosion of nervous energy that she couldn't seem to tame.

John used the heel of his hand to twist the metal caps from their glass bottles, then handed one to her. The strawberry-lime fizziness was a sweet, cool contrast to the salty chips. John took a deep draw from his soda, then set the bottle down to study her. She felt like a spotlight had suddenly been aimed her way, making her wish she had freshened up that lipstick after all.

"John…" she began—because that was the way she'd practiced it in front of her bathroom mirror that morning.

"I suppose I owe you an apology," he said, at the exact same moment.

"I know I'm only going to be at The Sunshine Clinic for a few… Wait…what?" she stuttered, flabbergasted that the prickly pediatrician she'd met a week ago was even capable of an apology.

He leaned in close enough to stir the hair at her temple when he spoke, launching her heart into a swift staccato.

"Listen, I probably shouldn't tell you this." He looked over both shoulders as if checking for eavesdroppers. "But The Sunshine Clinic…"

"Yes?"

"We're not really a medical clinic."

"What are you talking about?" Hints of sandalwood and orange spice from his aftershave were confusing her even more than this strange conversation.

"Remember those makeover shows? Where the show's producers took average people and gave them glamorous makeovers?"

She couldn't imagine where this was going. But it was interesting, so she grabbed another chip and waited.

"We're doing a show like that at the clinic. Hidden cameras and all that. But we're targeting medical professionals. It's called *Medical Makeovers 911* and you were our very first wardrobe intervention!" He leaned back in his chair, leaving a cool rush of air in his wake. "What did you think?"

His demeanor was typical Dr. J—calm, cool, unflappable. But there was an unmistakable glint of mischief in his gaze and she rather liked it.

She tapped her chin with one manicured fingernail, thinking fast on her feet. "Tackling the profession's lab coat problem? I see…"

"Exactly. They're so predictable."

She tilted her head, taking in this new, unexpected side of her colleague. So Dr. John Bennett had a sense of humor. Who would have guessed? Not her. But now she wanted to keep the game going, so she could tease out the smile making the corners of his mouth dance. "So donated cargo pants and faded tee shirts are…what? Med Chic?"

His eyes widened with delight at having a sparring partner. "Maybe Retro Rounding?"

"On-Call Casual? But wait…" She indicated his dark jeans and leather jacket with a wave of her hand. "What do you call this?"

"This?" He opened his jacket to check himself out. "I call this Hip-Hop Doc." Then he looked down at his red tee shirt, featuring a garish cartoon picture of a burrito. "With a side of kitsch."

She shook her head in mock disapproval. "Looks more like Grunge G.P. to me. With a side of goofy."

And then he laughed—a wondrous, husky sound that made Charlotte feel like she had won a fabulous prize. He tapped his bottle against hers.

"Touché. Sorry for the corny attempt at humor. Just my way of trying to make up for your first day getting off to such a rotten start. That was entirely my fault."

For the first time since she'd started working at the clinic, the pins-and-needles anxiety that she felt in John's presence faded. The whole world felt new and shiny, like Seattle's streets after a spring rainstorm. But dangerous too. Because it would be harder to stick to her No Dating Co-workers rule if her colleague was as charming as he was handsome.

She took a quick sip of her soda, hoping her attraction didn't show. "Well, it did seem like you were having a bad day."

John tilted his head with a soft half-smile.

"You were talking to someone when I came in," she clarified. "It didn't sound like it was going well."

He was thoughtful for a moment. "Oh, right! That was the principal at Piper's school." He dragged a hand down his face. "That kid's gonna be the death of me."

"I saw her picture on your desk. She doesn't look that scary."

"No?" He chuckled. "Try this on for size." He ticked a list off on his fingers. "Three schools and four nannies in seven months."

Charlotte finished her soda and set it aside. "She works fast. I'll give you that."

John's expression grew serious. "It's not her fault. My brother got himself into some trouble last year. He's been sentenced to five years in prison on drug charges. Because of that, my eleven-year-old niece must live with her bachelor uncle on his tiny sailboat."

*Bachelor uncle.*

So, he was single. Interesting...

*Not interesting! Irrelevant!*

"She doesn't even have a room to call her own. I've listed the boat for sale, and I have been looking for a new place. Something cozy, not too far from the clinic, with a little backyard where we can grow a few vegetables. Maybe even get a pet, like she's been begging for. But between my clinic hours and taking care of Piper, there hasn't been much time for house-shopping."

"So, that's why I'm here?" Charlotte deduced.

"That is indeed why you're here. Though I'm not used to sharing my turf with other doctors." He gave her a wry smile. "As you may have noticed."

"Yes, I may have noticed that," Charlotte agreed solemnly.

He tilted his soda bottle her way. "Enough about me. Just who exactly are you?"

"In case you've forgotten, I'm Dr. Charlotte Owens…"

He waved her off. "Not the boring stuff. I want to hear the good stuff. Like why a doctor who graduated top of her class has a resume full of locum assignments. And how you wound up in my little clinic, with nothing but an old wood door for your desk and a surly doctor in your face?"

She chuckled, enjoying their new camaraderie. "The old wood door is growing on me."

*And maybe the surly doc was too.*

She gave a casual shrug before delivering the canned description of her nomadic life that she had perfected over the years. "It's a great way to see the world…" *pause for a moment…* "without paying for an expensive hotel room!"

*Perfect. Now laugh and toss your hair over your shoulder, just like the carefree girl you are.*

John nodded but his gaze was serious, not quite joining in the fun. "So, you're a destination doc, then? I've read about that—doctors who use locum tenens assignments to see the world, complete with travel stipends and per diems for meals."

She shrugged. "It keeps the bills paid, right?" Charlotte reached for her soda again, but it was empty, which gave her hands nothing to do. "Just trying to keep life casual and fun, you know? No worries about hospital politics or micromanaging supervisors. I help where I'm needed, then spend my free time on the slopes or in the surf. The whole work-hard-play-hard thing, right?"

It was enough to leave it at that. He didn't need to know the truth. That she couldn't settle down in one place for long before she got an itchy sensation at the nape of her neck. Like a warning that something dangerous was headed her way. He didn't need to know why she couldn't have a favorite pie café, or a puppy, or spend the weekend painting her living room.

Because once upon a time, she'd had all those things, only to have them snatched away in the middle of the night by a police officer with a kind face who'd knocked on the door, then shattered her world.

She'd survived that once and learned how to live a life that couldn't be taken away.

Because she always left first.

By now people had usually asked all sorts of questions about her travels. Then told her how they wished they could go back in time, be a little more adventurous before the pressures of work and family settled them into rigid routines. That had inspired her to launch her travel blog, where she posted the pictures and stories of her travels around the world.

"I'm surprised you landed in Seattle," John said, his gaze intense and watchful. "Not exactly an international destination, is it? Unless you're an avid skier or snowboarder?"

Under different circumstances, Charlotte would have loved to take her snowboard out to one of Seattle's many ski runs. But that was not what this trip was about. "Seattle's my hometown, actually. I just came back because my father left me his house."

"I'm so sorry. I didn't realize you'd lost your father."

"Thanks, but I didn't really know him. He and my mom broke up before I was born."

John's brows narrowed. "Yet he left you his house? Why?"

It was a great question, but she had no idea why he'd left her his house. The letter the attorney had given her, with its promise of explanation, was still sitting in her kitchen, on top of the toaster oven where she had warmed her English muffin that morning.

"He never married or had more kids, so maybe I was his only choice."

That was just about all the personal chit-chat she cared to share. It was time to get back to the reason for this lunch—Angel's need for an EKG.

She took a deep breath. "John, I know I'm only here—"

"So it's just you and your mom, then? Or do you have siblings?"

The question stumped her for a minute. She couldn't understand why he was so interested in her family. "It was just me and my mom. But she died when I was thirteen, and I didn't have other family so I grew up in foster care."

Time to lead him back to safe territory. Where was their lunch, anyway?

"So, I've been thinking about Angel and—"

"What was she like? Your mom?"

Goodness, were they still talking about her? She'd much rather show him her latest social media posts, pictures of a mountain resort ski clinic in Colorado where she'd spent a month working. But something about his intense gaze made her doubt she could distract him so easily.

"She was...you know...nice. Like most moms are, I guess. Anyway, we don't have much time before we have to get back to the clinic, John, and I really think we should discuss—"

John leaned back in his chair and folded his arms in a relaxed, easygoing pose. "We've got plenty of time, Charlotte. All the time in the world, if we need it."

Charlotte bit her lip, out of ideas for how to get John to focus on anything but her. It was unnerving being the center of his attention. The way he was looking at her. Something about his gaze made the world feel like it had narrowed to just the two of them.

"Well, she was a single mom, you know. Things weren't easy for her...raising me on her own."

She waited for some kind of response, but he was placid, waiting for her to continue. She huffed an impatient sigh.

"We didn't have a lot of money, but I remember these silly little traditions she created for me. Like my birthday. Every year, on the night before my birthday, she'd let me stay up until midnight. We'd go to the local diner and have a midnight milkshake party so we could celebrate the exact moment I turned one year older."

These were memories she hadn't thought about for a long time. She smiled reflexively, remembering her mother's irrational excitement at sharing a simple milkshake with her.

John smiled in response, revealing a pretty irresistible dimple. "She sounds lovely, Charlotte."

Charlotte spun her empty soda bottle between her palms. "She was."

*And I miss her a lot.*

But she didn't want to dwell on that. Her life worked best when she stayed focused on the future, filling it with the destinations and assignments that kept her mind busy and her heart full.

She took a sip of water to regain her equilibrium. How did he do that? Somehow, in the space of five minutes, she had told John more about herself than she'd told anyone else. Unnerving, for sure.

It was high time to get back to the matter at hand. She cleared her throat and tried again. "John, I know I'm only here at The Sunshine Clinic for a few months—"

But then she felt a strange buzzing sensation under her hands, which she had splayed across the table.

"Sorry," John muttered, reaching for his cell phone. "Dr. Bennett speaking."

Maybe she should just send him an email. She was giving up hope that she and John were ever going to talk about Angel and how to pay for her EKG.

"Mm-hmm… Just a few hours, then?" John frowned and ran a hand through his hair. "Well, that's better than nothing, Cassie. And good luck with your exams!"

When he hung up, his relaxed vibe disappeared. He rubbed his forehead as if he had a headache. When he finally looked up, his face was tense in a way that was very un-Dr. J.

"That was my sitter," he explained. "I have been thinking about Angel's EKG. I want to be ready when she comes back to the clinic so we can get that test done quickly. We have a charity fund at the hospital that might cover Angel's testing. But the application is long, and I can't access her file away from the office, so I need to stay late to get it done. I was hoping my sitter would do a few nights this week, but she's studying for college entrance exams and can only give me one evening."

Just then, the server who'd taken John's order appeared with two red baskets. She was young and prettyand seemed to dawdle at their table just a bit too long, paying far more attention to John than was strictly necessary.

Charlotte could hardly blame the girl for flirting. John was a sexy catch and now, after chatting, she knew he had a heart of gold too. What girl wouldn't want to make a guy like John hers?

But that didn't justify the flare of jealousy that knotted her stomach. John was her colleague—and a temporary one at that. She shifted in her chair, trying to get comfortable, and that sent her knee crashing into John's again.

She should pull back into her tiny sliver of space.

But she didn't want to.

His leg was solid and warm. In some small way, her knee against his felt like she was laying claim to him. Even if it was just the claim of having a private lunch date.

"Nice to meet you," the server said, letting her hand trail against John's shoulder as she left.

Charlotte reached for another chip, desperate to burn off some angsty energy. But the basket was empty. John was watching her now, his expression both curious and challenging. But he didn't move away. If anything, his knee seemed to be returning the pressure.

What on earth was she doing? This was a working lunch—nothing more! Why on earth was she flirting with him?

She shifted her attention to her burrito, hiding any expression that would reveal the riot of emotions doing battle in her body. She tried to saw into her burrito with her plastic fork and knife, but the thick tortilla shell made a mockery of her efforts.

"That won't work. You gotta just go for it. Like this."

John demonstrated the technique by taking a huge bite of his burrito, making Charlotte regret her order. It was always awkward, eating in front of coworkers, but even more so when the stoic coworker in question had a smoldering sex appeal and was leaning his knee against hers.

She didn't want to think about that for too long, so she mimicked John's burrito technique, and the next thing she knew she had unleashed a hot, delicious mess of charbroiled pork and spicy red sauce all over her fingers. Before she could blush again, John laughed with abandon, making everything—the stress of her new job, the messy burrito, her unexpected jealousy—seem miraculous and wonderful.

She couldn't help but join in. Maybe everything was going to be okay. Surely these strange reactions to John would quiet down soon, and they would settle into a sensible friendship.

But then John passed her a stack of napkins, and his fingers grazed hers. That was when she knew she was wrong. Terribly, horribly wrong. Because that barely noticeable touch sent a hot charge of electricity racing from her fingertips to some place deep in her core. The sensation was not friendly. It was hot and demanding...impossible to ignore.

She couldn't downplay her body's reactions to John anymore. There was something about him that sent her body into a mutinous riot every time he was near.

Charlotte had a sudden unbidden image of John working alone after hours in the dark clinic, with nothing but empty takeout containers to keep him company. The urge to offer her help was so powerful she had to bite her lip to keep herself in check. Staying after-hours at the clinic with a colleague she found insanely attractive was a terrible idea. Quite possibly the worst idea of her life. If she wanted to get back some semblance of self-control, she needed to keep her distance and stick strictly to business. No more lunches alone, no more talk of anything other than clinic business, and certainly no being alone with John after hours.

*No. Dating. Colleagues. Remember that simple but oh-so-effective rule, Charlotte?*

John wadded up his napkin and placed it in the now-empty basket. "Well, it was just an idea. We'll just have to hope that Angel finds her way back to the clinic soon and is ready to give us her real name."

That was a long shot and they both knew it. But obviously John was concerned for Angel too and had found a way to get her EKG covered. Without charity funding, there was little they could do for Angel unless she literally collapsed on the street and needed emergency care.

So, while keeping her distance might keep Charlotte's heart safe, it would do nothing for Angel, who was at a great deal more risk.

"I could help," Charlotte blurted, and then squeezed her eyes shut, wondering if John would be shocked at her boldness.

But John didn't look shocked. If anything, he seemed pleased. "Are you sure?"

Invisible hands pushed her from behind.

*Go for it!* some long-dormant voice screamed in her head. *You know you like him. Maybe something good will happen.*

Or maybe things would end badly and she would ruin her professional reputation.

But her next assignment was already set, and the tiny dimples that shadowed his smile were making all her reasons pop like bubbles in the sun.

"Yeah, I'm sure," she said quickly, before she could change her mind.

# CHAPTER FOUR

JOHN SURVEYED THE preparations for his after-hours meeting with Charlotte. For the millionth time, he wished for a proper conference room, or even just an office.

*Rome wasn't built in a day.*

For Pete's sake, Rome wasn't his problem right now. What *was* his problem were these jittery, restless feelings that were driving him mad as his workday ended. He was spending entirely too much time double-checking that he had every form and supply they could possibly need. Not to mention stressing about whether he should order dinner in, or if that would look too much like a date.

Because this wasn't a date. This was strictly two professionals collaborating on a difficult case.

Oh, what a load of bunk. He spent entirely too much time thinking about Charlotte to believe that he wasn't interested. Of course he was interested—what man in his right mind wouldn't be interested in Charlotte? She was beautiful and smart, naturally warm, and adventurous. With little hints of vulnerability that she thought she kept hidden. So endearing.

Before John could stress on any more details, Charlotte showed up.

"Very efficient," she said, nodding to the supplies he had organized with military precision.

She brushed his shoulder as she passed, and the faint hint of her touch, plus her unique jasmine-infused scent, did nothing to quiet his nerves. If anything, her proximity set off an increasingly familiar war between his heart and his head, with his heart taking a strong lead today.

Sarah appeared in the doorway. "Do you two need anything before I go?"

It was kind of her to offer. But, as much as John appreciated Sarah's help, he also craved time alone with Charlotte, without the constant interruption of phone calls and texts and questions and emergencies. Even their lunch date had been a noisy, cramped affair, but it had also been intriguing. He couldn't stop thinking about the press of her knee against his. Had that been intentional? Maybe not. That table had been tiny—it was probably just logistics.

But he didn't think so. There had been something challenging and exciting in her eyes when their knees touched, and he strongly suspected she had been flirting.

That possibility had haunted his thoughts ever since the lunch and he was beyond annoyed with himself. He needed to focus on Angel's funding, not wonder if Charlotte had the hots for him. In another time and space, yes—he would pursue Charlotte with all he had. But that time and head-space belonged to Piper now, and it wasn't fair to start something with Charlotte that was destined to end badly.

The lunch date had been good. They had broken the ice and were on a friendlier footing now. No need to hope for anything more than that.

John separated the application form and handed her half. "We don't have much time, so I thought we could each take half and help each other as needed. I've got to warn you, though—this could take some time."

As John handed her a pen, a terrible thought occurred to him. Seattle was Charlotte's home-town, surely full of friends, classmates, and maybe a former lover or two?

The sudden hot rush of raw jealousy that roiled in his gut was ridiculous, but he had to ask any-way. "Unless you need to leave soon because someone is waiting?"

Charlotte's pen stilled, but she didn't look up.

"Nope," she said, and it seemed a bit too cheerful in John's opinion. "No one is waiting for me."

Good grief, what was wrong with him? The rush of relief he felt was just wrong. Someone like Charlotte should not go home to an empty house. She was beautiful, and smart, with a huge, warm heart for teens like Angel. But he couldn't deny that it pleased him to know that she was free. John had his faults, but dishonesty wasn't one of them.

Charlotte and her pen got back to work. He should do the same. But his mind was in a state of mutiny and his gaze lingered on her profile. He felt an invisible current buzzing between them that made him hyper aware of everything about her. The heat of her body, the rise and fall of her chest, the way she pursed her lips just so when she worked… His gaze lingered just a breath too long and she looked up to catch him staring.

Time froze for a moment, maybe two, before she gifted him a sweet, spontaneous smile. Then she shook her head in a scolding fashion and glanced him with her elbow.

"Come on, lazy bones. Get back to work."

A very sensible idea. He should totally do that. But the black squiggly marks on the pages before him could not compete with Charlotte for his attention. He shook his head to clear the fog.

"So, how did you end up living on a sailboat?" she asked. "It sounds quite romantic."

He laughed, thinking of his tiny living space, anchored just feet from his neighbors, with the constant briny scent of old boats and sea water.

"It started as a way to save money on rent while I was in med school. And I don't know about romantic... Last week I had the scare of my life. I woke up in the wee hours of the morning to a terrible commotion on the deck. I thought someone was trying to break in! Piper hid in the bathroom while I went to check it out, baseball bat in hand."

Charlotte waited, her eyes wide. "What happened?"

He laughed. "It was just a sea lion, looking for shelter from predators. Or a free meal."

"A case of barking and entering, then?"

"You could say that." He chuckled.

She shook her head as she refocused on the paperwork before her. "You know, in all the travel adventures and mishaps I've written about on my blog, I don't believe I have a sailing story. Maybe I could interview you sometime? Get a few pictures and put it on my blog?"

Before John could think it through, he blurted, "Better than that—I'll take you sailing!"

Her laugh was spontaneous and relaxed. "That would be great."

John was sorely tempted to bang his head against the table a few times. Maybe that was what it would take to knock some sense into him.

He quickly changed the conversation to keep himself out of trouble.

"But, as much as I love sailing, *The House Call* is no place for a tween girl to grow up. She needs privacy and space…a backyard. Even that pet she's been begging for."

And as much as he hated the idea of being anchored to a mortgage and property taxes, Piper's need for stability was more important than his whimsical dreams of adventure.

He hated it, but a familiar pang of nostalgia roiled in his gut. Nostalgia for his life before Piper, when he had been free to live as he pleased. With his mother gone and his brother grown, it had felt like the past was finally behind him. Finally, it was time for him to pursue his own dreams, with no fear of hurting or disappointing anyone.

But, like the Greek god Icarus, his dreams had taken him too close to the sun, searing his wings until they could hold him no more. It was his brother, though, not him, who'd crashed to the earth, no longer buoyed up by John's promise to be his keeper.

What a terrible thing it was…watching others pay for his mistakes.

Charlotte laid her pen down and tilted her head. "So, do I have this right? You started to take care of your brother when you were probably still wearing action hero pajamas. Then you started a clinic to make sure Seattle's homeless teens received good medical care. And now you're raising your niece."

He felt hypnotized by those indigo-blue eyes. Utterly incapable of looking away.

"I have to ask…" She leaned forward, and the slight movement was enough to stir the air between them, filling the space with her intriguing jasmine scent. "Just who takes care of Dr. J?"

Long-buried emotions rumbled deep in his gut. Her question touched a soft, raw place in his heart that was best left alone. In all the years he had tried to fill his father's shoes no one had ever asked about him, or the sacrifices he'd had to make. When kids his age had been buzzing about baseball tryouts or running off to spend a hot summer day at the nearby creek, he'd had to focus on his little family, making sure Michael was safe so his mother could work hard… so hard…making sure they had a roof over their head and some food in the refrigerator. It had never occurred to him to want more. Or maybe it had and he'd just learned to be numb long ago. Because there hadn't ever been any "more" to be had.

Charlotte was waiting patiently for answers he didn't have. Everything about her felt receptive and warm. She wanted to know him—and, as much of a revelation as that was, it was even more of one to realize he wanted to be known by her.

He coughed and shifted in his chair. "No one, I guess. It's just me and Piper."

"And before that just you and your brother?"

He nodded. It was just the three of them when his dad had skipped out, leaving his mom three months behind on rent and a boatload of bills. But he didn't want to dive into all that. It was getting late, and he wanted to focus on Angel's application—not the mess of responsibilities that his father had left on his young shoulders.

When they'd finished the application John walked Charlotte to her car, grateful for her help but still haunted by her question.

*Just who takes care of Dr. J?*

All his life he'd done his best to fill the void his father's absence had left behind. It was second nature for him to take care of Michael, the teens, and now Piper...to make sure she didn't fall into the same abyss as her father.

He had no regrets for his decisions so far, but was this his destiny? It often seemed that way. He was Piper's guardian for the next few years. Then Michael would return and need help getting his life back on track. The clinic would always need him to fight for money and resources. And someday Sarah would retire, leaving him without a trusted partner to figure this out.

Charlotte glanced up at him as they walked. She was wearing a wool pea coat, dark leggings, and black boots. Her hair was pulled up in her trademark messy bun that left tendrils of loose curls framing her face. Beneath the weak lighting of the parking lot's lamps, her blue eyes were as dark and stormy as the sea he loved. She gave him a little smile and then he knew. He wasn't imagining things, and her knee against his had not been an accident. That electric buzz he felt when she was near…? She felt it too. He was sure of it.

Her car chirped twice as she unlocked it with her remote and the interior lights came on. She arranged her things in the passenger seat, then met him at the driver's side. She reached for the door handle, then paused and turned back, her eyes wide with questions. She seemed less confident out here in the dark, just the two of them alone, the moment full of possibility.

Her question still lingered in his heart. What about him? When *would* it be his turn to find happiness?

He stepped forward, drawn to her warmth, wanting to touch her, hold her. Maybe now was his time. Right now…with her.

His cell phone beeped twice—the distinctive tone that signaled a text from his sitter. A sign that he was lingering too long in this quiet space with Charlotte. And a reminder of what was at stake. He was Piper's guardian because of the mistakes he had made with her father. He had to do better by Piper. He just had to.

Maybe later would be his time. When Michael came home. Or when Piper was older.

His jaw clenched with frustration. Yes, that was what he had. A whole basket of *maybes* to keep him warm at night.

Charlotte was practically in his arms, her gaze raking his face, trying to make sense of the emotions he couldn't hide. But as much as he wanted to feel her warm body against his, he needed to do the right thing—because following his desires would only hurt her in the end. After years of practice, he thought he'd become numb to the resentment of turning his back on what he wanted. But the effort of leaving Charlotte had his fingers curling into tight, hard fists.

*Deep breath. Count to three. Then open the car door and send her off with a brisk goodnight.*

Quick and painless. Like ripping off a Band-Aid.

But in the end his body betrayed him. He found himself bending to graze her lips with a featherlight kiss, stealing something small and warm for himself. Her lips were soft and receptive, a safe harbor on this bitterly cold night. His hand wandered of its own accord, finding her hair, then her neck, trailing over it with his fingers, setting loose a flurry of goosebumps in his wake. Her gloved hand found and grasped his, as if steadying herself. How his body raged for more—a deeper kiss, a longer night...

But he had to put a stop to this. He'd already gone too far.

"I'm sorry," he whispered, though he lacked the strength to explain why.

Before his heart could make more trouble, he turned on his heel and strode back to the clinic. An icy wind kicked up, slicing through his thin tee shirt and raking his face with its cruel, cold claws.

Her car door slammed, making him pause at the clinic's entrance. When her engine revved, he fought off the urge to call her back. Instead, he channeled his frustration into a ferocious pull on the clinic door that made it bang against the cement support post with a satisfying crack.

Then he ducked back into the clinic.

Back where he belonged.

Charlotte stopped by the coffee station before her last appointment of the day. It had been a long, grueling day, thanks to an influenza outbreak.

But Sarah had made things a little better by leaving a basket of home-baked treats near the coffee pot.

Charlotte was unwrapping an enticing blueberry muffin when she heard John approach. Her spine spontaneously stiffened at the sound of his footsteps.

All weekend she had been unable to escape her thoughts of John and that phantom kiss. She could still feel how his lips had brushed hers, so light she'd wondered if it was a dream.

It made her feel foolish to be thinking this way, unable to shake thoughts of him no matter what she tried. Her weekend had been a frenzy of cleaning and organizing, followed by long runs through the upscale neighborhood of her father's home. All so she could escape the awful yearning that his teasing kiss had left behind.

But even when she had worn herself out she'd still been able to remember the way she'd felt, pressed to John's chest. Like he was a mighty fortress, sheltering her from harm.

*This must stop.*

That was what she had vowed that morning on her way to work. She needed to come to her senses and put a stop to whatever this was between them. Infatuation? A crush? Whatever. They were both adults with sexual needs. Obviously they had developed some harmless attraction. So what? Attractions weren't destiny. They could be fun, or they could be annoying, but they were always meaningless so long as you didn't act on them.

From now on she would stick to her side of the clinic. No more lunches with John. No more after-hours work sessions. She would just focus on her patients and confer with John only when absolutely necessary.

And now here he was, standing behind her, his breath stirring her hair. Ready or not, it was time to put her new resolve to the test.

"Afternoon," John said. "How was your weekend?"

He reached across her for the cream and sugar packets, sending notes of sandalwood and citrus into her space. Her traitorous body went on full alert, forcing her to close her eyes against the rush of desire.

Sticking to her side of the clinic was going to be a challenge.

"Very busy," she croaked.

Her hamstrings still ached from the long miles she had logged, trying to outrun her thoughts of him.

For a long minute John doctored his coffee with two creams and one sugar, as was his habit. Charlotte willed herself back to her office, where she'd be safely sheltered from his tempting masculine aura. But her body seemed frozen in place, forcing her into an inner battle of self-control.

Just when she'd mustered enough willpower to grab her coffee cup and leave, he stopped her with a question.

"Do you have a moment? There's something I'd like to discuss."

*Alone? In your office?*

Her resolve was too new and shiny for this level of challenge!

"Of course," she whispered.

She followed him on autopilot, trying to ignore how the soft, well-washed denim of his jeans hugged every masculine curve of his backside.

He closed the door behind her. For one wild moment she thought he might push her up against the wall, crush her mouth with his, and finish what he'd started in the parking lot last week.

And if he did? Would she politely demur and explain her new sensible plan for self-preservation?

No, she would not do that. She would lose her ever-loving mind—that she was sure of. And then she would need a new plan.

What on earth was wrong with her? Vowing to retreat one minute…willing to toss the rules out the window the next.

*Casual and fun!*

That was her motto when it came to romance.

*Easy-breezy, no promises, no demands.*

But when it came to John, what she felt was anything but casual or fun. It was intense and greedy…like a wild animal she couldn't control.

John leaned against his exam table. She stood near the door and felt a brief impulse to bolt before things got any more complicated.

She took a deep breath to steady herself.

*It was just a silly little kiss*, she chided herself. *He probably doesn't even remember it.*

"Thanks for your time," John said. He crossed his arms over his chest, making his leather jacket strain against his bulky arms. "We should talk about what happened last week. After we finished Angel's application."

*Crap.* He wanted to talk about the kiss.

"Okay," she whispered.

"I was out of line, kissing you like that. I apologize for being inappropriate, and I genuinely hope I didn't make you uncomfortable."

*Uncomfortable? No, sir.*

There were a lot of things that kiss had made her feel, but uncomfortable was not one of them.

"Listen, Charlotte… I hope I'm not out of line to say this. You're a beautiful woman, and I'm very attracted to you."

She bit her lip, unsure how to respond. Of course, she knew he felt something for her— that was obvious from the kiss. But hearing him say it out loud…even the way her name rolled off his lips…she felt a strong desire to throw the rules out the window and just let her body take the lead.

The only thing that stopped her was his expression. He didn't look like a hopeful lover confessing his feelings. More like a fugitive confessing his crimes.

"But I have Piper in my life now. She's still adjusting to the trauma of what happened with her father. It's just a terrible time for me to be…"

Charlotte felt her heart sink. Which made no sense since she had come to work determined to keep her distance from John.

But there was a tiny piece of her heart that had spent the weekend wondering if John had thought of her half as much as she had obsessed over him.

And now she knew. He *had* been thinking about her. A lot.

About what a mistake it had been to kiss her.

He didn't want her in his bed, or maybe even in his life.

She could practically feel her heart latching every window and bolting every door. Every beat screamed *Mayday! Mayday! Mayday!* as her body stiffened for battle.

She jutted out her chin and sharpened her

sword. "It's fine," she said coolly. "I didn't think it meant anything. In fact, I hardly remember it."

John stuffed his hands in his pockets and looked down at his shoes. "Right... I'm glad you understand."

Charlotte fought off the urge to snort. She understood just fine.

*Inconvenient. Unwanted. Go away.*

Sarah knocked and poked her head around the door. "Sorry to interrupt. Dr. Owens, your patient is ready." Then her gaze ping-ponged between them. "Unless you want me to reschedule?"

Charlotte pushed herself off the wall. "No need, Sarah. I think we're done here."

*So done.*

But she couldn't help but steal a glance at John. He had his back to her, hands still stuffed deep in his leather jacket as he looked out the window. She heard his long, audible sigh just before she left.

*He was probably relieved that it was over.*

Well, she was too. This was what she got for even *thinking* about breaking the rule that had kept her heart safe all these years.

Lesson learned—thankfully before any real damage had been done. She should be dancing a jig down the hall. *GypsyMD* was a free-spirited gal. No strings holding her down, thank you very much.

But instead of relief or joy she was left with a bitter taste in her mouth and one burning question.

Why did getting what she wanted feel so bad?

# CHAPTER FIVE

CHARLOTTE STOPPED BY the coffee station for the cup of coffee she hadn't got. Drat, the pot was empty. She didn't have time to make another, so she headed to her exam room where Sam, a fifteen-year-old boy complaining of headaches, was waiting.

Sarah had put an asterisk next to the symptoms, which was her way of signaling that the teen was making a complaint about one thing but probably needed to be seen for something else. This sometimes happened when a patient had a private concern or didn't know exactly what they needed.

Sam was seated on the exam table facing the door when Charlotte entered. He wore combat boots and camouflage pants—the sort of things he could find at a military surplus store. His sweatshirt was zipped up, the hood pulled far over his head. It looked like he had created a safe cocoon for himself.

"Hey, Sam."

She was about to ask about his headaches when she noticed a strong odor in the room. Infection? Poor hygiene? No, more like decay. And the closer she got to the thin boy with the big brown eyes, the stronger the scent was.

"So, Sarah tells me you're not feeling well."

Over the past few weeks Charlotte had learned to keep her questions open-ended, even if her patient had written something specific on their intake form. It allowed the teen more space to share what was wrong, and often one symptom was really three or four.

The boy bit his lip and looked away. "My feet hurt."

"Okay. Let's get those boots off so I can take a look."

Charlotte kept her voice as light and casual as she could, trying to distract herself from the over-powering odor. Her brain was already reviewing the possibilities. He could have an out-of-control fungal infection. Or boots that needed to be replaced. Maybe a bacterial infection that had gotten out of hand.

The boy just sat there, looking straight down at the floor, not moving. His hood was draped over his face now, hiding him from the world and from her.

She washed her hands slowly, planning how to proceed. Charlotte was accustomed to having parents in the room with her patients, who could provide a full medical history and ensure compliance. But here it was just her and Sam.

Her first instinct was to lecture him about all the bad things that might happen if she didn't treat whatever problem he had. But nothing about his body language or demeanor said that he was resistant or rebellious.

Instead, he looked ashamed—which broke her heart. Why should he feel one second of shame for something that wasn't his fault?

*What would John do?*

She was surprised when that thought jumped into her head, considering how infuriated she'd been with him just a few minutes ago. But whatever her personal issues were with John, he was a hero to the teens who came to the clinic. They trusted him implicitly, and he'd earned that trust by being honest and reliable. If John were here, he wouldn't lecture Sam—that was for sure. He would slow things down...way down...so it seemed like he had all the time in the world to spend with the boy.

That was probably why he was always running late. But it was also why the teens trusted him so much.

Time to borrow a page from John's playbook.

"Sam, I'm going to take your boots off now, okay?"

Charlotte took one foot in her hands. Sam didn't resist or pull away, so she felt she was on the right track. The boot was old, and very worn, the sole pulling away from the upper. She untied the laces slowly. She would have liked to keep up a steady stream of mindless chit-chat to set his mind at ease.

*So, how's school? What's your favorite subject? Do you have any pets?*

But none of those questions felt right. She didn't know if Sam had a bed of his own, let alone pets or the ability to get to school every day.

As soon as she tried to remove his boot, she saw Sam's first problem. The boots were at least two sizes too small for him. As she tugged and pulled on the boot Sam winced in obvious pain.

"My goodness, Sam! How do you get these off every day?"

He shot her a deer-in-the-headlights look. That was when she realized he probably didn't take his boots off every day. Because it was too painful.

"I'm sorry...this might hurt a bit. You ready?"

He peered at her through long bangs, fear shadowing his eyes.

"I promise you'll feel better when this is done. Okay?"

He bit his lip, then looked away. He gave her a faint nod again.

She applied steady, even pressure as she pulled

and wiggled. Eventually the boot gave way—at the same time Sam cried out in pain. Any feeling of triumph that she might have felt at winning the boot war was instantly overshadowed by waves of the strong smell of infection. Charlotte forced herself not to react. Sam knew darn well the odor was coming from him. He didn't need her to remind him.

"Okay, Sam, one more time."

She repeated the process for his other boot, then began her assessment.

Sam's socks were in tatters, barely covering the sores that covered his feet. The sores had broken down the skin and were causing tissue loss, which was the source of the odor. She couldn't imagine how Sam managed to get around on feet that were in this condition.

Charlotte could feel Sam's eyes on her, fearing judgement or ridicule. This, she realized, was the moment when John had the most impact on the teens. When someone had revealed their greatest source of shame and pain, what did you say?

She slowly and gently released his feet, then looked up at him, feeling the weight of the world—Sam's world—on her shoulders. He just wanted to hear that everything would be okay. That was all any of the teens who came to the clinic wanted.

Charlotte shrugged and smiled. "I can fix this, Sam. No problem."

Sam bit his lip again, then nodded and visibly relaxed. Charlotte started by soaking his feet in an Epsom bath to help with the inflammation. He had a severe case of trench foot—a condition she'd honestly never expected to see outside of a medical textbook. But it made sense. Winter was Seattle's rainy season. And, while Charlotte loved to listen to the sounds of a rainstorm while she cooked dinner or read a book by the fire, days of rain were a nightmare for homeless teens. Their clothing, sleeping bags and footwear all got soaked. If they didn't have a safe, dry place to go, and extra pairs of dry socks and shoes, this was what happened.

She gently toweled his feet off, avoiding the blisters. "Does this hurt, Sam?"

He shook his head. "Not really. My feet used to hurt a lot, but then I decided to keep my boots on all the time. Pretty soon I stopped feeling anything at all."

That was not a good sign. Losing feeling meant his feet had been wet long enough to cause damage to his circulation and nerve function. As he healed, the feeling would return with a vengeance, which meant days of intense pain.

Charlotte sprayed his feet with antibiotic, then handed him a pair of new, clean socks. "I'm going to give you several pairs of dry socks, Sam, and we'll find some shoes that fit you from our donation box. You're going to need to keep your feet clean and dry, so they can heal. I'll make sure you get some antibiotic spray, too, and some pain relievers. I'd like to see you again next week, if that's all right?"

"Sure."

He slid off the table and gingerly landed on his feet. She handed him a pair of throwaway slippers to wear with his socks. Not a fashionable look, but that was probably all he could handle until his feet were in better shape.

"The best thing is to keep your feet clean, elevated, and exposed to the air for healing. Are you staying someplace where you can be warm and dry, Sam? In a shelter, maybe? Couch surfing with friends?"

His lips were a flat, tight line again as he shook his head.

"Let's go see Sarah, then. She has a way of finding shelter space when no one else can."

Sam's medical needs would help him get placed higher on the waiting lists too. With any luck he'd have a safe place to be while Social Services worked on finding a longer-term solution for him.

Charlotte left Sam with Sarah, after a hug and

a reminder to schedule his follow-up for the following week.

Sarah looked more frantic than usual. "Oh, honey, have you heard the news?"

"No?"

"It's Piper. She's had some kind of accident at school. John dashed off to meet the ambulance at the hospital. I'm afraid it's too late to have an on-call doctor fill in. Can you manage these last appointments on your own?"

There were two teens in the waiting area. One was stretched out on the vinyl chairs, grabbing a nap, while the other flipped through the pages of a magazine that was probably two years old.

"Of course—but what happened?"

"I don't know yet. John tore out of here twenty minutes ago." She waved her cell phone. "I'm going to wrap things up here, then head to the hospital. Want me to wait for you? Or will you meet us there?"

Charlotte froze with uncertainty. No matter how angry she had been at his apparent rejection of her as a romantic partner, she knew how much John loved his niece. Seeing her injured and in pain was probably killing him.

But that didn't mean he wanted her at the hospital. He'd made it clear that they were workmates, nothing more.

"I'm not sure yet," Charlotte said, still not able

to give a firm no. Because, as much as she wanted to push him away, she couldn't forget how he'd looked when he'd ended their kiss that night at the clinic. And that strange apology that didn't make sense... Was he really sorry he had kissed her? Or sorry that he had to stop?

She didn't have to decide right now. She could see these last two patients while Sarah went to John. Maybe Piper's accident wasn't that serious. Or maybe John would make his intentions known with a text or a phone call.

Sarah promised to let her know any news, then left for the hospital. Charlotte locked the front door behind her before returning to her exam room. She tried to focus on her last two patients, hoping that work would be her refuge from intrusive thoughts about John. Her heart might be closed off to any romantic entanglements with him, but that didn't mean she didn't care. He was a genuinely good man, who gave his best to everyone who counted on him. He deserved the support of friends at a time like this.

But did she belong at the hospital while he was facing a crisis? Well, the answer to that was probably no. He hadn't texted her since he'd left the clinic.

Besides, this was a family emergency—and she wasn't family. That was the price of being the Queen of Easy-Breezy. No messy commitments...no risk of loss. Just the way she liked it. But it also meant that no one ever thought to call on her for help, because she was always on her way somewhere else.

After she'd seen her patients, she locked up the clinic and headed to her car. It was strange, not seeing John's black SUV in its usual parking spot.

*He's fine. You're fine. Everybody's fine. Just go home.*

But it was impossible to imagine being back in her huge, empty house with a takeout order. Acting like it was just a normal night.

But that was what he wanted. For them to be just colleagues. That was what they both wanted.

*You can't have your cake and eat it too, Owens.*

A funny little phrase that meant she had to accept the limits of being colleagues. A sensible and wholly unsatisfying arrangement.

She made her way through the parking lot to the exit. Turned her left-hand signal on and waited for an opening in the traffic.

And then her phone chimed.

A text message. From John.

Hey.

That was all.

It was enough. She changed her turn signal from left to right and headed to the hospital.

* * *

Charlotte found John in the pediatric waiting room. Her heart gave an involuntary squeeze when she saw his bulky frame folded into a hard plastic chair. His eyes were closed, and he had his head resting on one hand, a day's worth of beard shadowing his jaw. All traces of the calm, cool and collected doctor she worked with every day were gone. He just looked weary and vulnerable.

She touched him lightly on the knee. "John?"

He woke up, dazed, looking at his surroundings in confusion.

Charlotte slid into the chair next to him. "What happened?"

John rubbed his eyes. "Bike accident at school. Piper was messing around, I guess, and went over the handlebars. Compound fracture of her fibula." He sighed and leaned back in his chair, the very image of weary exhaustion. "She'll need to stay a night or two for observation after her surgery, to make sure she doesn't have head trauma too. Then I can take her home."

Sarah appeared with a tray laden with mugs of coffee and half a Boston cream pie. Charotte had worked at the clinic long enough to know that in Sarah's worldview, there wasn't a problem in the world that couldn't be improved with hot coffee and a slice of pie.

"Home?" Sarah snorted. "To what? That sardine can you call home?"

"Yes, back to *The House Call*. Where else?" John clutched his coffee mug like it was a life preserver.

Sarah was having none of it. "That is a terrible place for Piper to recover. She has a broken leg, for Pete's sake! How is she going to get on and off the boat?"

"I'll help her."

Sarah rolled her eyes. "And what about bathing? She needs a bathtub where she can soak but keep her leg elevated and dry. And how comfortable is she going to be on a tiny little berth instead of a real, soft bed? What about the damp? And the mold?"

Sarah made good points. Charlotte had seen firsthand at the clinic how much longer it took their patients to recover from viruses and injuries because they didn't have the right environment to rest and recover.

Just then Charlotte looked up to find Sarah pinning her with a pointed stare. A *very* pointed stare.

"If only John had a friend with a spare bedroom or two. That sure would be helpful."

Charlotte felt her eyebrows dart upwards. Good grief, was Sarah suggesting that John and Piper stay with her?

No. That was crazy. Especially after they had just agreed to stay in their professional lanes. She and John barely knew each other. And Piper didn't know her at all. It would be strange, and awkward, and the complete opposite of keeping their distance as they had agreed.

It would also be helpful and kind and generous. All the things she had wanted this forced trip back to Seattle to be about.

Sarah was right. She had heard Charlotte complain enough about her father's home and its endless renovations. Every problem solved seemed to reveal two more. But renovations or not, the house was massive, with plenty of room for John and Piper. They could even have their own bathrooms, complete with luxurious marble baths and heated floor tiles.

She had no excuse not to offer the use of her home—except for her bruised ego and her desire to keep complications to a bare minimum.

She took a deep breath, then jumped in with both feet. "You could stay with me."

John looked up from his coffee, stunned and confused.

"My father's house—I mean, my house. It's huge and... Well, wait..."

She found her phone and navigated to the professional photos her real estate agent had sent a few days earlier in preparation for the house sale.

She flipped through the photos with John. "There's a bedroom off the kitchen that would be perfect for Piper, with its own bathroom. I could ask the work crew to add handrails to the bathtub if you want." She scrolled to the photos of the owner's suite. "And you could have this room...just down the hall from Piper."

"I don't know, Charlotte. This seems..."

"Weird?"

Because it was. It was extremely weird to invite a coworker of any kind, let alone one she had kissed and then agreed to avoid, to share her home for a few weeks.

He smiled. "Yes, but I was thinking more that it's an imposition."

"Not really. Honestly, the house is so huge I'll probably hardly know you're there."

*Oh, so not true.*

She would be acutely aware of his presence, but he didn't need to know that.

"I don't know... Maybe I could find a short-term rental for a month or two."

"Oh, John," Sarah huffed, crossing her arms across her chest. "You are not going to find a short-term two-bedroom rental on short notice. Stop being such a stubborn mule."

Emotions played out on John's face like a movie screen.

*Stubborn, protective, uncertain, confused.*

She knew what he was feeling because she felt it too. Inviting him to stay with her after they'd agreed to ignore their attraction felt like asking for trouble. But there were bigger issues at play than their feelings.

"Listen, John. This house I've inherited… Well, it's complicated. Let's just say that I've learned that my father chose his wealth over me when I was young. So I have resented the hell out of this house and all the suffering it represents for me and my mom."

She spontaneously grabbed his hand for emphasis, feeling strength in his broad palm and fingers.

"Using the house to help you and Piper would make me so happy. In some small way, it would make up for my father's selfishness, if that makes sense."

John's eyes were full of questions that she couldn't possibly answer right now.

He opened his mouth to protest, but then his shoulders slumped in resignation. "Maybe you're right. It would be good for Piper."

For the second time that day Charlotte got her way, yet she felt no sense of triumph. Already her emotions were a jumble of attraction and fear of getting hurt. Sure, they had agreed to keep things professional, but that was going to be a lot harder if John was showering and sleeping and living just down the hall from her.

A doctor in green scrubs approached. "Dr. Bennett?"

John jumped to his feet. "That's me."

"Piper's out of surgery. Everything went very well. Would you like to see her?"

"Yes, please!" He turned back to Charlotte. "One more thing… Thank you."

The next thing she knew he had drawn her to him, enfolding her in a warm hug that seemed to narrow the world down to just the two of them. She tried to return the hug like a friendly co-worker would, but when she felt the tension coiled in the muscles of his back her hands just itched to massage his worry away.

"For everything," he whispered against her ear.

Then he released her and followed the surgeon, leaving her to wonder what else he was grateful for.

# CHAPTER SIX

How HAD HE made such a mess of things?

Charlotte's kitchen was in total chaos. John had used every surface to make the dough and homemade sauce for his infamous pizza recipe. The kitchen was warm and infused with the tantalizing aroma of cheese and pepperoni. The price of his efforts was flour spilled on the floor and tomato sauce splashed on the counter.

But that wasn't the mess he was worried about.

That particular complication was still at the clinic. He and Piper had moved into Charlotte's home during the day, while Charlotte was at work. Because he had taken family leave as soon as Piper was injured, he had not seen Charlotte since the night at the hospital when she'd invited him and Piper to stay with her while Piper recovered.

That must have been so uncomfortable for her. He knew Sarah had strongarmed her into the invitation. It was for Piper's sake that he'd agreed to stay, but he was still looking for a short-term rental. It was the right thing to do—especially since he had made such a huge deal about sticking to the boundaries of their working relationship.

What a hard conversation that had been. The last thing he'd wanted was for Charlotte to feel he was rejecting her—he wasn't! And he didn't want her to think he regretted that kiss. He just regretted the timing. Had they met last year—or a few years later, when Michael was reunited with his daughter—maybe a relationship would have worked out.

But Piper had to come first. She was just a kid, trying to make sense of a world that had turned upside down on her. If he hadn't gotten so caught up in his dream of starting The Sunshine Clinic maybe he would have seen the signs that his brother was in trouble. It was his fault that Piper had lost the dad she loved with all her heart, if only temporarily. He couldn't take the chance that surrendering to his chemistry with Charlotte might make him miss signs of trouble with Piper too.

But he could at least apologize for making such a mess of things with Charlotte. Hopefully his homemade pizza and a nice bottle of Chianti would smooth things over. Put them back on good footing as colleagues and hopefully even friends.

"More pizza?"

Piper didn't even look up. She was sitting on

one of the stools that flanked the kitchen bar. She had a laptop balanced on her lap and her leg, now wrapped in a new white cast, was propped on the chair next to her. Her fingers flew over her keyboard as she played some online game.

He sighed, missing the chatty girl he'd used to visit in California. There was little chance she'd want to watch a movie or play a board game with him tonight. Not with the fate of the universe playing out on her computer screen.

The oven alarm went off, signaling that the last pizza was done. This one was for Charlotte—his attempt to mimic the spinach and feta pizza she sometimes ordered for lunch at the clinic. Not quite as obvious as a big bouquet of flowers, but hopefully the effect would be the same.

He slid the pizza off the pizza stone and onto a large serving platter. Then opened the bottle of Chianti so it could breathe before Charlotte got home.

"Charlotte will be here soon. Do you want to stay and hang out with us?"

Piper looked up and seemed to give it a good think. But then she bit her lip and shook her head. She tucked her tablet under her arm and slid off the stool, refusing his offer to help her back to her room.

Damn, he wished he could connect with her somehow.

"Hey," Charlotte said from the doorway.

John had seriously underestimated how seeing her again would affect him. She had her hair pulled back in a casual ponytail, revealing the sharp curve of her jaw and the length of her smooth neck. Her cargo pants hugged her curves just right, and her soft, peach-toned tee shirt brought out the color in her cheeks.

"Hey, yourself," John said, resisting the urge to welcome her home with a soft, warm kiss.

Exactly the kind of urge he'd feared when Sarah had proposed this arrangement.

Her gaze slowly scanned the kitchen. John hoped she wouldn't take offense at the mess of flour and sauce and pans all over her counters. But when her gaze settled back on him, she just smiled.

"This is nice, John. The house actually feels cozy."

He knew just what she meant. Once Piper was settled in her room, he had taken a tour of the downstairs. He knew Charlotte's home was under renovation, and he wanted to know which areas were too dangerous for Piper to navigate on crutches. Thankfully the crew seemed to be focusing on Charlotte's basement this week, working to remedy some water damage.

The house was just as Charlotte had described—spacious and grand in many ways, but also cold.

Maybe it was because many of the rooms were empty, cleared of furniture in preparation for the eventual house sale. But in a way John couldn't describe, the house felt like an empty shell. As if no one had ever really lived there. It troubled him that this was where Charlotte ended her days after caring for their patients at the clinic.

John held up the pizza. "Made your favorite."

She cocked her head. "You made a pizza just for me?"

"It was the least I could do, considering Piper and I have taken over your castle."

She smiled as she looked around. Piper's homework waited on the counter...a single shoe had been kicked off by the door. "I like what you've done with the place. Speaking of Piper—where is she? I'd love to meet her."

"She's either battling aliens or role-playing in an alternative universe at the moment. I'm sure she'll join us later, when she sees the chocolate eclairs we're having for dessert."

John reached into the glass display case that was suspended over the kitchen island. He found two wine glasses among the stacks of porcelain dinnerware and poured her a glass of wine. He detected a hint of her perfume as she took the glass. Something sweet and mysterious, plus those jasmine notes that always trailed after her. For just a moment, he could imagine this as his life. Making dinner for Charlotte, with Piper safe and sound down the hall. Just like a real family.

Whoa! What on earth was he thinking? He and Piper hadn't even spent a night in Charlotte's home and he was already thinking of them as a family! He turned away from Charlotte, hoping she wouldn't see the intense emotions playing out in his heart.

"I have some good news," she said, reaching past him for plates.

Her arm brushed his as she passed, setting every hair on his arm to attention.

"I could use some good news." John busied himself with finding cutlery and napkins for dinner. He had to get these unruly emotions under control.

Charlotte added pizza slices to two plates. "The chair of pediatrics signed off on Angel's charity application. It's being forwarded to the financial services department for processing. Once we get official approval, I'll set up Angel's EKG."

That was good news indeed. But the rush of relief he should have felt was muted from the stress of his week.

Charlotte took a small bite of pizza, then closed her eyes with pleasure. "*So* delicious, John. I think this is the first homemade meal I've had since I came to Seattle."

"Seriously? You don't cook?"

"I move around too much to justify hauling around heavy kitchen mixers or a full set of saucepans. Besides, there's no better way to experience a new place than through its food." She set her glass down and crossed her arms on the counter. "I thought you'd be more excited about Angel's application. Is something wrong?"

Was something wrong? What a funny question. Six months ago, his life had been simple enough. He'd worked too much, then spent all his free time preparing *The House Call* for its next adventure. Now he was living as a guest in the house of a colleague he was incredibly attracted to, thanks to his failure to keep his niece safe, no matter how hard he'd tried.

"No, everything's fine."

Because it had to be. His life and his problems had nothing to do with Charlotte. She was a free spirit, destined to spend just a month or two in Seattle before she flew off to more exciting destinations and assignments. She didn't need to be burdened with his problems.

"I see." She drummed her nails against the counter. Then she cocked her head and smiled playfully. "Don't mind if I do."

He mimicked her head-tilt. "Don't mind if you do, what?"

"Have that second glass of wine you want to offer me."

She peered past his shoulder to the half-full bottle of Chianti he had placed out of reach.

He shook his head with chagrin. "What is it about you that makes my manners disappear?"

That was a rhetorical question, of course. He knew exactly why he acted like an angsty teen whenever she was around. Because he liked her. A lot. She was beautiful, smart, and when he wasn't acting like an idiot, they had a really cool vibe between them.

He poured her another glass of wine, then topped off his own. He kept her company while she ate a second slice of pizza and caught him up on the clinic's schedule for the upcoming week.

When she'd finished, she blew him a chef's kiss. "That was delicious, John. Thank you." She folded her napkin, pushed it aside and leaned back in her chair. "All right, Bennett... Start talking."

"About what?"

"About whatever's making you look as mopey as a hound dog, as Sarah would say."

"Do I?"

He ran a hand across his jaw, stubble chafing his palm. He'd been too busy tending to Piper to focus on himself for these past few days. Charlotte waited, both hands cupping her wine glass. Her expression was patient and attentive. For one moment John was so tempted to let down his guard. To share his worries about Piper and his fears that he would fail as her guardian. But that wasn't fair to Charlotte. Why would a free spirit like her want to get wrapped up in his problems?

"I'm probably just tired," he said, offering his best attempt at a smile.

She eyed John for a long minute, as if she was weighing the merit of his reply. Finally, she shrugged and swirled the wine in her glass. "Sorry, Bennett. I just don't buy it."

John chuckled, surprised at her response. "Don't buy what?"

"The baloney you're peddling here. I know you're upset about something."

John couldn't imagine how she was so certain.

Reading his expression, she clarified. "It's this funny thing you do with your eyebrows when you're upset. You kind of squash them together... like this."

She mimicked the look for John, pushing her eyebrows together furiously while pursing her lips at the same time. She looked like one of the angry characters in Piper's video games.

John couldn't help but laugh. "I do not look like that!"

She sat back with an amused smile. "Yeah, you kind of do. But it's okay. You're still my favorite workmate."

He shook his head as he looked down at his glass. She was teasing him, and he rather liked it. It felt good to have someone in his life who knew him well enough to tease.

She leaned forward, resting her chin on her hand. It only made her look even more enticing. "Sometimes sharing our burdens makes the load a little lighter, yes?"

Why did she have to be so beautiful? Everything about her was warm and appealing. It was almost impossible not to lean into the moment. Maybe he could allow himself the indulgence of believing, just for an hour or so, that he didn't have to bear his burdens alone.

"Piper goes back to school on Monday," he said.

"And this is a bad thing?"

"Normally, no." The truth was he was dying to get back to the clinic. "But Piper didn't have a bike accident at school. She ran away."

Cripes, it was awful saying the words out loud.

"She showed up for her first period class, so she was there for the attendance check, but then she and a friend slipped away before the next period. They rode their bikes over a mile to a local bike park, to try out some tricks they saw on social media. It was all fun and games—until Piper's bike went one way and she went the other."

He closed his eyes against the image of her flying over the handlebars to land against a concrete barrier.

"John, that's terrible. But she's all right now, right? And what about you? Are you okay?"

"No," he shot back, immediately regretting his sharp tone. "How could I let this happen?"

Charlotte's brows knitted in confusion. "I don't understand. You weren't even there. So, how could this be your fault?"

"Because it's my job to protect her! It's up to me to choose the right sitter, the right school, the right...everything! If the school failed to keep her safe, then I failed her too. Because at the end of the day I'm all she has."

And that was his fault too, but his throat and chest were so tight he could hardly speak, let alone tell Charlotte the role he'd played in Piper's new reality.

John stood abruptly and cleared their dishes. He knew he was being too rough, clashing cups against plates and making a terrible racket. But it was oddly satisfying, the way the external clatter matched his inner turmoil. He felt Charlotte watching him, but she didn't say anything. What could she say? These problems were his to bear, and he shouldn't have burdened her with them at all.

He dropped the dishes in the sink and turned the water on full blast. Soon he had a sink full of hot, soapy water. Charlotte appeared at his side and cupped his shoulder with her soft hand. He closed his eyes against the swell of emotion her touch inspired. Somehow she was slipping past his defenses into the closed-off places of his heart, surprising and jarring him at the same time.

"Look, I don't have kids, or anything, so maybe I'm out of line here. But it seems to me that you've done an amazing job of being her safe place to land after her father went to jail. She's still grieving about her father and the loss of the home she knew. What about a therapist? Someone she can talk to and sort things out?"

John fiddled with the cloth napkins now stained with pizza sauce and wine. "We've tried a half-dozen therapists. She won't talk to them. She just clams up and stares out the window."

"Maybe you haven't found the right therapist?"

"Maybe," John muttered, then set about cleaning up the mess he had made.

Charlotte joined him, silently drying dishes while he worked out his frustrations with soap and a cleaning wand. He shouldn't have unloaded on her like that. Just a few days ago he'd been insisting that they needed to stick to being work colleagues, and now he was using her as a sounding board. This wasn't what she'd wanted when she invited him and Piper to stay here, he was sure of that.

When every dish was washed and put away,

John checked his watch. "It's getting late. I'll get Piper to join us for eclairs and coffee."

"Looking forward to it!" Charlotte said.

But John didn't find Piper sprawled on the bed with her computer or her books, like he'd expected. She wasn't in the bathroom either. The bed was still made and her suitcase sat next to the dresser, still waiting to be unpacked. But her shoes and jacket were missing.

John's heart jumped into his throat. Had she run away again?

He dashed back to the main living area, hoping against hope that Piper had somehow transported herself to the living room without him noticing. His mind was working overtime. She had a broken leg, for Pete's sake—how far could she go?

Unless all that time on her computer meant she'd been talking to someone online? Someone who could pick her up and...

John shifted to emergency mode. "She's gone!" he shouted. His throat was tight with terror.

But Charlotte was gone too.

"Out here!" he heard Charlotte call. "Bring your coat!"

John dashed outside to find Charlotte sitting in an Adirondack chair, wrapped in a plaid blanket. She was watching Piper approach a scraggly cat.

Charlotte smiled warmly at John and tapped the chair next to hers.

John sank into the chair, feeling a little wobbly with relief. "So, who's this?"

"I just call him Cat. The lawyer doesn't know if he belonged to my father or not. He visits every day, but he won't come into the house."

"What's wrong with his eye?" Piper studied the cat like he was something foreign and exotic.

Now that he was adjusting to the dimmer light outdoors, John could see what Piper was talking about. It was a tabby cat. Not young, but not a senior either. It was thin enough to count its ribs, and one eye had been scarred shut.

"I'm not sure. Maybe a fight. Or an accident. Doesn't look like he had proper veterinary care, so the eye is permanently damaged."

Piper was quiet. Then she reached out to touch the skinny creature.

"Don't!" John cried.

One bite and Piper could get Cat Scratch Disease, or rabies, or an infection of her bloodstream.

Charlotte laid her hand on John's to calm him. "Put your fingers out so he can sniff. Cat will let you know if he's feeling social or not."

John would still rather shoo the cat away, but before he could say so the cat began rubbing his face all over Piper's fingers and hand.

Piper looked up with a delighted smile. "He likes me!"

"Indeed, he does," Charlotte said. "And so far you are the *only* one he likes."

"He won't let you pet him?"

"Nope. I'm only allowed to feed him, and even then he seems to think he's doing me a favor."

The tabby was going mad on Piper now, even allowing her to scratch under his chin. A distinct rumbling sound rose from the cat's skinny belly, making Piper smile wider than John had ever seen. It was good to see her happy, even if it took a down-on-his-luck cat to make it happen.

"Why doesn't he have a real name?"

"I guess because I can't keep him. Seems better for his future family to have the honor of naming him."

Piper's smile faded. "Why can't you keep him?"

"Because soon I'll sell this house and get back to my real life. It's hard to have a pet when you move around a lot."

And there it was. The reminder he needed. Charlotte was amazing as a colleague and a friend. Her generosity in sharing her home with him and Piper was more than he'd ever expected. But he couldn't lean into this. As wonderful as it was to share an evening with Charlotte, this was just a sabbatical of sorts. He had a real life too, and it couldn't include Charlotte. He was the oak tree, deeply rooted to the earth, while she was a bird that flew where it wished. Their time together would be wonderful, but short, because that was what they were made for.

Charlotte's expression had turned thoughtful. "You know, Piper, seeing how Cat seems to like you so much, maybe you can help me…"

She cast John a sideways glance that made him wonder what she was up to.

"Cat's not going to get a good home if he's dirty and unfriendly. He obviously likes you, so maybe you could help me earn his trust? Then I could take him to a veterinarian for some good medical care. And together we could help him gain some weight, brush out his coat, and learn some basic manners."

John instantly understood her plan. When the doors to someone's heart were locked up tight, like Piper's after what had happened with her father, sometimes you had to find another way in. Piper wasn't willing to talk to a therapist about her adjustment issues, but maybe she would open up to Charlotte. Especially if the goal wasn't for her to open up, but just to help a scruffy old cat who had given up on people.

Piper was somber as she considered the offer. "He needs a better name."

Charlotte's laughter was lovely and spontaneous. "Are you negotiating your terms? Okay, it's a deal. You can name the cat whatever you want if you help me get Cat ready for his new forever family."

Cat stood and arched his back, then dropped to his forearms for a deep stretch. Maybe that meant he liked the deal too.

Piper followed Cat to the edge of the yard, watching as he easily scaled the fence and disappeared.

Charlotte called out a warning for her to stay away from the dilapidated greenhouse which clearly had not been used for a decade or more, then whispered under her breath, "Maybe the best therapist for Piper has four legs and a tail?"

Maybe so. But how was Piper going to help with Cat once they moved to a short-term rental?

She wouldn't. Not only would it be awkward and uncomfortable to set up frequent visits, there was no guarantee that Cat would be in a social mood when they visited.

So if he wanted Piper to have a chance to connect with Cat, and maybe even Charlotte, he was going to have to spend just about every minute of his day in close proximity to the woman who had captivated his imagination but was strictly off-limits.

Charlotte's hand still warmed John's arm, triggering that feeling he couldn't quite name. He searched his memory bank for another time in his life when he'd felt like this, but he came up blank.

There was a sense of relief, yes—but why? And it was mixed with some emotion that made him feel warm despite the chilly night air. As if they were a team, dedicated to helping Piper. Which meant he didn't have to go it alone.

"I think you're right. Sometimes we find help where we least expect it."

John tucked her hand into his chest, then closed his eyes and let the warmth infusing his body chase the evening chill away.

Charlotte broke down the last cardboard box and stacked it with the others for the recycling bin. The clinic's supply closet was restocked, ready for the week's work. She stretched her back and hamstrings, then grabbed a bottle of cold water from the kitchen.

She still needed to finish the draft of a federal grant report by the end of the week. John hated the mandatory reporting that came with federal funding, and she kept messing up her billing codes, so they had agreed to trade their most dreaded tasks.

Charlotte thought ahead to the end of the day, when her work would be done. Her travel journal had been badly neglected since she'd come back to Seattle. The house renovations would be done in less than a month, around the same time Piper's cast should be off. It was high time for her to start researching everything the Caribbean cruise ship had to offer.

She also needed to update her blog, *GypsyMD*. She didn't have a million followers, but those who did follow her were loyal, and loved following her adventures as a traveling doctor. If she couldn't give them an exciting glimpse into her nomadic life now, she could at least give them some teasers for her forthcoming exciting travels aboard *The Eden*.

It would be a welcome distraction from the simmering tension she felt with John in the house. It was one thing to work with him at the clinic, when they were both busy and focused on their patients. Quite another to see him padding about her house barefoot and wearing fitted jogging pants low on his hips. More than once she'd had to take a cold shower after work to get her mind out of the gutter.

Charlotte found Sarah and John in the lobby. John was sorting medical supplies into piles, while Sarah filled plastic sandwich bags with handfuls of supplies. Once a month The Sunshine Clinic closed early, so John could do street call work, where he went deep into Seattle's industrial district looking for homeless teens, sharing information about the clinic and providing medical care if needed.

John noticed her. "Hey, could you hand me those flyers?"

He pointed to a table behind Charlotte. She handed him a stack of blue flyers secured with a thick rubber band.

"Fifty!" Sarah said with finality.

She scooped up handfuls of the filled sandwich bags and dropped them into an open backpack at the end of the table.

"Perfect," John said. "We'll leave half at The House of Hope and place the others at gas stations and convenience stores in the area."

He finished stuffing the backpack with clean socks and toiletry kits.

Charlotte took a closer look at the bags Sarah was holding. They were filled with travel-sized medicines and ointments, along with a toothbrush, alcohol wipes, and a business card with the clinic's address and operating hours.

"Hey, this is your cell phone number!"

She was incredulous that John would share his personal number, rather than using the clinic's answering service for emergencies.

"If a kid needs us, I want to know. Not rely on an operator to decide if their call is important enough to page me." He shrugged on his backpack. "Ready?"

From beneath the table he hoisted a second

backpack, already filled with supplies, and held the straps out to Charlotte.

She shrugged on the backpack and groaned under its weight.

"Sorry!" John chuckled. "You're carrying the bottled water."

"Thanks a lot," Charlotte mock-complained, but she was secretly glad.

The struggle of hauling water bottles all over Seattle would be a welcome distraction from her frequent thoughts about John.

They headed into the street while Sarah stayed behind to handle phone calls and walk-ins. John gave Charlotte a lanyard that identified her as medical staff. He was hauling a wheeled blue ice chest, filled with more cold water and snack packs of apples, string cheese, crackers, and peanut butter.

Their first stop was The House of Hope, where they dropped off flyers and first aid kits. The shelter was decorated for Valentine's Day, with pink and white hearts taped in the windows. Charlotte couldn't see the kitchen, but she could smell the sweet scent of fresh-baked cookies and hear teens chattering and laughing amid the clatter of dishes being washed.

The shelter director insisted they take a few cookies for the road. Charlotte's frosted sugar cookie had *Be Mine* shakily piped by a young baker's hand. John's had a chubby Valentine cherub, his bow and arrow pointing Charlotte's way.

Not that he needed any help from Cupid. Ever since John's SUV had joined her rental in the garage, her feelings of agitation and restlessness had only multiplied. She wasn't herself when he was around. She felt awkward and overly self-aware.

John was walking ahead of her now, hauling the cooler and considering their next stop. Charlotte gazed down at his backside, admiring the muscular curves that flexed the limits of his denim jeans. *Damn.* She couldn't help but remember the night they'd worked late. That passionate but fleeting kiss...the feel of her fingers kneading his thick, silken curls.

She forced her gaze back to the work at hand. These distractions weren't going to help anyone. John had made his feelings perfectly clear. He might have enjoyed that kiss as much as she had, but moving forward was not an option.

They headed deeper into Seattle, stopping at churches, gas stations and the community center to drop off flyers and first aid kits. Clerks and volunteers suggested places where they had seen teens who might need their help. Charlotte had to walk fast to keep up with John, as he seemed determined to investigate every lead before dark.

The sun edged closer to the horizon. Charlotte jiggled her pack. "I have a few water bottles left."

John rubbed his chin. "One last stop, then—the skate park. We'll pass out the rest of our supplies, then head back to the clinic."

Despite the waning sun, the skate park was in full swing. Kids gathered in big and small groups, boasting and laughing, skateboards resting under skinny arms or leaned up against the fence. John focused on two girls near a cherry tree, its branches bare for a winter rest.

The girls, wary at first, soon warmed to John's gentle curiosity. The taller girl in skinny jeans said she knew about the clinic but didn't have plans to visit anytime soon.

"Keep the card," John said, pointing to the kit. "In case you need us."

She tucked the card in her back pocket. "Okay. But you guys should check on Tommy."

The shorter girl, with chipped, bubblegum-pink nail polish, pointed to a white cargo van. "Yeah, he's pretty sick."

The van was parked at the back of the parking lot. Based on the flat rear tire and the tall weeds growing through the front fender, it seemed it hadn't been moved in a long time. The rear door was open and Charlotte could see a boy, lanky and thin, lying on his side with his back to the world.

She and John approached the van slowly, calling the boy's name. It took almost a dozen attempts before Tommy moaned and turned their way.

"Hey, Tommy." John's voice was warm and soothing. "My name is John. I'm a doctor, and so is my partner, Charlotte. Your friends are very worried about you."

The boy opened his eyes but seemed too exhausted to keep them that way. He threw an arm across his face. "Man, I am *so* tired. I've been sleeping for *days*."

Charlotte scanned the boy from head to toe, assessing his condition. Her first impression was that he was a fast-growing adolescent who needed more calories than he was getting. His sandy brown hair needed a shampoo, and his jeans were frayed at the bottom. But what really concerned her was the beads of sweat on his forehead and his too-pale skin. Tommy was a very ill boy.

"Okay if I check you out?" John asked.

But Tommy didn't answer. He had already slipped back into unconsciousness.

Charlotte fished the blood pressure meter and thermometer from her pack. She accepted a pair of latex gloves from John, then took Tommy's temperature. One hundred and one degrees. Elevated, yes, but not dangerous. Ditto for his blood pressure and heart rate.

John gently pinched the skin on the back of Tommy's hand. It stayed tented. "He's dehydrated."

Charlotte draped her stethoscope around her neck and considered the boy. Tommy's eyes, when open, were vacant and confused. He clearly needed more than fluids and rest, but his vitals were that of a relatively healthy teenager. What could be wrong?

If only she had an army of highly trained doctors and nurses, ready to run any test she wanted. Or the benefit of a full medical history delivered by a parent or guardian who was intimately familiar with his history. But out here, bent over a sick boy in a rusty van, all she had was her intuition and the equipment she could carry in a backpack to save a boy who was deteriorating before her eyes.

But she also had John.

"Let's try an orthostatic," she said.

"That's pretty old school."

"I know, but it's worth a shot."

Tommy was beyond the typical age range, but it was possible that his body retained a child's ability to hide symptoms of serious infection. If so, getting him to stand would overwhelm his defenses and reveal how sick he really was.

John helped her to get Tommy to struggle to his feet. He was so weak John had to support his full body weight while Charlotte checked his vital signs again. She frowned at the new num-bers. His blood pressure had plummeted while his heart rate had soared to one hundred and fifty beats per minute.

Alarm bells rattled her core. "Sepsis," she mut-tered.

John's gaze darkened. They both knew that without immediate medical intervention the in-flammation raging through his body could dam-age his internal organs to the point of death.

Charlotte reached for her cell phone to call 911, but John growled, "No time!" All traces of the easygoing Dr. J were gone.

They maneuvered the moaning boy back into the van, barely aware of the growing crowd of teens gathered around watching them, silent and somber.

Charlotte dug through the cooler for the IV bag of antibiotics and saline, while John started a large bore catheter. They worked carefully, la-ser-focused on starting the IV fluids that would fight off whatever systemic infection was shut-ting Tommy's organs down.

John held a stethoscope to Tommy's chest while Charlotte called for an ambulance. Soon she heard the high-pitched wail of a screaming siren headed their way. Tommy's breathing had slowed ever so slightly. There was even a hint of pink in his cheeks. Charlotte allowed herself a tiny sigh of relief. Tommy was still in danger, but this baby step of improvement was a relief.

The ambulance crew arrived, and John completed the handover, squeezing Tommy's hand as he was loaded into the ambulance. The teens drifted away slowly, murmuring in hushed whispers.

With the crisis behind them, Charlotte's adrenaline rush was soon replaced by a crushing fatigue. She dropped like a stone onto a rickety wood bench. John sat next to her, the bench groaning under the extra weight.

"Will we ever see him again?" She felt cold and numb as she contemplated the near tragedy.

"Probably not."

Her stomach clenched with delayed fear. "That was too close, John. We almost lost him."

To her dismay, her voice was shaking, betraying emotions she couldn't control. She didn't realize her hands were shaking too until John folded both of his around hers, buttressing them against the late-day chill that seemed to rise from the damp earth beneath their feet.

"I know."

His voice was so calm. Like he had seen this a thousand times before—which maybe he had. But how could he stand it?

"I don't get it, John. What happened? How can a boy be *that* sick with no one to care for him?"

John's jaw clenched for just a second. "I don't know, Charlotte. Asking why too often can drive you crazy. These kids are like ghosts. You see them going to school, working a part-time job, trying to fit in. They work hard to hide what they lack. Teenage bravado, maybe, or an instinct to hide weakness on the street. I don't really know."

His grasp tightened around her hands, and she looked up to see his clenched jaw.

"But I do know this. They're worth saving. Every last one of them."

John released one hand so he could trace her cheek with his finger.

"What about you, Charlotte? Are you worth saving?"

Charlotte gasped at his question. "What are you talking about? I'm nothing like Tommy! He's completely alone in the world, with no one to look out for him except us. I have…"

She trailed off. Who did she have? Who could she count on to come to her aid at any time of the day or night, no questions asked?

She had thousands of followers who loved to live vicariously through her travel blog. But they didn't know her.

Even the friends she met every year or two for an exotic vacation didn't know her all that well.

Certainly not well enough to drop everything in their life for her if she were sick or injured.

Which was by design—so that she didn't have to feel the pain of saying goodbye to someone she cared about.

But she had never asked herself why she kept saying goodbye in the first place.

"So who would be there for you if you were as sick as Tommy? Who would refuse to leave your side until you were strong enough to take care of yourself?"

"I *am* strong enough to take care of myself!" She always had been—ever since her mother had died.

That was enough to trigger the memory of that terrible night. First the policeman, who'd delivered the terrible news. He'd asked if there was anyone he could call for her, but there had been no one. It had always been just her and her mom. A tiny family of two, complete in and of themselves. But she was gone and so the social workers came.

She had only been allowed to take what would fit in the trash bag they gave her. She'd packed as if she'd be gone for just a night or two, leaving so much behind. Pictures and collected seashells. Her mother's recipe collection and Charlotte's saved art projects. Ticket stubs and favorite slippers and the soft blanket they'd snuggled under for their movie nights.

John's steady gaze was stripping her bare. All

he wanted was her truth. But she wasn't sure she knew it anymore.

She was certain of one thing. She was tired of running. She could feel it in her bones.

Because what was the worth of a life spent living like a tourist? That was what she was, essentially. What was she missing by being always on the road, never dug in? Was she happy never making a difference in anyone's life because she was always on the move, always planning her next adventure, always one step ahead of heartbreak and hurt?

Instead of a family she had a travel blog. Instead of love she had a well-worn passport.

It had been enough for a long time…when she was defining herself after her years in foster care.

But what about now?

She sighed and looked down at the hands that enveloped hers. Hands that belonged to a good man who always stayed, no matter how it might crush his heart with despair.

She checked her neck—there was no itching, no feeling of imminent danger. For the first time in a long time, maybe forever, she felt like she was right where she wanted to be.

# CHAPTER SEVEN

BY THE TIME Charlotte and John got back to the clinic, it was long past dark. The clinic was locked and Sarah's car was gone. Charlotte had barely spoken after Tommy's perilous rescue and now, under the parking lot's lamps, John noted dark shadows under her eyes. He didn't press her for conversation as they unpacked the coolers and prepped for the next day.

"See you at the house," she mumbled as she rooted through her purse for her car keys.

John's stomach fluttered with alarm. Everything from her slumped shoulders to her slow gait screamed fatigue. His partner was far too tired to be behind the wheel of a car.

"Let me drive you home," he said.

"I'm fine," she countered, but it sounded like a reflex.

John paused, considering his options. Just long enough for her to unsuccessfully smother a huge yawn.

She gave him a sheepish half-smile. "Maybe you're right."

She dropped her keys into his hand and followed him to the car. John slid into the driver's seat and pressed the car's ignition button. The radio picked up Charlotte's playlist, playing an R&B song that was a soothing balm after their long day.

John turned on the car's heater, then checked his texts. Piper had gone to a friend's house after school, her first ever playdate since she had moved in with John. Living with Charlotte and finding camaraderie with a cat who didn't know where he belonged either had helped her find her bearings a bit, and helped John to see that in his desire to protect Piper he might have accidentally smothered her. If she was going to heal, he had to help Piper find her own village of friends and caring adults. And maybe a dumb cat too.

John texted the friend's mother to let her know he was on his way to pick up Piper.

She was blossoming at Charlotte's house. Sometimes John woke on his days off to find Piper's bedroom empty. Instead of the rush of alarm he'd felt that day when he'd been having pizza with Charlotte, he knew exactly where to find her. In Charlotte's kitchen, perched on the counter, helping to stir eggs or just chatting away while Charlotte made breakfast. Sometimes they both worked on the cat, brushing his fur out or showing him the joy of feather wands.

Their work seemed to be paying off. John could no longer count Cat's ribs at a glance. Cat was filling out with a steady diet of good food and extra treats.

In time, it had become natural to start their mornings in Charlotte's kitchen, with sunlight streaming through the windows while soothing music played on the speaker. Charlotte and Piper had little jokes that he didn't understand. But he liked to watch them while he pretended to read the news on his phone. Their easy camaraderie and quick laughter mixed with the music and the smell of coffee brewing and the sizzle of eggs and bacon on the stove. They were like threads in a tapestry, all woven together into something that felt warm and nurturing.

As they left the clinic, John realized he was famished. Charlotte must be too. Had they eaten lunch? He couldn't remember. But it was far too late for a restaurant, and local fast food was awful. They needed something simple, but quick. He spotted a coffee shop ahead, its interior lighting glowing amber against the dark, wet streets of Seattle, and drove in.

The aroma of fresh brewed coffee and sweet treats paired with the intense grinding and hissing of professional-grade coffee machines met him at the door. A glass display case was filled with croissants and bagels, sandwiches, fruit tarts, and a dizzying array of baked goods. John had no idea what Charlotte liked, so he chose a little of everything, then capped it off with two herbal teas.

Back in the car, Charlotte sniffed the steam escaping the takeout lid. "Mmm, chamomile," she breathed. "Perfect choice."

Just then it started to rain. Huge, fat drops that thumped on the windshield and roof of the car. He dialed the heat up two degrees and headed for their shared, temporary home.

The tea seemed to revive Charlotte. She peered into the backseat. "What smells so good?"

His best guess was the toasted buttered bagel, because the smell of it was making his stomach growl too.

She reached for the bag and the next thing he knew she was offering him half.

She groaned with pleasure at her first bite. "It's like you picked my favorite before I even knew it was my favorite!"

Was it ridiculous to feel this much pride at pleasing her? Maybe so, but he couldn't deny the shiver of pleasure that spiraled up his spine.

When they picked her up, Piper was equally pleased with the bag of goodies. She happily snacked on the chocolate chip muffin he had selected just for her and spent the trip home regal-

ing them with stories of her adventures with her
new best friend.

John guided the car out of the rain and into the
garage. He silenced the engine, then checked the
backseat, wondering what had happened to Piper's happy chatter. She was sleeping, curled into
a tight ball, still holding her half-eaten muffin.

"Out like a light," Charlotte whispered.

"She must have had fun."

John plucked her from the backseat while
Charlotte held her injured leg for support. They
worked silently to tuck Piper into bed.

"Wait," Charlotte whispered. "I have something for her."

A few minutes later she was back, with a small
gift bag that she gave to John.

"That's really thoughtful, but shouldn't it wait
till morning?"

Charlotte shook her head with a smile. "She
needs it now."

It was a nightlight in the shape of a lighthouse,
its beacon providing a soft amber glow to illu-
minate the nooks and crannies of Piper's room.

"Ever since you and Piper moved in, I've been
searching for a sailboat nightlight, to remind her
of *The House Call*. But when I saw this one, I
thought it was a good second choice." She looked
down at the sleeping girl between them. "I like

lighthouses. They can guide you back home, wherever that home might be."

They unloaded the car, and he followed her to the kitchen, where Charlotte busied herself with gathering up the takeout order and her purse.

Just when John was about to wish her goodnight, she held up the takeout bag.

"Want to join me for dinner?"

It was the exact opposite of what he should do. He liked her too much...was too keenly aware of her scent and her movements, the tiny freckle on her chin, her favorite music and how she liked her coffee.

But the stress of Tommy's rescue lingered in the knotted muscles of his shoulders and neck. It had been a close call—far too close for John's comfort. It would be nice to share the end of the day with someone who understood.

He must have hesitated a breath too long, because she looked down with a pained expression and toyed with a thread on her pants. He could hear what she didn't want to say out loud.

She didn't want to be alone.

"Of course," he said, aiming for the same casual tone. "I don't want to be alone either."

Which was a funny thing. Between Piper, the teens at the clinic, Sarah, and his colleagues at the hospital, John was rarely physically alone. But sometimes he felt like being in a crowd only amplified how isolated he felt. He was there, but not truly seen—or understood. It hadn't been until Charlotte joined the clinic that he'd had reason to question the grind of his life. Charlotte and her piercing questions had let him know she saw exactly who he was and what he had sacrificed to be what others needed him to be.

When Charlotte was close, he felt like he was more than a doctor, his brother's keeper, Mr. Responsible. She made him feel like he was a man with dreams of his own that mattered.

Charlotte set the café bag on the marble countertop and began searching for plates and cutlery.

They usually used the kitchen for their breakfast dates, but he wanted something more intimate and comfortable for tonight. He looked past the kitchen into the family room. It was smaller and seemed less formal than the great big room at the front of the house. There were pretty French doors that opened out to the lawn and the woods beyond. And a brick fireplace—though that had been painted white too. Still, this was a space he could work with.

He found a plush navy-blue comforter and a few candles in the hallway linen closet. In just a few minutes he had started a fire and lit a row of candles on the mantel. He shook out the comforter and laid it on the floor, just as Charlotte rounded the corner holding a tray laden with food.

"Voila!" John said. "Who says you can't have a picnic in the rain?"

She froze, considering the scene, and for a moment John feared he'd made a mistake. But her surprise quickly warmed into a smile.

"Lovely!" she pronounced. "I didn't think this house could be cozy, but you pulled it off."

"At least in this room." John settled on the comforter. "So, do they have any leads?"

She joined him. "Leads...?"

"The police. I imagine they must have an all-points bulletin out on your missing furniture."

She laughed, and John decided he could happily spend the rest of his life making that happen.

"No, it's all gone. I sold it—as per the plan. The last thing to go is the house." She bit into a berry tart and sighed with pleasure.

John chose a turkey sandwich from the serving tray. "When will you sell the house?"

"When we don't need it anymore."

When *we* don't need it anymore. He realized what was holding her back. "You're waiting because of me and Piper?" Guilt overshadowed the pleasure of being alone with her.

But she waved off his concern. "Don't be silly. I'm thrilled to see this house put to good use. You can stay as long as it takes for Piper to heal.

I don't start with *The Eden* until the spring, so there's plenty of time."

Her mention of her next adventure was an unwelcome reminder of the invisible clock that held power over his life. Funny how he had balked at the prospect of sharing his clinic with another doctor. Everything was so different now. It was getting easy to imagine Charlotte as his partner at work.

And now, with the firelight casting a soft glow on her hair and the curves of her face, it was getting easy to imagine her in his bed too.

"So, why do you think he left you all this—after years of…?" His hand found her knee, embraced its curve.

"Of wanting nothing to do with me?" She smiled and stretched. Her hand found its way to his, landing light as a butterfly atop the one he had clasped around her knee. "I really don't know. I imagine it's in the letter."

"What letter?"

"The letter my father left for me. It's in the kitchen, on top of the toaster. Maybe I'll read it someday. Then again, maybe not."

"You don't want to know?"

She plucked at a loose thread on the comforter, her jaw tight with tension. "If I read his letter, it feels like I'm letting him have his say. I'm not sure I want him to have that space in my head."

She took a deep breath and softened. "I don't know. Maybe in time I'll get curious. But for now, I just want to sell this monstrosity of a home so I can donate the proceeds to charity."

*And get back to my real life.*

He heard the words, even if she didn't say it out loud.

"So, no settling down for you, then? White picket fence, two-point-five kids, that sort of thing?"

Why on earth should his body be so coiled with tension? Her future personal plans were none of his concern. But once again his body was betraying him, revealing the disconnect between his sensible thoughts and what his heart truly wanted.

"When I was young I was rather angry about how my life had turned out. Bouncing from house to house in foster care was rough. But when I learned about locum tenens jobs, and how I could help kids anywhere in the world, I realized those foster care experiences could be turned into something positive. Not everyone can live like a nomad, with their whole life stored in a single suitcase. But thanks to those foster care years, I can."

"And being such a wanderer...does it suit you?"

The fire had warmed the room now. Its flames were casting dancing shadows on the wall. A log snapped loudly and shifted in the grate. The candles flickered in time with the steady beat of the rainstorm outside. This moment felt insulated and private, as if he had somehow managed to stop time so that the entire world had narrowed to just the two of them in the little cocoon he had created.

Maybe it was this sense of otherworldliness that made it seem so natural for him to brush an errant strand of hair from her eyes. She didn't flinch a bit. She just held his gaze, steady and thoughtful. Her chest rose and fell with each breath, her gold pendant reflecting the firelight.

"Until now," she whispered.

"Charlotte?" His heart was a thief, stealing the moment to claim its deepest desire. "Did you really forget our first kiss? That night at the clinic?"

She tilted her head, baring her delicate throat. "I thought it was a dream."

John leaned into her. Close enough that he could feel her breath as her chest rose and fell. "I think I want to renegotiate the terms of our agreement."

She closed her eyes, her soft, pink mouth waiting. "What agreement?"

"Exactly."

Charlotte felt his lip brush hers. His mouth was firm and warm, with a touch of intensity that quickened her pulse. She shifted toward him, felt his hand find her waist, his heat radiating through her thin shirt. It was gentle, this kiss, more like a gift or an offering than a runaway train of fiery passion. But Charlotte was keenly aware of everything about him. The musky sweet taste of his kiss. The scruff of his beard against her soft skin. The press of her breasts against his solid chest.

Her hand found the curve of his shoulder, followed it to the nape of his neck. Her fingers buried themselves into his hair, mapping him like he was a treasure to explore. Long-buried desires rose from deep in her core and rippled through her so that she opened to him fully, kissing him deeply. Their passions rose and she craved the feel of his bare skin. She wanted the length of his naked body pressed against hers so that there was nothing between them.

He had exposed what she wanted most. Someone who would touch her, love her, like this. Make her believe, even if it was just a dream, that she might be worthy of someone like him.

As if she had spoken aloud, he pulled her closer, tucking her into the curves of his body, and their tongues slowly danced as she wished the moment would never end.

But it did end—though not for long minutes—with Charlotte pulling away to catch her breath. She reached for her tea, needing something to soothe her parched, dry throat. But the tea did little to dampen the fire his touches had stoked.

She risked a glance at John, feeling as naked as if he had stripped every garment from her body. Their former agreement, as flimsy as it had been, was officially null and void. If they weren't co-workers committed to keeping their attraction in check, what were they?

She opened her mouth to ask, but something in John's expression stopped her. He was listening to something beyond the room.

"Piper? I'm in here."

She appeared at the door a moment later, rubbing her eyes, clearly a bit confused as to where she was. John rose to his feet and met her at the doorway.

"I had a bad dream," she said, on the verge of tears.

John swept her up for a hug and murmured comforting words. He gave Charlotte an apologetic smile as he took Piper back to her room, promising he would stay with her until she fell asleep.

Charlotte stayed behind to watch the fire slowly die. What on earth were she and John doing? He was committed to his niece and she was a mere visitor to Seattle and his clinic.

If this were just a fling, she might not feel this angsty mix of desire and apprehension.

If she had any sense at all, she'd put a firm end to whatever this was between them.

But she couldn't. Not after that kiss. John had set something loose in her that was not willing to be shut away again.

The time for good sense had come and gone. From here on out she was in uncharted territory.

# CHAPTER EIGHT

"GOOD MORNING, DR. OWENS. This is Julia, with Seven Seas Cruise Line International. We emailed your employment contract two weeks ago but have not received your signed copy. Could you please complete that at your earliest convenience?"

The cruise ship human resources director left her contact information and hung up.

Charlotte deleted the message and drummed her fingernails against her desk. Her assignment as ship's doctor for a major cruise line was less than a month away. By now she should have a full itinerary planned for herself, detailing all the excursions and sights she wanted to see while she cruised the Caribbean.

She wrote herself a reminder note and pinned it to the bulletin board above her desk. This weekend. She would definitely look at that contract this weekend.

From the corner of her eye, movement caught her attention. A paper plane had landed on her desk. Its pilot followed close behind and dropped into the chair next to her.

"Guess what that is."

"The winning lottery numbers?"

John groaned. "I wish... That, my friend, is everything you never wanted to know about the hospital gala."

Charlotte unfolded the airplane. It was John's invitation to the hospital's thirty-seventh annual fundraising gala, with all funds raised going to support the hospital's outreach programs—including The Sunshine Clinic.

John looked less than pleased.

"That bad, huh?"

"Tuxes are involved."

Charlotte thrilled at the image of her scruffy colleague all packaged up in a smart tuxedo. "I think I'd be willing to pay to see that."

"You don't have to pay. Just say yes."

"To what?"

"Come with me to the gala. Be my date. You don't even need a pumpkin carriage. The hospital has negotiated a corporate rate for hotel rooms, so guests won't need to drive if they've had a drink or two."

"What about Piper?"

"Sarah's practically begged me to let her stay overnight with her. A chance for her to spend time with her 'adopted grandchild' before she moves south to be closer to her children when she retires."

So, they would be alone for the night...

Their gazes met and held a second too long. Ever since that kiss by the fireplace John had been extra careful about Piper. With her father in jail and having had two moves in one year, he was cautious about revealing their status as a couple.

Which made sense to Charlotte too. It wasn't fair to let Piper get invested in them as a couple when it was destined to end in a few weeks. So that meant, other than stolen kisses when Piper was busy or in bed, their love life was mostly a cauldron of barely repressed desire.

A night away in a hotel room sounded very good to Charlotte.

But John misread her long silence. "Of course, you'll have your own room. At my cost. My way of saying thank you for accompanying me."

That wasn't what she was worried about, but this wasn't the time or place to discuss it. Not with Sarah manning the front desk behind them and a whole waiting room full of noisy teens.

The front door flew open and crashed against the wall.

"Hey, Doc! I got a kid who needs help here!"

Charlotte felt a rush of adrenaline at seeing Angel again. Finally! She and John had been waiting weeks for her to return to the clinic. Now that her charity funding was approved, all they needed to do was get her to see the cardiologist.

But that would have to wait. Angel had a girl with her. Fourteen, maybe fifteen years old, was Charlotte's best guess. And very sick. Even from a distance Charlotte could see from her hot cheeks and glassy, unfocused gaze that she was in a lot of pain.

"I'll think about it." Charlotte said. She patted John's shoulder, then went to the girls.

"This one needs help for real," Angel said. All her swagger had disappeared and she seemed genuinely afraid for her friend.

"I can see that," Charlotte said. "Come on in."

She led them to her room and asked the girl to get on the exam table.

She took her vitals, noting her high temperature on a chart.

"What's your name, honey?" she asked as she checked the girl's lymph nodes around her neck. The swelling there indicated her immune system had been working overtime to fight off some kind of infection or virus.

"Lily," the girl whispered. She was cradling the right side of her head in one hand and looked absolutely miserable.

"Does your head hurt?"

Charlotte cataloged the possibilities. She worried Lily had meningitis, and the swelling around her brain and spinal cord was causing extreme discomfort. But a bad virus could cause nasty headaches and a fever too.

"My ear..." Lily whimpered.

Charlotte's heart squeezed with sympathy for this girl who was suffering.

"We'll get you something for the pain in just a minute," she promised as she retrieved the otoscope.

Lily was hesitant to stop guarding her ear, but Angel turned out to be an unexpected ally.

"It's okay," Angel soothed. "Dr. Owens is one of the good ones."

Charlotte blushed with pride at Angel's compliment. Earning the trust of a streetwise kid like Angel was no easy feat. She just hoped Angel would trust her referral to a cardiologist too.

Lily's ear was practically on fire with infection. The delicate tissue of her middle ear was red-hot, bulging with inflammation. Despite Lily's whimpers, Charlotte gently moved the otoscope up and down, to the left and right, exploring the extent of the infection.

"Lily, could you wait a moment? I need to consult with my partner, Dr. J."

*My partner.*

Two words Charlotte had never said in her adult life.

John joined her in the hallway for an impromptu consultation.

"I'm pretty sure she has mastoiditis," she told John. "I didn't think that happened outside of medical school lectures. Can you confirm?"

John followed her back to the exam room and examined Lily's ear for a second time. He sighed deeply and clicked off the otoscope.

"I'm sorry, Lily, but we can't treat this here. You have an ear infection that has spread to a hollow bone behind your ear called the mastoid bone. Now it's filled with infection, and it could rupture any minute. If that happens, the infection could get into the covering around your brain and cause meningitis."

Lily was in so much pain she didn't care what happened next so long as they didn't touch her ear again.

John called for an ambulance to transport Lily to the hospital, leaving Charlotte free to focus on Angel.

"Thanks so much for bringing her in, Angel," she said. "She really needed a friend like you."

Angel gave her a shy smile.

"I'm really glad to see you again. How have you been feeling?"

Angel bit her lip. "I still get a little dizzy sometimes."

"Well, then, I hope you'll think this is good

news. The hospital wants to pay for your EKG testing, and we have a cardiologist who can see you on short notice. In fact, she could see you today."

Charlotte hoped that wouldn't scare Angel away, but she had to ask. Lily's ear infection was just one more example of what happened when kids didn't get good medical care fast enough.

Charlotte beamed when Angel sheepishly agreed to go.

She would have loved to drive Angel to the specialist herself, but hospital rules made that impossible. Instead, she gave Angel a bus pass and directions to the hospital. She watched Angel head off for a long multi-bus trip on her own, carrying a plastic bag that Charlotte had filled with chilled water and snacks.

*Free transportation*
*In-house EKG testing*

Charlotte mentally added two more items to her running list of services she would like to add to the clinic. She didn't know why she did this, except that she kept discovering more hidden needs in this little medical center.

But that was just the beginning. She'd been there long enough to know the kids needed far more than medical care to get their lives stabilized. They needed help getting proper identification, mental health services, and a nutritionist who could address the malnutrition that afflicted nearly every kid she worked with.

Sarah interrupted her musings. "Charlotte, I don't know what to do. Piper's school is on the phone and I can't reach John."

Charlotte felt her chest tighten. "Is Piper okay?"

"She's fine…she's fine. But she's gotten herself into another scrape at school and the principal wants her to go home. John's still at the hospital with Lily. They weren't too keen about admitting one of our patients without a consult from the emergency department attending."

"When will he be back?"

"No telling, love. Hospital admissions can take—"

"Forever," Charlotte finished.

Charlotte texted John but didn't get any more of a response than Sarah had. He was probably focused on getting Lily admitted as quickly as possible.

"Page the on-call pediatrician and ask them to come in. I'm going to get Piper. Tell John if you see him first."

John had added Charlotte to the school's list of Piper's "safe persons," so the principal was able to give Charlotte a report on Piper's latest scuffle. This one had earned her a three-day suspension from school, and the principal said she would like to see John "at his earliest convenience."

*That does not sound good.*

Charlotte knew that Piper's future at the school was hanging on a thread.

She took Piper home and headed to the kitchen, where she kept the first aid kit.

"Let's take a look, okay?" She indicated the scrapes on Piper's arms and knuckles.

Piper shrugged and hoisted herself up to sit on the kitchen counter.

Charlotte used antibacterial soap to clean her scrapes. "What happened anyway?"

"Some girl said something I didn't like."

"If anyone at school is bullying you, your uncle will help you. You know that, right?"

Piper jutted her chin and looked away. "No one's bullying me."

"So what happened, then?"

Piper shrugged. "I just didn't like the way she looked at me."

"That's it? All this because someone looked at you funny?"

"I guess…"

Charlotte rinsed the cuts with disinfectant, then applied a thin layer of antibiotic ointment while she tried to understand this version of Piper. With Charlotte, she'd always been a sweet kid. Gentle with Cat, helpful at home. Always polite, though a bit subdued. This combative side of Piper just didn't make sense.

Charlotte used her knuckles to gently guide Piper's head up and her gaze to her own. "Hey, kid. What's happened here? Why are you in trouble all the time?"

Piper's eyes brimmed with tears. "It won't make sense."

"Try me."

Piper took a deep breath, looked out the window. "I don't mind being in trouble."

"How come?"

"Cause if I get in enough trouble, they'll have to send me to jail." Piper shifted her gaze back to Charlotte. "Then I could be with my dad."

Understanding rolled through Charlotte's body like a gentle wave. Everything—the fighting and rule-breaking, even Piper's running away from school—made sense when viewed from the limited perspective of an adolescent girl's view of the world.

Charlotte set the last Band-Aid in place. "Does your Uncle John know that's what you want?"

"No, but he never asks either."

With that, she slid off the counter, tucked Cat under her arm, and went to her room.

By the time John got home, Piper had fallen asleep, with Cat tucked in a tight ball at her feet.

Charlotte warmed up some leftovers and kept John company while he ate. She filled him in on Piper's troubles at school and what she had learned from their talk.

"Has she seen her dad since he went to jail, John?"

John's expression was pained. "I haven't wanted to do that to her. I see Michael every month, but the whole process of getting through security... the environment...it's all so bleak."

"To you and me, sure. But she needs to see him, John. And he needs to see her too."

"I know." John sighed and let his head fall back to rest on the couch.

Charlotte settled in next to him. "What are you afraid of?"

"That she'll blame me for her father being there."

Charlotte handed him a glass of wine. She studied his profile, illuminated by the cozy fire that John had started when he got home. "Why would she blame you, John?"

John exhaled in a long, low sigh. "When our mother died, she left us a little money. Michael used his to go to art school in California. I used mine as seed money for the clinic. I thought that we were all grown up, and it was safe for me to focus on my dreams. Michael came home after a year, bringing baby Piper with him."

He smiled at the memory and Charlotte could see he loved being an uncle.

"But he seemed different. Moodier, and more prone to angry outbursts. I thought it was due to his breakup with Piper's mother and that he'd get better in time."

"But he didn't?" Charlotte surmised, hoping her patient demeanor would encourage conversation.

"No, he didn't. He got a lot worse over time. I saw him and Piper as often as I could, but the clinic was just taking off and I wanted it to be a success."

He set his wine glass on the table and leaned forward, rolling his neck to release the tension stored there.

"What I didn't realize was that Michael was undiagnosed bipolar. And his wild mood swings were driving him to spend more time with people who weren't good for him. One night..." John paused to gather his thoughts. "One night he called me for help. Said he really needed to see me. But it was the night of the hospital gala, and the chair of pediatrics wanted me to represent the clinic. I was already in my tuxedo, and the mayor was going to be there. There was no way I could skip the event."

Charlotte felt dread rolling off John in waves.

It was clear he hated even thinking about that night, let alone speaking of it out loud.

"That was the night Michael was arrested. If I had just answered his call instead of letting it go to voicemail! If I had just listened more, or been a better brother, maybe I would have realized Michael had bipolar disorder! Instead, it took a prison psychiatrist who doesn't even know him to diagnose what was in front of me all along."

John rolled his head to look at her. She saw hints of the boy he'd once been in those eyes, forced to grow up too fast. He was drop-dead handsome, but that wasn't what pulled at her heart. It was the vulnerability that he was too tired to hide. She never saw this side of him at the clinic. He was too busy being strong for the teens.

She reached out to cup his face with her hand, felt his stubble rough on her palm. He laid his hand over hers, capturing her. Then brought her hand to his mouth. She could feel his warm breath as he kissed her fingers, one by one.

She waited until he seemed calm. "That's a sad story, John," she said. "And I'm sorry that happened to your family. But just because you *feel* guilty, it doesn't mean you are."

Something that looked a little like hope sparked in his eyes.

"Thank you," he said. "I just wish things could have been different."

John turned her hand, revealing her wrist so he could kiss it, then followed a path up her arm, leaving gentle kisses in his wake. She could see a tiny scar on his chin and she itched to trace it with her fingers, hear the story of its origin.

"What's the story with this necklace?" John said, thumbing the pendant lying against her chest. "I've never seen you take it off."

Her hand flew to the pendant, as if making sure it was still there. "Really? I'm sure I have."

"You haven't." He pressed her hand to his heart. "I'm very perceptive about these sorts of things."

"It was my last birthday gift from my mother." The pendant featured a moon tarot card—a reminder that in the face of uncertainty, she should trust her intuition. She moved away from him and thumbed it unconsciously...her version of a worry stone.

John said nothing but his gaze was kind and patient. She knew he was waiting for more. And if the man had the courage to share his most painful secret with her, she supposed she could do the same.

"I was thirteen when she died."

He whistled, soft and low. "That's a tough age to lose a parent, Charlotte. That kind of thing can leave some emotional scars."

She shrugged and swirled her wine glass,

watching the ruby-red liquid cling to the glass. "I suppose...if you let it."

He cocked his head. "Why did you grow up in foster care? Couldn't Social Services find your father?"

His question took her by surprise—so direct and to the point. She was tempted to evade the question, just so she wouldn't have to tell him the truth, but that didn't seem fair after he had just bared his soul.

"A couple of months ago I would have told you no. But I just recently learned that my father did indeed know that I existed and that my mother had died." She drained the last of her wine for a bit of courage. "He opted to terminate his parental rights."

John's eyebrows rose perceptibly. "Are you serious?"

When she nodded, his usual calm, tell-me-anything demeanor disappeared. He leaned forward and took her hand in his again, grasping it firmly as if he feared she might float away.

"That's awful, Charlotte. No man should ever abandon his child. You did not deserve that."

Charlotte shrugged. "It worked out okay in the end. Because of my foster care years, I've built a pretty exciting life for myself as a traveling doctor. I'd say that's a win-win."

John's eyes never left her face. "Losing your

mother as a teen and having your father's rejection send you into foster care is not a win-win, Charlotte."

She was about to come up with another quip, to lighten the moment, but his expression said *Don't*. So, she sat frozen, not knowing what to do other than sit there with the truth that she had just shared. Her father hadn't wanted her—even when she'd needed him very badly.

John didn't say a word. It was uncomfortable at first, just sitting in silence, letting the pain of that admission swirl about in her chest. She was gripped with a strong impulse to get up and get busy. Clear the table, stoke the fire, build an addition to the house... Anything other than just sit and feel the pain of abandonment.

John stroked the back of her hand with his thumb, and she took great solace in his quiet way of saying she wasn't alone. But his words were the sweetest balm of all, letting her know that he saw what she truly feared.

"There was nothing wrong with you, Charlotte." His gaze was serious, piercing. He spoke slowly, emphasizing every word. "That was all on him. It had *nothing* to do with you."

Charlotte's pulse quickened at his perception. His eyes were as intense as she had ever seen them. As sexy as she had always found him, this level of connection was a whole new level of temptation.

Which brought its own set of problems.

She didn't think she'd be able to get by with stolen kisses and furtive glances for much longer.

Not when their attraction was deepening into something that she found quite irresistible.

# CHAPTER NINE

CHARLOTTE STOOD IN front of the floor-length mirror in her hotel room, fearing she might have made a mistake. When shopping for a dress for the hospital's fundraising gala, she'd thought the floor-length, off-the-shoulder black crepe gown was a sensible choice. Paired with a little purse and crystal-embellished silver high heels, she'd thought she would make an elegant but feminine statement.

And she had achieved that for sure.

With a serious side dish of sexy.

A slit in the dress ran from the hem to her hip, much higher than she remembered when she'd tried it on, and it would undoubtedly afford a generous view of her leg as she danced. The sleeveless top showed off her neck and shoulders, along with a tantalizing glimpse of cleavage.

This was a far cry from the donated cargo pants and faded tee shirt she had worn on her first day at the clinic. Maybe too far.

She loved the way the crepe whispered when

she moved, but the way it hugged and amplified every feminine curve was making her doubt herself. This dress didn't hint at exotic travel and rugged adventure. It spoke of romance and intrigue, fantasy and fascination. It felt a little dangerous, this dress. Like it could take her places she'd never gone before.

*Stop*, she whispered to her reflection.

This dress symbolized her new mission of pursuing the life she wanted, not just running from what she feared. And tonight she wanted to feel elegant and pretty.

She swished the dress some more, just for the fun of it, then started working on arranging her hair into a French braid updo. She felt like a princess tonight. A princess who wasn't going to wait for the king to rescue her. She was going to save herself, slay her dragons, and then claim her prize.

She was setting the last pin in place when there was a sharp knock at the door.

She strode to the door, feeling the cool air of the hotel room on her exposed leg.

"Good evening, Dr. Bennett."

She had no idea why she went all formal like that. Maybe because she was wearing formal wear. Or maybe because the man on her threshold oozed class and elegance in a tuxedo that had been perfectly tailored to his masculine, bulky build. Powerful, sophisticated, and elegant, this new version of her colleague left her speechless.

John seemed to be having trouble finding his words too, because he just stood at the threshold of her room, his mouth open, while he scanned her from head to silvery strappy toe.

"Dr. Owens. I mean, Charlotte. I think... Wow." He shook his head and tried again. "You look quite stunning, Charlotte."

An all-glass elevator was their carriage as they traveled down from Charlotte's room to the gala downstairs, affording a generous view of the hotel's lobby as they descended. Women in beautiful gowns roamed the halls and the boutique had stayed open late, offering high-end accessories and expensive jewelry. She thought she recognized one of the women as an on-call doctor who sometimes helped at the clinic.

"Oh, look. Isn't that...?"

But John wasn't paying any attention to the activity in the lobby. Instead, he was focused on the small stack of notecards in his hand. It must be the notes for his speech as he whisper-practiced the words that he hoped would inspire donors to support The Sunshine Clinic and the other outreach programs of the hospital.

The champagne reception was in full swing when they found their way to the ballroom. Waiters swooped here and there with trays full of champagne and hors d'oeuvres, while a lone pianist played smooth background music. John flagged down a waiter and took two tall flutes of champagne for himself and Charlotte.

"Come on, let me introduce you to some people," he said.

They moved from group to group, meeting the many specialists who made the hospital one of the top-rated in North America. Then they found their way to one of the round tables, where placards printed with their names marked their assigned places.

John and Charlotte took their seats. A server soon appeared, pouring ice water into their glasses and offering a basket of assorted breads and butter. Introductions revealed that they were sharing their table with a heart surgeon and her husband, a nurse practitioner who worked in cancer care, and the Pattersons, who had an entire wing of the hospital named after them for their generous donations.

"I'm sorry, dearie, what did you say your name was?" Mrs. Patterson asked, leaning in toward Charlotte. She cupped a hand around her ear, clearly hard of hearing.

"Dr. Charlotte Owens. I'm a locum pediatrician at The Sunshine Clinic for Kids."

"Oh, that's nice. How many kids do you two

have?" she asked, her fingers curved round the top of her purse.

"Oh, no!" Charlotte laughed. "We're not married."

Mrs. Patterson beamed. "Aw, you're newlyweds, then? The babies will be here soon enough."

Charlotte just smiled back. There didn't seem to be any point in correcting her again.

John leaned over and kissed her cheek, which made Mrs. Patterson beam even more.

All too soon, the chairman of the hospital board introduced John. Charlotte gave his hand a little squeeze for good luck as he headed for the stage.

John scanned his notecards one last time. This event was all about asking the community to support the hospital with generous donations. He didn't know why the chair of pediatrics had asked *him* to be the keynote speaker this year. Asking strangers to donate thousands of dollars was way outside his comfort zone. As was admitting that he couldn't do the important work of The Sunshine Clinic on his own.

But the teens needed him to be their voice.

He arranged the cards in a neat little stack, tucked them in his pocket and adjusted the microphone.

"My name is Dr. John Bennett and I really

hate asking for help. When I was young, asking for help was terrifying. I was afraid my family might be split up if anyone knew that we sometimes couldn't pay the phone bill or afford more than the basics. Now I'm a doctor, and I take care of kids who also hate asking for help. But unlike me, who at least had a family, they're alone in the world and don't know who to trust. I want to be that person for them. The one who helps them see they deserve so much more than just basic survival. That it's safe for them to dream and set goals. That they can count on us to be there. Ultimately, I want them to understand that it's not just okay to ask for help, it's their basic human right to get it. But to do that work, I have to ask for *your* help. Because I can't do it alone—no matter how much I think I want to."

John went on to describe the vision he had for The Sunshine Clinic. Expanding it into a one-stop health clinic able to address all the medical and mental health needs of teens in crisis. Finding ways to expand its reach in Seattle and beyond, so more teens could get the support they needed. He finished by telling them about Matthew and Sam and Angel, giving human faces to the dry statistics he had captured on the index cards in his pocket.

He refocused on the audience. He felt utterly drained after exposing his deepest thoughts and desires to virtual strangers. But he also felt liberated. Whatever happened next would be what it was.

He was about to leave the stage when, from the back of the room, he heard the sound of someone clapping. Soon it was followed by another person, and then another. One by one, everyone in the room rose to their feet, clapping and smiling. There were more than a few hankies out, dabbing at damp eyes.

John was mystified. It took him a full minute to realize that the standing ovation was for him.

His throat grew tight with emotions he was having a hard time containing.

He saw Charlotte standing next to Mrs. Patterson, patting her shoulder as she dabbed her eyes with a hanky. Charlotte gave him a shaky smile through her own shimmering tears as she clapped. *Well done*, she mouthed, and he suddenly felt blissfully, crazily, unbearably happy.

With the speeches done, the lights were dimmed and the on-stage curtains parted to reveal a DJ with her equipment surrounding her. She played songs that were energetic, with a strong background beat for dancing.

John offered Charlotte his hand. "Dance with me?"

For the next hour, they burned off the nervous energy of the night, dancing and spinning and

singing along with the lyrics. Charlotte pulled out
the pins that held her French updo in place, letting
her dark waves spill down over her shoulders and
driving John crazy. It felt so good to let himself
go, to dance and move with Charlotte until they
were both damp with exertion.

There was a slight pause, and then the first
notes of a slow ballad played. Charlotte gave John
a small smile, then nodded toward the table, indicating that she was ready to head back. She was
probably right. This was a professional event. The
two of them slow-dancing together would definitely activate the hospital's gossip network. But
he was surprised at the sudden wave of resistance
that washed over him. He was so tired of ignoring his heart's deepest desires.

He stopped in his tracks. "No, please stay," he
said, catching her hand.

She gave him a nervous smile. "With all these
people?"

"Why not?" he said, tugging her to him. "You
are my wife, after all."

She hesitated for a moment, then her eyes lit up
with understanding. "That's right—we're newlyweds! At least in Mrs. Patterson's mind."

"That's good enough for me."

She laughed, and then she was in his arms.
John felt her hand curve over his shoulder as he
claimed the small of her back. Their free hands

met, their fingers intertwined, and then they were dancing to the music, their bodies in perfect sync.

As they circled the floor—first right, then left, then right again—John felt her body slowly melt into his.

She pulled away from his shoulder to look up at him. Her mouth was candy-apple-red, plump and full. An irresistible feast waiting to be devoured.

"We danced like this at our wedding reception, didn't we?" she said. Her eyes were hesitant, as if she was not sure he'd want to play the game.

He lightly traced the curve of her jaw with his finger. "We did. And we were perfect, Charlotte. As if we'd been dancing together for a thousand years."

The dance floor was more crowded now. He tucked her closer and her body became like a reed, bending and swaying with his as they smoothly moved between the other couples.

Charlotte moved so elegantly with the music. There was something very ethereal about the way she danced, as if she were a mirage that could disappear at any moment.

*Please stay,* he thought.

A yearning rose from deep in his heart—for what, he couldn't say, but he knew it was awfully important. His heart beat faster with the wanting of her.

Charlotte was gazing at him with a wistful

look in her eyes. She caught her bottom lip between her teeth before asking, "And our wedding night...were we perfect then too?"

His heart literally stopped for a full beat as he realized what she was asking. There was a hint of challenge in her eyes mixed with nervousness. Because it *was* a challenge—and he knew it. They had been dancing around the question of their relationship ever since they'd met. John knew their attraction was undeniable, but so was the force of the fears that repelled them when they got too close.

They moved in rhythmic circles, gazes locked, bodies melded. She matched his movements perfectly, so that he couldn't tell if he was leading or following. Everything blurred together—he and Charlotte, the past and the present, hopes and fears...

He took a deep bracing breath and stepped into the unknown, with all its wild, sweet possibilities. "Better than perfect, Charlotte. We were real."

He heard Charlotte's breath catch in her throat. He could practically feel the want humming in her body, vibrating into his. She stopped dancing for a moment, gazed at him directly, without artifice or fear. For a moment he feared he had taken the game too far and she would disappear in his arms like smoke.

But instead she raised herself on tiptoe and

whispered in his ear. A sudden hot rush of desire swept through his body like a tsunami. He nodded and led her to the edge of the dance floor. He knew they should probably say their goodbyes to coworkers and donors.

John hovered between responsibility and desire.

Oh, to hell with doing the right or proper thing. All he wanted was Charlotte.

He grabbed Charlotte's hand and led her out of the ballroom, letting his heart guide the way.

# CHAPTER TEN

Mercifully, they had the elevator to themselves. John punched the button for their floor. For a moment they stood side by side, shoulder to shoulder, watching the numbers climb on the indicator. Soft music played in the background—something kind of jaunty. The entire scene was surreal, and out of sync with the urgent, pressing need she felt deep in her belly.

Neither reached for the other's hand or stole a kiss. Which was good, she thought, because just one touch would be like dropping a match on a pile of dry kindling. It wouldn't surprise her if they both went up in flames.

At last, there was a soft *ding*, signaling their floor, and the elevator doors slid open. Then John grabbed her hand and led her down the hallway to his room. With one quick swipe of his key card, the door swung open and John pulled her across the threshold.

Finally, they were alone.

As soon as the door clicked shut, John's hands

found her waist and guided her backwards, until her back was pressed up against the door. His mouth, hard and needy, found hers, shocking her breath into silence. Her body instantly responded to his. Her mouth opened to him, tasting a hint of whiskey on his lips and beneath that, the taste of him. Wild and masculine, thrilling and real. It was almost too much, all these sensations at once, and she whimpered against his mouth, needing more.

Her hands moved of their own accord, traveling the length of his arms to the breadth of his shoulders, the strong muscles of his back. But that wasn't enough—not nearly enough—and she tugged at his shirt, freeing it so she could slide her hands beneath to explore the warm, firm flesh of his belly and back.

John groaned against her lips, his breath jagged and harsh. "I've wanted to make love to you since the day you walked into my clinic."

Charlotte took a ragged breath. "Really? Because I thought you hated me."

John nipped her bottom lip, making her gasp with the shock of it, then followed with light kisses and nibbles that made a shiver of pleasure race up her spine.

"None of that is important now. Only this. Only us."

He braced both of his arms on the wall, creating a cocoon just for them, then moved his mouth over hers. She closed her eyes and let him take her deeper, until all she could see and sense was him, all around her.

She opened her eyes to find his gaze, steady and strong. He encircled one of her wrists and guided her to the sleeping area. She followed him to the foot of the king-sized bed that dominated the room. He kissed her again, this time gently, with great deliberation.

"I want to take this slow, Charlotte. I've waited so long to touch you. I need to know you, see you… I don't know if that makes sense, but…" He trailed off as he bent to kiss her again, his hands reverent as they cupped her face.

So, this was what it felt like to be cherished. To have someone make you feel like you were the most important person in the world. It felt good to be seen, but also vaguely dangerous. She stood on tiptoe, her hands on John's as they framed her face, as if he were her only chance of surviving the raging rivers of doubt that threatened to drown her.

And then he was undressing her. Slowly spinning her till her back was to him, finding the zipper cleverly hidden in the side seam of her dress. There was a sharp, hissing sound, then her dress fell in a crumpled heap at her feet. The cool air of the room rushed over her body, tensing her nipples and sending goosebumps down her back.

John's mouth found her flesh...the graceful curve where her shoulder met her neck. His mouth was warm...so warm compared to the cool room. His fingertips stroked the delicate flesh over the curve of her breasts, teasing the place just above her lacy strapless bra. It made her shiver with pleasure again.

"Look at us, Charlotte," John said, his voice husky. "We're perfect."

There was a mirror across from the bed. There she was, nearly naked and wrapped in John's arms. They fit together so perfectly, her head to his shoulder, his strength to her grace. She felt the symmetry of them, and it was so tempting to lean into him and this image, believing it would be enough to sustain them.

She turned away from the mirror, offering her profile. "The light... Can we turn it off, please?"

Not because she was ashamed, but because she wanted to block out the entire world so that all she could feel and taste was John.

He switched off the table lamp, then opened the heavy draperies so the soft glow of Seattle's nightlife was their only illumination.

Then he was back, pulling her to him, and she had her chance to even the playing field. She quickly unbuttoned his shirt, sliding her hands up and over his shoulders, letting the shirt slide from his back to finally reveal the strength she'd lusted for these last long months. He was as beautiful a man as she'd ever seen, his muscles full and firm, his belly taut with tension.

He guided her to the bed, following her down till they lay together. He continued his slow, deliberate exploration, his tongue finding the soft flesh curving up from her bra, driving her crazy with little licks and nibbles. She arched her back, silently begging for more, and he obliged, unclasping her bra and then flinging that useless garment across the room. It made her laugh a little, his wanton playfulness, but when his mouth found her breast and began a careful exploration of her hidden pleasure points she couldn't laugh anymore. She could barely think.

Had she ever been loved like this before? Definitely not. It was like he was creating her with every touch, every kiss, every stroke of his fingertips. Finding everything good and tender she'd kept hidden away and sculpting it out of the raw material that was her life. She felt found, and she knew it was because John was the first to ever look.

She moaned as his thumb found her nipple and teased even more pleasure from her already heated body. Such a flood of sensations—the roughness of his fingers, the softness of his tongue, the solid weight of his body on hers, the beat of their hearts together... The air seemed to crackle with electricity as he hooked her lace panties with his finger and slid them off her legs. Then his hands were everywhere, exploring, finding, teasing, setting off a deep ache that started in her core and rolled out in gentle waves to every inch of her body.

He strummed her desire ever higher, till she was fisting the sheets beneath her, arching toward a release that seemed tantalizingly out of reach.

"John...!" she cried out, and she didn't know if she was begging for mercy or begging for more. "More..." she panted into the night, her skin slick with sweat.

More sensation, more pleasure, more touch and more tingles, and more long, slow, wet kisses that wiped her memory clean.

*I want more*, she thought.

So much more that all her doubts and fears were overcome by the raging desire she felt for him. But she couldn't say all the things in her heart. All she could do was call his name.

And then he was there, as if he had read every thought in her head, stretching the full length of his body with hers, the weight of him so reassuring in the midst of this storm that was sweeping through her, threatening to sweep her out to sea. She grasped tight to his body, finding refuge and calm there in his steady heartbeat and patient hands.

*More...*

John eased her onto her back. She could feel the heat of his body under her hands, hear his jagged breath against her ear. Proof that he wanted her as much as she wanted him, and it only made her crazier.

"Please..." she whispered against his kiss, and she couldn't stop herself from grinding against him, which made him growl with need.

She hooked one leg over his, felt his body shift under hers as he reached across the bed. She heard a drawer open, then the rip of foil, before his weight was fully on her again. With the moonlight bathing their bodies in a luminous glow, he found her, and she arched to meet him. The sensations that followed were so sublime Charlotte felt utterly incapable of speech or thought. Gentle and slow, he rocked her into the night. Every sigh took her home, back to a place and time when she'd felt loved and protected.

He gathered her close and rocked her until her mind was quiet and her heart full. So full she feared it would explode into a thousand points of brilliant light. And when the warm feelings in her body heated to their inevitable flashpoint, it was his body she clung to. Every shuddering wave wiped her slate clean, leaving her raw and exposed, defenseless in his arms. He cried out her name soon after. She opened her eyes and found his gaze, deep and intense, his pupils dark with pleasure.

Later, when their hearts had slowed to a normal rhythm, he spread the comforter over both of them and tucked her into the curve of his body. She listened as his breaths grew long and deep. It was tempting to let the rise and fall of his chest soothe her to sleep...

But this wasn't her room. She didn't belong there—not all night. Somehow falling asleep in his arms seemed too intimate despite their intense sexual encounter.

The digital clock marked another minute's passing.

*One more minute. I'll leave when the clock is at the half-hour.*

Sixty seconds later, she swore she'd leave when five minutes had passed.

But it was many minutes later when she sighed, knowing she couldn't linger in John's warm bed any longer.

He was surely deep in sleep by now.

It was time for her to go.

As if reading her mind, John tightened his arm around her, pressing her against his chest.

"Just stay," he whispered against her hair. "All you have to do is stay."

Charlotte's body went still, but her mind was running wild. It was so tempting to stay there, curled up against John. His body was warm and she could smell his uniquely masculine scent on his skin and her pillow.

*"Just stay"* was closing her eyes and drifting into sleep, safe and peaceful in John's arms.

*"Just stay"* was sharing coffee with him the next morning, planning their next date and sending sexy text messages between patients.

*"Just stay"* was having a future, adopting a puppy, spending their weekends painting the living room.

But *"just stay"* could also be police officers and stolen futures and having everything she knew and counted on wiped out in a split second. There was no way she could have love without accepting the risk of losing it forever.

Her body remained rigid as her mind battled furiously with itself. Want versus need...hope against fear.

The room's heater clicked on. Beyond the door she could hear a faint peal of laughter as other hotel guests found their way back to their rooms.

*He doesn't mean forever. Just for tonight.*

She could do this... just for tonight. She let herself slowly relax into John, melting into the warm cocoon he had created for her. And as the sun's first rays cast a faint, pink glow in their room she finally closed her eyes and drifted into sleep.

A week later found John in an exceedingly good mood. He'd come to work late, on account of taking Piper to the doctor to have her cast removed. She'd lost a little muscle tone after weeks of resting her leg, but that didn't stop her from jumping out of his SUV and skipping her way into school.

John's gait was positively jaunty as he crossed the waiting room. "Morning, Sarah," he said, swinging his backpack up to land on the reception counter. "What have I missed?"

"Not much," Sarah said. "Charlotte seems to have things under control this morning. Now, what's happened to put you in such a good mood? You look like the cat who's just eaten the canary."

"Which would not be good news for the canary, now, would it?" John said, his body pulsing with anticipation.

After weeks of consideration, he'd finally made a grand decision. There was no point in trying to hide it from Sarah. She was the eyes and ears of the place, able to ferret out anything out of the ordinary.

John opened his backpack and carefully withdrew the forms he'd spent the previous night working on. He handed them over to Sarah and waited for her response.

She popped her bifocals on the end of her nose and perused the documents, then handed them back. "It's about time, if you ask me."

He should have known better than to expect flattery or compliments from Sarah. She was old-school about that sort of thing, believing that excessive praise made a person go soft.

Still, he had thought she would be a little more excited, considering how often she had harped at him to add a second doctor to the clinic.

"It's not official, of course," he cautioned, tapping the forms into a tidy stack. "I need to talk to Charlotte first, before I submit this to Human Resources. I don't want just any doctor to work here on a permanent basis. So if Charlotte's not interested in staying long-term, then these forms will wind up in the trash."

It felt like a long shot—maybe the longest shot he'd ever taken. But after the night they'd spent together after the gala, he couldn't imagine living life as if everything was the same. These past few weeks of living with Charlotte and Cat had made him realize that maybe all his protectiveness over Piper was a mistake. All this time he had thought that he needed to ignore his growing feelings for Charlotte, so that Piper would be safe. But Piper was healing much faster now that they lived with Charlotte. Maybe, he thought, his job wasn't to protect her from anything that might hurt her. Maybe his job was to help her find a tribe of friends and family who would pick her up if she took a fall.

Sarah crossed her fingers for good luck for him as she reached to take a call. "Oh, one more thing," she said. "Your first patients of the day are waiting in your exam room."

John nodded and headed to the workstation he shared with Charlotte. Soon he'd be able to trade the old wood door for a real built-in office area. He had gathered all the supplies and just needed to carve out some time on the weekend to get the work done.

Still whistling, he carried on preparing for the day. He stopped by the coffee station first, then reviewed the day's cases.

He was just about to set off for his exam room when he noticed a bright pink note pinned to Charlotte's bulletin board.

*Return cruise ship contract ASAP!*

It was written in Charlotte's neat script. There were about fifty exclamation marks for emphasis.

He stopped whistling mid-note and his heart took a nosedive toward his stomach. He plucked the note from the board and examined both sides, though he had no idea what he expected to see.

So, she was still excited about working on the cruise ship. She hadn't spoken of it in so long, he'd thought maybe she was losing interest in the prospect. An assumption on his part and apparently an incorrect one at that.

He put the note back and slumped in his chair to recover. Was everything just the same for her, then? Their night at the hotel had meant nothing?

Not that she owed him anything after their shared night together. They were both grown adults, free to spend their nights where they wished. But for John, going back to the status quo was not going to be easy. He was falling for her, pure and simple. And now that he had seen how well Piper was doing with Charlotte in their lives, his fear that falling for Charlotte might hurt Piper was losing its grip on him.

He sighed and scrubbed his face with his hands. He had patients waiting. He couldn't mope here like a lovestruck teenager, hoping for a different outcome if he waited long enough.

He looked at the forms he had so meticulously completed the night before, asking the hospital to make Charlotte's job permanent.

Should he even ask her if she wanted to stay? Or were the fifty exclamation marks on that note all the answer he needed?

He contemplated that for a long minute—then dropped the forms in the trash can next to his desk.

# CHAPTER ELEVEN

JOHN WAS IN LOVE.

She was beautiful and funny and had the cutest one-toothed smile he'd ever seen.

Babies weren't John's usual patient demographic, but this particular baby was snuggled in her big sister's arms. Rosa was seventeen years old and had brought baby Anna to the clinic because she was worried about her.

"She does this strange eyelid fluttering thing," Rosa said, her brow furrowed with worry. "It used to only happen when we were outside, on sunny days. But now it happens a lot inside too, especially when she's first waking up in the morning. I've rinsed her eyes and tried some of those eye drops made for babies from the drugstore. But nothing is helping."

John gently took the baby from Rosa. His heart went out to the girl. She looked as nervous and worried as any mother would. Speaking of mothers—where was Anna and Rosa's mom? That was always a tricky question, and one he'd have to approach carefully.

John lay Anna on the table and started with a basic exam. The baby girl was in excellent health. Her cocoa-brown skin was smooth and nourished, and her plump, round belly said she was getting plenty of calories every day. He noted her tiny clean white socks and the warm yellow sweater over her jumper. Someone was taking very good care of Anna.

"Sorry, Miss Anna, but I have to shine this bright light in your eyes," John crooned to the baby.

Anna flailed her arms wildly and blew a raspberry kiss, which John took as her tacit approval. Shining his ophthalmoscope in each of her chocolate-brown eyes, he determined that her basic brain function was fine and she didn't show any signs of neurological disease. The eyes themselves were fine too, without evidence of injury or disease.

But during the exam Anna had had several short episodes of her eyes rolling upward, paired with rapid-fire eyelid flutters. Each episode lasted just a second or two and didn't seem to bother Anna in the slightest.

"Does Anna ever seem spaced out to you? Like she's daydreaming and you can't get her attention?"

Rosa nodded. "Yeah. Sometimes when I'm feeding her she'll just stare off in the distance for a little bit, like she's thinking about something. Is that important?"

"It could be." John finished the exam and passed Anna back to Rosa for snuggles. Anna giggled wildly when she saw her sister, clapping her chubby hands with delight.

"Silly girl," Rosa said, giving her sister a gentle nose-bop with her finger. "I never left you!"

*And you never would*, John thought, instinctively knowing that for some reason Rosa had stepped in as Anna's mother and was doing the best she could with only the knowledge and resources she had as a teenager.

"So, what do you think is wrong?" Rosa asked.

Baby Anna began fussing in Rosa's arms. The long wait to see John had surely extended into her lunchtime. Rosa opened her backpack with one hand and tugged out a small cooler where a chilled bottle waited. She shook it to mix the formula, then offered it to Anna, who greedily sucked at the nipple.

John made some notes in the baby's brand-new client record before focusing on Rosa. "There's a couple of possibilities. Your sister's eye-blinking could be a sign of a behavioral tic. Most kids outgrow those in a year or less. But if not, she could have a condition of the nervous system called

Tourette Syndrome. But the fact that your sister also had periods of spacing out makes me suspicious that she's having seizures. Those spacing out spells could be absence seizures, which are like brief electrical storms in the brain that impair your sister's consciousness for anywhere from ten to forty-five seconds. The blinkies might only be eyelid myoclonia, a small seizure that doesn't impair her in any way, but all that seizure activity is not good for her brain."

Rosa was wide-eyed now, and clearly afraid. "Is she going to be okay?"

"I think her prognosis is excellent. But we need to get those seizures under control—and that means she needs to see a neurologist for testing and treatment."

Rosa's expression fell. "Oh, I don't think my family has the money for anything like that, Dr. J."

John closed his laptop and rolled a stool over so he could meet her eye to eye. "Well, let's talk about that, Rosa. And then let's talk about you."

A half-hour later John walked Rosa to the reception area and asked Sarah to set up a neurology appointment for Anna. The baby was asleep now, her dark lashes like fringes on her tiny, plump cheeks.

"And let's reach out to the hospital's Social Services, too," John told Sarah. "I'd like a social worker to contact Rosa regarding subsidized childcare options for Anna." He turned to Anna. "No more skipping school to take care of your sister, okay?"

Rosa's eyes were shiny with misty unshed tears. "Thank you so much, Dr. J. I don't know what we would have done if you weren't here."

John squeezed her elbow. "That's what we're here for."

John returned to his desk to type up the notes from the appointment. Seeing Rosa had triggered so many memories for him. He was glad he could be there for her, but it brought back memories of all his lost years. How much he had given up to try and protect his brother as best he could.

He thought of Rosa and the worry that had etched her young face. Would she blame herself for Anna's seizures? When in fact the culprit would be a rogue gene, either inherited or mutated, that had set the path in place before Anna was even born.

There wasn't anything Rosa could do to change her sister's fate. Was it possible that there wasn't anything John could have done to change his brother's fate either? Maybe Michael, like Piper, needed more than just John in his life, trying to shoulder all the burdens on his own.

Maybe he needed more in his life too. More love, more connection, more community, more support. Certainly the last few months with Charlotte had opened his heart to magical new possibilities. Thanks to her, he had been able to speak from the heart at the gala about the work they did at the clinic, garnering historic levels of donations for The Sunshine Clinic. Thanks to her, Piper's laptop sat ignored for much of the day while she played with Cat or invited a friend over for manicures and "girl talk"—whatever that was.

Was he really going to let all that walk out of his life without a fight?

The papers he'd discarded before seeing Rosa were still in the trash. He pulled them out, smoothed the corners with the palm of his hand. His heart wavered. This was a crazy idea. Did he seriously think that *GypsyMD* would want to trade her life of exotic travel and adventure for a grounded life in Seattle with him and Piper?

But he couldn't forget how it had felt to hold Charlotte in his arms that night at the hotel. To feel the struggle in her body for so many long minutes when he'd asked her to stay. He'd feared she might just flip the covers back and leave anyway. But though she'd never said a word, he'd felt the answer in her body as she'd finally softened against his chest. It had stirred his protective side, knowing that she was choosing to trust him, and he'd wanted to be worthy of that trust that night and for all the nights ahead.

That was the part of him that knew he had to ask Charlotte to stay—even if it ended in rejection. Because he deserved to have this chance. And so did she.

John slid the paperwork back inside his backpack. He would ask Charlotte tonight, after Piper went to bed, if she would consider staying in Seattle permanently.

But, drat, it was Thursday—the day he played basketball with the teens at the community center after work. He rarely missed these games. The kids had come to count on him being there every Thursday—it was a sort of unofficial office hour, when they could ask questions or check him out in a more relaxed setting.

Trust was so important in his work with these teens. Making those games every Thursday was one of the ways he earned that trust.

Okay, tomorrow, then. He'd take the paperwork home but wait until the next day to ask Charlotte to consider staying in Seattle.

Charlotte's pink note fluttered when the heat pump clicked on. It felt like a taunt. Was he sure he had until tomorrow? This note was pinned to her bulletin board to make sure she didn't forget. That meant she was going to sign that contract soon.

But if it was still taped there, she hadn't signed it yet. He still had a chance.

Enough contemplating, it was time for action.

He borrowed her notepad to write her another note.

*You are cordially invited for a sunset cruise aboard The House Call. Dress is resort casual. Dinner will be served. Don't be late!*

He taped that note on top of hers, to make sure she noticed it first. Then added fifty-one exclamation points for good measure.

Mickey's Café and Tiki Bar was a harborside restaurant located at the marina where John docked *The House Call*. He and Piper were frequent visitors. Piper loved the strawberry milkshakes and John loved the breathtaking views of the harbor, where he and Piper would watch various water vessels come and go. Making up outlandish stories about the people aboard and their adventures was their favorite game.

But tonight it was just him and Charlotte. He had asked Sarah if she would mind keeping Piper at her place overnight again, so he and Charlotte could sail alone.

He could feel the cold bottle of champagne he had stored in his backpack pressing against his spine. The paperwork he needed to submit to make Charlotte's position at the clinic permanent was safely stored in a different pocket. With any luck, he'd be able to pop the champagne later, to celebrate the start of a new adventure for both of them.

But first dinner. John ordered several sandwiches and side dishes as part of the café's signature "picnic to go" special, which they offered to their seafaring customers. Everything was packed into an adorable wicker picnic basket which, it was understood, customers would return to the restaurant on their way out of the marina.

John watched Charlotte as they headed toward the dock where his boat waited. With her hair down and the breeze rustling its loose, dark waves, she was truly stunning tonight.

Moose, the marina cat, was serving his self-appointed role as sentry. He was perched on a post, big, fluffy and regal. Local lore said that petting Moose before a trip would keep sailors and boats safe at sea. Charlotte obliged with a long session of ear-rubs.

John and Charlotte held hands as they followed the walkway to John's boat. It was six-thirty— half an hour past the time he usually went to the community center. Some of the regulars would be there by now, warming up and trading friendly taunts for the game ahead. More teens would trickle in over the next half-hour, greeting each other with hearty jests or tentative smiles. John knew he was the glue that held the whole evening together, helping shy kids find their place on the team and giving the strongest players a good workout.

Charlotte put her hand on his arm. "You good?"

He was doing it again—ruminating on all the people he wanted to save instead of just being with his people.

Tonight was about him and Charlotte. And Piper too, even though she wasn't there.

Charlotte spun so that she was facing him, blocking his path. "We don't have to do this, you know."

"What are you talking about?"

"Sailing. I'd love to go, but I have a feeling you'd feel better if you were at the community center."

He started to protest but realized it was pointless. Charlotte could read him like a book. "How did you know?"

"It's this funny thing you do with your face when you're worried. Want me to demonstrate?"

He laughed, remembering her demonstration of his scowling face. "No, thanks. I'm good."

John contemplated the possibility of making it to the community center to check on the teens and then getting back in time for a quick sail around the bay. He couldn't deny the nagging feeling that he was letting the teens down.

He shook off these familiar demons. He loved those weekly basketball games, but that didn't mean he should be there every single week. If he was going to build a bigger life for him and Piper, and eventually his brother, he needed to stop carrying the weight of the world on his shoulders all the time.

He gave Charlotte's hand a little shake. "Come here."

He pulled her in close and circled his arm around her waist. He could feel her smooth, warm skin through her shirt. He nuzzled her neck, deeply inhaling the sweet scent of Charlotte mixed with jasmine and the briny scent of the sea. All his favorite things mixed together in one intoxicating fragrance.

"This is the only place I want to be." He pulled back so he could see her eyes. "Okay?"

"Okay," she said, leaning into him until her forehead rested against his chest.

He stroked the back of her neck for a moment, feeling a new warmth take root in his heart and expand to fill his entire body. It chased away the guilt and fear, so that all that was left was a profound gratitude that of all the clinics in all the world, this gorgeous woman had found her way to The Sunshine Clinic.

"All right," he said, placing his knuckles under her chin so he could guide her gaze to his. "Are you ready to learn the ropes, so to speak?"

"Sure!" She laughed. "I've had a lot of travel

adventures in my life, but this will be my first time sailing."

They boarded *The House Call* and he showed her how to prepare the ropes for their voyage. Then he used the onboard motor to navigate out of the marina and into the harbor.

If he had more time, he'd take her far beyond the harbor. Past the sea lions basking on buoys and the seawall that protected the shoreline from storm surge flooding. Past the sailboats and houseboats and the seaside mansions. And past the fishing trawlers, their nets heavy with catch. He'd take her out to the Puget Sound where, if the winds were favorable, he would shut off the engine and hoist the sails and harness the power of nature to explore the islands and ports off the coastline of Seattle.

But there was little wind, so Charlotte's first sailing lesson couldn't include hoisting a sail. She accepted the consolation prize of navigating via the onboard motor while John set out their picnic dinner from Mickey's Café. With their plates full, and the boat floating far from the shoreline, they sat on the deck to eat dinner, their legs dangling over the water.

John didn't think this moment could be any more perfect. There was the feel of Charlotte's hip and shoulder against his, the distant lights of other ships in the harbor reflecting off the water, and the very light breeze that rippled the water and made Charlotte shiver in the night. All the things he'd always wanted...all in one place. There was only one thing that would make this night more perfect.

He was about to reach for his backpack, with its contract and champagne, when Charlotte glanced up at him, her shoulder pressed to his. Their gazes met and something in her eyes made his pulse quicken. There was a sultry glint to her eyes that made it too easy to imagine her naked in his berth, stretched out on the navy-blue comforter, her hair wild and tousled against the pillow.

Oh, what he would give to have the length of her gorgeous naked body pressed against his in the same bed where he had spent so many lonely nights. He could imagine it all quite perfectly— and suddenly it was all he wanted.

He raised his fingers to stroke her cheek delicately, as if she were a very fine statue meant to be kept safe behind velvet ropes. He felt that way sometimes...that she was not really for him. Then he dropped his head to kiss her, deliberately and carefully, with great reverence.

Her lips were warm against the cold night. The soft meeting of their mouths made his soul sigh with pleasure. How could he ever doubt that she was for him? They fit together too perfectly and understood each other too well. Even their jagged edges were like the pieces of a puzzle, fitting together to make sense out of the fragments of their past.

Charlotte scooted closer to him, eventually working her way into his lap. Now she was everywhere...in his arms...deepening the kiss... asking for more. And he wanted to give her everything he had—tonight and all the nights after. His mouth became hungry and hot. He wanted to somehow pull her into his very soul. Charlotte was here, in his arms, filling all the empty places in his heart and soul.

*I believe in this. I believe in us. I believe in forever.*

"John..." she whispered against his ear.

Her hands had burrowed their way beyond his coat, under his shirt, and were now stroking his skin, taking his temperature higher. He knew what she was asking of him and he wished he could figure out a way to hoist both of them up from where they sat so he wouldn't have to let her go.

"Mm-hmm..." he replied.

It was all he could manage. Because Charlotte was kissing him everywhere now, and it felt so good to be loved this much. He believed that was what this could be. Love—pure and simple.

"Make love to me again..." she breathed, stirring all those lovely memories of their night at the hotel, when she had thrilled him just by asking for what she wanted.

Oh, he should do that. They should make love tonight, and then in the morning, and probably midday tomorrow for good measure.

He whispered against her lips. "Charlotte?"

"Mm-hmm…?"

He stopped her gently, pressing his fingertips against her chest with just the tiniest bit of pressure.

She broke away, but her eyes were hazy and unfocused with desire. "Hmm…?"

He traced his thumb against her bottom lip, willing himself to propose the idea of her staying long-term. But she was doing something with her fingers, tucking them into the waistband of his pants, finding the warm, hidden skin there with her sea-cooled fingers. It made him burn all over for her, and to wish for a better space to continue their explorations.

"Hold that thought," he said—then crushed her mouth with his. He felt like a starved man who would never get his fill.

Somehow they struggled to their feet without breaking their kiss. Charlotte wrapped herself around him, matching his hungry kisses with her own before leading him downstairs to his berth.

Then she jumped on the bed and landed on

her knees. And she laughed and laughed, telling him to, "Get in here, slowpoke!" She pulled her sweater off in one fluid motion, revealing her luscious curves and the sweet tease of her white lace bra.

He unbuttoned his shirt as fast as he could, but the last button was stubborn. He had no choice but to pull his shirt apart with one ferocious yank, sending the button flying across the room to land with a soft *plink*. Her eyes widened with delight as she moved aside to make room for him in the berth.

But before he could join her there was a ferocious buzzing in his back pocket—the insistent chime of a five-alarm fire bell. It was the distinctive tone he had chosen for calls from the hospital.

Charlotte froze on the bed. Their gazes met and locked. They both knew this wasn't any routine call from the hospital. Not this late on a weeknight.

He answered it. "This is Dr. Bennett."

He listened for many long minutes, asked routine questions about the patient's status. Eventually he turned away from Charlotte, so she wouldn't see what this call was doing to him.

"Thanks for calling. I'm on my way."

John disconnected the call and paused, taking one last minute for himself. One last minute of feeling loved and hopeful about his future. One last minute of living in a watercolor dreamworld where he had a vibrant, if hazy, future with Charlotte.

"What is it, John? What's wrong?"

He darkened the phone before sliding it into his pocket. He felt the mask of Dr. J slipping back into place.

"We have to head back."

"Why?" She held her sweater to her chest. "What's wrong? Is it Piper?"

John made the adjustments that would fire the engine back into life. He didn't want to talk. He just wanted to get moving...get back to work. It seemed to be the only thing the universe was willing to trust him with.

"John?" She was more insistent now, sensing the magnitude of the change in their tiny space.

"It's Angel. She went to the community center looking for me because she was feeling very sick."

"Is she okay?" Charlotte slipped her sweater back on.

"I don't know. She collapsed at the center and was rushed to the emergency room."

# CHAPTER TWELVE

THE HOSPITAL'S WAITING room was filled with teens that Charlotte recognized from The Sunshine Clinic. She wanted to go with John to get an update on Angel's status, but seeing the stress and worry on these young faces, she knew she needed to stay with them.

Unlike on most of her temporary assignments, where she was the outsider looking in, the teens here had adopted her as part of their ever-shifting, highly flexible family unit. Not a family like any she had seen in movies or on television, but a family all the same.

Maybe that was why she hadn't responded to *The Eden* yet. The beauty and adventure of the Caribbean still called to her, but she felt a strange and utterly unfamiliar pull to stay in Seattle. She was falling for John—she knew that—and for his precocious, lovable niece. But there was more holding her in Seattle. Forces she couldn't understand, but which made it impossible for her to just board *The Eden* and leave it behind.

She didn't know exactly what she would do, but she knew she needed to call the cruise ship's human resources department and ask for an extension before signing her contract. It would give her more time to think and decide what she wanted to do.

Now, looking at the pale, strained expressions of the teens who had witnessed Angel's collapse, she finally understood why she felt pulled to stay. She was needed here. Piper, and the teens, and even that silly Cat, all needed her.

The only person she wasn't sure about was John. He was so self-sufficient...so insistent on doing things his way and on his own. Would he welcome her decision to stay in Seattle? Or was their love affair nothing more to him than a fling with a doctor he was sure would leave?

But she pushed those thoughts to the back of her mind as the teens told her what they had seen—how Angel had gone to the community center, pale and confused, looking for John. How she'd left and some of the teens had followed her, sensing something was wrong, and how they'd found her in the parking lot, unconscious and cold.

"It was so scary," one of the girls said. She had her arms wrapped around herself, rocking back and forth.

"Where was Dr. J anyway?" one of the boys

demanded. "He's always at our Thursday night games!"

John returned to the waiting room and the teens gathered around him for news and information. He did his best to get them caught up on Angel's status, assuring them that Angel was going to be okay.

He caught eyes with Charlotte and nodded toward the nurses' station.

"I'll be back in a second, kids. Let me just get Dr. Owens caught up."

Charlotte followed John to a quiet alcove near the nurses' station.

"The EMTs said when they found Angel she was unconscious but breathing on her own. Other than her fast heart rate, her other vital signs were good. She regained consciousness on the way to the ER, but complained of dizziness and a small headache. The ED attending wants to keep her for a few hours for observation. But if she remains medically stable, they plan to release her by morning."

Charlotte grabbed his arm. "We can't let them do that, John. Angel could have a genetic heart defect. Maybe Brugada Syndrome? I don't know… But I do know that if they release her tonight without more testing her heart could be a ticking time bomb in her chest."

John ran a hand through his hair. "I know. But

without a full family medical history they're not
going to admit her to the hospital for testing. Especially not without health insurance."

"I'm going to talk to the attending," Charlotte
snapped.

John caught her arm at the wrist before she
could stalk down the hall.

"Hey." John pinched the bridge of his nose. "I
think it might be time for me to take over Angel's care again."

"What are you talking about?"

John slipped his hands into his leather jacket.
"I feel that I've been losing sight of some of my
priorities, you know? That I might be getting out
of touch with the teens. Your house will be done
in the next few weeks. Who knows what's next
for you?"

Charlotte's brow furrowed in frustration. "I
haven't signed my contract."

"I know. But you could if you wanted to. You
can go anywhere you want, Charlotte, or you can
stay right here. I don't have those choices. I've
got people who count on me to be there for them,
and lately—like tonight—I've been letting them
down."

Charlotte felt a familiar heat creeping up the
back of her neck, and that prickly, itchy sensation following close behind.

"Having you here these past few months has

been…" John stopped to cough, his voice breaking. "Amazing. Charlotte, I can't thank you enough for all you've done for Piper, Angel, the teens…and me."

Charlotte wanted to press her hands to her ears.

*Please stop talking…please stop talking… please stop talking.*

"I don't ever want my life to be the way it was before, Charlotte. Falling in love with you has made me realize that I deserve more. The trouble is, I don't know how to get what I most want— you—without hurting someone. Like I did tonight."

*Toughen up, Owens. This isn't your first rodeo. Yes, he said he loved you, but now he's changed his mind. So what? It's not like you haven't been here before. If your own father didn't want to claim you, why would John or anyone else?*

"Now that Piper's leg is healed, she and I can move back onto *The House Call* tomorrow. It will make it easier for me to get the work done on it so I can list it for sale and buy a proper home."

That bitter voice was back in her head.

*I told you so. I told you so. I told you so.*

Then suddenly he was in front of her, cupping her face between his hands, right there, where everyone could see them.

"Charlotte, listen to me. This isn't goodbye. I just need a little time to straighten things out."

She took his hands from her face, put them back at his sides. "It's all right, John. I understand just fine. Take all the time you need. I'll wrap things up at the clinic this week and let the cruise ship know that I've completed my assignment."

"Wait... You're leaving?"

"Yes—that's generally what people do when they're no longer needed."

"I never said that."

"You don't have to say the words out loud, John. It's written all over your face. You might love me, but you're never going to trust me. Not with the hard stuff. Not with the people who matter to you. You want to save the world all alone, like some kind of superhero. But I never wanted a superhero, John. I just wanted you."

She gathered her purse and coat, eager to escape with her dignity intact. She did not want to weep in front of John or any of the hospital staff. That would have to wait until later, when she was far away from here and could put all this behind her.

John stopped her before she could storm down the hall. "Maybe you didn't want a superhero, Charlotte, but did you really want me? Imperfect, fallible, sometimes not sure what's the right thing to do? Because you sure seem willing to bolt as soon as things are less than perfect."

Charlotte looked down at his hand on her arm.

"Well, I guess we've both had a chance to speak our mind. I'm going to go see Angel now. Even if she isn't my patient anymore, I still care what happens to her."

"Charlotte!" John protested.

But then the attending appeared at John's elbow, ready to discuss Angel's case.

John looked helplessly back and forth between the attending and Charlotte. "Just...wait for me, okay?" he said.

He followed the attending out of the waiting room, all of his attention concentrated on being briefed about Angel's progress.

Charlotte watched him leave, her heart breaking into a million tiny pieces.

She made it past the reception desk and the triage area before the tears she'd held back spilled down her cheeks. She needed a few minutes to pull herself together before she saw Angel.

She paused in the hallway outside the treatment bays, leaning against the wall, her jacket folded over her arms. A nurse passed by and gave her a compassionate smile and squeezed her arm. She probably thought Charlotte had just received some terrible news about a family member. And that wasn't too far from the truth. Because what she'd had with John and Piper over the past few months had been the closest thing to family she'd had since her mother died.

"Dammit," she said, searching her bag for a clean tissue.

How many times would she have to learn the same painful lesson over and over again? Love didn't stay—at least not for her. Her fate lay in pursuing adventure, not sticking around and waiting to be rejected. She'd *known* this when she'd come here, yet she'd insisted on taking a chance.

Charlotte checked her appearance in the glass window of a treatment room. Her nose was red and her skin a bit blotchy, so she dusted some powder over her face and fluffed her hair until she felt presentable. Then she searched the emergency department until she found Angel's room. She looked tiny and wan on the hospital gurney, her face the same pale shade as the white blanket draped over her thin frame.

"Hey, Angel," Charlotte said, sitting at the end of her bed. "How are you feeling?"

Angel took a deep sip of the soda that a nurse must have given her. "Mostly good," she said, her voice lacking its usual bravado. "Maybe a little dizzy. And I have a headache."

Definitely symptoms of Brugada Syndrome, the genetic heart defect that Charlotte had feared Angel might have. But the only way to know for sure was to have Angel admitted to the hospital for extensive testing.

"The doctor said I could go home tonight. That's good, right?"

Charlotte tilted her head with a soft smile. "Usually that would be great news, Angel. But in your case that's not what I want for you."

Charlotte explained the medical condition that might be causing Angel's symptoms.

"But the only way we can get these tests done is if you let us know who you are. Then we can get a full medical history. That is, if you're okay with us talking to your family?"

Angel's expression darkened. "I don't want to be a burden to them."

"Why would helping you be a burden to your family?"

Angel looked away, out the window, her hands moving restlessly over the blankets that covered her legs. "I have three sisters, and my mom was having a hard time taking care of all of us. I thought it would be easier if I left. I'm almost fifteen now...old enough to get a job, take care of myself. It's one less mouth for my mom to feed, right?"

"Does she know where you are?"

Angel's jaw quivered. "No. I don't want her to worry. I can take care of myself now."

"Based on what you've told me so far, Angel, I'm pretty sure she wants to hear from you. And I'm certain she would want you to get help with these heart problems you're having." Charlotte pulled a pad of paper from her purse, and a pen, putting them in front of Angel. "I don't know exactly why you don't want anyone to know your real name, but I know the power that comes with seizing control of something when your world feels like it's spinning out of control. Not showing your true self does protect you from being hurt again. But it also makes you invisible. And invisible people can't be loved, because no one knows who they really are."

Angel met her gaze now, and Charlotte felt like there was a flicker of understanding in her eyes.

"Let me help you, Angel. Me and Dr. J and all the doctors here. We all want you to be safe and healthy."

Angel took a deep breath, then picked up the pen and began writing, the pen's nib making scratching sounds against the paper. Then she handed it to Charlotte.

Charlotte read the paper and smiled. "It's nice to finally meet you, Kaitlyn Webb."

A few hours later, John left the emergency room feeling like a bus had run over him slowly and repeatedly. It had been a long, grueling night of trying to convince the attending that Angel's case was more serious than simple fainting.

It was only because Charlotte had got Angel's

real name that he'd been able to call her mother and get a full medical history. Learning that her father had died in his forties of a heart attack had been enough for the attending to order more testing. Thankfully Angel would spend the next few nights in the hospital, where she would be safe and sound.

He had immediately looked for Charlotte, to share the good news, but she'd been nowhere to be found in the hospital. She hadn't responded to his texts or calls either. His last hope had been to find her car next to his at the hospital, where they had hurriedly parked when they'd come back from the marina.

But her car wasn't there.

He felt his blood run very cold. Memories of their fight about Angel's care had haunted him all night. Had he really needed to make his stand so soon after learning the news of Angel's collapse? He'd been shaken and worried, not in the best frame of mind to tell the woman he loved that he needed a little time and space to straighten out his life.

But he did. He had been living in a strange limbo for years now, and he'd never seen it until he'd fallen in love with Charlotte. Only then had he seen how his old, limiting beliefs were holding him back from living the full life he deserved. So long as he felt it was up to him and him alone to care for the teens and for Piper, he'd never be able to make room in his life for anything more interesting than a houseplant.

He checked his phone again—still no response to his texts. This was unlike Charlotte, who was as obsessive about returning calls and texts as he was. He started his car and headed for her house. Suddenly it felt very urgent that he find Charlotte right away.

Charlotte's car was in the garage. That was a good sign. But he felt very uneasy at finding her in her bedroom, with a suitcase on the bed.

"How's Angel?" she asked. But she remained where she was, her back to him as she gazed out the window.

Something wasn't right.

He moved slowly, assessing the situation. "She has an excellent prognosis, thanks to you getting her real name." His eyes roamed the room, saw the empty hangers in the closet and the counters cleared of perfume and makeup. "What's going on, Charlotte?"

She turned to him, her eyes red and puffy. "I have to go, John."

He took it all in. This seemed like an awfully strong reaction to him asking for a little space to get his life straightened out.

"I thought your assignment with *The Eden* didn't start until next month."

She sniffed and turned away. "I never signed the contract."

"So, where will you go?"

"I don't really know."

John had a well-honed radar after years of working with teens who were too young or too traumatized to verbalize their needs. He was good at reading between the lines...hearing the truth in what wasn't spoken aloud.

All this time he had believed Charlotte was someone with wanderlust in her soul—*GypsyMD*, keeping life casual and fun. But now he thought she might be something different.

"A little Greyhound therapy, then?"

She sniffed again. "What?"

"Greyhound therapy. That's what we call it at the clinic. Some of our kids think if they pack up their stuff and jump on a Greyhound bus they can leave all their problems behind. Start fresh somewhere else."

"I don't think that."

"No? Then what's happening here?"

She sat on the bed, her fingers curling round the mattress edge. When she spoke, her words were too soft for him to understand.

He took a step forward, straining to understand. "I'm sorry... You don't know how to... what?"

"I don't know how to *stay*!" she exploded, and the tears started again.

She resumed packing, channeling her nervous energy into cramming sweaters into her large suitcase. "I'm just not built like you, John. If I stay in one place for too long I start to get nervous and jumpy. Like I'm a fish in a blender... just waiting for fate to push the button. I love you, and Piper, and the teens—and even that crazy Cat who won't go away. But I'm not sure that's enough."

None of that made sense. They had worked together for months and she'd seemed perfectly comfortable at the clinic and at her house. The big change had come tonight, when he'd asked for space to straighten out some of the messes in his life. Which made sense, considering she had been doubly traumatized at a young age. First, by losing her mother to a car accident and then by her father's rejection.

What better way to make sure she was never abandoned again than to refuse to stay? Charlotte didn't travel because she had wanderlust in her soul. She traveled to avoid the connections that would break her heart if she lost them.

Every cell in his body wanted him to gather her into his arms and promise her that she was safe. That he wasn't going anywhere, and she could stop running now.

But he doubted she would listen. Not when she was this upset.

John considered his options, then headed over to the chair she had in her bedroom. He pulled it away from the wall, sat down and stretched his legs out. He opened his phone and navigated to the apps. Soon the room was full of the sound of bells and dings and whistles.

Charlotte stopped packing and looked at him. "What are you doing?"

"Some fruit-matching game that Piper taught me."

"What?"

The sounds of several bells chiming at once filled the room. "See, I just matched five lemons there—so now I have five hundred points."

Charlotte stood across from him, her arms full of sweaters. The expression on her face was pure confusion.

"Just something to do. You know... While I wait."

"Wait for what?"

He laughed. "For you, of course. Oh, wait—I need this pineapple." He made a few finger-swipes and then there were more bells and whistles. "See, the way I figure it, you can go as far away as you want. Travel all seven oceans... cross the continents. Hell, you can go to the moon. But when you've gotten all that out of your system you *will* come back to me. Because there is nothing in this universe that is stronger than the love we made the night of the hospital gala. Nothing, not even your fear, can overpower that. So do what you must. I'll be right here waiting for you. For as long as it takes."

For several long minutes Charlotte stood staring at him in disbelief. John willed himself to focus on the stupid game. Whether she left or stayed—that was up to her. But he wasn't lying. He really would wait for her. Even if he was an old man when her stubborn heart finally accepted what he already knew was true.

There was no other woman on this earth for him but her.

After a very long, uncomfortable silence, she set the sweaters down. Not in the suitcase, he noticed, which seemed like a good sign.

She finally looked at him. She looked exhausted and a little fragile.

He dropped the phone and went to her, gathered her in his arms, ready to buttress her against all the hurts of her past. She lifted her head and waited. He bent his head to kiss her, long and slow. He wanted to soothe her pain away, calm her stormy emotions and welcome her home.

But there was a strange and bitter taste in this kiss.

He searched for the sweetness he always

found in her, but found only sadness, longing, and goodbye.

Disbelief churned in his gut, making him feel sick and sad. He wanted to shake her and beg her to stay. She didn't have to go, no matter how many times she told herself she did. She could stay if she wanted. Didn't she know that? She could break the rules that were holding her hostage.

He pulled away and searched her face. That was when he knew he wasn't going to win this fight. Her mind had been made up ever since she'd left the hospital...maybe ever since she'd arrived in Seattle.

She stepped away. Touching her fingers to her mouth. Pressing her lips as if imprinting their last sad kiss there. Then she turned back to her suitcase, pushed the sweaters down, and zipped the mammoth case shut.

Every cell in his body wanted him to fight for her. But that would mean fighting *against* her, because the enemy he wanted to defeat was buried deep in her heart.

*Just stay!* he wanted to scream. *That's all you have to do...just stay!*

She wrestled the suitcase off the bed.

This was happening whether he liked it or not.

He sat helpless and stunned as she escaped the room and his life. There wasn't a thing he could do to change her mind. He knew better than to even try.

All he could do was wait. And hope that the trade winds would soon blow her back to him.

# CHAPTER THIRTEEN

CHARLOTTE TOOK A break from eating to stretch. Her body was so achy these days. She often wondered if she was coming down with a cold, but the sniffles never came. She was probably just tired from the last few weeks.

It had been a whirlwind of goodbyes as she'd ended her assignment at The Sunshine Clinic and put her father's house on the market. She had opted to stay at a hotel until John moved out of the house and into a cute little brick house near the hospital, with plenty of room for Piper and Cat.

Charlotte had seen Angel—now Kaitlyn—one last time before she'd left for *The Eden*. Angel had come by with many of The Sunshine Clinic's regular patients to say goodbye to her. She'd had her aunt with her, with whom she was now living, and was sporting a new pacemaker that protected her heart from going into cardiac arrest. Testing had revealed she did indeed have Brugada Syndrome, and it was probably the reason her father had died so young.

But all that was behind her now. *GypsyMD* was back! Traveling the Caribbean on an unbelievably swanky cruise ship that provided every luxury and amenity she could imagine.

She looked at the dinner her medical assistant had brought. Caesar salad and roasted chicken with a few petits fours for dessert. All perfectly prepared by an award-winning chef.

But absolutely nothing looked appetizing.

*"You need to eat something,"* her assistant had urged.

Charlotte knew she was right. She had lost ten pounds since leaving Seattle and judging from the total loss of her appetite she might lose ten more. Now her cute summer dresses just hung on her frame, when she bothered to put them on at all. All she really wanted to wear was her gray sweatpants and an old band tee shirt she'd found at the thrift store.

All this because she had tried giving up her nomadic ways to give love a chance and it had failed spectacularly.

When she had accepted the cruise ship assignment, she had planned to lose herself in everything the Caribbean cruise had to offer. Surely a few days of sea mist and warm sun would restore her soul? Then she would be ready to take advantage of the many port excursions and tours that were part of cruise life. She just had to pick which ones.

She pushed her untouched dinner away and thumbed through the brochures listlessly. Cave tubing. A historical Mayan ruin site tour. Barrier reef snorkeling. A jungle Jeep tour.

She didn't know what was wrong with her. By now her notebook should be full of ideas and itineraries, all arranged in priority order because there was never enough time to do everything she wanted. But her notebook remained blank. All she could think about was how much Piper would love cave tubing if she were here. Or how John would make his corny jokes during the Mayan ruin site tour to keep things lively.

Nothing sounded good unless she could share it with her people.

She shook off the thought. She didn't have people anymore, but what she did have was a tidy sum of money from the sale of her father's home. The money was sitting in her account, waiting to be donated to a worthy charity. She opened a new page in her notebook and wrote *Charity* across the top. If she figured out where to donate the money, maybe that would clear her head to focus on her next adventure.

There was a knock at the door. Her medical assistant said, "Dr. Owens, we have a patient complaining of chest pain."

That wasn't good. So far Charlotte's work on *The Eden* had been fairly uneventful. Plenty of sunburn cases, indigestion, and a few folks who had forgotten to pack their medicines. Nothing truly serious had happened while she was onboard, and she was hoping to keep it that way.

"Okay, please put them in Exam Room One."

"I did that. But just so you know, she's brought her husband and family with her."

"Good. I'm glad she has support." Charlotte closed up her notebook and draped her stethoscope around her neck.

"Her *very large* family," the medical assistant said with a wink.

Sure enough, the hallway outside the exam room was packed with family members of every age. The youngest was a baby, who had fallen asleep on her mother's shoulder. Everyone was wearing Hawaiian-themed shirts—which would have been a festive sight if it hadn't been for the worry on their faces.

"Excuse me," Charlotte said repeatedly as she pushed through the small crowd.

She finally made it into the exam room where an older lady was lying on the bed, her eyes closed, holding hands with a gentleman who looked to be around her age and very worried.

"Mrs. Patterson?" Charlotte said, recognizing the elderly woman who had shared her table at the hospital's fundraising gala.

The man at her side gave her shoulder a gentle shake. She opened her eyes and said, a little too loud, "What?"

The man gestured to her ear, then made a hand sign as if turning a dial up.

"Oh!" the woman said, before reaching behind her ear. Lily could see the half-moon shape of a hearing aid perched on her ear and knew Mrs. Patterson was adjusting the volume.

"The doctor's here," the man said, before taking her hand in his.

he woman squinted her eyes before she smiled in recognition. "Ah, the newlywed lady doctor. How's your husband?"

Charlotte's heart squeezed hard with a fresh wave of pain. Just seeing Mrs. Patterson brought back a flood of memories of that night with John...especially the way they'd danced together in the ballroom, and how they'd spent their time later, in his room.

Charlotte just smiled to hide her distress. She didn't want to spend time explaining her situation. Especially when Mrs. Patterson was complaining of chest pain.

"I think what's important here is you, Mrs. Patterson."

Her husband had both of his hands clasped around hers. "She started complaining of chest pain about an hour ago. We had such a lovely dinner, and then we did some dancing."

"A lot of dancing!" Mrs. Patterson laughed.

"We're celebrating our fiftieth anniversary," Mr. Patterson explained. "Our family planned this cruise as a kind of family reunion and wedding anniversary celebration."

"How lovely," Charlotte said. "I'm sure you don't want to spend your anniversary down here in the medical clinic, so let's get you checked out and on your way, shall we?"

Mrs. Patterson's vital signs were all quite stable, which made Charlotte feel a lot better. If Mrs. Patterson was having a heart attack she would likely have an irregular heartbeat, clammy skin, or shortness of breath. Still, heart attacks could be sneaky, with no warning signs, so she'd need to do an EKG to monitor Mrs. Patterson's heart activity.

The cruise ship's medical clinic had a portable EKG monitoring system that was easy and compact to use. Recordings were stored on the cloud, so if it was necessary to arrange a helicopter evacuation to a land-based hospital, a patient's test results could easily be accessed by the hospital's emergency room. This was the kind of technology that Charlotte had wanted to add to

The Sunshine Clinic. But it was expensive, and few teens needed an EKG on a regular basis, so hospital funding would never include these types of extra services.

"So, tell me how you two lovebirds met," Charlotte said as she set up the electrodes that would monitor Mrs. Patterson's heart.

She would need to be monitored for at least an hour, so Charlotte wanted to keep her mind busy and distracted from the testing at hand.

"Well, we very nearly didn't!" said Mr. Patterson, giving his wife a sweet smile. "Thanks to my wife's stubborn streak."

Mrs. Patterson laughed and waved him off. "Heavens, am I ever going to live that down?"

Charlotte pulled up a chair and made herself comfortable. "You'd better tell me the story now. You've piqued my curiosity!"

"It was all my fault," Mrs. Patterson said, folding her hands across her chest. "I went to a Halloween party with some friends in high school. When I walked in the door there was the most handsome cowboy I'd ever seen, dancing his heart out in the living room. My own heart quite literally skipped a beat when he looked my way. But he was dancing with two witches at the same time. Beautiful girls, hanging on his every word, and I decided right then and there that he must be some kind of heartbreaker who collected girl-friends like trophies."

"So when I asked this beautiful lass out on a date the next weekend she roundly turned me down," Mr. Patterson said. "And the next time and the next time and the time after that. It was embarrassing!"

Mrs. Patterson fixed her pale blue eyes on Charlotte's. "I was certain that he was only pursuing me for the challenge of it. That as soon as I said yes he'd pull his love-'em-and-leave-'em routine on me too. A routine I hadn't actually seen, by the way, but was sure he was guilty of." She patted her husband's hand affectionately. "As it turned out the two beautiful ladies he was dancing with were his cousins, visiting from out of town for a long weekend."

"I've never collected girlfriends!" Mr. Patterson said indignantly. "I've got my hands full with this one!"

The long-married couple gazed at each other as if they'd just met a few hours earlier. Charlotte smiled at their obvious love for each other.

"And to think," Mrs. Patterson said, "if I hadn't ever learned the truth about you, none of this would have happened!" She waved her hand to indicate the family members who were standing around or sitting on the floor, waiting for news of her health.

An hour later, Charlotte removed the electrodes and gave the Mrs. Patterson the good news that her heart was strong and healthy. "You may have just overdone it with the anniversary celebrations," she told her. "Take it easy for the next few days, don't hit the all-you-can-eat buffet too hard, and come back to see me if anything seems amiss."

The Pattersons and their multi-generational family left the clinic in much better spirits than when they'd entered. And Charlotte's heart felt lighter too, now she knew the couple would be able to enjoy their anniversary trip and hopefully many more years together.

Charlotte closed up the clinic and headed back to her cabin. Her mind was full of the story that Mrs. Patterson had shared. Especially how the Pattersons' love story would never have happened if she hadn't learned the truth about her hopeful suitor.

Then she thought of Angel—Kaitlyn—and how she'd risked her health because she'd thought she was a burden to her family.

And Piper, who'd assumed that getting herself into trouble at school would get her reunited with her father.

And John, who'd thought asking for help for the clinic would be a sign of weakness, when in fact the Seattle community very much wanted to take care of its at-risk teens.

*How many self-destructive things do we do when we don't know the truth?* Charlotte wondered.

Which made it impossible to avoid thinking about her own decisions—especially the ones that had led her here.

*"This isn't goodbye, Charlotte. I just need a little time..."*

John had straight out told her what he needed. But all she'd heard were echoes of her father's rejection and abandonment. She hadn't been able to get past her own fears and really listen to what John needed. So she had made decisions for him, for both of them, that were really just about protecting her ego.

*It's too late. He wouldn't want to see me now after what I did to us.*

And there they were again. Her assumptions and beliefs about what John would do, without ever giving him a chance to speak for himself.

The truth was, she didn't know what he would say. Maybe she was right. Maybe he never wanted to see her again.

It would break her heart if that were true, but she still had to try.

She had to be stronger than her fears if she ever hoped to have a real life for herself. A life that looked like the Pattersons', full of love and a devotion so strong that it created two more generations.

But before she went back to Seattle there was one more truth she needed to face. One more person she had not allowed to have his say.

Charlotte closed the door to her cabin and went to the closet. She had packed up in a hurry once her father's house had sold, so she wasn't sure what documents had come with her and which ones were packed away in storage. She flipped past her medical license, the house sale contract, her employment contract with *The Eden*. Towards the back, she finally found what she was looking for.

She held the envelope, its ivory paper thick and expensive, for several long minutes. She ran her finger across her name, *Dr. Charlotte Owens*, written in her father's script across the front. It felt like her entire life had come down to this one letter.

She took a deep breath and flipped it over, running her finger under the seal to break it.

The new built-in desk was an excellent addition to the office, giving John and the clinic's second doctor a dedicated space for their computer and files. Much classier than the old door he'd lain across two sawhorses.

He wished Charlotte were here to see it.

The very thought of her was enough to form a thick lump in his throat. His body still felt utterly exhausted from the hard work of grieving over their breakup.

He'd kept hoping she'd come back, or call, or in some way reach out to him...give them a second chance. But she was gone in every sense of the word.

She hadn't even updated her travel blog, which had worried him at first. But the hospital had assured him that they had spoken to her when she'd ended her assignment, so he knew she was okay. She just didn't want to speak to him.

Sarah poked her head into John's office. "Don't forget that meeting with the chief at two o'clock this afternoon!"

"I won't," John assured her. "Now go on with yourself. There's a retirement with your name written all over it."

He got up to walk her to the door, knowing that otherwise Sarah would find a hundred more little tasks she needed to do before she officially retired.

"Oh, John..." Sarah lamented. "I can't imagine not seeing you and the kids every day. Are you sure you're going to be all right?"

John stooped to give her a kiss. "I'll be fine, Sarah, though I'm sure going to miss you. Without you, I don't think The Sunshine Clinic would ever have happened."

Sarah reached out to give John one of her signature bear hugs, and he gratefully accepted.

"You would have found a way, John. You always do."

John walked Sarah to her car and wished her well. He had a new medical assistant now, and a new receptionist to replace Sarah now she'd announced she was finally ready to retire. She meant it this time.

There had been other changes to the clinic too. Like the breathing treatment area that Charlotte had suggested, and a steady stream of nursing students who worked every afternoon to earn practicum hours toward their degrees and provided John with free staffing. There was a nutritionist who came every Friday afternoon, and there were plans to add a dentist and a hygienist two or three days a week.

But the best thing of all was the ten-year plan that the hospital had developed for The Sunshine Clinic, with John's input taking priority. In due time, the clinic would move into a bigger building that could accommodate more doctors, nurses, and other specialists, who would provide all the services John had always dreamed of.

It was like a dream come true, and it had all

started the night he'd given his speech from the heart at the fundraising gala.

As it turned out there were a lot of doctors and administrators who wanted to help Seattle's disadvantaged teens. They just hadn't known that John needed more donations, more volunteers, and a bigger budget—because he had never asked. Now that the hospital's board of directors were aware of his ambitions and needs, a lot more funding and support had been sent his way.

Which was why he had a monthly meeting with the chief of pediatrics to discuss the clinic's progress and growth. But the chief's emails had been rather cryptic of late, hinting at some new initiative the hospital had in mind for the clinic. Despite his best efforts, John hadn't been able to get his boss or any of his colleagues to spill any beans about this new plan.

John gathered his files and notes for the meeting. Then paused in the hallway outside the door he still thought of as Charlotte's office. But Charlotte wasn't there anymore, and she wasn't coming back. He had a new part-time pediatrician now, who worked a few afternoons a week, and on-call doctors filling in the rest of the time. It was more help than he'd had since he started the clinic, but it wasn't Charlotte...

John usually made good use of his driving time by listening to pediatric medicine podcasts, so he could keep up with the latest research and treatment options. But he just wasn't in the mood today, so he searched the radio until he found a smooth jazz station. It reminded him of the night he had driven Charlotte home from the clinic after their street call work. It had felt so good to take care of her when she was so exhausted after Tommy's close call with death.

But it didn't feel good to remember their fight at the hospital when Angel had collapsed.

*"You might love me, but you're never going to trust me...not with the people who matter to you."*

A superhero. That was what she'd called him. She'd said that he just wanted to save the world alone, like some kind of superhero.

That was crazy, he'd thought when she'd first left. The last thing in the world he felt like was a superhero of any kind. Superheroes didn't have brothers who fell apart right in front of them, or nieces who wanted to fight their way into jail.

But that had been a few months ago, and he saw things differently now. Especially now he knew how much his colleagues wanted to help the clinic once he had told them the truth during his speech at the gala. He really couldn't do everything he wanted for the teens all by himself.

So, Charlotte was right.

He had fallen head over heels in love with her. But he hadn't been willing to fully trust her with all of his vulnerabilities. To let her know that he needed her at the clinic and in his life.

John pulled into one of the parking spaces at the hospital for medical staff and made his way to his boss's office. Her assistant directed him to the conference room and offered him a coffee while he waited.

"She'll just be a few moments. She's invited a guest to join you today. Someone who is familiar with the new community initiative the hospital wants to explore."

It was really driving John crazy that no one would tell him what was going on. It had been like this for weeks—ever since the hospital had gained a new donor who was apparently putting some stipulations on their donation. John hoped it wasn't going to become a problem.

Eventually John had waited long enough to need a refill on his coffee. He was doctoring his coffee with two creams and sugar when he heard the conference room door open.

"Hey, Dr. Fagan," John said, without looking up. "Can I get you a coffee?"

"Sure. Two creams, please. But I guess you already know that."

John's world froze as he recognized her voice. He slowly turned and faced her. She was even more beautiful than he remembered, her long hair falling in waves around her face and her skin now tanned from the time she had spent in the Caribbean.

"What are you doing here?" he managed to say, amazed that his brain was still able to form words.

"I have something to show you," she said, tucking her hair behind her ear.

"I can't go anywhere right now. I'm about to have a meeting with the chief of pediatrics and a new donor to the clinic."

She smiled and, damn, if his heart didn't skip a beat. "I believe I *am* that donor, John. And I'd like to show you what I've donated."

This entire situation had rendered John mute, and he had no choice but to follow her like an obedient puppy. She led him out of the conference room to the elevators outside the chief's office. It was too soon and too awkward for any kind of conversation, so he simply stood in silence next to her, smelling that jasmine-scented perfume she favored, which stirred memories of their last elevator ride together.

Those memories were too provocative, so he forced himself to concentrate on the ever-decreasing floor numbers as they descended to the parking garage.

"Where are we going?" he asked, as she walked him out of the garage toward a fenced lot next to the hospital. This was where the hospital's ambulances parked when they were off duty.

"This way," she said.

When they rounded the corner, John was shocked to discover the chief of pediatrics was there, along with other colleagues from the pediatrics department. And Sarah too.

They were all flanking a large blue vehicle that John had never seen before, but which bore the name of his clinic. Only it said *The Sunshine Mobile Clinic for Kids*.

John looked to Charlotte. "I don't understand..."

Dr. Fagan appeared at his side, all smiles and handshakes. "Congratulations, John. You're the proud owner of a new forty-foot mobile health clinic, equipped with two exam rooms, an on-board laboratory, and telehealth equipment so your patients can access specialists all over North America. All thanks to the extremely generous donation of your former locum tenens Dr. Owens. I've been trying to woo her to come back and work for us full-time, but she's playing hard to get. Maybe you'll have better luck."

With that, Dr. Fagan opened the door to the mobile clinic so that the pediatric team could get their first tour, leaving John and Charlotte alone.

John searched for the right words. "This is amazing, Charlotte. Thank you so much. But I don't understand..."

"It was my father's letter, I guess."

"You read it, then?"

"Yes, and now I want to read it to you."

She led John by the hand to a picnic table under some trees and sat across from him. She pulled a letter from her purse, then smoothed the paper with her hands. Her voice was shaky but clear as she read to him the words she had avoided for so long.

*Dear Charlotte,*

*Words cannot express my regret at having to write this letter. If I had lived my life properly, a letter such as this would never be necessary. Unfortunately, I made choices I deeply regret. And, while I can never take back the harm I have caused you, I can at least give you a full accounting of the details.*

*I met your beautiful mother the summer before I went to college. I was bright and energetic, destined to attend a good college and become a good attorney, like my father and his father before that. Your mother waited tables at a café my friends and I liked to visit, and I thought she was just about the most amazing creature I had ever seen. What started as a harmless flirtation blossomed into a full-blown love af-*

*fair. She was all I could think about every minute of every day.*

*A few weeks before I was scheduled to leave for college, we discovered your mother was pregnant. And while I was thrilled, and confident we'd find a way to raise you while finishing our educations, my parents had a very different reaction. They gave me an ultimatum—I could choose you and your mother and forfeit the family trust fund that would pay for my college. Or I could walk away from both of you and everything would be as if it had never happened.*

*I think my choice is obvious, and I will never be able to make up for the hard years you and your mother endured. There is no excuse for what I did. I was young and afraid and convinced I couldn't survive without my family's support.*

*Years later, when your mother died, I forfeited my parental rights rather than face you. I couldn't imagine that you wouldn't hate me for my choices. I foolishly assumed that you would be placed with a relative on your mother's side. That was not the case, as I learned much later, when making plans for my estate.*

*In the end, Charlotte, all of my choices were for naught. The legal career I valued*

*above you failed me when my business part-
ner embezzled funds, leaving our firm des-
titute and in legal jeopardy. Everything I
worked for slipped through my fingers like
sand. And why shouldn't it? A house that's
built on a shaky foundation is destined to
fall in times of trouble.*

*Now, at the end of my life, all I have left
in the world is this house, and it's in about
as good of shape as I am. I hope in some
small way it will bring good to your life.
And I hope that you'll be smarter than I was.*

*Charlotte, when something—or someone—
good comes your way, you grab on tight and
don't ever let it go.*

Charlotte folded the letter into thirds and
slipped it back into its envelope. John noticed
how worn the paper was and suspected that she
had read and reread the letter many times.

"It was Mrs. Patterson who inspired me to read
the letter. You remember her from the gala, right?
She was on a cruise with her family on *The Eden*
and had a bit of a health scare. She was fine,
thank goodness, but talking to her and her husband and meeting her family made a bit of an
impression on me."

Charlotte paused to tuck some errant strands

of hair behind her ear. She seemed different now, he noticed. More confident than he remembered.

Despite their many months apart, John had the strongest urge to pull her into his arms, tuck her against his chest. He knew how hard that must have been for her, reading a letter from the man who was responsible for the hardest years of her life. But she wasn't his to comfort anymore, so he willed his hands to remain at his sides while she spoke.

"I'm afraid I'm guilty of making the same mistakes as my father," Charlotte said, her blue eyes dark and solemn. "I fell in love with you and Piper and The Sunshine Clinic. I knew you were my home, John, and that I belonged here. But at the first sign of trouble I dived back into the life I knew instead of doing what was right. I should have been there for you after Angel's collapse, even if you needed some space to deal with your emotions. Instead, I balked and bolted, so I didn't have to risk you rejecting me."

"I was never going to abandon you, Charlotte. I just didn't know how to love you without someone getting hurt or overlooked."

She reached out for his hand. "I know that now. Which is why I wanted to donate the proceeds of my father's house sale to The Sunshine Clinic. Now you can bring those corny jokes to even more at-risk teens in Seattle, whether they want to hear them or not."

He pulled her to him now, close enough that he could see the dark circles of her pupils and the lush, full lips that he longed to kiss. "I don't suppose I could interest you in an exciting travel assignment on the streets of Seattle?"

She tilted her head up in an unmistakable invitation to pick up where they had left off. "I don't suppose you could keep me away, Dr. Bennett."

Finally, she was his. Really, truly his. And it seemed like the heavens should open so that legions of angels could tumble from the sky and serenade them where they stood. But that didn't happen, so he settled for a long, sweet, slow kiss that would start the next chapter of their lives.

# EPILOGUE

*One year later*

CHARLOTTE HAD JUST smashed a perfectly good bottle of champagne.

It was a beautiful Saturday in June, and John and Charlotte had invited all their friends, who were really their family, to join them for an official christening ceremony for their new sailboat, *Two Docks and a Boat*.

Piper was hosting her first playdate on their new, larger sailboat. She practically beamed as she showed her friend how to dock and tie off the boat, along with all the other boating chores she'd learned since living with John.

Piper's friendships were blossoming at school, and playdates like these were becoming a regular occurrence in her life. She and John were visiting Michael regularly now and had invited Charlotte to join them for their next visit. Charlotte was looking forward to meeting her future brother-in-law, and eventually helping him start his life over with her and John for support.

John was busy on the deck of their new boat, cooking burgers for a summer picnic. Charlotte went up behind him and gave him a hug. "Look what we've done here," she said.

John paused in his work and watched the party unfold. The air was filled with the chatter of excited teens, many from the clinic, catching up with Angel/Kaitlyn and her new life.

Seagulls circled overhead, hoping for their chance at a stolen hamburger bun, while the sun shone over it all.

"We made this," Charlotte said, her heart full to bursting. "Our own little family."

John slipped an arm around her and grazed his lips against hers. "You think you'll miss jungle tours in the Caribbean? Or snow-skiing in Vail?"

Charlotte chuckled. "Definitely!" She looked down at the hand that John had splayed protectively against her belly. "But I think our little guy will provide enough adventure for me for quite some time."

John nuzzled her ear. "Should we tell everyone now or later?"

She leaned back against him, loving the solid strength of him. "Later, I think."

For now, she wanted to bask in the quiet refuge of his arms, safe in the knowledge that she had found her way home.

\* \* \* \* \*

# MEDICAL

Life and love in the world
of modern medicine.

## Available Next Month

All titles available in Larger Print

**Forbidden Nights With The Paramedic**  Alison Roberts
**Rebel Doctor's Baby Surprise**  Alison Roberts

.......................................................................................................

**Rescued By The Australian GP**  Emily Forbes
**An ER Nurse To Redeem Him**  Traci Douglass

.......................................................................................................

**Marriage Reunion With The Island Doc**  Sue MacKay
**Single Mum's Alaskan Adventure**  Louisa Heaton

Keep reading for an excerpt of a new title
from the Special Edition series,
FLIRTING WITH DISASTER by Elizabeth Hrib

# Chapter One

Nothing would humble a person faster than taking a toddler on an airplane. Of that, Sarah was certain. Controlling said toddler in a confined space for any length of time should've been considered an act of God.

"Share?" Parker said, standing on his seat and shoving a chubby fist full of animal crackers into her face.

"Oh, thank you, baby," Sarah said, taking a cracker. "Let's sit down now, okay?"

Parker flopped down with all the grace of a newborn elephant, jamming the rest of the crackers into his mouth. She'd given him the window seat, hoping to contain his shenanigans. Thankfully, the stranger on the end of their aisle—Pamela—was an older woman who had raised six children and a plethora of grandchildren. She had promptly assured Sarah that the antics of one curly haired two-year-old would be no bother.

Parker picked up the tablet she'd brought along for this exact situation, and she helped him string the kid-sized headphones over his ears again. If anything was going to save her and the rest of the passengers on this plane from a spontaneous toddler meltdown, it was *CoComelon*.

While Sarah was busy untangling the cord of the headphones from between Parker's fingers, a flight attendant rushed past their row. Sarah and Pamela both turned, watching the woman head toward the very back of the plane. Every head in every row snapped around too, morbidly drawn to the sight of panic.

"I wonder what that's all about," Pamela murmured.

"I have no idea." The sight of a flight attendant running was enough to send Sarah's heart racing, but when no overhead announcement was made, she settled back in her seat, trying to ignore the concerned whispers that flitted about.

She turned and watched a familiar yellow school bus scroll across the screen of the tablet, smiling as Parker began imitating the actions to one of his favorite songs. She ran a gentle hand through his hair. Parker had inherited her unruly brown curls. Between those and his bright blue eyes, she could already tell he was going to be a heartbreaker. The hint of mischief so often worn in the turn of his tiny smile didn't bode well for her either. Where that smile went, some sort of destruction usually followed.

"I don't know how you would ever say no to him," Pamela commented, idly flipping through her magazine now that the buzz at the back of the plane had died down. "He is darn cute."

"Oh, I can't," Sarah laughed. "He definitely has me wrapped around each of his little fingers."

"Well, you're certainly braver than I was at your age. I don't think I took any of my kids on a plane until they were about six or seven. Maybe even a little older."

"He's been on a plane before," Sarah said. "But he wasn't quite one yet. I fed him during takeoff, and he slept the entire flight."

"You do a lot of traveling?"

Sarah nodded. "For work."

"Oh," Pamela said with interest. "What do you do?"

"I'm a travel nurse, so every time I pick up a new contract, I have to relocate. Sometimes it's close enough to drive. But usually not." Sarah had spent this last contract in Washington State and the one before that in Texas.

"My, he'll be a well-traveled gentleman before he starts school," Pamela said.

"That's the plan."

Sarah had recently decided to take a break from work in order to spend some quality time with Parker and visit her best friend, Kate. She might've also been using this trip to avoid having to make a decision about where they should go next. The reality was that Parker was getting older. In another couple of years, he would be ready to start school. The next contract she picked up had to be one she was willing to endure long term. It meant settling down, and that was something Sarah was decidedly bad at.

Just the thought of it made her wrinkle her nose.

She enjoyed the *traveling* part of travel nursing. The part that allowed her to pick up and relocate any time she wanted. To start fresh in a new city or a new state. Sometimes even a new country, depending on the kind of contract she accepted. Shortly after finishing nursing school, Sarah had spent nine glorious months working in Australia. Of course, that was long before Parker had been born. In those days she'd been single and mingling all over the place. Now she had to worry about bath time and sleep schedules and stepping on pointy toys in the dark. With those kinds of priorities, she now kept her contracts stateside.

The plane shifted, flying through a bout of turbulence, and Parker's eyes widened considerably. Sarah reached to put his seat belt back on as he looked out the window. He wasn't all that fascinated by the clouds, still too young to understand the concept of being thirty-six thousand feet in the air. He had, however, been completely thrilled by all the work trucks on the tarmac when they'd boarded the plane.

"Truck?" he asked, looking up at her.

"We'll see the trucks when we land," she said, though she doubted he could hear her over *CoComelon*. The flight from Washington to Michigan, where Kate's family lived, was a little over four hours. They'd already survived about three-quarters of it without any meltdowns. Another hour and a bit and they'd be back on the ground. Until then, she prayed to whatever gods who were listening that Parker held it together.

He yawned and slumped his head against her, rubbing his face into her arm. She silently thanked whoever had just answered her prayer. Now was the perfect time for a nap. Sarah sat very still, not wanting to do anything to inadvertently excite him. Toddlers were funny like that. One second they'd be half asleep, their eyelids drooping, and the next they'd be bouncing off the furniture. Sarah didn't know where the sudden burst of energy had come from, she just knew this plane was not big enough to accommodate it. Parker yawned again, his eyes starting to close.

Sarah had the urge to take his headphones off to make him more comfortable, but she knew if she tried to separate the boy and his tablet, there would be hell to pay. So she let him fall asleep with them on. The idea of being lulled to sleep by *CoComelon* was her idea of hell. But if it kept Parker happy, who was she to interfere?

His head bobbed, almost colliding with the tablet where it was perched on his knees. Sarah gently maneuvered him so that he was leaning on the armrest of the seat instead. After a moment, Parker grew still, and Sarah carefully turned the volume down a couple notches.

She let out a sigh of relief, half expecting someone to congratulate her. No one ever did, though she'd always thought these moments of successful parenting deserved a trophy. Now that Parker was asleep, Sarah pulled a book from her bag and relaxed against her seat. For the first time since the plane had taken off, she no longer felt like a linebacker that had to be ready to stop an escaping toddler.

As she prepared to sink into the romantic entanglements of the very muscled man on the front cover of her book, another flight attendant went rushing past their row toward the back of the plane. A moment later a second flight attendant chased after her.

"Okay, something is definitely going on," Pamela said, putting her magazine aside.

Sarah had always been told not to panic on a plane unless the flight attendants were also panicking. She wasn't sure this qualified as panicking, but something was clearly wrong.

Sarah and Pamela both turned around, as did many of the other passengers. Whatever it was, it was at the very, *very* back of the plane, too far for either of them to see properly. Sarah settled back in her seat, picking up her book, reading the same passage over and over again. There was a distinct murmur of commotion coming from the back of the plane that was hard to ignore.

"You think someone's getting sick?" Pamela wondered. "The last plane I was on, a kid had really bad motion sickness and threw up the whole flight. The entire plane smelled like puke."

Sarah wanted to point out that a full flight-attendant response seemed like overkill for a little motion sickness, but she also didn't want to worry Pamela. "Maybe," she mumbled, turning back to her book.

Then a voice played overhead: "If there is a medical professional on board, please hit your Call button now. We have an in-flight medical emergency."

Sarah perked up at the announcement, her pulse racing the same way it did when she was at work in the middle of a trauma. Despite all her experience, there was a small part of her that hoped someone else hit their Call button. Asking for medical help at this altitude did not bode well.

Pamela glanced around the plane, then back to Sarah. "I think you're up."

"Looks like it." Sarah raised her arm, hitting the button.

A flight attendant hurried down the aisle toward her.

"I'm an ER nurse," Sarah said. "Not sure how much help I'll be, but—"

"Oh, good," the flight attendant said. "Please come with me."

Sarah glanced back at Parker. He was still asleep, and she thanked the headphones for that.

"I'll keep an eye on him," Pamela promised. "You go deal with whatever is happening back there."

"Thanks," Sarah said, sliding past Pamela into the aisle. Dozens of eyes turned her way as she followed the flight attendant. Never in her life had she felt so on display. Toward the back of the plane, the passengers were less interested in her and more interested in what was happening. Some people had stood up, craning their necks to try to get a better view, ignoring repeated requests from the flight attendants to sit down. With everything she'd seen in her line of work, Sarah had learned never to underestimate the power of human curiosity. She was just glad that she hadn't spotted any phones recording yet.

"The pilot is getting in contact with a medical crew on the ground," the flight attendant told her. "But if you could be their eyes and ears…" She trailed off as Sarah nodded.

When they reached the back of the plane, a group of passengers and crew were crowded around a seated middle-aged man. Sarah spotted the two other flight attendants that had rushed by her row earlier. Ignoring the crowd, she immediately started assessing the man with what she liked to think of as her nursing brain. That was the part of herself that automatically started filing away bits and pieces of information, trying to anticipate the diagnosis and what the doctor would order as a result. She'd already determined that the man was in some sort of serious pain based on how he was hunched over and knuckling his chest. A fine film of sweat covered his forehead. Immediate red flags started jumping out at her, and before anyone said anything, she already knew they were likely dealing with some sort of cardiac situation.

Sarah managed not to swear out loud. Instead, she prayed to the god of planes, trains and automobiles that this man was not having a heart attack in the air.

The flight attendants made room for her, and Sarah knelt down beside him. "Hi," she said, taking the man's wrist gently, feeling for his pulse. "My name's Sarah. I'm a nurse. Can you tell me your name?"

"Jack," he gasped, sitting back in his seat and wincing at her.

Sarah finished counting his pulse, noting his short, quick respirations. "Nice to meet you, Jack. Can you tell me what's going on?"

"My chest," he said. "I've got pain in my chest."

"And it just started suddenly?"

He nodded.

"Can you show me where exactly?"

Jack tapped the center of his chest. "Here."

"Does the pain move? Down your arm? Into your shoulders? Anywhere else?"

He shook his head. "No. I don't think so."

There was a first aid kit open on the floor, and Sarah spotted a blood pressure cuff and a stethoscope. She took those out of the kit and wrapped the cuff around Jack's arm. "I'm going to take some vitals, okay?"

Jack nodded as Sarah pumped up the blood pressure cuff and stuck the stethoscope into her ears. She placed the diaphragm over his pulse point, listening for the familiar swish of blood as she watched the pressure gauge on the cuff.

Sarah let the cuff deflate and strung the stethoscope around her neck as she dug around for an oxygen saturation probe. She found one in the kit and clipped it on the end of Jack's finger.

"If you had to rate your pain out of ten, Jack, with ten being the worst amount of pain and one being the least, what number would you give it?"

"Five," he said. "Maybe a six."

Considering his complaints of chest pain, most of his vitals were relatively stable. His respirations were elevated, and he was clearly having some trouble catching his breath, but that could be explained away easily by the pain and anxiety he was likely feeling. Chest pain could mean a lot of things—a heart attack, angina, indigestion. The hard part up here was going to be ruling things out. If this were a hospital, Sarah would be preparing him for an ECG and hooking him up to all sorts of monitors. There were specific protocols to follow when dealing with chest pain. But up in the air, this was going to be a whole different kind of emergency.

"Jack, do you have a history of high blood pressure?" she asked.

"Not usually."

"Cholesterol?"

"My doc said it was a little high last time I was in for a checkup."

"Do you smoke?"

He nodded. "Thirty years."

"Drink alcohol?"

"Socially."

"The pilot has a doctor on the line," one of the flight attendants interrupted. She held the phone they used to speak to the flight deck to her ear.

*Perfect,* Sarah thought, and she jumped into report mode, rhyming off her preliminary assessment. "Tell the doctor we've got a middle-aged man with sudden onset of acute centralized chest pain. Rated six out of ten. Pain does not radiate. Patient is diaphoretic, clutching his chest and short of breath. Vitals as follows: heart rate 88. Blood pressure 135 over 75. Respirations 22. Oxygen saturation is 95% on room air."

The flight attendant repeated what Sarah said word for word. She looked confused. "They want to know about his history?"

"Patient reports no history of high blood pressure. Discussed high cholesterol with family doctor during last visit," Sarah said. "Patient has a thirty-year history of smoking."

"The doctor wants to know if you've given any medications?"

"No meds given." She looked at Jack. "Do you have medication allergies?"

He shook his head.

"Do you take any blood thinners?"

"No."

Sarah started to rifle through the first aid kit again, looking for familiar drugs. "I've got aspirin and nitro on hand," she said.

"The doctor said give 325 milligrams of aspirin," the flight attendant relayed.

Another flight attendant handed her a bottle of water, but Sarah refused it. She gave Jack the aspirin. "I want you to chew this to get it in your bloodstream faster."

He did, making a disgruntled face.

The flight attendant on the phone was nodding along to the voice on the other end. "The doctor also said to give 0.4 milligrams of nitroglycerin."

Sarah took the other med. "Jack, I want you to put this under your tongue and let it dissolve, okay?"

He nodded, taking the pill. Sarah inflated the blood pressure cuff again and placed the stethoscope back into her ears. As she performed another set of vitals, she noted Jack's breathing ease. If the nitroglycerin was going to help with the chest pain, they would know soon.

"How's your pain?" she asked Jack after another minute.

"Better," he said. "It's getting better. Maybe a three out of ten."

Sarah relayed the improvement and the new set of vitals to the doctor via the flight attendant.

"He said administer another dose of nitroglycerin. And then buckle up."

Sarah raised a brow.

"Well, the captain said that last part," the flight attendant clarified. "We're going to be landing soon. An ambulance will meet us on the ground."

Sarah nodded. She administered one more dose of nitroglycerin, then climbed into the empty seat beside Jack, reaching for the seat belt.

"Not how you figured you'd spend the flight, huh?" he said to her, looking better than he had ten minutes ago.

"No, I actually thought I'd have my toddler hanging off me the entire time, so this is definitely an improvement."

Jack smiled, putting his head back, letting the medications work. There was still the chance that he'd suffered or was currently suffering a heart attack, but hopefully it was just angina and once he was assessed at the hospital they would get him on some regular medication.

He took her hand and squeezed it. "Well," he said, "I certainly appreciate you being here."

One of the flight attendants returned with a form for Sarah to fill out. She documented her assessment, the doctor's orders, the medications given and Jack's vital signs. As the plane prepared to land, she kept a close eye on him, hoping they would touch down before anything else went wrong. The flight attendants scurried back to their seats as the plane began its descent.

And it was at that moment exactly, while Sarah was trapped at the back of the plane, that Parker woke up and started to scream.

# Subscribe and fall in love with a Mills & Boon series today!

You'll be among the first to read stories delivered to your door monthly and enjoy great savings.

# MILLS & BOON

## JOIN US

**Sign up to our newsletter to stay up to date with...**

- Exclusive member discount codes
- Competitions
- New release book information
- All the latest news on your favourite authors

Sign up at **millsandboon.com.au/newsletter**